厚德博學
經濟匡時

匡时 大学通识系列

语 言 与 跨 文 化 交 流

诺贝尔文学奖作家作品选读

丁 冬 沈娴敏◎编著

上海财经大学出版社

图书在版编目(CIP)数据

诺贝尔文学奖作家作品选读:英文/丁冬,沈娴敏编著. —上海:上海财经大学出版社,2020.12

(匡时·大学通识系列·语言与跨文化交流)

ISBN 978-7-5642-3684-7/F·3684

Ⅰ.①诺… Ⅱ.①丁…②沈… Ⅲ.①世界文字-现代文学-作品综合集-高等学校-教材-英文 Ⅳ.①I11

中国版本图书馆 CIP 数据核字(2020)第 241014 号

□ 责任编辑 李志浩

□ 封面设计 张克瑶

诺贝尔文学奖作家作品选读

丁 冬 沈娴敏 编著

上海财经大学出版社出版发行

(上海市中山北一路 369 号 邮编 200083)

网 址:http://www.sufep.com

电子邮箱:webmaster @ sufep.com

全国新华书店经销

上海华业装璜印刷厂印刷装订

2020 年 12 月第 1 版 2020 年 12 月第 1 次印刷

710mm×1000mm 1/16 23.5 印张(插页:2) 459 千字

定价:79.00 元

前言

诺贝尔文学奖自1901年颁奖以来,已走过了一百多年的征程,也一直被视为世界范围内文学领域的最高奖项,应该说诺贝尔文学奖是对作家文学创作最高级别的认可和嘉奖。根据创立者诺贝尔的个人遗嘱,诺贝尔文学奖授予“最近一年来在文学方面创作出具有理想倾向的最佳作品的人”。文学奖由瑞典文学院评议后决定获奖人选,由于许多重大成果并非在一年内就可以确认,“最近一年”的时间限制条件被适当放宽为“最近的成就”或“最近才显示出重大意义的老成果”。瑞典文学院将“文学”定义为“不仅是纯文学”(诗歌、小说、剧本),“而且是因其形式和风格而具有文学价值的其他文字作品”。[①] 诺贝尔文学奖获奖作品的主题大多涉及全球人类所面临的共同问题,其中的人文关怀和对社会现实的体察是全世界人类共同的精神财富。阅读这些作品不仅能够提高读者的文学修养,而且能够增进读者对战争、生态危机、伦理等普世性问题的认识,有助于开阔视野、完善自我,培养世界公民和人类命运共同体意识。

本书的编写有以下几个目的:向中国高校的大学生普及诺贝尔文学奖获奖作家的生平和写作风格;普及一定的文学要素、文学流派和文学原理等知识,教会学生更加专业地鉴赏和分析一部文学作品;渗透相关文史哲的理论,比如后现代主义历史观、女性主义批评、存在主义哲学等,进一步完善中国大学生的人文知识结构,使得他们能够从文学作品中透视作家对于现代社会的思考,包括现代性的危机、资本主义制度、战争、性别与种族问题等。

为了尽可能达到这些目标,本书的每个单元都选取一个核心主题,并围绕这一主题组织相关材料,这些主题构成一条贯穿全套教材的线索;同时,有关“文学鉴赏”的基本元素,包括基本的文学概念、相关的文学理论,以及适当的鉴赏策略等,都被分成若干个点,由浅入深、由易及难地分布在各个单元的问题讨论及拓

---

① 以上内容参考自诺贝尔文学奖官网 https://www.nobelprize.org/prizes/literature/。

展阅读中。每个单元由以下六个组成部分:第一部分为作者生平简介及代表作介绍;第二部分为文本导读,包括本单元选段的主要故事情节、历史文化背景、相关的评论;第三部分为文章选段;第四部分为针对选段的学生讨论话题;第五部分为与该作家作品相关的文学批评或社会思潮介绍;第六部分为拓展阅读书目推荐。

在获诺贝尔文学奖的诸多作家和纷繁浩瀚的作品中遴选出适合高校课堂教学的作家作品实属不易。在兼顾作品主题的共鸣度、语言难易度的考量下,本书选择了13位获奖作家,大致涵盖20世纪以来的各个历史时期和主要文学流派。本书的第一单元介绍泰戈尔的诗歌《吉檀迦利》及其体现的诗人对人与自然的解读。第二单元关注萧伯纳的《卖花女》,探讨剧中所反映的社会阶层不平等的问题。第三单元对托马斯·曼的《死于威尼斯》进行解读,了解其对理性和感性这一哲学命题的探讨。第四单元选自赛珍珠的《大地》,检视西方人眼中的中国形象。第五单元为福克纳的《献给艾米丽的一朵玫瑰花》,介绍南方哥特文学的基本特点。第六单元包含丘吉尔在第二次世界大战期间所做的两次重要演讲,让学生感受英语语言的魅力。第七单元为海明威的《士兵之家》,探讨海明威基于冰山理论的小说创作美学。第八单元选自加缪的《局外人》,探讨存在主义哲学家对荒谬和存在的哲学思考。第九单元为托尼·莫里森的《最蓝的眼睛》,借此探讨美国社会种族、性别、阶级等社会问题。第十单元是波兰女诗人辛波斯卡的诗歌选读,了解她如何借助反讽艺术揭示日常生活中的智慧。第十一单元介绍莫言的《红高粱》,了解莫言语言的丰富多样性和他的民间叙事。第十二单元为加拿大女作家艾丽丝·门罗的短篇小说《办公室》,探讨作家的女性主义思想。第十三单元为白俄罗斯女作家阿列克谢耶维奇的《切尔诺贝利的悲鸣》选段,探讨报告文学的基本特征以及作者的复调叙事。

本书以作家的获奖时间为序进行编排,尽可能涵盖文学的多种文类,涉及体裁包括长篇小说、短篇小说、诗歌、剧本、演讲、报告文学。本书对于作家的选择也兼顾各种国籍,除了优秀的英美代表作家之外,还有印度的泰戈尔,波兰的辛波斯卡,中国的莫言,白俄罗斯的阿列克谢耶维奇。除了选取经典的作家比如泰戈尔、萧伯纳等,还选取了四位近二十年内获奖的作家。在选择作品时编者也考虑到了文本和当下社会的联系,强调经典文学作品的当下观照,见证经典文学永恒的魅力。

本书的第3、5、7、8、9、10、12章由丁冬老师整理编写，第1、2、4、6、11、13章由沈娴敏老师整理编写。特别感谢上海财经大学通识教育中心及上海财经大学外国语学院相关专家老师的指导和意见。感谢上海财经大学出版社诸位编辑的辛勤劳动。本书旨在为中国高校的广大师生提供一个了解诺贝尔文学奖作家作品的窗口。由于篇幅所限，不可能介绍所有获奖作家及其作品，对书中所涉及内容也无法作详尽无遗的评述。本书尽力为读者提供相关获奖作家和作品的概貌及主题，为读者进一步学习和研究文学提供学术探讨的基础，希望对文学尤其是外国文学感兴趣的一般读者和专业研究人员也能具有参考价值。限于编者的学术水平，书中错误在所难免，其中各种不足之处，恳请专家、学者和广大读者不吝指正。

丁 冬

2020年6月5日于上海

Table of Contents

Chapter 1 Tagore and His Song Offerings

Ⅰ.作者简介

拉宾德拉纳特 · 泰戈尔 Rabindranath Tagore(1861—1941),出生于印度加尔各答一个贵族家庭,他的父亲是梵社的宗教领袖。泰戈尔有较好的家教氛围,他的大部分教育都在家完成,他反对死记硬背的传统教育。年轻时,他广泛旅行,曾陪伴父亲到喜马拉雅山。泰戈尔很早就开始用孟加拉语写作,创作了散文、诗歌、歌词、戏剧等。十七岁时泰戈尔被送到英国接受正规教育,表现出了对文学的极大兴趣。除了文学活动,他还对社会改革感兴趣,比如创办尊重学生个性的实验学校。他也经常参加印度民族主义运动,甘地是他的挚友。泰戈尔在1915年被英国政府封为爵士,但几年内他辞去了这一荣誉,以抗议英国在印度的殖民政策。

在他的家乡孟加拉邦(现在的孟加拉国),泰戈尔的文学才华很早就得到了认可。他翻译了一些自己的诗歌,很快就在西方广为人知。他是印度文学和文化史上浓墨重彩的一笔,而对于全世界来说,他则是印度精神遗产的代言人。

泰戈尔创作的各种文学体裁中最广为人知的是他的诗歌。在他 50 多卷的诗集中,有《马纳奇》(*Manasi*,1890)、《金舟》(*Sonar Tari*,1894)、《新月集》(*The Crescent Moon*,1903)、《吉檀迦利》(*Gitanjali*,1910)、《园丁集》(*The Gardener*,1913)、《飞鸟集》(*Stray Birds*,1916)等。泰戈尔的很多英文诗集大多是从原孟加拉语的诗集编辑而来,和原文并不完全一一对应。虽然在中国泰戈尔的《飞鸟集》知名度最高,但是在国际上,他的《吉檀迦利》是最受欢迎的,"吉檀迦利"在孟加拉语中意为"献祭之歌"。除了诗歌之外,泰戈尔的文学成就还包括戏剧《暗室之王》(*Raja*,1910)、《邮局》(*Dakghar*,1912)等。他还著有几卷短篇小说和一些小说,其中包括《家与世界》(*Ghare-Baire*,1916)等。

此外,泰戈尔还写了音乐剧、舞蹈剧、各类散文、旅行日记和两本自传。泰戈尔于 1913 年获得诺贝尔文学奖,他是第一位获得此殊荣的非欧洲人。泰戈尔 60 多岁时对视觉艺术着迷,创作了 2 500 幅绘画作品。此外,他谱的曲子被两个国家选为国歌:印度国歌《人民的意志》和孟加拉国国歌《金色的孟加拉》。

泰戈尔的诗歌在西方广受好评的主要原因在于他对传统诗学的创新。正如 1913 年诺贝尔文学奖评委会的评价所言:他的诗歌深刻、感性、新鲜而优美,既有纯熟的技巧,也有深刻的思想,并且通过他特有的英语表达,使之成为西方文学不可或缺的一部分("his profoundly sensitive, fresh and beautiful verse, by which, with consummate skill, he has made his poetic thought, expressed in his own English words, a part of the literature of the West")。①

泰戈尔的很多英文诗歌非常完美地融合了东西方文化,诗歌节奏平衡,就像叶芝评论的:"同时结合了诗歌的柔性优雅和散文的雄健力量。"泰戈尔的诗歌语言精确、经典,并且对英语进行了创新性使用。对于诗歌创作,泰戈尔认为他只是一个中间人,他描绘的只是他与生俱来所认知的世界。他没有以天才或者创造者自居,这一点和西方对于文学创作的观点截然不同。西方的文学暗合了启蒙主义以降的人本主义思想,强调要征服自然来为我们所用。而泰戈尔的哲学则完全相反:他不赞成将自然和人对立起来,强调要亲近自然,从自然中汲取力量,所以他的诗歌中充满了自然的意象,比如印度广袤的森林。他认为身处和谐的大自然中,人类可以获得心灵的平静。

---

① 本书中作家生平信息和诺贝尔授奖词均参考自诺贝尔文学奖官网内容(https://www.nobelprize.org/prizes/literature/),后文不再另做说明。

Ⅱ. 内容提要

《吉檀迦利》是泰戈尔最重要的作品之一，也是因为此作品，他获得了1913年的诺贝尔文学奖。这本诗歌集中的很多作品都完成于泰戈尔人生最艰难的时期，在此期间，他的父亲、妻子、女儿、儿子相继离世。他将这些巨大的痛苦凝练成为美丽动人的诗句，作为对痛苦的反思和对于神的献祭，并将这本诗集命名为《吉檀迦利》。

《吉檀迦利》共有103首诗歌，每一首都可以独立存在。诗集的前7首解释了泰戈尔创作这些诗歌的理由及神和世人的密切联系。第8首至第35首则描绘了诗人对于神的殷切期望。第36首至第56首的主题是和神的相见。第57首至第85首则转而描绘神的降临给世人带来的喜悦。第86首至第100首是对于死亡的颂歌，诗人在这些诗歌中渴望得到永生，并且歌颂了人和神的和谐共处。诗集的最后三首诗歌总结升华了整本诗集。

《吉檀迦利》的语言优雅，内涵丰富。诗人描绘了人和神和谐共处、相互融合的理想状态。为了描写这种状态，泰戈尔在诗歌中注入了一些现实的自然意象。另一方面，诗歌中关于神的描写又是神秘甚至是虚空的。这两种文学风格的组合成就了泰戈尔独一无二的写作特色。诗歌既简洁又纯真，同时诸多修辞手法的运用又赋予诗歌极大的文学性。

本书选取了诗集中的四首诗歌，第11首和第35首从不同角度描绘了神的形象，第79首间接描绘见到神的喜悦，第92首的主题则探讨了死亡的内涵。

Ⅲ. 诗歌选篇

11

Leave this chanting and singing and telling of beads! Whom dost thou worship in this lonely dark corner of a temple with doors all shut? Open thine eyes and see thy God is not before thee!

He is there where the **tiller**① is tilling the hard ground and where the path-maker is break-

① 农夫。

ing stones. He is with them in sun and in shower, and his garment is covered with dust. Put off thy holy **mantle**① and even like him come down on the dusty soil!

Deliverance②? Where is this deliverance to be found? Our master himself has joyfully taken upon him the bonds of creation; he is bound with us all for ever.

Come out of thy **meditations**③ and leave aside thy flowers and incense! What harm is there if thy clothes become **tattered**④ and stained? Meet him and stand by him in toil and in sweat of thy brow.

35

Where the mind is without fear and the head is held high,
Where knowledge is free,
Where the world has not been broken up into fragments by narrow domestic walls,
Where words come out from the depth of truth,
Where tireless striving stretches its arms towards perfection,
Where the clear stream of reason has not lost its way
Into the **dreary**⑤ desert sand of dead habit,
Where the mind is led forward by thee
Into ever-widening thought and action—
Into that heaven of freedom, my Father, let my country awake.

79

If it is not my portion to meet thee in this life then let me ever feel that I have missed thy sight—let me not forget for a moment, let me carry the **pang**⑥s of this sorrow in my dreams and in my wakeful hours.

As my days pass in the crowded market of this world and my hands grow full with the daily profits, let me ever feel that I have gained nothing—let me not forget for a moment, let me carry the pangs of this sorrow in my dreams and in my wakeful hours.

When I sit by the roadside, tired and panting, when I spread my bed low in the dust, let me

① 袍子。
② 解脱。
③ 冥想。
④ 破烂的。
⑤ 沉寂的。
⑥ 剧痛。

ever feel that the long journey is still before me—let me not forget a moment, let me carry the pangs of this sorrow in my dreams and in my wakeful hours.

When my rooms have been **deck**①ed out and the flutes sound and the laughter there is loud, let me ever feel that I have not invited thee to my house—let me not forget for a moment, let me carry the pangs of this sorrow in my dreams and in my wakeful hours.

92

I KNOW that the day will come when my sight of this earth shall be lost, and life will take its leave in silence, drawing the last curtain over my eyes.

Yet stars will watch at night, and morning rise as before, and hours **heave**② like sea waves **cast**③ing up pleasures and pains.

When I think of this end of my moments, the barrier of the moments breaks and I see by the light of death thy world with its careless treasures.

Rare is its lowliest seat, rare is its meanest of lives.

Things that I longed for in vain and things that I got—let them pass.

Let me but truly possess the things that I ever **spurn**④ed and overlooked.

Ⅳ. 思考题

1. What images does Tagore adopt to describe the ideal realm of God?
2. Can you summarize the features of the ideal God in these poems?
3. What literary devices does Tagore use in these poems?

Ⅴ. 文学批评

如何读诗

Read a poem with a pencil in your hand. Mark it up; write in the margins; react to it; get involved with it. Circle important, or striking, or repeated words. Draw lines to con-

① 装饰。
② 起伏。
③ 抛起。
④ 蔑视。

nect related ideas. Mark difficult or confusing words, lines, and passages. Read through the poem several times, both silently and aloud, listening carefully to the sound and rhythm of the words.

EXAMINE THE BASIC SUBJECT OF THE POEM

Consider the title of the poem carefully. What does it tell you about the poem's subject, tone, and genre? What does it promise? (After having read the poem, you will want to come back to the title in order to consider further its relationship with the poem.)

What is your initial impression of the poem's subject? Try writing out an answer to the question, "What is this poem about?"—and then return to this question throughout your analysis. Push yourself to be precise; aim for more than just a vague impression of the poem. What is the author's attitude toward his or her subject?

What is the poem's basic situation? What is going on in it? Who is talking? To whom? Under what circumstances? Where? About what? Why? Is a story being told? Is something—tangible or intangible—being described? What specifically can you point to in the poem to support your answers?

Because a poem is highly compressed, it may help you to try to unfold it by paraphrasing the poem aloud, moving line by line through it. If the poem is written in sentences, can you figure out what the subject of each one is? The verb? The object of the verb? What a modifier refers to? Try to untie any syntactic knots. Is the poem built on a comparison or analogy? If so, how is the comparison appropriate? How are the two things alike? How different? What is the author's attitude toward his subject? Serious? Reverent? Ironic? Satiric? Ambivalent? Hostile? Humorous? Detached? Witty? Does the poem appeal to a reader's intellect? Emotions? Reason?

CONSIDER THE CONTEXT OF THE POEM

Are there any allusions to other literary or historical figures or events? How do these add to the poem? How are they appropriate? What do you know about this poet? About the age in which he or she wrote this poem? About other works by the same author?

STUDY THE FORM OF THE POEM

Consider the sound and rhythm of the poem. Is there a metrical pattern? If so, how regular is it? Does the poet use rhyme? What do the meter and rhyme emphasize? Is there any alliteration? Assonance? Onomatopoeia? How do these relate to the poem's meaning?

What effect do they create in the poem? Are there divisions within the poem? Marked by stanzas? By rhyme? By shifts in subject? By shifts in perspective? How do these parts relate to each other? How are they appropriate for this poem?

How are the ideas in the poem ordered? Is there a progression of some sort? From simple to complex? From outer to inner? From past to present? From one place to another? Is there a climax of any sort? What are the form and genre of this poem? What should you expect from such a poem? How does the poet use the form?

LOOK AT THE WORD CHOICE OF THE POEM

One way to see the action in a poem is to list all its verbs. What do they tell you about the poem? Are there any difficult or confusing words? Even if you are only the slightest bit unsure about the meaning of a word, look it up in a good dictionary. If you are reading poetry written before the twentieth century, learn to use the Oxford English Dictionary, which can tell you how a word's definition and usage have changed over time. Be sure that you determine how a word is being used—as a noun, verb, adjective, adverb—so that you can find its appropriate meaning. Be sure also to consider various possible meanings of a word and be alert to subtle differences between words. A good poet uses language very carefully; as a good reader you in turn must be equally sensitive to the implications of word choice.

What mood is evoked in the poem? How is this accomplished? Consider the ways in which not only the meanings of words but also their sound and the poem's rhythms help to create its mood.

Is the language in the poem abstract or concrete? How is this appropriate to the poem's subject? Are there any consistent patterns of words? For example, are there several references to flowers, or water, or politics, or religion in the poem? Look for groups of similar words.

Does the poet use figurative language? Are there metaphors in the poem? Similes? Is there any personification? Consider the appropriateness of such comparisons. Try to see why the poet chose a particular metaphor as opposed to other possible ones. Is there a pattern of any sort to the metaphors? Is there any metonymy in the poem? Synechdoche? Hyperbole? Oxymoron? Paradox? A dictionary of literary terms may be helpful here.

FINISHING UP

Ask, finally, about the poem, "So what?" What does it do? What does it say? What is its purpose?

Ⅵ. 拓展阅读

Ana Jelnikar's "WB Yeats's (Mis) Reading of Tagore: Interpreting an Alien Culture" (*University of Toronto Quarterly* 77.4 (2008): 1005-1024).

Edward John Thompson's *Rabindranath Tagore: Poet and Dramatist* (Oxford University Press, 1948).

Rabindranath Tagore's *Gitanjali* (Simon and Schuster, 2013).

Ⅶ. 参考文献

Tagore, Rabindranath. *Gitanjali*. Simon and Schuster, 2013.

"How to Read a Poem." Retrieved June 7th, 2020, https://writing.wisc.edu/handbook/assignments/readingpoetry/.

Chapter 2 George Bernard Shaw and His Social Critique

Ⅰ.作者简介

萧伯纳 **George Bernard Shaw**（1856—1950）出生在都柏林一个公务员家庭。由于不喜欢传统的教育模式，萧伯纳没有接受正规的教育。年轻的时候，他去往伦敦，并在房地产行业干了一段时间。19 世纪八九十年代，萧伯纳成为著名的音乐和戏剧评论家，并成为费边社（Fabian）的一名杰出成员，为此他写了许多宣传小册子。他最开始步入文坛是以小说家的身份，但是并不太成功。作为易卜生新戏剧的狂热倡导者，萧伯纳决定用剧本对当时的英国戏剧进行批评，并以此来针砭时弊。其中，《鳏夫之家》（*Widower's Houses*）和《沃伦夫人的职业》（*Mrs. Warren's Profession*）猛烈抨击了社会虚伪，而在《武器与人》（*Arms and the Man*）和《掌握命运的人》（*The Man of Destiny*）等剧中，他的批评则不那么激烈。萧伯纳是一位十分激进的理性主义者，他漠视传统，用敏锐的思维和机智的语言把舞台变成一个思想的论坛。在萧伯纳后期的戏剧中，有时候论证会超过戏剧文本本身,比如作品《长生》(*Back to Methuselah*);不过在同一时期,他创作了代表作《圣女贞德》(*Saint Joan*),在这部剧中,他重写了著名的法国少女英雄贞德的故事,并将其从中世纪延伸到当时的社会,借古讽今。

萧伯纳的其他重要剧目还有《恺撒和克娄巴特拉》(*Caesar and Cleopatra*),这是一部充满现代典故的历史剧。在萧伯纳最成功的"问题剧"之一《芭芭拉少校》(*Major Barbara*)中,观众的注意力被机智的论证所吸引,即人类只能通过政治活动而不是个人来实现审美救赎。《医生的困境》(*The Doctor's Dilemma*)虽然被萧伯纳戏称为悲剧,却是一部真正的喜剧,它的幽默是针对医学界的。《念珠菌》(*Candida*)以社会对性关系的态度为讽刺对象,《皮格马利翁》(*Pygmalion*)以语音学研究对中产阶级道德和阶级差异进行了巧妙处理。正是戏剧冲突、喜剧效果和社会批判的结合赋予了萧伯纳喜剧独特的风格。

萧伯纳于1925年获得诺贝尔文学奖,"因为他的作品具有理想主义和人性的双重特征,其辛辣的讽刺作品往往充满了独特的诗意美"("for his work which is marked by both idealism and humanity, its stimulating satire often being infused with a singular poetic beauty")。萧伯纳的作品结合敏捷的思维和令人捧腹的幽默,用充满人文关怀的笔触探讨了社会问题。萧伯纳声称他的幽默笔触是为了更好地传递他激进的思想,文字对他来说是最好的武器。萧伯纳在英国戏剧界树立了自己的标杆,他是易卜生的拥护者,也是当时肤浅流行剧的反对者。萧伯纳的剧本创作往往不遵循传统的约定俗成,他的剧作的新奇之处不在于结构和形式,而在于作者直截了当地将自己的思想嵌合在文学作品中,将想法通过文字付诸实践。

Ⅱ. 内容提要

《皮格马利翁》也被译作《卖花女》,是一部五幕剧,创作于1912年,1913年首次在德国演出。在希腊神话中,皮格马利翁爱上了他创作的一尊栩栩如生的女性雕像,并给她取名为加拉泰亚。"皮格马利翁"这个词后来演变成一个塑造某种东西的人,这也是该剧的主题。作为一部审视社会问题的戏剧,《卖花女》对构成阶级制度基础的社会优越性提出了质疑。它揭示了演讲和礼仪是如何维持阶级差异的,然而这种预先判断充满了任意和武断,即把一个人的价值建立在他的或她的发音上。

故事情节以语音学教授亨利·希金斯遇见单纯的卖花女伊丽莎·杜利特尔开始。他吹嘘自己能教她说正规的英语,从而帮她爬上更高的社会阶层。因此伊丽莎第二天来到希金斯家,要求希金斯教她像淑女一样说话。希金斯的朋友皮克林上校提出,如果希金斯能在六个月后的一次花园聚会上把伊丽莎冒充成公爵夫人,就可以支付实验费用。虽然希金斯在言语方面成功地改变了伊丽莎,但他粗鲁的举止和脏话并没有教会她相应的社交礼仪。在希金斯母亲的聚会上伊丽莎粗俗的表达差点暴露了她的真实社会地位。经过训练,伊丽莎在花园派对上成功地伪装成了淑女,但希金斯并没有以礼相待。伊丽莎感到失望和羞辱,决定离开希金斯,不再愿意被当作仆人对待。她认为社会阶层不是由一个人的发音决定的,而是由一个人受到的尊重决定的。与此同时,一个富有的美国人给了伊丽莎的父亲一笔钱,这笔意外之财使他从一个酒鬼一下子变成了一个中产阶级。

剧本并没有明确交代伊丽莎和希金斯的结局。萧伯纳在后记中写道,他计划的结局是伊丽莎将会嫁给小资产阶级的弗雷迪,和他开一家花店,而不是继续忍受希金斯。《卖花女》后来被好莱坞改编成音乐喜剧《窈窕淑女》(1956),但影片呈现了与剧本完全不同的结局。

本书所选的是剧本的第二幕,伊丽莎来到希金斯家,解释了她想改变口音的原因。他们达成协议,希金斯同意训练她的口音。与此同时,伊丽莎的父亲来到希金斯家里企图勒索钱财。杜利特尔和希金斯就中产阶级道德问题进行了辩论。

Ⅲ. 作品:《卖花女》第二幕

[Next day at 11 a. m. Higgins's laboratory in Wimpole Street. It is a room on the first floor, looking on the street, and was meant for the drawing-room. The double doors are in the middle of the back hall; and persons entering find in the corner to their right two tall file cabinets at right angles to one another against the walls. In this corner stands a flat writing-table, on which are a **phonograph**[①], a **laryngoscope**[②], a row of tiny organ pipes with a **bellow**[③]s, a set of lamp chimneys for singing flames with burners attached to a gas plug in the wall by an indiarubber tube, several tuning-forks of different sizes, a life-size image of half a human head, showing in section the vocal organs, and a box containing a supply of wax cylinders for the phonograph.]

[Further down the room, on the same side, is a fireplace, with a comfortable leather-covered easy-chair at the side of the **hearth**[④] nearest the door, and a coal-scuttle. There is a clock on the mantelpiece. Between the fireplace and the phonograph table is a stand for newspapers.]

[On the other side of the central door, to the left of the visitor, is a cabinet of shallow drawers. On it is a telephone and the telephone directory. The corner beyond, and most of the side wall, is occupied by a grand piano, with the keyboard at the end furthest from the door, and a bench for the player extending the full length of the keyboard. On the piano is a dessert dish **heaped**[⑤] with fruit and sweets, mostly chocolates.]

[The middle of the room is clear. Besides the easy chair, the piano bench, and two chairs at the phonograph table, there is one stray chair. It stands near the fireplace. On the walls, engravings; mostly Piranesis and **mezzotint**[⑥] portraits. No paintings.]

[PICKERING is seated at the table, putting down some cards and a tuning-fork which he has been using. HIGGINS is standing up near him, closing two or three file drawers which are hanging out. He appears in the morning light as a robust, vital, **appetizing**[⑦] sort of man of forty or **thereabouts**[⑧], dressed in a professional-looking black frock-coat with a white linen collar and black silk tie. He is of the energetic, scientific type, heartily, even violently interested in everything that can be studied as a scientific subject, and careless about himself and other people, including their feelings. He is, in fact, but for his years and size, rather like a very **impetuous**[⑨] baby "taking notice" eagerly and loudly, and requiring

---

① 留声机。
② 喉镜。
③ 手拉风箱。
④ 壁炉。
⑤ 堆放。
⑥ 镂刻的。
⑦ 有魅力的。
⑧ 附近,差不多。
⑨ 冲动的。

almost as much watching to keep him out of unintended mischief. His manner varies from genial bullying when he is in a good humor to stormy **petulance**① when anything goes wrong; but he is so entirely frank and void of malice that he remains likeable even in his least reasonable moments.]

HIGGINS.

[as he shuts the last drawer] Well, I think that's the whole show.

PICKERING.

It's really amazing. I haven't taken half of it in, you know.

HIGGINS.

Would you like to go over any of it again?

PICKERING.

[rising and coming to the fireplace, where he plants himself with his back to the fire] No, thank you; not now. I'm quite done up for this morning.

HIGGINS.

[following him, and standing beside him on his left] Tired of listening to sounds?

PICKERING.

Yes. It's a fearful strain. I rather fancied myself because I can pronounce twenty-four distinct vowel sounds; but your hundred and thirty beat me. I can't hear a bit of difference between most of them.

HIGGINS.

[chuckling, and going over to the piano to eat sweets] Oh, that comes with practice. You hear no difference at first; but you keep on listening, and presently you find they're all as different as A from B. [MRS. PEARCE looks in: she is Higgins's housekeeper] What's the matter?

MRS. PEARCE.

[hesitating, evidently **perplexed**②] A young woman wants to see you, sir.

HIGGINS.

A young woman! What does she want?

MRS. PEARCE.

Well, sir, she says you'll be glad to see her when you know what she's come about. She's quite a common girl, sir. Very common indeed. I should have sent her away, only I

---

① 暴躁,易怒。
② 疑惑的。

thought perhaps you wanted her to talk into your machines. I hope I've not done wrong; but really you see such **queer**① people sometimes...you'll excuse me, I'm sure, sir...

HIGGINS.

Oh, that's all right, Mrs. Pearce. Has she an interesting accent?

MRS. PEARCE.

Oh, something dreadful, sir, really. I don't know how you can take an interest in it.

HIGGINS

[to PICKERING] Let's have her up. Show her up, Mrs. Pearce [he rushes across to his working table and picks out a cylinder to use on the phonograph].

MRS. PEARCE

[only half resigned to it] Very well, sir. It's for you to say. [She goes downstairs].

HIGGINS.

This is rather a bit of luck. I'll show you how I make records. We'll set her talking; and I'll take it down first in Bell's visible Speech; then in broad Romic; and then we'll get her on the phonograph so that you can turn her on as often as you like with the written transcript before you.

MRS. PEARCE

[returning] This is the young woman, sir.

[The FLOWER GIRL enters in state. She has a hat with three **ostrich**② feathers, orange, sky-blue, and red. She has a nearly clean apron, and the shoddy coat has been tidied a little. The **pathos**③ of this **deplorable**④ figure, with its innocent vanity and consequential air, touches PICKERING, who has already straightened himself in the presence of MRS. PEARCE. But as to HIGGINS, the only distinction he makes between men and women is that when he is neither bullying nor **exclaiming**⑤ to the heavens against some featherweight cross, he coaxes women as a child coaxes its nurse when it wants to get anything out of her.]

HIGGINS

[**brusquely**⑥, recognizing her with unconcealed disappointment, and at once, baby-

① 奇怪的。
② 鸵鸟。
③ 可怜,悲悯。
④ 可怜的。
⑤ 惊叫。
⑥ 粗暴地。

like, making an intolerable grievance of it] Why, this is the girl I jotted down last night. She's no use: I've got all the records I want of the Lisson Grove **lingo**①; and I'm not going to waste another cylinder on it. [To the girl] Be off with you: I don't want you.

THE FLOWER GIRL.

Don't you be so **saucy**②. You ain't heard what I come for yet. [To MRS. PEARCE, who is waiting at the door for further instruction] Did you tell him I come in a taxi?

MRS. PEARCE.

Nonsense, girl! What do you think a gentleman like Mr. Higgins cares what you came in?

THE FLOWER GIRL.

Oh, we are proud! He ain't above giving lessons, not him: I heard him say so. Well, I ain't come here to ask for any **compliment**③; and if my money's not good enough I can go elsewhere.

HIGGINS.

Good enough for what?

THE FLOWER GIRL.

Good enough for ye...oo. Now you know, don't you? I'm come to have lessons, I am. And to pay for em too: make no mistake.

HIGGINS.

[stupent] WELL!!! [Recovering his breath with a **gasp**④] What do you expect me to say to you?

THE FLOWER GIRL.

Well, if you was a gentleman, you might ask me to sit down, I think. Don't I tell you I'm bringing you business?

HIGGINS.

Pickering: shall we ask this baggage to sit down or shall we throw her out of the window?

THE FLOWER GIRL.

---

① 外国话,别人听不懂的语言。
② 冒失的。
③ 恭维,赞美。
④ 喘气。

[running away in terror to the piano, where she turns at bay] Ah...ah...ah...ow...ow...ow...oo! [Wounded and **whimpering**①] I won't be called a baggage when I've offered to pay like any lady.

[Motionless, the two men stare at her from the other side of the room, amazed.]

PICKERING.

[gently] What is it you want, my girl?

THE FLOWER GIRL.

I want to be a lady in a flower shop stead of selling at the corner of Tottenham Court Road. But they won't take me unless I can talk more genteel. He said he could teach me. Well, here I am ready to pay him...not asking any favor...and he treats me as if I was dirt.

MRS. PEARCE.

How can you be such a foolish ignorant girl as to think you could afford to pay Mr. Higgins?

THE FLOWER GIRL.

Why shouldn't I? I know what lessons cost as well as you do; and I'm ready to pay.

HIGGINS.

How much?

THE FLOWER GIRL.

[coming back to him, triumphant] Now you're talking! I thought you'd come off it when you saw a chance of getting back a bit of what you chucked at me last night. [**Confidentially**②] You'd had a drop in, hadn't you?

HIGGINS.

[**peremptorily**③] Sit down.

THE FLOWER GIRL.

Oh, if you're going to make a compliment of it...

HIGGINS.

[thundering at her] Sit down.

MRS. PEARCE.

[severely] Sit down, girl. Do as you're told. [She places the stray chair near the hearthrug between HIGGINS and PICKERING, and stands behind it waiting for the girl to

---

① 抽噎。

② 秘密地。

③ 独断地。

sit down].

THE FLOWER GIRL.

Ah...ah...ah...ow...ow...oo! [She stands, half rebellious, half bewildered].

PICKERING.

[very **courteous**①] Won't you sit down?

LIZA.

[coyly] Don't mind if I do. [She sits down. PICKERING returns to the hearth-rug].

HIGGINS.

What's your name?

THE FLOWER GIRL.

Liza Doolittle.

HIGGINS.

[Declaiming **gravely**②] Eliza, Elizabeth, Betsy and Bess, They went to the woods to get a birds nes':

PICKERING.

They found a nest with four eggs in it:

HIGGINS.

They took one apiece, and left three in it. [They laugh heartily at their own wit.]

LIZA.

Oh, don't be silly.

MRS. PEARCE.

You mustn't speak to the gentleman like that.

LIZA.

Well, why won't he speak sensible to me?

HIGGINS.

Come back to business. How much do you propose to pay me for the lessons?

LIZA.

Oh, I know what's right. A lady friend of mine gets French lessons for eighteen pence an hour from a real French gentleman. Well, you wouldn't have the face to ask me the same for teaching me my own language as you would for French; so I won't give more than

---

① 有礼貌的。

② 严肃地。

a shilling. Take it or leave it.

HIGGINS.

[walking up and down the room, rattling his keys and his cash in his pockets] You know, Pickering, if you consider a shilling, not as a simple shilling, but as a percentage of this girl's income, it works out as fully equivalent to sixty or seventy guineas from a millionaire.

PICKERING.

How so?

HIGGINS.

Figure it out. A millionaire has about 150 pounds a day. She earns about half-a-crown.

LIZA.

[haughtily] Who told you I only...

HIGGINS.

[continuing] She offers me two-fifths of her day's income for a lesson. Two-fifths of a millionaire's income for a day would be somewhere about 60 pounds. It's handsome. By George, it's enormous! It's the biggest offer I ever had.

LIZA.

[rising, terrified] Sixty pounds! What are you talking about? I never offered you sixty pounds. Where would I get...

HIGGINS.

Hold your tongue.

LIZA.

[weeping] But I ain't got sixty pounds. Oh...

MRS. PEARCE.

Don't cry, you silly girl. Sit down. Nobody is going to touch your money.

HIGGINS.

Somebody is going to touch you, with a broomstick, if you don't stop **snivelling**[①]. Sit down.

LIZA.

[obeying slowly] Ah...ah...ah...ow...oo...o! One would think you was my father.

---

① 抽泣。

HIGGINS.

If I decide to teach you, I'll be worse than two fathers to you. Here [he offers her his silk handkerchief]!

LIZA.

What's this for?

HIGGINS.

To wipe your eyes. To wipe any part of your face that feels moist. Remember: that's your handkerchief; and that's your sleeve. Don't mistake the one for the other if you wish to become a lady in a shop.

[LIZA, utterly bewildered, stares helplessly at him.]

MRS. PEARCE.

It's no use talking to her like that, Mr. Higgins: she doesn't understand you. Besides, you're quite wrong: she doesn't do it that way at all [she takes the handkerchief].

LIZA.

[snatching it] Here! You give me that handkerchief. He give it to me, not to you.

PICKERING.

[laughing] He did. I think it must be regarded as her property, Mrs. Pearce.

MRS. PEARCE.

[resigning herself] Serve you right, Mr. Higgins.

PICKERING.

Higgins: I'm interested. What about the ambassador's garden party? I'll say you're the greatest teacher alive if you make that good. I'll bet you all the expenses of the experiment you can't do it. And I'll pay for the lessons.

LIZA.

Oh, you are real good. Thank you, Captain.

HIGGINS.

[tempted, looking at her] It's almost **irresistible**①. She's so deliciously low—so horribly dirty...

LIZA.

[protesting extremely] Ah... ah... ah... ah... ow... ow... oooo!!! I ain't dirty: I washed my face and hands afore I come, I did.

---

① 不可抵挡的。

PICKERING.

You're certainly not going to turn her head with flattery, Higgins.

MRS. PEARCE.

[uneasy] Oh, don't say that, sir: there's more ways than one of turning a girl's head; and nobody can do it better than Mr. Higgins, though he may not always mean it. I do hope, sir, you won't encourage him to do anything foolish.

HIGGINS.

[becoming excited as the idea grows on him] What is life but a series of inspired follies? The difficulty is to find them to do. Never lose a chance: it doesn't come every day. I shall make a duchess of this draggletailed **guttersnipe**①.

LIZA.

[strongly deprecating this view of her] Ah...ah...ah...ow...ow...oo!

HIGGINS.

[carried away] Yes: in six months...in three if she has a good ear and a quick tongue...I'll take her anywhere and pass her off as anything. We'll start today: now! this moment! Take her away and clean her, Mrs. Pearce. Monkey Brand, if it won't come off any other way. Is there a good fire in the kitchen?

MRS. PEARCE.

[protesting]. Yes; but...

HIGGINS.

[storming on] Take all her clothes off and burn them. Ring up Whiteley or somebody for new ones. Wrap her up in brown paper till they come.

LIZA.

You're no gentleman, you're not, to talk of such things. I'm a good girl, I am; and I know what the like of you are, I do.

HIGGINS.

We want none of your Lisson Grove **prudery**② here, young woman. You've got to learn to behave like a duchess. Take her away, Mrs. Pearce. If she gives you any trouble **wallop**③ her.

LIZA.

---

① 贫民窟的孩子。

② 假正经。

③ 痛打。

[springing up and running between Pickering and Mrs. Pearce for protection] No! I'll call the police, I will.

MRS. PEARCE.

But I've no place to put her.

HIGGINS.

Put her in the dustbin.

LIZA.

Ah...ah...ah...ow...ow...oo!

PICKERING.

Oh come, Higgins! Be reasonable.

MRS. PEARCE.

[resolutely] You must be reasonable, Mr. Higgins: really you must. You can't walk over everybody like this.

[HIGGINS, thus scolded, subsides. The hurricane is suceeeded by a **zephyr**① of amiable surprise.]

HIGGINS.

[with professional exquisiteness of **modulation**②] I walk over everybody! My dear Mrs. Pearce, my dear Pickering, I never had the slightest intention of walking over anyone. All I propose is that we should be kind to this poor girl. We must help her to prepare and fit herself for her new station in life. If I did not express myself clearly it was because I did not wish to hurt her delicacy, or yours.

[LIZA, reassured, steals back to her chair.]

MRS. PEARCE.

[to PICKERING] Well, did you ever hear anything like that, sir?

PICKERING.

[laughing heartily] Never, Mrs. Pearce: never.

HIGGINS.

[patiently] What's the matter?

MRS. PEARCE.

Well, the matter is, sir, that you can't take a girl up like that as if you were picking up a pebble on the beach.

---

① 和风。

② 抑扬顿挫。

HIGGINS.

Why not?

MRS. PEARCE.

Why not! But you don't know anything about her. What about her parents? She may be married.

LIZA.

Garn!

HIGGINS.

There! As the girl very properly says, Garn! Married indeed! Don't you know that a woman of that class looks a worn out drudge of fifty a year after she's married.

LIZA.

Who'd marry me?

HIGGINS.

[suddenly resorting to the most thrillingly beautiful low tones in his best **elocutionary**① style] By George, Eliza, the streets will be strewn with the bodies of men shooting themselves for your sake before I've done with you.

MRS. PEARCE.

Nonsense, sir. You mustn't talk like that to her.

LIZA.

[rising and squaring herself determinedly] I'm going away. He's off his **chump**②, he is. I don't want no balmies teaching me.

HIGGINS.

[wounded in his tenderest point by her insensibility to his elocution] Oh, indeed! I'm mad, am I? Very well, Mrs. Pearce: you needn't order the new clothes for her. Throw her out.

LIZA.

[whimpering] Nah...ow. You got no right to touch me.

MRS. PEARCE.

You see now what comes of being saucy. [Indicating the door] This way, please.

LIZA.

[almost in tears] I didn't want no clothes. I wouldn't have taken them [she throws

---

① 演讲的。
② 呆子。

away the handkerchief]. I can buy my own clothes.

HIGGINS.

[deftly retrieving the handkerchief and intercepting her on her reluctant way to the door] You're an ungrateful wicked girl. This is my return for offering to take you out of the gutter and dress you beautifully and make a lady of you.

MRS. PEARCE.

Stop, Mr. Higgins. I won't allow it. It's you that are wicked. Go home to your parents, girl; and tell them to take better care of you.

LIZA.

I ain't got no parents. They told me I was big enough to earn my own living and turned me out.

MRS. PEARCE.

Where's your mother?

LIZA.

I ain't got no mother. Her that turned me out was my sixth stepmother. But I done without them. And I'm a good girl, I am.

HIGGINS.

Very well, then, what on earth is all this **fuss**① about? The girl doesn't belong to anybody...is no use to anybody but me. [He goes to MRS. PEARCE and begins coaxing]. You can adopt her, Mrs. Pearce: I'm sure a daughter would be a great amusement to you. Now don't make any more fuss. Take her downstairs; and...

MRS. PEARCE.

But what's to become of her? Is she to be paid anything? Do be sensible, sir.

HIGGINS.

Oh, pay her whatever is necessary: put it down in the housekeeping book. [Impatiently] What on earth will she want with money? She'll have her food and her clothes. She'll only drink if you give her money.

LIZA.

[turning on him] Oh you are a brute. It's a lie: nobody ever saw the sign of liquor on me.

[She goes back to her chair and plants herself there defiantly].

---

① 大惊小怪。

PICKERING.

[in good-humored **remonstrance**①] Does it occur to you, Higgins, that the girl has some feelings?

HIGGINS.

[looking critically at her] Oh no, I don't think so. Not any feelings that we need bother about. [Cheerily] Have you, Eliza?

LIZA.

I got my feelings same as anyone else.

HIGGINS.

[to PICKERING, reflectively] You see the difficulty?

PICKERING.

Eh? What difficulty?

HIGGINS.

To get her to talk grammar. The mere pronunciation is easy enough.

LIZA.

I don't want to talk grammar. I want to talk like a lady.

MRS. PEARCE.

Will you please keep to the point, Mr. Higgins. I want to know on what terms the girl is to be here. Is she to have any wages? And what is to become of her when you've finished your teaching? You must look ahead a little.

HIGGINS.

[impatiently] What's to become of her if I leave her in the gutter? Tell me that, Mrs. Pearce.

MRS. PEARCE.

That's her own business, not yours, Mr. Higgins.

HIGGINS.

Well, when I've done with her, we can throw her back into the gutter; and then it will be her own business again; so that's all right.

LIZA.

Oh, you've no feeling heart in you: you don't care for nothing but yourself [she rises and takes the floor resolutely]. Here! I've had enough of this. I'm going [making for

① 抗议。

the door]. You ought to be ashamed of yourself, you ought.

HIGGINS.

[snatching a chocolate cream from the piano, his eyes suddenly beginning to twinkle with mischief] Have some chocolates, Eliza.

LIZA.

[halting, tempted] How do I know what might be in them? I've heard of girls being drugged by the like of you.

[HIGGINS whips out his penknife; cuts a chocolate in two; puts one half into his mouth and bolts it; and offers her the other half.]

HIGGINS.

Pledge of good faith, Eliza. I eat one half you eat the other.

[LIZA opens her mouth to **retort**①: he pops the half chocolate into it]. You shall have boxes of them, barrels of them, every day. You shall live on them. Eh?

LIZA.

[who has disposed of the chocolate after being nearly choked by it] I wouldn't have ate it, only I'm too ladylike to take it out of my mouth.

HIGGINS.

Listen, Eliza. I think you said you came in a taxi.

LIZA.

Well, what if I did? I've as good a right to take a taxi as anyone else.

HIGGINS.

You have, Eliza; and in future you shall have as many taxis as you want. You shall go up and down and round the town in a taxi every day. Think of that, Eliza.

MRS. PEARCE.

Mr. Higgins: you're tempting the girl. It's not right. She should think of the future.

HIGGINS.

At her age! Nonsense! Time enough to think of the future when you haven't any future to think of. No, Eliza: do as this lady does: think of other people's futures; but never think of your own. Think of chocolates, and taxis, and gold, and diamonds.

LIZA.

---

① 反驳。

No: I don't want no gold and no diamonds. I'm a good girl, I am. [She sits down again, with an attempt at dignity].

HIGGINS.

You shall remain so, Eliza, under the care of Mrs. Pearce. And you shall marry an officer in the Guards, with a beautiful moustache: the son of a **marquis**①, who will disinherit him for marrying you, but will **relent**② when he sees your beauty and goodness...

PICKERING.

Excuse me, Higgins; but I really must interfere. Mrs. Pearce is quite right. If this girl is to put herself in your hands for six months for an experiment in teaching, she must understand thoroughly what she's doing.

HIGGINS.

How can she? She's incapable of understanding anything. Besides, do any of us understand what we are doing? If we did, would we ever do it?

PICKERING.

Very clever, Higgins; but not sound sense. [To ELIZA] Miss Doolittle...

LIZA.

[overwhelmed] Ah...ah...ow...oo!

HIGGINS.

There! That's all you get out of Eliza. Ah...ah...ow...oo! No use explaining. As a military man you ought to know that. Give her her orders: that's what she wants. Eliza: you are to live here for the next six months, learning how to speak beautifully, like a lady in a florist's shop. If you're good and do whatever you're told, you shall sleep in a proper bedroom, and have lots to eat, and money to buy chocolates and take rides in taxis. If you're naughty and idle you will sleep in the back kitchen among the black beetles, and be walloped by Mrs. Pearce with a broomstick. At the end of six months you shall go to Buckingham Palace in a carriage, beautifully dressed. If the King finds out you're not a lady, you will be taken by the police to the Tower of London, where your head will be cut off as a warning to other **presumptuous**③ flower girls. If you are not found out, you shall have a present of seven-and-sixpence to start life with as a lady in a shop. If you refuse this offer you will be a most ungrateful and wicked girl; and the angels will weep for you.

---

① 侯爵。
② 变得宽厚。
③ 荒谬的。

[To PICKERING] Now are you satisfied, Pickering? [To MRS. PEARCE] Can I put it more plainly and fairly, Mrs. Pearce?

MRS. PEARCE.

[patiently] I think you'd better let me speak to the girl properly in private. I don't know that I can take charge of her or consent to the arrangement at all. Of course I know you don't mean her any harm; but when you get what you call interested in people's accents, you never think or care what may happen to them or you. Come with me, Eliza.

HIGGINS.

That's all right. Thank you, Mrs. Pearce. Bundle her off to the bath-room.

LIZA.

[rising reluctantly and suspiciously] You're a great bully, you are. I won't stay here if I don't like. I won't let nobody wallop me. I never asked to go to Bucknam Palace, I didn't. I was never in trouble with the police, not me. I'm a good girl...

MRS. PEARCE.

Don't answer back, girl. You don't understand the gentleman. Come with me. [She leads the way to the door, and holds it open for ELIZA].

LIZA.

[as she goes out] Well, what I say is right. I won't go near the king, not if I'm going to have my head cut off. If I'd known what I was letting myself in for, I wouldn't have come here. I always been a good girl; and I never offered to say a word to him; and I don't owe him nothing; and I don't care; and I won't be put upon; and I have my feelings the same as anyone else...

[MRS. PEARCE shuts the door; and ELIZA'S plaints are no longer audible. PICKERING comes from the hearth to the chair and sits astride it with his arms on the back.]

PICKERING.

Excuse the straight question, Higgins. Are you a man of good character where women are concerned?

HIGGINS.

[moodily] Have you ever met a man of good character where women are concerned?

PICKERING.

Yes: very frequently.

HIGGINS.

[dogmatically, lifting himself on his hands to the level of the piano, and sitting on it with a bounce] Well, I haven't. I find that the moment I let a woman make friends with me, she becomes jealous, exacting, suspicious, and a damned nuisance. I find that the moment I let myself make friends with a woman, I become selfish and **tyrannical**①. Women upset everything. When you let them into your life, you find that the woman is driving at one thing and you're driving at another.

PICKERING.

At what, for example?

HIGGINS.

[coming off the piano **restlessly**②] Oh, Lord knows! I suppose the woman wants to live her own life; and the man wants to live his; and each tries to drag the other on to the wrong track. One wants to go north and the other south; and the result is that both have to go east, though they both hate the east wind. [He sits down on the bench at the keyboard]. So here I am, a confirmed old bachelor, and likely to remain so.

PICKERING.

[rising and standing over him gravely] Come, Higgins! You know what I mean. If I'm to be in this business I shall feel responsible for that girl. I hope it's understood that no advantage is to be taken of her position.

HIGGINS.

What! That thing! Sacred, I assure you. [Rising to explain] You see, she'll be a pupil; and teaching would be impossible unless pupils were sacred. I've taught scores of American millionairesses how to speak English: the best looking women in the world. I'm seasoned. They might as well be blocks of wood. I might as well be a block of wood. It's...

[MRS. PEARCE opens the door. She has ELIZA'S hat in her hand. PICKERING retires to the easy-chair at the hearth and sits down.]

HIGGINS.

[eagerly] Well, Mrs. Pearce: is it all right?

MRS. PEARCE.

[at the door] I just wish to trouble you with a word, if I may, Mr. Higgins.

HIGGINS.

Yes, certainly. Come in. [She comes forward]. Don't burn that, Mrs. Pearce. I'll

---

① 暴君的。

② 冷酷地。

keep it as a curiosity. [He takes the hat].

MRS. PEARCE.

Handle it carefully, sir, please. I had to promise her not to burn it; but I had better put it in the oven for a while.

HIGGINS.

[putting it down hastily on the piano] Oh! thank you. Well, what have you to say to me?

PICKERING.

Am I in the way?

MRS. PEARCE.

Not at all, sir. Mr. Higgins: will you please be very particular what you say before the girl?

HIGGINS.

[sternly] Of course. I'm always particular about what I say. Why do you say this to me?

MRS. PEARCE.

[unmoved] No, sir: you're not at all particular when you've mislaid anything or when you get a little impatient. Now it doesn't matter before me: I'm used to it. But you really must not swear before the girl.

HIGGINS.

[indignantly] I swear! [Most emphatically] I never swear. I **detest**① the habit. What the devil do you mean?

MRS. PEARCE.

[stolidly] That's what I mean, sir. You swear a great deal too much. I don't mind your damning and **blasting**②, and what the devil and where the devil and who the devil...

HIGGINS.

Really! Mrs. Pearce: this language from your lips!

MRS. PEARCE.

[not to be put off]...but there is a certain word I must ask you not to use. The girl has just used it herself because the bath was too hot. It begins with the same letter as bath. She knows no better: she learnt it at her mother's knee. But she must not hear it

---

① 憎恶。

② 爆破。

from your lips.

HIGGINS.

[loftily] I cannot charge myself with having ever uttered it, Mrs. Pearce. [She looks at him steadfastly. He adds, hiding an uneasy conscience with a judicial air] Except perhaps in a moment of extreme and justifiable excitement.

MRS. PEARCE.

Only this morning, sir, you applied it to your boots, to the butter, and to the brown bread.

HIGGINS.

Oh, that! Mere alliteration, Mrs. Pearce, natural to a poet.

MRS. PEARCE.

Well, sir, whatever you choose to call it, I beg you not to let the girl hear you repeat it.

HIGGINS.

Oh, very well, very well. Is that all?

MRS. PEARCE.

No, sir. We shall have to be very particular with this girl as to personal cleanliness.

HIGGINS.

Certainly. Quite right. Most important.

MRS. PEARCE.

I mean not to be **slovenly**[①] about her dress or untidy in leaving things about.

HIGGINS.

[going to her solemnly] Just so. I intended to call your attention to that [He passes on to PICKERING, who is enjoying the conversation immensely]. It is these little things that matter, Pickering. Take care of the pence and the pounds will take care of themselves is as true of personal habits as of money. [He comes to anchor on the hearthrug, with the air of a man in an unassailable position].

MRS. PEARCE.

Yes, sir. Then might I ask you not to come down to breakfast in your dressing-gown, or at any rate not to use it as a napkin to the extent you do, sir. And if you would be so good as not to eat everything off the same plate, and to remember not to put the porridge

---

① 邋遢的。

saucepan out of your hand on the clean tablecloth, it would be a better example to the girl. You know you nearly choked yourself with a fishbone in the jam only last week.

HIGGINS.

[routed from the hearthrug and drifting back to the piano] I may do these things sometimes in absence of mind; but surely I don't do them habitually. [Angrily] By the way: my dressing-gown smells most damnably of **benzine**①.

MRS. PEARCE.

No doubt it does, Mr. Higgins. But if you will wipe your fingers...

HIGGINS.

[yelling] Oh very well, very well: I'll wipe them in my hair in future.

MRS. PEARCE.

I hope you're not offended, Mr. Higgins.

HIGGINS.

[shocked at finding himself thought capable of an **unamiable**② sentiment] Not at all, not at all. You're quite right, Mrs. Pearce: I shall be particularly careful before the girl. Is that all?

MRS. PEARCE.

No, sir. Might she use some of those Japanese dresses you brought from abroad? I really can't put her back into her old things.

HIGGINS.

Certainly. Anything you like. Is that all?

MRS. PEARCE.

Thank you, sir. That's all. [She goes out].

HIGGINS.

You know, Pickering, that woman has the most extraordinary ideas about me. Here I am, a shy, **diffident**③ sort of man. I've never been able to feel really grown-up and tremendous, like other chaps. And yet she's firmly persuaded that I'm an arbitrary overbearing bossing kind of person. I can't account for it.

[MRS. PEARCE returns.]

MRS. PEARCE.

---

① 石油精。
② 不和善的。
③ 没有自信的。

If you please, sir, the trouble's beginning already. There's a dustman downstairs, Alfred Doolittle, wants to see you. He says you have his daughter here.

PICKERING.

[rising] Phew! I say! [He retreats to the hearthrug].

HIGGINS.

[promptly] Send the blackguard up.

MRS. PEARCE.

Oh, very well, sir. [She goes out].

PICKERING.

He may not be a blackguard, Higgins.

HIGGINS.

Nonsense. Of course he's a blackguard.

PICKERING.

Whether he is or not, I'm afraid we shall have some trouble with him.

HIGGINS.

[confidently] Oh no: I think not. If there's any trouble he shall have it with me, not I with him. And we are sure to get something interesting out of him.

PICKERING.

About the girl?

HIGGINS.

No. I mean his dialect.

PICKERING.

Oh!

MRS. PEARCE

[at the door] Doolittle, sir.

[She admits DOOLITTLE and retires].

[ALFRED DOOLITTLE is an elderly but vigorous dustman, clad in the costume of his profession, including a hat with a back brim covering his neck and shoulders. He has well marked and rather interesting features, and seems equally free from fear and conscience. He has a remarkably expressive voice, the result of a habit of giving vent to his feelings without reserve. His present pose is that of wounded honor and stern resolution.]

DOOLITTLE.

[at the door, uncertain which of the two gentlemen is his man] Professor Higgins?

HIGGINS.

Here. Good morning. Sit down.

DOOLITTLE.

Morning, Governor. [He sits down **magisterially**①] I come about a very serious matter, Governor.

HIGGINS.

[to PICKERING] Brought up in Hounslow. Mother Welsh, I should think. [DOOLITTLE opens his mouth, amazed. HIGGINS continues] What do you want, Doolittle?

DOOLITTLE.

[menacingly] I want my daughter: that's what I want. See?

HIGGINS.

Of course you do. You're her father, aren't you? You don't suppose anyone else wants her, do you? I'm glad to see you have some spark of family feeling left. She's upstairs. Take her away at once.

DOOLITTLE.

[rising, fearfully taken aback] What!

HIGGINS.

Take her away. Do you suppose I'm going to keep your daughter for you?

DOOLITTLE.

[remonstrating] Now, now, look here, Governor. Is this reasonable? Is it fair to take advantage of a man like this? The girl belongs to me. You got her. Where do I come in? [He sits down again].

HIGGINS.

Your daughter had the audacity to come to my house and ask me to teach her how to speak properly so that she could get a place in a flower-shop. This gentleman and my housekeeper have been here all the time. [Bullying him] How dare you come here and attempt to blackmail me? You sent her here on purpose.

DOOLITTLE.

[protesting] No, Governor.

HIGGINS.

---

① 威严地。

You must have. How else could you possibly know that she is here?

DOOLITTLE.

Don't take a man up like that, Governor.

HIGGINS.

The police shall take you up. This is a plant...a plot to **extort**[1] money by threats. I shall telephone for the police [he goes resolutely to the telephone and opens the directory].

DOOLITTLE.

Have I asked you for a brass farthing? I leave it to the gentleman here: have I said a word about money?

HIGGINS.

[throwing the book aside and marching down on Doolittle with a poser] What else did you come for?

DOOLITTLE.

[sweetly] Well, what would a man come for? Be human, governor.

HIGGINS.

[disarmed] Alfred: did you put her up to it?

DOOLITTLE.

So help me, Governor, I never did. I take my Bible oath I ain't seen the girl these two months past.

HIGGINS.

Then how did you know she was here?

DOOLITTLE.

["most musical, most melancholy"] I'll tell you, Governor, if you'll only let me get a word in. I'm willing to tell you. I'm wanting to tell you. I'm waiting to tell you.

HIGGINS.

Pickering: this chap has a certain natural gift of **rhetoric**[2]. Observe the rhythm of his native woodnotes wild. "I'm willing to tell you: I'm wanting to tell you: I'm waiting to tell you." Sentimental rhetoric! That's the Welsh strain in him. It also accounts for his mendacity and dishonesty.

PICKERING.

---

① 敲诈。
② 修辞。

Oh, PLEASE, Higgins: I'm west country myself. [To DOOLITTLE] How did you know the girl was here if you didn't send her?

DOOLITTLE.

It was like this, Governor. The girl took a boy in the taxi to give him a **jaunt**[①]. Son of her landlady, he is. He hung about on the chance of her giving him another ride home. Well, she sent him back for her luggage when she heard you was willing for her to stop here. I met the boy at the corner of Long Acre and Endell Street.

HIGGINS.

Public house. Yes?

DOOLITTLE.

The poor man's club, Governor: why shouldn't I?

PICKERING.

Do let him tell his story, Higgins.

DOOLITTLE.

He told me what was up. And I ask you, what was my feelings and my duty as a father? I says to the boy, "You bring me the luggage," I says...

PICKERING.

Why didn't you go for it yourself?

DOOLITTLE.

Landlady wouldn't have trusted me with it, Governor. She's that kind of woman: you know. I had to give the boy a penny afore he trusted me with it, the little swine. I brought it to her just to oblige you like, and make myself agreeable. That's all.

HIGGINS.

How much luggage?

DOOLITTLE.

Musical instrument, Governor. A few pictures, a trifle of jewelry, and a bird-cage. She said she didn't want no clothes. What was I to think from that, Governor? I ask you as a parent what was I to think?

HIGGINS.

So you came to rescue her from worse than death, eh?

DOOLITTLE.

---

① 远足。

[appreciatively: relieved at being understood] Just so, Governor. That's right.

PICKERING.

But why did you bring her luggage if you intended to take her away?

DOOLITTLE.

Have I said a word about taking her away? Have I now?

HIGGINS.

[determinedly] You're going to take her away, double quick. [He crosses to the hearth and rings the bell].

DOOLITTLE.

[rising] No, Governor. Don't say that. I'm not the man to stand in my girl's light. Here's a career opening for her, as you might say; and...

[MRS. PEARCE opens the door and awaits orders.]

HIGGINS.

Mrs. Pearce: this is Eliza's father. He has come to take her away. Give her to him. [He goes back to the piano, with an air of washing his hands of the whole affair].

DOOLITTLE.

No. This is a misunderstanding. Listen here...

MRS. PEARCE.

He can't take her away, Mr. Higgins: how can he? You told me to burn her clothes.

DOOLITTLE.

That's right. I can't carry the girl through the streets like a blooming monkey, can I? I put it to you.

HIGGINS.

You have put it to me that you want your daughter. Take your daughter. If she has no clothes go out and buy her some.

DOOLITTLE.

[desperate] Where's the clothes she come in? Did I burn them or did your missus here?

MRS. PEARCE.

I am the housekeeper, if you please. I have sent for some clothes for your girl. When they come you can take her away. You can wait in the kitchen. This way, please.

[DOOLITTLE, much troubled, accompanies her to the door; then hesitates; finally turns confidentially to HIGGINS.]

DOOLITTLE.

Listen here, Governor. You and me is men of the world, ain't we?

HIGGINS.

Oh! Men of the world, are we? You'd better go, Mrs. Pearce.

MRS. PEARCE.

I think so, indeed, sir. [She goes, with dignity].

PICKERING.

The floor is yours, Mr. Doolittle.

DOOLITTLE.

[to PICKERING] I thank you, Governor. [To HIGGINS, who takes **refuge**① on the piano bench, a little overwhelmed by the proximity of his visitor; for DOOLITTLE has a professional flavor of dust about him]. Well, the truth is, I've taken a sort of fancy to you, Governor; and if you want the girl, I'm not so set on having her back home again but what I might be open to an arrangement. Regarded in the light of a young woman, she's a fine handsome girl. As a daughter she's not worth her keep; and so I tell you straight. All I ask is my rights as a father; and you're the last man alive to expect me to let her go for nothing; for I can see you're one of the straight sort, Governor. Well, what's a five pound note to you? And what's Eliza to me? [He returns to his chair and sits down judicially].

PICKERING.

I think you ought to know, Doolittle, that Mr. Higgins's intentions are entirely honorable.

DOOLITTLE.

Course they are, Governor. If I thought they wasn't, I'd ask fifty.

HIGGINS.

[revolted] Do you mean to say, you callous **rascal**②, that you would sell your daughter for 50 pounds?

DOOLITTLE.

Not in a general way I wouldn't; but to oblige a gentleman like you I'd do a good deal, I do assure you.

PICKERING.

Have you no morals, man?

---

① 避难。

② 无赖。

DOOLITTLE.

[unabashed] Can't afford them, Governor. Neither could you if you was as poor as me. Not that I mean any harm, you know. But if Liza is going to have a bit out of this, why not me too?

HIGGINS.

[troubled] I don't know what to do, Pickering. There can be no question that as a matter of morals it's a positive crime to give this chap a farthing. And yet I feel a sort of rough justice in his claim.

DOOLITTLE.

That's it, Governor. That's all I say. A father's heart, as it were.

PICKERING.

Well, I know the feeling; but really it seems hardly right...

DOOLITTLE.

Don't say that, Governor. Don't look at it that way. What am I, Governors both? I ask you, what am I? I'm one of the undeserving poor: that's what I am. Think of what that means to a man. It means that he's up agen middle class morality all the time. If there's anything going, and I put in for a bit of it, it's always the same story: "You're undeserving; so you can't have it." But my needs is as great as the most deserving widow's that ever got money out of six different charities in one week for the death of the same husband. I don't need less than a deserving man: I need more. I don't eat less hearty than him; and I drink a lot more. I want a bit of amusement, cause I'm a thinking man. I want cheerfulness and a song and a band when I feel low. Well, they charge me just the same for everything as they charge the deserving. What is middle class morality? Just an excuse for never giving me anything. Therefore, I ask you, as two gentlemen, not to play that game on me. I'm playing straight with you. I ain't pretending to be deserving. I'm undeserving; and I mean to go on being undeserving. I like it; and that's the truth. Will you take advantage of a man's nature to do him out of the price of his own daughter what he's brought up and fed and clothed by the sweat of his brow until she's growed big enough to be interesting to you two gentlemen? Is five pounds unreasonable? I put it to you; and I leave it to you.

HIGGINS.

[rising, and going over to PICKERING] Pickering: if we were to take this man in hand for three months, he could choose between a seat in the Cabinet and a popular **pulpit**[1] in Wales.

PICKERING.

What do you say to that, Doolittle?

DOOLITTLE.

Not me, Governor, thank you kindly. I've heard all the preachers and all the prime ministers...for I'm a thinking man and game for politics or religion or social reform same as all the other amusements...and I tell you it's a dog's life anyway you look at it. Undeserving poverty is my line. Taking one station in society with another, it's...it's...well, it's the only one that has any ginger in it, to my taste.

HIGGINS.

I suppose we must give him a fiver.

PICKERING.

He'll make a bad use of it, I'm afraid.

DOOLITTLE.

Not me, Governor, so help me I won't. Don't you be afraid that I'll save it and spare it and live idle on it. There won't be a penny of it left by Monday: I'll have to go to work same as if I'd never had it. It won't **pauperize**[2] me, you bet. Just one good **spree**[3] for myself and the missus, giving pleasure to ourselves and employment to others, and satisfaction to you to think it's not been throwed away. You couldn't spend it better.

HIGGINS.

[taking out his pocket book and coming between DOOLITTLE and the piano] This is irresistible. Let's give him ten. [He offers two notes to the dustman].

DOOLITTLE.

No, Governor. She wouldn't have the heart to spend ten; and perhaps I shouldn't neither. Ten pounds is a lot of money: it makes a man feel prudent like; and then goodbye to happiness. You give me what I ask you, Governor: not a penny more, and not a penny less.

PICKERING.

Why don't you marry that missus of yours? I rather draw the line at encouraging that

---

① 讲道坛。
② 使贫穷。
③ 狂欢做乐

sort of immorality.

DOOLITTLE.

Tell her so, Governor: tell her so. I'm willing. It's me that suffers by it. I've no hold on her. I got to be agreeable to her. I got to give her presents. I got to buy her clothes something sinful. I'm a slave to that woman, Governor, just because I'm not her lawful husband. And she knows it too. Catch her marrying me! Take my advice, Governor: marry Eliza while she's young and don't know no better. If you don't you'll be sorry for it after. If you do, she'll be sorry for it after; but better you than her, because you're a man, and she's only a woman and don't know how to be happy anyhow.

HIGGINS.

Pickering: if we listen to this man another minute, we shall have no convictions left. [To DOOLITTLE] Five pounds I think you said.

DOOLITTLE.

Thank you kindly, Governor.

HIGGINS.

You're sure you won't take ten?

DOOLITTLE.

Not now. Another time, Governor.

HIGGINS.

[handing him a five-pound note] Here you are.

DOOLITTLE.

Thank you, Governor. Good morning.

[He hurries to the door, anxious to get away with his booty. When he opens it he is confronted with a dainty and exquisitely clean young Japanese lady in a simple blue cotton kimono printed **cunningly**① with small white jasmine blossoms. MRS. PEARCE is with her. He gets out of her way deferentially and apologizes]. Beg pardon, miss.

THE JAPANESE LADY.

Garn! Don't you know your own daughter?

DOOLITTLE.

[exclaiming simultaneously] Bly me! it's Eliza!

HIGGINS.

---

① 精巧地。

[exclaiming simultaneously] What's that! This!

PICKERING.

[exclaiming simultaneously] By Jove!

LIZA.

Don't I look silly?

HIGGINS.

Silly?

MRS. PEARCE

[at the door] Now, Mr. Higgins, please don't say anything to make the girl **conceited**[①] about herself.

HIGGINS.

[conscientiously] Oh! Quite right, Mrs. Pearce. [To ELIZA] Yes: damned silly.

MRS. PEARCE.

Please, sir.

HIGGINS.

[correcting himself] I mean extremely silly.

LIZA.

I should look all right with my hat on. [She takes up her hat; puts it on; and walks across the room to the fireplace with a fashionable air].

HIGGINS.

A new fashion, by George! And it ought to look horrible!

DOOLITTLE.

[with fatherly pride] Well, I never thought she'd clean up as good looking as that, Governor. She's a credit to me, ain't she?

LIZA.

I tell you, it's easy to clean up here. Hot and cold water on tap, just as much as you like, there is. Woolly towels, there is; and a towel horse so hot, it burns your fingers. Soft brushes to scrub yourself, and a wooden bowl of soap smelling like primroses. Now I know why ladies is so clean. Washing's a treat for them. Wish they saw what it is for the like of me!

HIGGINS.

---

① 自负的。

I'm glad the bath-room met with your approval.

LIZA.

It didn't: not all of it; and I don't care who hears me say it. Mrs. Pearce knows.

HIGGINS.

What was wrong, Mrs. Pearce?

MRS. PEARCE.

[blandly] Oh, nothing, sir. It doesn't matter.

LIZA.

I had a good mind to break it. I didn't know which way to look. But I hung a towel over it, I did.

HIGGINS.

Over what?

MRS. PEARCE.

Over the looking-glass, sir.

HIGGINS.

Doolittle: you have brought your daughter up too strictly.

DOOLITTLE.

Me! I never brought her up at all, except to give her a lick of a strap now and again. Don't put it on me, Governor. She ain't accustomed to it, you see: that's all. But she'll soon pick up your free-and-easy ways.

LIZA.

I'm a good girl, I am; and I won't pick up no free and easy ways.

HIGGINS.

Eliza: if you say again that you're a good girl, your father shall take you home.

LIZA.

Not him. You don't know my father. All he come here for was to touch you for some money to get drunk on.

DOOLITTLE.

Well, what else would I want money for? To put into the plate in church, I suppose. [She puts out her tongue at him. He is so **incensed**① by this that Pickering presently finds it necessary to step between them]. Don't you give me none of your lip; and don't let me

---

① 激怒的。

hear you giving this gentleman any of it neither, or you'll hear from me about it. See?

HIGGINS.

Have you any further advice to give her before you go, Doolittle? Your blessing, for instance.

DOOLITTLE.

No, Governor: I ain't such a mug as to put up my children to all I know myself. Hard enough to hold them in without that. If you want Eliza's mind improved, Governor, you do it yourself with a strap. So long, gentlemen. [He turns to go].

HIGGINS.

[impressively] Stop. You'll come regularly to see your daughter. It's your duty, you know. My brother is a clergyman; and he could help you in your talks with her.

DOOLITTLE.

[evasively] Certainly. I'll come, Governor. Not just this week, because I have a job at a distance. But later on you may depend on me. Afternoon, gentlemen. Afternoon, ma'am. [He takes off his hat to MRS. PEARCE, who disdains the salutation and goes out. He winks at HIGGINS, thinking him probably a fellow sufferer from Mrs. Pearce's difficult **disposition**①, and follows her].

LIZA.

Don't you believe the old liar. He'd as soon you set a bull-dog on him as a clergyman. You won't see him again in a hurry.

HIGGINS.

I don't want to, Eliza. Do you?

LIZA.

Not me. I don't want never to see him again, I don't. He's a disgrace to me, he is, collecting dust, instead of working at his trade.

PICKERING.

What is his trade, Eliza?

LIZA.

Talking money out of other people's pockets into his own. His proper trade's a **navvy**②; and he works at it sometimes too...for exercise...and earns good money at it. Ain't you going to call me Miss Doolittle any more?

---

① 性情。

② 挖土工。

PICKERING.

I beg your pardon, Miss Doolittle. It was a slip of the tongue.

LIZA.

Oh, I don't mind; only it sounded so genteel. I should just like to take a taxi to the corner of Tottenham Court Road and get out there and tell it to wait for me, just to put the girls in their place a bit. I wouldn't speak to them, you know.

PICKERING.

Better wait till we get you something really fashionable.

HIGGINS.

Besides, you shouldn't cut your old friends now that you have risen in the world. That's what we call **snobbery**①.

LIZA.

You don't call the like of them my friends now, I should hope. They've took it out of me often enough with their ridicule when they had the chance; and now I mean to get a bit of my own back. But if I'm to have fashionable clothes, I'll wait. I should like to have some. Mrs. Pearce says you're going to give me some to wear in bed at night different to what I wear in the daytime; but it do seem a waste of money when you could get something to show. Besides, I never could fancy changing into cold things on a winter night.

MRS. PEARCE.

[coming back] Now, Eliza. The new things have come for you to try on.

LIZA.

Ah...ow...oo...ooh! [She rushes out].

MRS. PEARCE.

[following her] Oh, don't rush about like that, girl [She shuts the door behind her].

HIGGINS.

Pickering: we have taken on a stiff job.

PICKERING.

[with conviction] Higgins: we have.

Ⅳ. 思考题

1. How is class differentiation depicted in this excerpt? What are some contrasts between

---

① 势利。

Higgins and Eliza?

2. How do you understand the gender issue depicted in this act? Do you see different interpretations from various characters?
3. What do you think is the so-called middle-class morality? What is Shaw's attitude toward this social concept?

Ⅴ. 文学批评

悲剧六要素

One of the most important critical studies on drama is Aristotle's Poetics which studies the famous Greek dramatic art, tragedy. Aristotle argues that tragedy is a poetic mimesis which imitates universal ideas to bring about a "catharsis" of the spectators...to arouse pity and fear so as to purge them from such feelings in real life.

According to Aristotle, tragedy has six main elements: plot, character, diction, thought, spectacle (scenic effect), and song, of which the first two are most important. He considers the plot is the most important element of tragedy:

Tragedy is an imitation, not of men, but of action and life, of happiness and misery. And life consists of action, and its end is a mode of activity, not a quality. Now character determines men's qualities, but it is their action that makes them happy or wretched. The purpose of action in the tragedy, therefore, is not the representation of character: character comes in as contributing to the action. Hence the incidents and the plot are the end of the tragedy; and the end is the chief thing of all. Without action there cannot be a tragedy; there may be one without character…. The plot, then, is the first principle, and, as it were, the soul of a tragedy: character holds the second place.

Aristotle goes on to say that the plot must be a complete whole—with a definite beginning, middle, and end—and its length should be such that the spectators can comprehend without difficulty both its separate parts and its overall unity. Moreover, the plot requires a single central theme in which all the elements are logically related to demonstrate the change in the protagonist's fortunes, with emphasis on the dramatic causation and probability of the events. Aristotle emphasizes the importance of plot that it is beyond the control of the protagonist or any individual influence.

The second most important element of a tragedy is character, who must be a figure with whom the audience can identify and sympathize. Aristotle defines the ideal protagonist as "…a man who is highly renowned and prosperous, but one who is not pre-eminently virtuous and just, whose misfortune, however, is brought upon him not by vice or depravity but by some error of judgment or frailty; a personage like Oedipus." In addition, the hero should not offend the moral sensibilities of the spectators, and as a character he must be true to type, true to life, and consistent.

The hero's error or frailty (harmartia) does initiate the events of the tragedy but it is wrong to overemphasize his own personality. Instead, the hero's fate, despite its immediate cause in his finite act, comes about because of the nature of the cosmic moral order and the role played by chance or destiny in human affairs.

The remainder of the *Poetics* is given over to examination of the other elements of tragedy and to discussion of various techniques, devices, and stylistic principles.

The *Poetics* contains much valuable information about the origins, methods, and purposes of tragedy, and to some extent how the Greeks themselves reacted to their theater. In addition, the ideas and principles of the *Poetics* dominated the composition of tragedy in western Europe during the seventeenth, eighteenth, and nineteenth centuries.

Ⅵ. 拓展阅读

Charles Berst, Fred Marker, and Fred Berg's *The Cambridge Companion to George Bernard Shaw* (Cambridge University Press, 1998).

Milton Crane's "*Pygmalion*: Bernard Shaw's Dramatic Theory and Practice" (*Publications of the Modern Language Association of America* (1951): 879-85).

Timothy Chappell's *Values and Virtues*: *Aristotelianism in Contemporary Ethics* (Oxford University Press, 2006).

Ⅶ. 参考文献

Aristotle. *Poetics*. Trans. Malcolm Heath. Penguin Classics, 1997.

Chapter 3　Thomas Mann and Literary Classicism

Ⅰ. 作者简介

托马斯 · 曼 Thomas Mann（1875—1955），德国作家，1875 年生于德国北部吕贝克的一个望族，父亲曾任该市参议员和副市长。1891 年托马斯 · 曼的父亲去世，母亲带着他的弟弟妹妹迁往慕尼黑，他自己则继续留在吕贝克读中学。1894 年中学毕业后，他也去了慕尼黑，在一家保险公司当实习生，并在慕尼黑几所大学旁听历史和文学史课程，还参与编辑《二十世纪》和《痴儿》杂志。

处女作中篇小说《沦落》于 1894 年发表，1901 年发表成名作《布登勃洛克一家》。此后便专门从事创作。《布登勃洛克一家》描写的是吕贝克望族布登勃洛克一家四代人从 1835 年到 1877 年间的兴衰史。通过对布登勃洛克一家在垄断资产阶级家族的排挤、打击下逐渐衰落的历史描写，详细地揭示了资本主义旧的刻意盘剥和新的掠夺兼并方式的激烈竞争和历史成败，成为德国 19 世纪后半期社会发展的缩影。但因作者受叔本华、尼采哲学思想的影响，小说对帝国主义势力持无能为力的消极态度，对自由资产阶级抱无可奈何的哀婉情绪。

1905年，托马斯·曼同卡蒂娅普林斯·海姆结婚。尽管曼对自己的同性恋倾向不是一无所知，但他选择了压抑克制。他们生了六个孩子，三儿三女。除了长子克劳斯·曼，长女艾丽卡·曼也是一位作家、演员和社会活动家。克劳斯·曼和艾丽卡·曼都是公开的同性恋者。托马斯·曼1912年写成中篇小说《死于威尼斯》，被搬上银幕之后，引起了国际上对他同性恋身份的注视。

1924年他发表了长篇哲理小说《魔山》，进一步奠定了他在国际文坛上的地位。他在祖国德国的名声于20世纪20年代达到了最高峰，1929年荣获诺贝尔文学奖，理由是："由于他那本伟大小说《布登勃洛克一家》，它在当代文学中具有日益巩固的经典地位。"("principally for his great novel, *Buddenbrooks*, which has won steadily increased recognition as one of the classic works of contemporary literature.")

这之后，他担任了很有影响的德国文学艺术院的院长，虽然他对种种公务的缠身感到不满，但他意识到，这一职位使他在帮助其他作家方面有了更大的自由，也使他有了避开纳粹舆论界攻击的威望。1933年希特勒上台，他撰文谴责法西斯对德国文化的歪曲和破坏，被迫流亡国外，于1938年移居美国，1944年加入美国籍。

第二次世界大战期间，托马斯·曼发表了大量广播演说，反对希特勒法西斯主义。流亡期间他创作了大量作品。1933-1943年完成颂扬犹太人、反对纳粹种族主义的四部曲《约瑟和他的兄弟们》，包括《雅各的故事》(1933年)、《约瑟的青年时代》(1934年)、《约瑟在埃及》(1936年)和《赡养者约瑟》(1943年)。1939年发表长篇历史小说《绿蒂在魏玛》，1943-1946年完成反映艺术家悲剧的长篇小说《浮士德博士》(1947年)等。20世纪50年代发表长篇小说《被挑选者》(1951年)，反映他对战败的德国应采取宽容政策的主张。未完成的长篇小说《大骗子菲利克斯·克鲁尔的自由——回忆录第一部分》(1954年)再次探讨资本主义社会中艺术家的命运问题。1952年托马斯·曼移居瑞士。

托马斯·曼坚持写作，直至生命的最后一息，他还写了大量的评论文章和书信，在他漫长的文学生涯中总共写了二万多封信。他于1955年在瑞士苏黎世逝世。

Ⅱ.内容提要

中篇小说《死于威尼斯》讲述了正直而有名望的主人公阿申巴赫10年孜孜不倦地潜身于创作,一心想攀登艺术高峰的故事。长年累月的辛勤工作使阿申巴赫心力交瘁,为使紧张的大脑得以休息,他决定做一次旅行。阿申巴赫在威尼斯的饭店里偶遇一个非常俊美的波兰籍男孩塔齐奥,并深深被其吸引。他认为孩子是美的化身,因而陷入一种反常的情爱里不能自拔,但他只是默默尾随却不敢接近。不久,威尼斯瘟疫横行,外国游客纷纷回国,而阿申巴赫明知有染疾身亡的危险,却偏偏不肯离开,宁愿守在孩子身旁。阿申巴赫苦心经营了几十年的理性和意志帝国逐渐崩塌,他意乱情迷,荒诞不经,最终在最后一次追随塔齐奥时死在了沙滩上。

托马斯·曼本人称这部中篇小说为"名副其实的结晶体,这是一种结构,从许许多多的晶面上放射出光辉。它蕴含着无数隐喻;当作品成型时,连作者本人也不禁为之目眩"。他认为作品的主题是"死亡的诱惑力和神魂颠倒中的无秩序以及激情洪流具有毁灭性的突然入侵,这些战胜了井然有序、有条不紊、貌似时刻处于控制之中的平静生活"。当代秘鲁作家、诺贝尔文学奖获得者略萨认为这篇小说是史上最优秀的中篇小说之一。美国举行的一次文学作品评选则把该作品评为一百部同性恋小说之首,压倒三岛由纪夫的《禁色》和劳伦斯的《恋爱中的女人》。而著名意大利导演维斯康蒂根据小说改编拍摄的电影《威尼斯之死》也影响巨大,在电影史上占据着重要地位。

作者在小说中用精细的笔触描写了地中海的地景人情,刻画了作家在暗恋中的微妙心理和各种举动,并且从个人体验出发对艺术家心理和观念以及艺术追求历程进行了细致的再现。小说中的诸多意象——炎热的天气、老虎、丛林,以及各种形象怪诞的人等,都让作品笼罩着诡异而神秘的气氛,整部作品有着丰富的内涵和象征意义。

Ⅲ. 作品

ONE

Gustav Aschenbach, or von Aschenbach, as he had officially been known since his fiftieth birthday, set out alone from his residence in Munich's **Prinzregentenstrasse**① on a spring afternoon in 19... with the intention of taking an extended walk. **Overwrought**② from the difficult and dangerous labors of the late morning hours, labors demanding the utmost caution, **prudence**③, **tenacity**④, and precision of will, the writer had even after the midday meal been unable to **halt**⑤ the **momentum**⑥ of the inner mechanism. And so, shortly after tea he had sought the outdoors in the hope that open air and exercise might revive him and help him to enjoy a fruitful evening.

It was early May, and after a few cold, wet weeks a **mock**⑦ summer had set in. The English Garden, though as yet in tender bud, was as **muggy**⑧ as in August and full of vehicles and pedestrians on the city side. At **Aumeister**⑨, to which he had been led by ever more solitary paths, Aschenbach briefly scanned the crowded and lively open-air restaurant and the cabs and carriages along its edge, then, the sun beginning to sink. He stopped at the Northern **Cemetery**⑩ to wait for the **tram**⑪ that would take him straight back to town.

As it happened, there was no one at the tram stop. Nor was any vehicle to be seen on the paved roadway. There was nothing stirring behind the stonemasons' fences, where crosses, headstones, and monuments for sale formed a second, uninhabited graveyard, and the mortuary's Byzantine structure opposite stood silent in the glow of the waning day. Its

① 地名:慕尼黑摄政王街。
② 筋疲力尽。
③ 细致。
④ 毅力。
⑤ 停止,抑制。
⑥ 势头。
⑦ 似是而非的。
⑧ 闷热的。
⑨ 地名:奥迈斯特。
⑩ 公墓,墓园。
⑪ 电车。

façade displayed a selection of **symmetrically**① arranged **gilt**②-lettered inscriptions concerning the afterlife, such as "They Enter into the Dwelling Place of the Lord" or "May the Light Everlasting Shine upon Them," and reading the formulas, letting his mind's eye lose itself in the mysticism served to distract the waiting man for several minutes until, resurfacing from his reveries, he noticed a figure in the **portico**③, and something slightly out of the ordinary in the figure's appearance gave his thoughts an entirely new turn.

The man—of medium height, thin, beardless and strikingly **snub-nosed**④—was the red-haired type and had its milky, freckled complexion. The broad, straight-brimmed bast **hat**⑤ covering his head lent him a distinctly foreign, exotic air. He did, however, have the customary **knapsack**⑥ strapped to his shoulders, wore a yellowish belted suit of what appeared to be loden, and carried a gray waterproof over his left forearm, which he pressed to his side, and an iron-tipped walking stick in his right hand, and having thrust the stick diagonally into the ground, he had crossed his feet and braced one hip on its crook. Holding his head high and thus exposing a strong, bare Adam's apple on the thin neck rising out of his loose, open shirt, he gazed alert into the distance with colorless, red-lashed eyes, the two **pronounced**⑦ vertical **furrows**⑧ between them oddly suited to the short, turned-up nose. Thus—and perhaps his elevated and elevating position contributed to the impression there was something of the man, something lordly, bold, even wild in his **demeanor**⑨, for be it that he was grimacing, blinded by the setting sun, or that he had a permanent facial **deformity**⑩, his lips seemed too short: they pulled all the way back, baring his long, white teeth to the **gums**⑪.

Aschenbach's half-distracted, half-inquisitive scrutiny of the stranger may have been lacking in discretion, for he suddenly perceived that the man was returning his stare and was indeed so directly, so blatantly determined to challenge him publicly and force him to

① 对称地。
② 镀金的,金边的。
③ 门廊。
④ 塌鼻的。
⑤ 草帽。
⑥ 背包。
⑦ 明显的。
⑧ 皱纹。
⑨ 举止。
⑩ 畸形。
⑪ 牙龈。

withdraw it that Aschenbach, embarrassed, turned away and set off along the fence, vaguely resolved to take no further notice of him. A minute later he had forgotten the man.

It may have been the stranger's appearance that acted upon his imagination or some other physical or psychological influence coming into play, but much to his surprise he grew aware of a strange expansion of his inner being, a kind of restive anxiety, a **fervent**① youthful craving for faraway places, a feeling so vivid, so new or else so long outgrown and forgotten that he came to a standstill and—hands behind his back, eyes on the ground, rooted to the spot—examined the nature and his own feeling.

He had—at least since he could afford the advantages of traveling the world at will—regarded tourism as nothing but a hygienic **precaution**② to be taken from time to time. Preoccupied with the tasks imposed upon him by his ego and the European psyche, overburdened by the obligation to produce, and no lover of the external world, he is never so much as tempted to venture beyond Europe. Especially now that his life was on the decline and his fear of failing to achieve his artistic goals—the concern that his time might run out before he had accomplished what he needed to accomplish, he had confined his external existence almost exclusively to the beautiful city that had become his home and the rustic cottage he had built for himself in the mountains.

Thus the sudden impulse which had come over him was soon restrained and redressed by reason and the self-discipline he had practiced from an early age. He had intended to reach a certain point in his work, which was his life, before moving to the country, and the thought of leaving his desk for months to go wandering around the world seemed too frivolous and disruptive to be taken seriously. Yet he knew only too well the source of the sudden temptation. It was an urge to flee—he fully admitted it, this yearning for freedom, release, an urge to flee his work, the **humdrum**③ routine of a rigid, cold, passionate duty.

TWO

The author of "A Wretched Figure" that had earned him the gratitude of the younger generation by showing it a path to moral fortitude existing even beyond the depths of knowledge; and the thinker whose impassioned treatise, "Art and the Intellect," had led serious critics to rank him, on the strength of the work's rigorous logic and eloquent use of antithe-

---

① 狂热的。

② 养生之道。

③ 乏味的，平凡的。

ses, alongside **Schiller**① and his meditation "On Naive and Sentimental Poetry"—Gustav Aschenbach was born in L., a county town in the province of Silesia, the son of a senior official in the judiciary. His **forebears**② had been officers, judges, and civil servants, men who led disciplined, decently **austere**③ lives serving king and state.

Since his entire being was bent on fame, he proved himself if not quite precocious then at least, thanks to the resolute and precise persona he cultivated. Barely out of school he had acquired a name for himself. In the space of ten years he had learned to perform his professional duties and manage his fame from his writing desk and to make every sentence of his correspondence gracious and pregnant with meaning (letters had to be brief, because the demands made on the staunch and successful are many). The forty-year-old, worn down by the strains of his work, had to cope with a daily mail bearing stamps from all over the world.

Equidistant④ from the **banal**⑤ and the **eccentric**⑥, his talent seemed tailored to gain both the confidence of the general public and the demanding admiration of the **connoisseur**⑦. Since boyhood he had been pressed from all sides to achieve—and to achieve the extraordinary and thus had never known leisure, the carefree idleness of youth. When in about his thirty-fifth year he was taken ill in Vienna.

Wishing to bear on such frail shoulders the burdens imposed by his talent and wishing to go far, he had great need of discipline, and discipline was fortunately an inborn quality he had inherited from his father's side of the family. At forty at fifty and even when younger, at an age when others **dissipate**⑧ their talents, or blissfully **defer**⑨ their grand projects, he would start his day early by **dashing**⑩ cold water over his chest and back; then, having set a pair of tall wax candles in silver holders at the head of his manuscript, he would spend two or three fervent, conscientious hours offering up to art the strength he had

---

① 席勒(1759—1805),德国著名诗人、哲学家、历史学家和剧作家。
② 祖先。
③ 简朴的,苦行的,一丝不苟的。
④ 等距的。
⑤ 平庸的。
⑥ 古怪的。
⑦ 鉴赏家。
⑧ 驱散,挥霍。
⑨ 拖延。
⑩ 泼溅。

garnered① in sleep.

Once, in a less than conspicuous passage, Aschenbach stated outright that nearly everything great owes its existence to "despites": despite misery and affliction, poverty, desolation, physical debility, vice, passion, and a thousand other obstacles. But it was more than an observation; it was his experience, the very formula of his life and fame, the key to his work.

Gustav Aschenbach was the writer of all those who labor on the brink of exhaustion, the heavy-laden, the worn-down who yet hold their heads high, the moralists of achievement who, though slight of stature and **chary**② of means, manage to attain, for a time at least, the trappings of greatness by combining rapture of the will with clever management. They are the heroes of the age. And they all recognized themselves in his work, found themselves validated, celebrated, glorified therein; they rendered him thanks and proclaimed his name.

After several restless years of testing this place and that, he eventually chose Munich as his permanent residence and led a solid bourgeois existence there, enjoying the respect that is in certain cases **vouchsafed**③ by the intellect. The marriage he had contracted in his youth with a girl from a scholarly family was cut short, following a brief period of bliss, by the girl's death. It left him with a daughter, who was now married. He had had no son.

Gustav von Aschenbach was of somewhat less than medium height, dark, and clean-shaven. The head seemed a bit too large for the almost **dainty**④ body. The hair, brushed back, was thin at the crown but very thick and gray at the **temples**⑤ and framed a high, **rugged**⑥ looking forehead. The gold frame of the **rimless**⑦ spectacles cut into the root of a strong, nobly **aquiline**⑧ nose. The mouth was large—now **slack**⑨, now suddenly narrow

---

① 获得。
② 谨慎的。
③ 赐予。
④ 娇小的。
⑤ 鬓角。
⑥ 凹凸不平的，这里指皱纹密布的。
⑦ 无框的。
⑧ 钩的。
⑨ 松弛的。

and tight—the cheeks **sunken**① and furrowed. Important destinies must have passed through that head, which was often tilted **dolefully**②, yet it was art—not, as is commonly the case, a hard and turbulent life—that had formed the **physiognomy**③. On a personal level, too, art is life intensified: it delights more deeply, consumes more rapidly; it engraves the traces of imaginary and intellectual adventure on the **countenance**④ of its servant and in the long run, for all the **monastic**⑤ calm of his external existence, leads to self-indulgence, over-refinement, **lethargy**⑥, and a restless curiosity that a lifetime of wild passions and pleasures could scarcely engender.

THREE

Several matters of a mundane and literary nature kept him in Munich for approximately a fortnight after that walk and on a day between mid and late May he set off by night train for **Trieste**⑦, where he spent only twenty-four hours, boarding the ship for Pola the next morning.

What he sought was something exotic and distinctive yet of easy access, and so he stopped at an island in the Adriatic, not far from the coast of Istria, one that had acquired a following in recent years and featured beautifully jagged cliffs facing the open sea. But rain, a heavy atmosphere, the provincial closed society of the Austrian hotel guests, and the lack of a peaceful, intimate contact with the sea that only a soft, sandy beach can provide had soured him and kept him from feeling he had found his final destination.

He was troubled by an impulse to go he knew not quite where, and he was studying the ships' timetables. Where did one go when one wished to travel overnight to a unique, fairytale-like location? What was he doing here? He had come to the wrong place. That is where he should have gone. He lost no time in announcing his departure. A week and a half after his arrival on the island a swift motorboat bore him and his luggage across the

① 瘦削的。
② 伤感地，忧郁地。
③ 面相。
④ 面容。
⑤ 修道院的，平静的。
⑥ 困乏，嗜睡。
⑦ 的里雅斯特（意大利东北部港市）。

misty morning water back to the naval base and he **disembarked**① only to mount a **gang-plank**② leading to the damp deck of a steamer about to weigh anchor for Venice.

Aschenbach went on deck. With one arm propped on the railing he watched first the idlers **loitering**③ on the **quay**④ to watch the ship set sail, then the passengers on board. The second-class passengers, men and women both, were **squatting**⑤ on the forward deck, using their crates and **bundles**⑥ as rests. A group of young men on the upper deck, Pola shop assistants by the look of them, excited by the prospect of a jaunt to Italy, were making a great to-do about themselves and their venture, jabbering, laughing, indulging **smugly**⑦ in their gesticulations, and leaning over the railing to shout **jeers**⑧ at their friends, who were moving along the embankment, clutching their briefcases and shaking their canes menacingly at the holidaymakers.

One of them, wearing an extravagantly cut pale-yellow summer suit, a red necktie, and a Panama hat, outdid the others in his **raucous**⑨ show of **mirth**⑩. Once Aschenbach had had a closer look at him, however, he realized with something akin to horror that the man was no youth. He was old, there was no doubting it: he had wrinkles around his eyes and mouth; the crimson of his cheeks was **rouge**⑪; the brown hair beneath the straw hat **toupee**⑫; the neck—scrawny, **emaciated**⑬; the stuck—on mustache and imperial on his chin—dyed; the full complement of yellow teeth—a cheap **denture**⑭; and the hands, with rings on both forefingers, those of an old man. A shudder ran through Aschenbach as he watched him and his interplay with his friends. Did they not know, could they not see that

---

① 登陆。
② 跳板。
③ 游荡，闲逛。
④ 码头。
⑤ 蹲。
⑥ 箱子和行李包。
⑦ 洋洋自得。
⑧ 嘲笑，戏弄。
⑨ 喧闹的。
⑩ 欢乐。
⑪ 胭脂。
⑫ 假发。
⑬ 消瘦的。
⑭ 假牙。

he was old, that he had no right to be wearing their **foppish**① , **gaudy**② clothes, no right to be carrying on as if he were one of them? They seemed to be used to him and take him for granted, tolerating his presence and treating him as an equal, returning his pokes in the ribs without **malice**③. How could they? Aschenbach laid his hand on his forehead and shut his eyes: they felt hot for want of sleep. He had the impression that something was not quite normal, that a dreamlike disaffection, a warping of the world into something alien was about to take hold, however, he felt a floating sensation and, looking up panic-stricken, realized that the heavy, dingy bulk of the ship was slowly casting off from the stone **jetty**④.

The sky was gray, the wind humid. Harbor and islands left behind, all land soon disappeared from sight in the haze. Flakes of coal dust, bloated with moisture, settled on the swabbed deck, which refused to dry. Before an hour was up, a sailcloth awning was spread out: it had started to rain. Wrapped in his coat, a book in his lap, the traveler took his ease, the hours slipping by unnoticed. The rain had ceased; the awning been taken down. The horizon was now visible in its entirety. The vast disk of the barren sea stretched out beneath the **turbid**⑤ dome of the sky. But in empty, unarticulated space our senses lose the capacity to articulate time as well, and we sink into the immeasurable. Strange, shadowy figures—the superannuated dandy, the goateed purser from deep in the hold—passed through his mind with vague gestures and jumbled dreamlike utterances, and he fell asleep.

The engine stopped, **gondolas**⑥ pressed alongside, the gangplank was lowered, and **customs**⑦ officials came aboard and discharged their duties: disembarkation could proceed. Aschenbach let it be known that he wished to have a gondola convey him and his luggage to the **vaporetti**⑧ **pier**⑨ that ply between the city and the **Lido**⑩, for he intended to take up residence by the sea. His plan was approved, his request shouted to the water below, where the gondoliers were squabbling in dialect.

---

① 纨绔子弟的,花花公子的。

② 艳俗的。

③ 恶意。

④ 筑堤。

⑤ 浑浊的。

⑥ 贡多拉,威尼斯特有的一种小船,船身狭长,底部平坦,船首与船尾均较高。

⑦ 海关。

⑧ 交通汽艇。

⑨ 码头。

⑩ 海滨浴场。

Who has not battled a fleeting shudder, a secret dread and anxiety upon boarding a Venetian gondola for the first time or after a prolonged absence? That strange conveyance, coming down to us unaltered from the days of the ballads and so distinctively black, black as only coffins can be—it conjures up **hush-hush**① criminal adventures in the rippling night and, even more, death itself: the **bier**②, the obscure **obsequies**③, the final, silent journey. And has anyone observed that the seat in such a boat, that armchair **lacquered**④ coffin-black with its dull black upholstery, is the softest, most soothing, most voluptuous seat in the world? Aschenbach grew aware of this after settling down at the gondolier's feet opposite his luggage, which lay neatly assembled in the prow. The rowers were still squabbling, raucous and unintelligible, gesturing menacingly, but the strange silence of this city of water seemed to absorb their voices gently, disembody them, and scatter them over the sea. It was warm here in the harbor. Lulled by the **tepid**⑤ breath of the **sirocco**⑥, lolling on the cushions over the **pliant**⑦ element, the traveler closed his eyes and yielded to a **lassitude**⑧ as unwonted as it was sweet. "The ride will be brief," he thought. "Could it but last forever." Rocking tranquilly, he felt himself drift away from the throng and the jumble of voices.

How calm and yet calmer his surroundings became! There was nothing to be heard but the plash of the **oar**⑨ and the hollow thump of the waves against the prow, which rose up over the water, steep and black and reinforced at the tip like a halberd, and yet a third sound, a mutter, a murmur, the whisper of the gondolier talking to himself through clenched teeth, in fits and starts, the sounds extracted by the effort of his arms. Aschenbach glanced up and noted not without **consternation**⑩ that the **lagoon**⑪ was widening about him and the gondola making for the open sea. Clearly he could not relax all that much; he would have to see to the execution of his wishes.

---

① 极为秘密的。
② 棺材。
③ 葬礼。
④ 漆,上漆。
⑤ 微温的。
⑥ 热风。
⑦ 顺从的。
⑧ 倦怠。
⑨ 船桨。
⑩ 惊愕。
⑪ 咸水湖。

"To the vaporetto pier, I told you!" he said, half turning. The murmuring ceased, but no reply was forthcoming.

"To the vaporetto pier, I said!" he repeated, turning all the way round and peering up into the face of the gondolier, who loomed behind him on his raised plank against the pallid sky. He had a **disobliging**①, even brutal physiognomy and was dressed in navy blue, with a yellow **sash**② wound round his waist and a shapeless straw hat. The cast of the face and the curly blond mustache under the small snub nose made him look anything but Italian. Though rather **frailly**③ built—one would not have thought him particularly suited to his trade—he handled the oar with great energy, putting his whole body into every stroke. From time to time, his lips drawn back by the strain, he bared a set of white teeth. Knitting his reddish eyebrows, he looked over his charge's head and retorted in **curt**④, almost **churlish**⑤ tones, "You are going to the Lido."

"I am," Aschenbach parried, "but I hired the gondola to take me only as far as San Marco. I wish to transfer to the vaporetto."

"You cannot transfer to the vaporetto, sir."

"And why not?"

"Because the vaporetto takes no luggage."

That was so, Aschenbach remembered. He said nothing, but the **gruff**⑥ manner, so unlike the treatment foreigners usually receive from the natives, he found disagreeable.

"That is my business," he said. "Perhaps I wish to **deposit**⑦ my luggage there. You will turn back."

Silence. The oar plashed; the water thudded against the prow. Presently the muttering and murmuring commenced again: the gondolier was talking to himself between his teeth.

What was he to do? Alone on the water with this oddly obstreperous, uncannily determined man, the traveler saw no way of imposing his will. Besides, what a nice rest he could have if he did not lose his temper! Had he not wished the trip to last longer, last forever?

---

① 不招人喜欢的。
② 腰带。
③ 脆弱的。
④ 草率的。
⑤ 无礼的。
⑥ 冷淡的,生硬的。
⑦ 寄存。

It was wisest to let things take their course; what is more, it was highly pleasant. A sense of duty or pride, the recollection, as it were, that one might forestall such things, moved him to pull himself together, and he asked, "What do you charge for the trip?"

Looking straight past him, the gondolier answered, "You will pay."

The response called for was clear. "I shall not pay a thing," Aschenbach answered mechanically, "not a thing if you take me where I do not want to go."

"You want to go to the Lido."

"But not with you."

"I am rowing you well."

Fair enough, thought Aschenbach, relaxing. Fair enough. You are rowing me well. Even if you are after my purse and send me to **the House of Hades**① with a bash of the oar from behind, you will have rowed me well.

But nothing of the sort occurred. They even had company: a boatload of musical highwaymen, men and women both, singing to a guitar and a mandolin and sailing solicitously alongside the gondola, filling the stillness over the waters with their **venal**② for foreigners only poetry. Aschenbach tossed some money into the hat they held out. They immediately fell silent and departed whereupon he could hear the gondolier whispering again, carrying on his intermittent conversation with himself.

And so they arrived, bobbing in the wake of a vaporetto bound for the city. Two municipal officials, their hands behind their backs, were pacing up and down the embankment, looking out over the lagoon. Aschenbach left the gondola at the landing stage, assisted by the old man to be found at every landing stage in Venice, and, having run out of coins, crossed to the hotel opposite the pier to break a **banknote**③ and give the oarsman his just deserts. After being attended to in the lobby, he returned to find his belongings on a cart on the pier and the gondola and gondolier gone, nowhere to be seen.

"He took off," said the old man. "A bad lot that man. He had no license, sir. The only gondolier without one. The others phoned over to us. He saw the officials waiting for him, so he took off."

Aschenbach shrugged.

"You got a free ride, sir," the old man said, holding his hat out. Aschenbach tossed

① 冥王之府,地狱。

② 为钱而干的,以盈利为目的的。

③ 兑换零钱。

some coins into it. He gave instructions for his luggage to be taken to the Hotel des Bains and followed the cart along the avenue, the white-blossoming tree-lined avenue which, **flanked**① by **taverns**②, **bazaars**③, and boardinghouses, ran straight across the island to the beach.

He entered the spacious hotel from the back, the garden terrace, and made his way through the spacious lobby and vestibule to the office. Since he was expected, he was received with assiduous deference. The manager, a short, quiet, obsequiously courteous man sporting a black mustache and a frock coat of French cut, rode up to the second floor with him and showed him to his room, a pleasant place furnished with cherry-wood furniture and decorated with strongly scented flowers, its high windows offering a view of the open sea. He walked up to one of them after the manager had withdrawn, and while his luggage was being brought in and set down behind him he gazed out at the beach, which was all but devoid of people, it being afternoon, and the sunless sea, which at high tide was sending long, low waves against the shore in a calm, regular cadence.

The figures encountered on the journey—the repulsive old fop with his "sweetheart" drivel, the outlaw gondolier defrauded of his fee—still remained in the traveler's mind. Though neither difficult to explain rationally nor even thought-provoking, they were utterly **outlandish**④—or so he found them—and **unsettling**⑤. For the moment, however, he greeted the sea with his eyes, delighted that Venice was so near and easy of access, and at length he turned, washed his face, gave the **chambermaid**⑥ instructions for seeing to his comfort, and had himself conveyed by the green-clad Swiss lift attendant to the ground floor.

He took his tea on the seaside terrace, then went down and walked a good distance along the **promenade**⑦ in the direction of the Hotel Excelsior. Upon his return he thought it time to change for dinner. He did so in his usual slow and deliberate manner, for he was accustomed to work while attending to his toilet, yet he reached the lobby a bit too early, finding a goodly number of the guests, strangers to one another, feigning mutual indifference

① 两侧设有。
② 酒馆,客栈。
③ 集市。
④ 古怪的。
⑤ 使人不安的。
⑥ 女服务员。
⑦ 走道,通道。

as they waited together for the meal. He picked up a newspaper from the table, settled into a leather armchair, and cast an eye over the company, which differed largely from that of his previous hotel.

A broad, tolerant, all-encompassing horizon opened before him. Sounds of the major languages **mingled**① in muted tones. Internationally recognized evening dress, that uniform of civilization, made of the diversity a **semblance**② of **homogeneous**③ decency. He saw the dry, long face of an American, a large Russian clan, English ladies, and German children with French nurses. The Slav element seemed to prevail. Polish was being spoken in his immediate vicinity.

It came from a group of young people of various ages seated around a **wicker**④ table under the supervision of a governess or female companion: three girls, between the ages of fifteen and seventeen from the looks of them, and long-haired boy of about fourteen. Aschenbach noted with astonishment that the boy was of a **consummate**⑤ beauty: his face—pale and charmingly **reticent**⑥, ringed by honey-colored hair, with a straight nose, lovely mouth, and an expression of **gravity**⑦ sweet and divine recalled Greek **statuary**⑧ of the noblest period, yet its purest formal perfection notwithstanding it conveyed a unique personal charm such that whoever might gaze upon it would believe he had never **beheld**⑨ anything so accomplished, be it in nature or in art. Also striking were the clear and fundamental differences in the approach to child rearing that appeared to govern the dress and general behavior of the siblings. The **attire**⑩ of the three girls, the eldest of whom could be considered grown up, was austere and chaste: their identical habit-like slate-colored, knee-length dresses, sober and deliberately unbecoming in cut and brightened only by white turndown collars, suppressed and **nullified**⑪ any grace they might have had. Their hair, plastered down smoothly over their heads, made their faces as vacant and inexpressive as a

---

① 混合。
② 外表,外观。
③ 同质的。
④ 柳条编织的。
⑤ 完美的,无比的,至上的。
⑥ 含蓄的。
⑦ 庄重,严肃。
⑧ 雕像。
⑨ 看,注视。
⑩ 服装,衣服。
⑪ nullify:注销,销毁。

nun①'s. Surely a mother was at work here, and one who had no intention of applying to the boy the strict **pedagogical**② principles she deemed appropriate to the girls. In his life, softness and tenderness clearly held sway. His fair hair had been spared the **shears**③: it curled down over his forehead and ears and still lower onto his neck. The English sailor's suit—with its puffy sleeves narrowing to tight circles around the dainty wrists of the still childlike but slender hands and its braiding, bows, and embroideries—gave his delicate figure a rich and **pampered**④ appearance. He sat half facing his observer with one black leather shoe in front of the other, an elbow propped on the arm of his wicker chair, and a cheek resting against the closed hand in an attitude of **nonchalant**⑤ manner and completely devoid of the servile⑥ rigidity to which his female siblings seemed accustomed. Was he **ailing**⑦? His complexion stood out white as ivory against the darker gold of the surrounding curls. Or was he merely the **coddled**⑧ favorite, the object of a biased and volatile love? Aschenbach inclined towards the latter. Innate in nearly every artistic nature is a **wanton**⑨, treacherous **penchant**⑩ for accepting injustice when it creates beauty and showing sympathy for and paying **homage to**⑪ aristocratic privilege.

A waiter made the rounds, announcing in English that dinner was served, and the guests gradually disappeared through the glass door. Latecomers straggled past from the vestibule and lifts. Service had begun in the dining room, but the young Poles lingered at their wicker table, and Aschenbach, comfortably seated in his deep armchair and admiring the beauty before his eyes besides, waited with them.

The governess—a short, **corpulent**⑫, red-faced woman of not quite gentle birth—signaled them at last to rise. Arching her brows, she pushed her chair back and bowed when a tall woman dressed in grayish white and richly adorned with pearls entered the lobby.

---

① 修女,尼姑。
② 教学的。
③ 剪切,修剪。
④ 娇宠的。
⑤ 漫不经心的。
⑥ 奴性的。
⑦ 体弱多病的。
⑧ 宠爱的。
⑨ 任性的,荒唐的。
⑩ 倾向。
⑪ 崇拜,膜拜。
⑫ 肥胖的。

The woman's demeanor was cool and dignified; the look of her lightly powdered hair and the cut of her dress displayed the simplicity that prescribes taste wherever **piety**① is deemed an attribute of aristocracy. She could have been the wife of a high-ranking German official. The only aspect of her appearance evincing a certain fanciful sense of luxury was the jewelry, which was in fact nearly worthless and consisted of earrings plus a very long triple strand of gently shimmering pearls the size of cherries.

The siblings had risen quickly. They bent to kiss the hand of their mother, who, a reserved smile on her well-preserved yet somewhat weary and pointy-nosed face, looked past their heads and addressed a few words in French to the governess. Then she went over to the glass door. The children followed, the girls in order of age, the governess, and finally the boy. For some reason he looked back before crossing the threshold, and since there was no one else left in the lobby, his eyes, of an unusual twilight gray, met those of Aschenbach, who, his paper in his lap, was absorbed in watching the group make its exit.

There was certainly nothing the least bit remarkable about what he had seen. The children had not gone in before their mother; they had waited for her, greeted her deferentially, and observed the customary formalities when entering the dining room. Yet it had all been done so deliberately, with such concern for discipline, duty, and self-esteem that Aschenbach felt strangely moved. He hesitated a few moments more, then he too made his way to the dining room and was shown to his table, which, he noted with a brief stir of regret, was at some remove from that of the Polish family.

Tired yet mentally alert, he **whiled away**② the lengthy meal pondering abstract, even **transcendental**③ matters such as the mysterious connection that must be established between the generic and the particular to produce human beauty and moving on to general problems of form and art only to conclude that his thoughts and discoveries resembled certain revelations that come to us in dreams and after **sober**④ consideration prove perfectly **inane**⑤ and worthless. He lingered after dinner—sitting and smoking, strolling through the hotel grounds enjoying the evening fragrance—then retired early and spent the night in a deep sleep, unbroken, yet animated by a number of dreams.

---

① 虔诚。
② 消磨时间。
③ 超验的。
④ 清醒的,冷静的。
⑤ 空洞的。

The weather had not improved the next morning. The wind came from the land. The sea was dull and calm, shrunken almost, under a pale, overcast sky, the horizon blandly close; the sea had retreated so far from the beach that it left several rows of long sandbanks exposed. Opening his window, Aschenbach thought he could smell the **foul**① **stench**② of the lagoon.

A sudden **despondency**③ came over him. He considered leaving then and there. Once, years before, after weeks of a beautiful spring, he had been visited by this sort of weather and it so affected his health he had been obliged to flee. Was not the same fever setting in? The pressure in the temples, the heavy eyelids? Changing hotels again would be a **nuisance**④, but if the wind failed to shift he could not possibly remain here. To be on the safe side, he did not unpack everything. At nine he went to breakfast in the specially designated buffet between the lobby and the dining room.

The ceremonious silence on which grand hotels pride themselves prevailed. The waiters moved about the room noiselessly, on tiptoe. The clatter of tea things and a half-whispered word were the only sounds audible. In a corner diagonally opposite the door and two tables removed from his own, Aschenbach saw the Polish girls with their governess. Their ash-blond hair freshly plastered down, their eyes red, they sat perfectly erect in their stiff blue-linen dress with the small white turndown collars and cuffs, passing a jar of preserves round the table. The boy was absent. Aschenbach smiled. Well, well, little **Phaeacian**⑤! he thought. You seem to be the only one privileged to sleep his fill.

He took a leisurely breakfast, was given some forwarded mail by the porter—who had entered the room, braided cap in hand—then smoked a cigarette and opened one or two of the letters. And he was present for the entrance of the **slugabed**⑥ awaited in the corner.

He came through the glass door and walked straight across the quiet room to his sisters' table. His **gait**⑦ was extraordinarily graceful both in the way he held his upper

---

① 腐烂的。

② 臭气。

③ 失望。

④ 麻烦事。

⑤ 费阿刻斯人，是荷马史诗《奥德赛》中提到过的一个传奇民族。据说他们居住在东地中海的某个不知名的岛屿上，喜欢优越的生活胜于劳作，因此，费阿刻斯这个名字已经成为寄生虫，或爱享福的人的代名词了。

⑥ 睡懒觉的人。

⑦ 步态。

torso① and in the way he moved his knees and white-shod feet; it was a very light gait, at once delicate and proud, and **embellished**② by the childlike modesty with which, twice on his way across the room, he turned his head and raised, then lowered his eyes. Smiling and murmuring a word in his soft, fuzzy language, he took his seat, and now, especially as he had turned his full profile to the observer, the latter was once more amazed, indeed, **startled**③ by the truly godlike beauty of this mortal being. Today the boy was wearing a lightweight, washable outfit with a blue-and-white-striped middy blouse that had a red silk bow at the chest and a plain white stand-up collar. The collar, though none too elegant a match for the rest of the outfit, showed off the boy's fair, blossoming head in its consummate charm, the head of an **Eros**④ with the creamy glaze of **marble**⑤, eyebrows serious and finely traced, temples and ear covered darkly and softly at right angles by encroaching ringlets.

Good, good, thought Aschenbach with that cool, professional approval in which artists encountering a masterpiece sometimes shroud their delight, their excitement. Truth to tell, he went on thinking, were sea and shore not awaiting me, I should stay here as long as you! But he did leave, greeted by the staff as he passed through the lobby, then descending the large terrace and proceeding straight along the boardwalk to the beach. He was shown to his rented **cabana**⑥ by the barefoot old man serving there as bathing attendant, had his table and chair set up on a sandy wooden platform, and made himself comfortable in the chaise **longue**⑦ he had drawn onto the wax-yellow sand closer to the water.

"I shall stay, then," Aschenbach thought. "What better place could there be?" And folding his hands in his lap, he let his eyes run over the sea's great expanse and set his gaze adrift till it blurred and broke in the monotonous mist of barren space. He loved the sea and for deep-seated reasons: the hardworking artist's need for **repose**⑧, the desire to take shelter from the demanding diversity of phenomena in the bosom of boundless simplicity, a **propensity**⑨—proscribed opposed to his mission in life and for that very reason se-

---

① 躯干。
② 装饰。
③ 震惊。
④ 爱神,在希腊神话中形象为一个手拿弓箭、长有一对小翅膀的淘气小男孩。
⑤ 大理石。
⑥ 小屋。
⑦ 躺椅。
⑧ 安宁。
⑨ 倾向。

ductive—propensity for the unarticulated, the immoderate, the eternal, for nothingness. To repose in perfection is the desire of all those who strive for excellence, and is not nothingness a form of perfection? But as he dreamt his way deep into the void, the horizontal shoreline was suddenly intersected by a human form and, summoning his gaze back from the infinite and bringing it into focus, he saw none other than the beautiful boy coming from the left, walking past him in the sand.

He was barefoot in preparation for wading, his slender legs exposed to above the knee, and while his gait was slow it was as light and proud as if he were quite accustomed to going about shoeless. He looked over at the cabanas in the perpendicular row, but no sooner did he spy the Russian family going about its business in cheerful harmony than a storm cloud of angry disdain came over his face: the forehead wrinkled into a dark frown; the mouth rose up, pulling the lips to one side in a bitter grimace that rent the cheek; the brows grew so deeply furrowed that the eyes seemed to have sunk under the pressure, glowering out from beneath them, speaking the language of hate. He looked down, looked back again ominously, then thrust one shoulder forward in a show of repulsion and rebuff, and left his enemies behind.

A kind of delicacy or apprehension, something akin to deference or modesty, caused Aschenbach to turn away, as if he had seen nothing. Yet he was cheered and shaken at the same time, in other words, **elated**①. His eyes still **averted**②, Aschenbach listened to the boy's voice, the high, rather weak voice with which he greeted his playmates, who were busy building a sand castle. They responded, calling out his name or pet name several times, and Aschenbach listened to it with a certain curiosity, but could make out nothing more than two melodic syllables: "Adgio" or, more often, "Adgiu," with a final u they lengthened as they called. He liked the sound of it: he found its **euphony**③ appropriate to the object in question and, having repeated it to himself, turned back, contented, to his letters and papers.

With his portable writing case on his knees, he began attending to this or that item of correspondence with his fountain pen. But after no more than a quarter of an hour he decided it was a pity to divert his mind from the situation at hand, the most enjoyable he knew, to let it slip past for the sake of an indifferent pursuit. He tossed his writings aside

① 得意扬扬的。
② 回避，避免。
③ 音调。

and gazed back at the sea, but before long, distracted by the voices of the youngsters building the sand castle, he turned his head to the right along the back of the chair the better to follow once more the doings of the exquisite Adgio.

He located him at once: the red bow on his chest was unmistakable. Engaged with the others in laying an old plank as a bridge across the sand castle's water-filled moat, he gave directions by shouts and head signals. He had ten or so companions, boys and girls—some his own age, some younger—chattering **higgledy-piggledy**① in tongues: Polish, French, and even some Balkan languages. But his name was the most often heard. He was clearly sought after, courted, admired. One boy in particular, a Pole like him—a **stocky**② fellow who was addressed as something like Jasiu and who had black, slicked-down hair and was wearing a belted linen suit—appeared to be his closest friend. When the current stage of work on the castle came to an end, they walked along the beach with their arms around each other, and the fellow addressed as Jasiu kissed the beautiful boy.

Aschenbach was tempted to shake a finger at them. Then he breakfasted on some large, fully ripe strawberries he had purchased from a peddler. It had grown very hot, though the sun was unable to pierce the layer of haze in the sky. Lethargy fettered the mind even as the senses enjoyed the vast, benumbing pleasure of the ocean's calm. The serious Aschenbach found it a suitable, perfectly satisfying use of his time to guess at the name that sounded like Adgio, and with the aid of some Polish **reminiscences**③ he determined that it must be Tadzio, the pet name for Tadeusz, which becomes Tadziu in direct address.

Tadzio was bathing. Aschenbach, who had lost sight of him, spotted his head, then his arm rising paddle-like from the water far out at sea, the sea being most likely shallow for quite a distance. But already he seemed a cause for concern; already women's voices were calling out to him from the cabanas, its soft **consonants**④ and **long-drawn-out**⑤ final u making it at once sweet and wild: "Tadziu! Tadziu!" Back he came, running through the waves, his legs beating the resistant water into foam, his head flung back, and to see so vibrant a figure, with the grace and austerity of early manhood, fair as a gentle god, emerging

① 叽叽喳喳的。
② 健壮结实的。
③ 记忆。
④ 辅音。
⑤ 余音袅袅的。

from the depths of sea and sky, escaping the watery element—it was enough to inspire mythical associations, like the lay of a bard about times primeval, about the origin of form and the birth of the gods. His eyes closed, Aschenbach **harkened**① to the chant welling up within him and thought again that being here was good and he would stay.

Later Tadzio lay in the sand resting from his swim, wrapped in a white sheet drawn up under his right shoulder, his head reposing on a bare arm, and Aschenbach even when not observing him, when reading a few pages in his book—hardly ever forgot that he was there and that he had only to turn his head slightly to the right to glimpse the object of his admiration. He almost felt he was sitting there to keep watch over the boy as he rested—indulging in his own affairs, yet constantly guarding the noble figure a little way off to his right. And he **was infused with**② a paternal affection, the attraction that one who creates beauty by means of self-sacrifice feels for one who is **inherently**③ beautiful. After midday he left the beach, returned to the hotel, and went up to his room.

He spent two hours in his room and took the vaporetto across the foul-smelling lagoon to Venice in the afternoon. He got out at San Marco, had tea in the square, and then, in conformity with his daily program there, set off on a stroll through the streets. But this stroll brought about a major change in his mood and intentions.

A **repellent**④ **sultriness**⑤ permeated the narrow streets, the air so thick that the odors **emanating**⑥ from houses, shops, and food stalls—the vapor of oil, the clouds of perfume, and more-hovered like fumes without dispersing. Cigarette smoke hung in place dissipating slowly. Aschenbach felt more irritated than invigorated by the bustle of the crowd. The longer he walked, the more afflicted he was by that odious condition brought on by the combination of sea air and sirocco. He broke out into a disagreeable sweat. His eyes refused to function, his chest constricted, he felt feverish, the blood throbbed in his head. He fled the bustling commercial streets and crossed the bridges into the alleyways of the poor. There he was set upon by beggars, and the foul odor from the canals made breathing a torment. Leaning against the edge of a fountain in a quiet square, he wiped his forehead and realized he would have to travel on.

---

① 倾听。
② 充满了。
③ 固有的,内在的。
④ 令人厌恶的。
⑤ 闷热。
⑥ emanate: 发出,散发。

For the second time—and this time definitively the city had proved itself extremely harmful to him in such weather. Braving it out obstinately seemed unreasonable, the prospect of a shift in the wind being quite uncertain immediate decision was of the essence. Returning home was out of the question at this point: neither his summer nor his winter quarters were ready. But this was not the only place with sea and sand, and elsewhere they were to be had without the nefarious admixture of the lagoon and its feverous vapors. He recalled having heard the praises of a small seaside resort not far from Trieste. Why not go there?

Upon his return to the hotel, even before dining, he informed the office that unforeseen circumstances had compelled him to leave early the following morning. Regrets were tendered, the bill settled. He dined and spent the warm evening reading newspapers in a rocking chair on the back terrace. Before retiring, he packed all his belongings for departure.

He did not sleep particularly well, the imminent displacement having unnerved him. When he opened the windows in the morning, the sky was as overcast as it had been, but the air seemed fresher, and regret set in. If he had held off a bit, if he had not been so quick to lose heart, if he had instead tried to adjust to the air or wait for the weather to improve, he would now have been free of stress and strain and looking forward to a morning on the beach like the one the day before. Too late. He must go on wanting what he had wanted yesterday. He dressed and rode down to the ground floor at eight for breakfast.

The breakfast room was still empty when he went in. Several guests arrived while he sat waiting for his order. His teacup at his lips, he watched the Polish girls enter with their companion. Shortly thereafter the porter went up to him, cap in hand, to admonish him to depart: the motorcar was ready to drive the gentleman and several other passengers to the Hotel Excelsior, where the motor launch would be waiting to convey them to the station via the company's private canal. Time was pressing.

Aschenbach felt time was doing nothing of the sort: his train was not due to leave for more than an hour. He resented the way hotels prevailed upon their guests to vacate the premises prematurely and indicated to the porter that he wished to breakfast in peace. The man withdrew hesitantly only to reappear five minutes later. The motorcar could not possibly wait any longer, he said. Then let it go and take his trunk with it, Aschenbach retorted angrily; he would use the public vaporetto when the time came, and would he kindly leave the arrangements for his departure to him? The employee bowed. Glad to have fended off the man's tedious admonitions, Aschenbach finished his breakfast in a leisurely fashion;

he even had the waiter bring him a newspaper. Time was indeed short by the time he stood at last. And it so happened that at that very instant Tadzio entered through the glass door.

As he crossed the departing Aschenbach's path on his way to the family table, he modestly lowered his eyes before the man with the gray hair and lofty brow only to raise them again, soft and wide, in that charming way of his, and walk past. "Adieu, Tadzio!" Aschenbach thought. "It was all too brief." And, contrary to his custom, actually forming the words with his lips and uttering them to himself, he added, "God bless you."

He then went through the departure formalities—distributing gratuities and listening to the short, softspoken manager in the French frock coat make his farewell—left the hotel on foot as he had come, followed by the hotel porter with his hand luggage, and set out for the vaporetto landing along the white-blossoming avenue that cut across the island. Having reached it, he took a seat—and what ensued was a woeful **remorse**①.

For now that the city had twice made him ill, now that he had twice been forced to pick up and leave it, he would henceforth be obliged to consider it an impossible and forbidden destination, one he was not up to and could never think of revisiting. Indeed, he felt that should he leave now, shame and pride must prevent him from setting eyes again on the beloved city that had twice brought him low, and this conflict between the soul's inclination and the body's capabilities suddenly struck the aging man as so serious and significant, his physical defeat seemed so ignominious, in such urgent need of redress, that he could not comprehend the frivolous resignation with which he had decided to acknowledge and bear it with no true struggle.

Meanwhile the vaporetto was approaching the station and his pain and perplexity grew to the point of distraction. Tormented as he was, he felt it impossible to depart, yet none the less so to turn back. He entered the station racked by indecision. It was very late; he had not a moment to lose if he was to catch the train. He both wished to and did not. But time was pressing, goading him onward, and he hastened to purchase his ticket and then peered through the tumult for the hotel employee on duty there. The man appeared and informed him that the large trunk had been dispatched. Dispatched? Already? Yes, as ordered: to Como To Como? And after a flurry of comings and goings, **irate**② questions and embarrassed answers, it came out that back in the luggage room of the Hotel Excelsior the trunk had been thrown together with some other people's luggage and routed in a totally

① 懊悔,悔恨。
② 愤怒的。

misguided direction.

Aschenbach had difficulty maintaining the only plausible facial expression in the circumstances. A reckless joy, an unbelievable **glee**① took almost **convulsive**② hold of his breast. The hotel employee rushed off to do what he could to stop the trunk, but returned, as was to be expected, unsuccessful. Aschenbach accordingly announced that he was unwilling to travel on without his luggage and had decided to go back and wait at the Hotel des Bains until the article was retrieved. Was the hotel motor launch still at the station? The man assured him it was just outside, and in a torrent of Italian he induced the ticket clerk to take back the ticket Aschenbach had purchased. Then he swore that telegrams would be sent and no effort spared, nothing left undone to ensure that the trunk be recovered as soon as possible. And thus a most unusual thing came to pass: twenty minutes after arriving at the station the traveler found himself on the Grand Canal making his way back to the Lido.

What an oddly improbable, comically dreamlike adventure: taking brokenhearted leave of places forever and then, turned round and spirited back by fate, seeing them again within the hour! The waves beat against the concrete walls of the narrow canal that runs across the island to the Hotel Excelsior. There a motor omnibus stood waiting to take the returning guest straight to the Hotel des Bains on the road above the rippling sea. The small, mustached manager in the frock coat came down the steps to greet him. His room had of course been occupied, but another, equally suitable, would be ready immediately. And thus the fugitive was lodged once more, and in a room all but identical in situation and furnishing.

At noon he spotted Tadzio in his striped linen outfit and red bow returning from the sea to the hotel through the beach gate and along the boardwalks. From his lofty vantage point Aschenbach recognized him immediately, even before getting a clear view of him, and was on the point of thinking something like: So you're still here, too, Tadzio. But at that very moment he felt the casual greeting fade and vanish before the truth of his heart, he felt the **rapture**③ of his blood, the joy and agony of his soul, and acknowledged to himself that it was Tadzio who had made it so hard for him to leave.

---

① 欢乐。
② 抽搐,痉挛。
③ 狂喜。

He sat there perfectly still, perfectly invisible on his lofty **perch**①, gazing within himself. His features were keen, his eyebrows high, his lips drawn into an intelligent smile. Then he raised his head and with both arms, which had been hanging limply over the back of his chair, made a slow, rising, circular motion that brought the hands forward in such a way as to indicate an opening and spreading of the arms. It was a gesture of willingness, welcome, of calm acceptance.

FOUR

The soothing regularity of the existence quickly cast a spell over him: he was charmed by the soft, resplendent benignancy of it all. What a place indeed, combining as it did the appeal of a refined southern seaside resort with a strange, wondrous city in intimate proximity Aschenbach did not care for pleasure. It was the only place that could enchant him, relax his will, make him happy. Chiefly, however, and with a most felicitous regularity, it was mornings on the beach that afforded him extended opportunities for the study and reverence of the fair vision of Tadziu. Yes, it was the daily assurance of good fortune, the periodic recurrence of favorable circumstances that so filled him with contentment that made the place so precious to him and strung each sunny day so obligingly to the others.

He would rise early—as was his wont when under the unrelenting pressure of his work—and was one of the first on the beach, when the sun was still mild and the sea a dazzling white, still dreaming. He would greet the gate attendant amiably and nod another friendly greeting to the barefoot graybeard who readied his place for him pulled out the brown awning and moved the furniture out of the cabana—whereupon he settled in. He then had three or four hours during which the sun climbed to its zenith and grew to a frightening intensity, during which the sea turned a deeper and deeper blue, and during which he could watch Tadzio.

Soon the observer knew every line and pose of that body so noble, so freely exposed, joyfully welcoming anew each already familiar aspect of his beauty, and his wonderment and delicate sensual delight knew no bounds. Summoned to greet a guest paying his respects to the ladies at the cabana, the boy would run up out of the water—dripping wet perhaps, tossing back his curls—hold out his hand and—one foot planted on the ground, the other on tiptoe—execute a charming twist and turn of the body, gracefully restless, gra-

① 栖息处。

ciously diffident, and obliging from a sense of noblesse oblige. He would lie full length with his towel wrapped round his chest, a delicately chiseled arm resting in the sand, a hand cupping the chin, while the boy addressed as Jasiu squatted at his side, playing up to him, and there could be nothing more tantalizing than the smiling eyes and lips of the chosen one looking up at his inferior, his servant. He would stand at the edge of the sea, alone, removed from his family, quite near Aschenbach, erect, his hands clasped behind his neck, slowly rocking on the balls of his feet, staring out into the blue in reverie, while little waves rolled up and bathed his toes. The honey-colored hair fell gracefully in ringlets at the temples and the back of the neck, the sun glimmered in the down of the upper spine, the fine delineation of the ribs and symmetry of the chest stood out through the torso's scanty cover, the armpits were still as smooth as a statue's, the hollows of the knees glistened, and their bluish veins made the body look translucent. What discipline, what precision of thought was conveyed by that tall, youthfully perfect physique! Yet the austere and pure will laboring in obscurity to bring the godlike statue to light—was it not known to him, familiar to him as an artist? Was it not at work in him when, **chiseling**① with sober passion at the marble block of language, he released the slender form he had beheld in his mind and would present to the world as a mirror of spiritual beauty?

Mirror! His eyes embraced the noble figure standing there at the edge of the blue, and in a rush of ecstasy he believed that his eyes gazed upon beauty itself, form as divine thought, the sole and pure perfection that dwells in the mind. Was it not common knowledge that the sun diverts our attention from the intellectual to the sensual? It benumbs and bewitches both reason and memory so that the soul in its elation quite forgets its true nature and clings with rapt delight to the fairest of **sundrenched**② objects, yes, only with the aid of the **corporeal**③ can it ascend to more lofty considerations. **Cupid**④ truly did as mathematicians do when they show concrete images of pure forms to incompetent pupils: he made the mental visible to us by using the shape and coloration of human youths and turned them into memory's tool by adorning them with all the luster of beauty and kindling pain and hope in us at the sight of them.

Nothing gladdens a writer more than a thought that can become pure feeling and a

① 凿。
② 阳光照射的。
③ 身体，形体。
④ 丘比特，爱神。

feeling that can become pure thought. Just such a pulsating thought, just such a precise feeling was then in the possession and service of the solitary traveler: nature trembles with bliss when the mind bows in homage to beauty. He suddenly desired to write. It was something he was familiar with, something he knew from experience, and the desire to make it shine in the light of his words was suddenly irresistible. What is more, he longed to work in Tadzio's presence, to model his writing on the boy's physique, to let his style follow the lines of that body, which he saw as godlike, and bear its beauty to the realm of the intellect. Seated at his rough table under the awning, in full view of his idol, the music of his voice in his ears, he formulated that little essay—a page and a half of sublime prose based on Tadzio's beauty—the purity, nobility, and quivering emotional tension of which would soon win the admiration of many. It is surely as well that the world knows only a beautiful work itself and not its origins, the conditions under which it comes into being, for if people had knowledge of the sources from which the artist derives his inspiration they would oftentimes be confused and alarmed and thus vitiate the effects the artist had achieved. How strange those hours were! How curiously fruitful the intercourse of mind with body! When Aschenbach put away his work and quit the beach, he felt exhausted and, yes, spent, as if his conscience were **reproaching**① him after a **debauch**②.

The following morning he was going down the front steps, about to leave the hotel, when he spied Tadzio alone—nearing the beach gate on his way to the sea. The desire, the mere thought of taking the opportunity to make the casual, offhand acquaintance of the beautiful boy who had unknowingly so elated and moved him, to address him and take pleasure in his response and the look in his ayes—nothing could be more natural, more obvious. The boy was walking slowly—he could easily be overtaken—and Aschenbach merely accelerated his pace. He caught up to him on the boardwalk in back of the cabanas and was on the point of laying his hand on his head or shoulder—a phrase, some friendly words in French on his lips—when he felt his heart hammering wildly, from the quick pace perhaps, and he was so breathless that his voice would have been hoarse and strained had he tried to speak. He paused and struggled to get hold of himself, but suddenly feared he had been walking too long just behind the boy, feared the boy would notice, turn and look at him questioningly, so he had one more go at it, failed, surrendered, and walked past with downcast eyes.

---

① 责备。

② 做了坏事。

He had ceased keeping track of the time he allotted himself for leisure and gave no thought whatever to going home. He had had ample funds transferred here. His sole concern was that the Polish family would leave, but he learned **surreptitiously**[①], by inquiring casually of the hotel barber, that their arrival had barely predated his own.

There is nothing more curious or delicate than a relationship between people who know each other only by sight, who encounter and observe each other daily, hourly—yet are constrained by convention or personal caprice to keep up the pretense of being strangers, indifferent, avoiding a nod or word. There is a feeling of **malaise**[②] and overwrought curiosity, the hysteria of an unsatisfied, unnaturally stifled need for mutual knowledge and communication, and above all a sort of strained esteem. For a man loves and respects his fellow man only insofar as he is unable to assess him, and longing is a product of insufficient knowledge.

Some kind of relationship and acquaintance was bound to develop between Aschenbach and young Tadzio, and the older man was thrilled to discover that his interest and attention did not go wholly **unreciprocated**[③]. For example, what induced the beautiful boy, when appearing on the beach each morning, to shun the boardwalk behind the cabanas and saunter through the sand in front of them past Aschenbach's residence—sometimes coming needlessly close to him, all but grazing his table or chair—on the way to the family cabana? Was this the result of the attraction, the fascination of a superior emotion on a tender and thoughtless object? Aschenbach looked forward daily to Tadzio's entrance and at times pretended to be busy when it occurred and let the boy pass seemingly unnoticed. But at other times he looked up and their eyes would meet.

Once, however, one evening, something different happened. The Polish boy and his sisters together with their governess had failed to come to dinner in the main dining room, as Aschenbach noted with alarm. After the meal, worried about their absence, he was pacing in evening dress and a straw hat in front of the hotel at the foot of the terrace when all at once he spied the nunlike sisters with their companion and, four steps behind them, Tadzio, emerging into the light of the arc lamps. They were obviously on their way from the vaporetto landing, having dined in the city for some reason. It must have been cool on the water: Tadzio was wearing a navy blue pea jacket with gold buttons and a matching cap.

---

① 偷偷摸摸地。
② 不安。
③ 没有回应的。

Sunshine and sea air did not tan him, and his skin had the same yellowish marble hue as at the outset, but today he looked paler than usual, whether because of the cool air or the bleaching effect of the lamps' lunar light. His symmetrical eyebrows stood out more sharply; his eyes were a deep, dark shade. He was more beautiful than words can convey, and Aschenbach felt acutely, as he had often felt before, that language can only praise physical beauty, not reproduce it.

He was unprepared for the precious image: it had come unexpectedly, and he had not had time to put on a calm, dignified expression. Joy, surprise, and admiration may thus have shown openly in his face when his eyes met those of the boy who had disappeared, and at that instant it happened: Tadzio smiled, smiled at him, with an intimate, charming, **unabashed**① smile, his lips opening slowly. It was the smile of **Narcissus**② bending over the water mirror, the deep, **enchanted**③ smile with which he stretched out his arms to the reflection of his own beauty, an ever so slightly **contorted**④ smile—contorted by the hopelessness of his endeavor to kiss the lovely lips of his shadow.

The **recipient**⑤ of this smile hurried off with it as if it were a fatal gift. He was so shaken that he felt compelled to flee. Oddly **indignant**⑥ and tender **admonitions**⑦ welled up inside him: "You mustn't smile like that! One mustn't smile like that at anyone, do you hear?" He flung himself on a bench, frantically **inhaling**⑧ the plants' **nocturnal**⑨ fragrance. Then, leaning back, arms dangling, overwhelmed and shuddering repeatedly, he whispered the standard formula of longing—"I love you!"

FIVE

During the fourth week of his stay at the Lido, Gustav von Aschenbach observed some peculiar developments taking place in the world around him. First of all, it struck him that

---

① 不害羞的,坦率的。

② 纳西索斯,希腊神话中一位长相十分清秀的美少年,他对任何姑娘都不动心,只对自己的水中倒影爱慕不已,最终在顾影自怜中抑郁死去。死后化作水仙花,仍留在水边守望着自己的影子。Narcissus因而是"孤芳自赏者""自我陶醉者"的代名词。

③ 迷人的,醉人的。

④ 扭曲的。

⑤ 接受者。

⑥ 愤怒的。

⑦ 训诫,责备。

⑧ Inhale:吸入。

⑨ 夜间的。

even as the season advanced, the number of guests at his hotel was falling rather than rising and, in particular, the use of German around him had so ebbed and waned that the only sounds reaching his ear at meals and on the beach were foreign. Then one day while conversing with the barber, whom he now patronized frequently, he gleaned a rather unsettling piece of news.

Having mentioned a German family that had just departed after a short stay, he added in his chatty unctuous manner, "But you are staying on, sir. You have no fear of the disease." Aschenbach looked at him. "The disease?" The barber did not reply, acted busy, disregarded the question, and when it was put to him with more urgency he claimed to know nothing and attempted with embarrassed eloquence to change the subject.

That was at noon. A few hours later, the dead calm and burning sun notwithstanding, Aschenbach went into Venice, driven by a **mania**① to follow the Polish boy and his sisters, whom he had seen set off for the vaporetto landing with their companion. He did not find his idol at San Marco. However, while taking tea at his little round wrought-iron table on the shady side of the square, he suddenly whiffed an unusual aroma in the air, an aroma he now felt he had been inhaling for days without being conscious of it, a **cloying**② medicinal smell. He sniffed again and after some thought identified it, then finished his tea and left the square. In that cramped space the smell grew stronger. The street corners were plastered with printed notices warning the population on behalf of the city fathers against eating **oysters**③ and **mussels**④ and using canal water because of certain **gastric**⑤ disorders that were only to be expected given the weather conditions.

He went up to a shopkeeper and asked what he knew about the disagreeable odor. The man looked him up and down with heavy eyes and promptly roused himself "A precautionary measure, sir!" he answered, gesticulating. "A police **injunction**⑥ one can only obey. The atmosphere is oppressive; the sirocco is bad for the health. In short, you understand. Perhaps they are being overly cautious..."

Aschenbach thanked him and went on. On the vaporetto taking him over to the Lido

---

① 狂热。
② 发腻的。
③ 牡蛎。
④ 贝类。
⑤ 胃部的。
⑥ 命令。

he now caught a smell of **germicide**[①].

Back at the hotel, he headed straight for the newspaper table in the lobby and made a survey of what was available. He found nothing in the foreign-language papers. Those in his own language reported rumors, cited fluctuating figures, reproduced official denials, and questioned their **veracity**[②]. That explained the departure of the German and Austrian element. Nationals of other countries evidently knew nothing, suspected nothing, and were not yet concerned. "Nothing is to be said about it!" thought Aschenbach anxiously, tossing the papers back on the table. "It is to be hushed up!" So Aschenbach felt a **morose**[③] satisfaction at the officially concealed goings-on in the dirty alleyways of Venice, that nasty secret which had merged with his own innermost secret and which he, too, was so intent on keeping: he was in love and concerned only that Tadzio might leave, and he realized not without horror that in the event he would not know what to make of his life.

He had not been content of late to leave the possibility of seeing and being near the beautiful boy to chance or daily routine; he had pursued him, tracked him down. On Sundays, for instance, the Poles never came to the beach. Having surmised that they would be attending mass at San Marco, he would hurry there and, entering the golden dusk of the sanctuary from the square's torrid heat, locate the boy he had so missed.

Then, as the crowd poured through the opened portals into the radiant square teeming with pigeons, the **beguiled**[④] traveler would **lurk**[⑤] in the vestibule, hiding, lying in **ambush**[⑥]. He would watch the Poles go out of the church, watch the siblings take ceremonious leave of their mother, who then set off for home in the direction of the Piazzetta. Having ascertained that the boy, his nunlike sisters, and their governess would turn right and proceed through the clock tower gateway into the Merceria, he gave them a head start and then followed them, followed them **furtively**[⑦] on their stroll through Venice. He had to stop when they **tarried**[⑧], duck into food stalls and courtyards when they doubled back; he would lose them, pursue them, hot and exhausted, over bridges, and endure moments of

---

① 杀菌剂。
② 真实性。
③ 阴郁的。
④ 如痴如醉的。
⑤ 潜伏。
⑥ 埋伏。
⑦ 偷偷地。
⑧ 逗留。

mortal shame when seeing them suddenly come towards him in a narrow passageway from which there was no escape. Yet it cannot be said he was suffering: he was drunk in both head and heart, and his steps followed the dictates of the demon whose delight it is to **trample**① human reason and dignity underfoot.

Thus the **addled**② traveler could no longer think or care about anything but pursuing unrelentingly the object that had so inflamed him, dreaming of him in his absence, and, as is the lover's **wont**③, speaking tender words to his mere shadow. Loneliness, the foreign environment, and the joy of a belated and profound exhilaration prompted him, persuaded him to indulge without shame or remorse in the most distasteful behavior, as when returning from Venice late one evening he had paused at the beautiful boys door on the second floor of the hotel and pressed his forehead against the hinge in drunken rapture, unable to tear himself away even at the risk of being discovered and caught.

Yet he still had moments of pause and near **lucidity**④. Where is this taking me? he would think then with alarm. Where is this taking me? Like any man whose natural gifts aroused an aristocratic interest in his ancestry, he habitually called to mind his forebears. He thought of them again here and now—**enmeshed**⑤ as he was in so **illicit**⑥ an experience, involved in such exotic extravagances of emotion—thought of their imposing **fortitude**⑦, their **upstanding**⑧ manliness of character and gave a **dour**⑨ smile. What would they say? But what for that matter would they have said about his life as a whole, a life diverging from theirs to the point of degeneracy, lived under the spell of art! He too had served; he too, like so many of them, had been soldier and warrior, for art was war, a grueling struggle that people these days were not up to for long.

Thus did the man seek to defend himself and preserve his dignity. Yet at the same time he kept paying willful, **obstinate**⑩ attention to the **unsavory**⑪ events in the depths of

---

① 践踏。
② 糊涂的。
③ 习惯。
④ 明朗、清晰。
⑤ 沉浸于。
⑥ 不正当的。
⑦ 刚毅。
⑧ 正直的。
⑨ 阴沉的。
⑩ 固执的。
⑪ 令人讨厌的。

Venice, the adventure of the outer world that merged darkly with the adventure of his heart and fed his passion with vague, illicit hopes. Obsessed with the need to obtain new and reliable information on the status and progress of the disease, he riffled through the German papers in the cafés, the ones on the hotel newspaper table having disappeared for several days. They were all assertions and retractions: they would report twenty, forty, even a hundred or more deaths and instances of the disease, after which the existence of an epidemic was if not flatly denied then reduced to totally isolated cases introduced from outside.

In one evening, after dinner, it so happened that a small group of street singers from the city gave a performance in the front garden. The two men and two women stood by the iron post of an arc lamp, lifting their faces, white in the glare, to the large terrace, where the guests sat ready, over coffee and cold drinks, to submit to the exhibition of local color. The hotel staff—lift attendants, waiters, and office clerks had come out to listen at the doors to the lobby.

Mandolin, guitar, accordion, and squeaky fiddle soon came to life under the fingers of the beggar **virtuosi**①. But the true talent and leader of the ensemble was **unequivocally**② the other man—the one with the guitar and a kind of **baritone-buffo**③ character who, though he had no voice to speak of, was a gifted **mime**④ and possessed of remarkable comic energy. He often broke away from the group, his large instrument in tow, and made his way forward, where he was rewarded with laughter and encouragement.

Aschenbach sat at the **balustrade**⑤, occasionally cooling his lips with the mixture of **grenadine**⑥ and soda water sparkling ruby red before him in the glass. The sight of the **prancing**⑦ **jester**⑧ had twisted his features into a fixed, almost painful grimace. He sat on, indifferent, while inwardly he was thoroughly **engrossed**⑨: a mere six paces away Tadzio was leaning on the stone **parapet**⑩.

---

① 名家,艺人。
② 毫无疑问,清楚的。
③ 男中音。
④ 滑稽演员,模仿者。
⑤ 栏杆。
⑥ 石榴汁。
⑦ 欢腾的。
⑧ 小丑。
⑨ 全神贯注的。
⑩ 矮墙。

There he stood in the belted white suit he sometimes donned for dinner, **inexorably**①, innately graceful, his left forearm on the parapet, his feet crossed, his right hand on his hip—looking down at the **minstrels**② with an expression that was not so much a smile as an indication of aloof curiosity, of courteous acknowledgment. From time to time he drew himself up and, puffing out his chest, pulled the white blouse down through the leather belt with an elegant tug of both hands. But there were also times when—as the aging traveler noted **triumphantly**③, his mind reeling, yet terrified as well—he turned his head over his left shoulder—now wavering and cautious, now fast and **impetuous**④, as if to catch him off guard—to the place where his admirer was seated. Aschenbach did not meet Tadzio's eye, because a humiliating anxiety compelled the lover to put a curb on his glances. The women guarding Tadzio were seated at the rear of the terrace, and things had now reached the point where the lover needed to be concerned about standing out or arousing suspicion. Yes, several times now—on the beach, in the hotel lobby, in the Piazza San Marco—he had noted with a kind of numbness that they called Tadzjo back when he came near him, that they were intent on keeping him at a distance, and he could only acknowledge it as a terrible insult which racked his pride in hitherto unknown torment, yet which his conscience could not **gainsay**⑤.

In the meantime the guitarist had begun a solo to his own accompaniment. The lyrics of the song were merely silly, but in his **rendition**⑥—with the facial expressions and body movements he used, his suggestive **winks**⑦, and the way he licked the corners of his mouth—they became ambiguous, vaguely **obscene**⑧. Protruding from the soft collar of his open shirt, which clashed with his otherwise formal attire, was a scrawny neck with a **conspicuously**⑨ large Adam's apple. His pallid face, its beardless features giving no indication of his age, seemed lined with grimaces and vice, and the two furrows stretching defiantly, imperiously, almost savagely between his reddish brows contrasted oddly with the grin on

---

① 无情地,冷酷地。
② 江湖艺人。
③ 胜利地,洋洋得意地。
④ 迅疾的。
⑤ 否认,反驳。
⑥ 演奏。
⑦ 眨眼。
⑧ 下流的。
⑨ 显著地。

his mobile mouth. What made the solitary traveler focus all his attention on him, however, was the realization that the suspicious character seemed to bring his own suspicious atmosphere with him: each time the **refrain**① recurred, the singer set off on a grotesque march, making faces and waving, his path taking him directly under Aschenbach's seat, and each time he made his round a strong smell of **carbolic acid**② wafted its way up to the terrace from his clothes and body.

Once the ditty was over, he started collecting money. He went up to Aschenbach, he and his odor, which no one else appeared to mind.

"Tell me," said the solitary traveler in an almost mechanical undertone. "Venice is being **disinfected**③. Why?"

"It's the police," the joker answered hoarsely, "the rules, sir. It's the heat and the sirocco. The sirocco is oppressive. It's bad for the health..."...He spoke as if surprised one could pose such a question, and demonstrated the sirocco's pressure with the flat of his hand.

"So there is no disease in Venice?" Aschenbach asked very softly between his teeth.

The jester's muscular features settled into a grimace of comic helplessness. "Disease? Of what sort? Is the sirocco a disease? Or our police—are they a disease? You must be joking! A disease? How can you say such a thing? A preventative measure, can't you see? A police order to combat the effects of the oppressive weather conditions." He gesticulated.

"Very well," said Aschenbach, softly and tersely again, quickly dropping an unduly large coin into the hat. He then dismissed the man with his eyes. The man obeyed, grinning and bowing. But no sooner had he reached the steps than two hotel employees pounced upon him and started cross-examining him in whispers, their face hard against his. He shrugged, reassuring them, swearing he had been **discreet**④.

The guests dispersed and Tadzio had long since abandoned the balustrade, yet to the displeasure of the waiters the solitary traveler sat on at his table with the remainder of the grenadine. Night proceeded; time dissolved. There had been an **hourglass**⑤ in his

---

① 副歌。
② 石碳酸。
③ 消毒。
④ 谨慎的。
⑤ 沙漏。

parents' house many years before, and all at once he could see the fragile yet momentous little device as if it were standing before him. The rust-colored sand would run soundless and fine through the narrow glass neck, and when the upper bulb was nearly empty a small raging **whirlpool**① would form there.

In the afternoon of the very next day the ever obstinate traveler took another step in his investigation of the outside world, and this time with the utmost success: he went into the British travel agency located just off Saint Mark's Square and, after changing some money at the cash desk, assumed the expression of a suspicious foreigner and asked his awkward question of the clerk who had waited on him. "No cause for alarm, sir," he began. "A routine measure, nothing serious. They often issue such orders to forestall the deleterious effects of the heat and the sirocco..." when his blue eyes met the stranger's weary, somewhat mournful gaze directed at his lips with mild contempt, the Englishman blushed. "That," he went on in a low voice and with a certain animation, "is the official explanation, which one finds it **expedient**② to accept here. But I can tell you that there is more to it than meets the eye." And then in his honest, genial way he told Aschenbach the truth.

For several years now Indian **cholera**③ had displayed a growing tendency to spread and migrate. Emanating from the humid **marshes**④ of the **Ganges Delta**⑤, rising with the **mephitic**⑥ exhalations of that lush, uninhabitable, primordial island jungle shunned by man, where tigers crouch in bamboo thickets, the epidemic had long raged with unexpected **virulence**⑦ through Hindustan, then moved eastward to China, westward to Afghanistan and Persia, and, following the main **caravan**⑧ routes, borne its horrors as far as Astrakhan and even Moscow. But while Europe **quaked**⑨ at the thought of the **specter**⑩ invading from there by land, it had been transported by sea in the ships of Syrian merchants and shown up in several Mediterranean ports simultaneously. Then in mid-May of this year, on one

---

① 旋涡。
② 有利的,权宜之计。
③ 霍乱。
④ 沼泽。
⑤ 印度的恒河三角洲。
⑥ 恶臭。
⑦ 毒性,毒力。
⑧ 旅行商队。
⑨ 发抖。
⑩ 幽灵。

and the same day, the dread **vibrios**① had been discovered in the blackened, wasted corpses of a ship's boy and a grocer woman in Venice. The cases were kept secret. Within a week, however, there were ten of them, then twenty, thirty, and in different districts to boot. A man from a provincial town in Austria, returning home from a few days' holiday in Venice, died with unmistakable symptoms, and the first rumors of an outbreak in the city on the lagoon made their way into the German press. The Venetian authorities issued a statement to the effect that health conditions had never been better, then took the most essential precautions against the disease. But some food must have been contaminated—vegetables, meat, or milk—because, denied or concealed as it was, death ate a path through the narrow streets, and the premature summer heat, which had warmed the water in the canals, was particularly **conducive to**② its spread.

The epidemic even seemed to be undergoing a revitalization. Recovery was rare: eighty out of a hundred of those infected died, and died a horrible death, because the disease would strike with the utmost ferocity, often taking its most dangerous form, the "dry" form, as it was called. In such cases the body was unable to expel the massive amounts of water secreted by the blood vessels, and within a few hours the patient would **shrivel up**③ and choke—convulsed and groaning hoarsely—on his own blood, now thick as **pitch**④. But fear of the overall damage that would be done—concern over the recently opened art exhibition in the Public Gardens and the tremendous losses with which the hotels, the shops, the entire, multifaceted tourist trade would be threatened in case of panic and loss of confidence—proved stronger in the city than the love of truth and respect for international **covenants**⑤: it made the authorities stick stubbornly to their policy of secrecy and denial. After thus summarizing the main points, the Englishman concluded, "You would do well to leave, and today rather than tomorrow. The imposition of a **quarantine**⑥ is **imminent**⑦."

"Thank you," said Aschenbach, and left the office.

Feverish with agitation, triumphant in his possession of the truth, a repulsive taste in his mouth, and fantastic horror in his heart, the solitary traveler paced up and down the

① 霍乱病菌。
② 有利于。
③ 枯萎,蔫掉。
④ 沥青。
⑤ 规定,协议。
⑥ 隔离。
⑦ 迫在眉睫。

flagstones of the magnificent square. He was trying to come up with a decent and purificatory mode of action. After dinner that evening he could go over to the woman in pearls and deliver the speech he was now formulating: "Permit me, Madam, stranger that I am, to give you a piece of advice. You must leave, leave immediately, with Tadzio and your daughters! Venice is **infested**①." He might then lay a farewell hand on the head of Tadzio, turn on his heel, and flee the **quagmire**②. Yet at the same time he felt infinitely far from seriously wishing to take such a step. It would lead him back, restore him to himself, but there is nothing so distasteful as being restored to oneself when one is beside oneself. "Nothing is to be said about it!" he whispered wildly. And added, "I shall say nothing." The consciousness of his collusion, his share of guilt intoxicated him as small quantities of wine intoxicate the weary brain. The image of the infested and abandoned city throbbing wildly in his mind kindled hopes unfathomable, beyond reason, and outrageously sweet. What was that serene happiness he had dreamed of a moment before compared with such expectations? What were art and virtue to him given the advantages of chaos? He said nothing and stayed on.

That night he had a terrifying dream...

The stricken man awoke from his dream unnerved and shaken. He no longer **shunned**③ the curious glances of the people around him: whether he aroused their suspicion was of no concern to him. They were fleeing, were they not, leaving Venice: many of the cabanas were vacant, a number of tables in the dining room unoccupied, and in the city there was scarcely a foreigner to be seen. The truth seemed to have leaked out despite the **tenacious**④ solidarity among interested parties in their attempt to ward off panic. But the woman in pearls stayed on with her family either because the rumors had not reached her or because she was too proud and fearless to notice them. Thus Tadzio stayed on, and Aschenbach, in his **beleaguered**⑤ state, occasionally had the feeling that flight and death might eliminate all life standing in his way and leave him alone on this island with the beautiful boy; indeed, when he sat in the morning by the sea, his gaze—heavy and fixed—resting on the object of his desire, or when, as evening fell, he resumed his undignified

① 病毒滋生的,大批为患的。
② 泥潭,沼泽地。
③ 躲避。
④ 顽强的。
⑤ 着魔的。

pursuit through the narrow streets **clandestinely**①.

Like any lover, he wished to please and dreaded the thought that it might be impossible. He added cheery, youthful touches to his wardrobe, wore jewels, and used scent; he spent long hours several times a day at his toilet, coming to table **bedizened**②, excited, and tense. Gazing at the sweet youth who had won his heart he was sickened by his aging body: the sight of his gray hair, his **pinched**③ features filled him with shame and despair. He felt an urge to revitalize himself, restore himself physically, and patronized④ the hotel barber with increasing frequency.

Draped in the hairdressing gown, leaning back in the chair under the barber's ministering hands, he peered in **dismay**⑤ at his image in the looking glass.

"Gray," he said, with a grimace.

"Slightly," the fellow replied. "And all for a bit of **negligence**⑥, a disregard for externals, which is understandable. After all, we are only as old as we feel in our minds and hearts, and, in certain circumstances gray hair can be an untruth. A man like you, sir, has every right to his natural hair color. Will you permit me simply to restore to you what is yours?"

"How so?" asked Aschenbach.

The eloquent barber rinsed his client's hair in two kinds of liquid—one clear, the other dark—and it was as black as it had been in his youth, whereupon he set it in soft waves with his curling iron and stepped back to observe the results.

"All that is left to be done," he said, "is to freshen up the face a bit."

And like someone who cannot stop, is never satisfied, he passed with energetic solicitude from one treatment to the next. Aschenbach, reclining comfortably, unable to resist, indeed, full of hope for the outcome, watched his eyebrows arch more distinctly and evenly, his eyes grow longer, their brightness enhanced by a light line beneath the lids, and farther down, where the skin had been brownish and leathery saw a blush of sparingly applied carmine, saw his lips, anemic only a moment before, swell raspberry-red and the furrows in his

① 秘密地。
② 盛装打扮。
③ 短缺的,匮乏的。
④ 光顾。
⑤ 气馁,惆怅。
⑥ 疏忽。

cheeks and around his mouth, the wrinkles under his eyes vanish beneath face cream and the glow of youth he saw, his heart pounding, a young man in his prime. The cosmetician finally proclaimed himself satisfied by thanking him with the abject courtesy characteristic of such people when serving their clients. "A **trifling**① readjustment," he said, putting the finishing touches on Aschenbach's appearance. "Now the gentleman need have no **qualms**② about falling in love." The **spellbound**③ lover left, **agitated**④ and confused, yet as happy as in a dream. His necktie was red, his broad-brimmed straw hat wound round with a gaudy striped ribbon.

A tepid storm wind had come up, and while the rain was light and intermittent the air was humid, thick, and pregnant with noisome fumes. Besieged by fluttering, clattering, whistling noises, feverish under his rouge, Aschenbach had the feeling that an evil breed of wind spirits was carrying on in space, monstrous sea creatures rooting in, gnawing at, befouling the condemned man's victuals. For the salty weather had robbed him of his appetite, nor could he help imagining food to be tainted by infection.

Trailing the beautiful boy one afternoon, Aschenbach penetrated the stricken city's tangled core. His sense of direction having failed him—the alleys, canals, bridges, and tiny squares in the labyrinth were too much alike—he was no longer certain of even the compass points; all he cared about was keeping track of the vision he was so ardently pursuing and, forced by ignominious vigilance to flatten himself against walls and take cover behind the people ahead of him, he was long unaware of the fatigue, the exhaustion that emotion and **unremitting**⑤ tension had wreaked upon his body and mind. Tadzio walked behind his family, usually letting the governess and his nunlike sisters pass ahead of him when the street narrowed and, sauntering along on his own, he would turn his head periodically to glance over his shoulder with his unusual twilight-gray eyes and make certain his admirer was still following him. He would see him and did not betray him.

"For beauty, Phaedrus, mark thou well, beauty and beauty alone is at once divine and visible; it is hence the path of the man of the senses, little Phaedrus, the path of the artist to the intellect. For surely thou knowest that we poets cannot follow the path of beauty

---

① 微不足道的。
② 不安,疑虑。
③ 入迷的。
④ 激动的。
⑤ 不懈的。

lest Eros should join forces with us and take the lead; For how can a man be worthy as an educator if he have a natural, inborn, incorrigible penchant for the abyss? Much as we renounce it and seek dignity, we are drawn to it. Thus do we reject, say, analytical knowledge: knowledge, Phaedrus, lacks dignity and rigor; it is discerning, understanding, forgiving, and wanting in discipline and form; it is in sympathy with the abyss; it is the abyss. We do therefore firmly resolve to disavow it and devote ourselves henceforth to beauty alone, which is to say, simplicity grandeur and a new rigor, a second innocence, and form. But form and innocence, Phaedrus, lead to intoxication and desire; because we are incapable of taking to the heavens, we are capable only of taking to **profligacy**①. Now I shall go, Phaedrus, and thou shalt remain. And when thou seest me no more, then thou too shalt go."

Several days thereafter Gustav von Aschenbach left the Hotel des Bains later in the morning than usual, as he had been feeling **indisposed**②. He was suffering from dizzy spells that were only partly physical: they were accompanied by a precipitously mounting anxiety and feelings of hopelessness. He noticed a large assemblage of luggage waiting to be dispatched in the lobby, asked a doorman which guests were departing, and was given the aristocratic Polish name he had secretly expected to hear. He received the news with no change in his sunken features but with that slight lift of the head one uses to show one has registered something one does not need to know, and then asked, "When?"

"After lunch," he was told, and he nodded and went down to the sea.

It was desolate there. An autumnal, off-season mood seemed to lie upon the once so colorful and animated, now all but deserted pleasure haunt, its sand no longer kept clean. A camera, apparently abandoned, stood on its **tripod**③ at the edge of the water, the black cloth draped over it flapping noisily in the chilly wind.

Tadzio, with the three or four playmates left to him, was moving about on the right in front of the family cabana, and Aschenbach, resting on his longue about midway between the sea and the row of cabanas, a blanket over his knees, was watching him once again. Their play, which went unsupervised, the women being presumably occupied with travel preparations, looked **unruly**④ and was getting out of hand. That stocky fellow with the

---

① 挥霍,放荡。

② 不适的。

③ 三脚架。

④ 放肆的。

belted linen suit and black, slicked-down hair the one they addressed as Jasiu—aroused and blinded by a handful of sand thrown in his face, had forced Tadzio into a wrestling match, which ended in the swift defeat of the beautiful yet weaker boy. But now that it was time to part, the **underling's**[①] **deferential**[②] sentiments seemed to have turned to brutal cruelty as he sought revenge for his long enslavement, and the **victor**[③], far from releasing his victim, knelt on his back and drove his face so relentlessly into the sand that Tadzio, already breathless from the struggle, appeared in danger of suffocating. His efforts at shaking off the burden of his attacker were convulsive and ceased for moments at a time, recurring only as twitches. Horrified, Aschenbach was about to spring to his aid when the **ruffian**[④] finally let him free. Tadzio, very pale, raised his body halfway and sat motionless for several minutes, leaning on one arm, hair disheveled and eyes darkening. Then he got to his feet and walked slowly off. The boys called out to him, cheerily at first, then anxiously, **imploringly**[⑤]; he did not hear. The dark boy, who must have felt immediate remorse at having gone so far, ran after him and tried to make peace. A heave of the **shoulder**[⑥] **rebuffed**[⑦] him. Tadzio moved on at an angle towards the water. He was barefoot and wearing the striped linen suit with the red bow.

There he stood a moment, gazing out into the distance, then turned to the left and began moving slowly along the long, narrow strip of exposed land. Separated from the shore by a broad stretch of water and from his companions by a proud frame of mind, he walked on, a highly aloof and isolated figure, his hair streaming, in the sea, in the wind, before the misty infinitude. Again he paused to gaze into the distance. And all at once, as if driven by a memory, an impulse, he twisted his body at the waist, hand on hip, into a graceful turn and glanced over his shoulder towards the shore. There sat the observer as he had sat before, when those twilight-gray eyes had first glanced back from the threshold and met his. His head, reclining on the back of the chair, had slowly followed the figure moving there in the distance; now it rose as if to meet the eyes again and sank down on his chest, so that the eyes stared up from below while the face displayed the slack, self-absorbed expression

① 地位低下的。
② 恭敬的。
③ 胜利者。
④ 暴徒,恶棍。
⑤ 恳求地。
⑥ 耸肩。
⑦ 拒绝。

of deep slumber. But to him it seemed as if the pale and charming **shepherd**① of souls out there were smiling at him, beckoning to him, as if, releasing his hand from his hip, he were pointing outward, floating onward into the promising immensity of it all. And, as so often, he set out to follow him.

Minutes passed before people rushed to the aid of the man, who had **slumped**② sideways in his chair. He was carried to his room. And that very day a respectfully stunned world received word of his death.

Ⅳ. 思考题

1. Summarize the plot of the novella.
2. How is Aschenbach characterized? Comment on Mann's characterization.
3. There are repeated images of grotesque figures in the story. What kind of purposes do those images serve?
4. What do you make of Aschenbach's affection toward Tadzio? The tale and the film are commonly acknowledged as gay novel and gay film. Do you agree or disagree?
5. What is the theme behind the story?

Ⅴ. 文学批评

文学古典主义

Literary Classicism refers to a style of writing that consciously emulates the forms and subject matter of classical antiquity. For the purposes of Western literature, this means Greek and Roman drama, poetic forms like the epic, and literary theory as expounded in Aristotle's "Poetics." Classicism developed during the Renaissance and Enlightenment eras, and continued to shape literature into the 20th century.

Seventeenth century French writers were the first to align with classical standards as part of an organized literary movement. An appreciation for the ideals of antiquity began when classical translations first became widely available during the Renaissance. Literary

---

① 牧羊人,这里是引导者的意思。
② 躺,倒。

classicism appeared in dramatic works modeled on Greek masters, such as Aeschylus and Sophocles, and sought to embody Aristotle's Three Unities. These called for literary works to have a single plotline, a single location and a compressed time span. Literary classicism expanded from drama into poetry during the Enlightenment, when it became known as Neo-classicism, and prose during the 18th century Augustan Age of English literature.

Ⅵ. 拓展阅读

Ritchie Robertson's "Classicism and its Pitfalls: *Death in Venice*" (*The Cambridge Companion to Thomas Mann*. Ed. Ritchie Robertson. Cambridge University Press, 2004: 95-106.)

Ⅶ. 参考文献

Matus, Douglass. "Examples of Literary Classicism." Retrieved June 7th, 2020, https://penandthepad.com/examples-literary-classicism-19902.html.

托马斯·曼. 托马斯·曼散文. 黄燎宇译. 北京:人民文学出版社,2014.

Chapter 4　Pearl. S. Buck and Her Vision of China

Ⅰ. 作者简介

赛珍珠 Pearl S. Buck,(1892—1973),美国作家,以其在中国的生活小说而闻名。赛珍珠的父母是长老会传教士,她从小在中国东部镇江长大,最初是由母亲和一位中国家庭教师教育的,15 岁时被送到上海的一所寄宿学校。两年后,她进入了弗吉尼亚州林奇堡的兰多夫 · 麦肯女子学院读书,并于 1914 年毕业。

1925 年,赛珍珠回到中国,在中国大学教授英语文学。在此期间,她短暂回到了美国继续在康奈尔大学学习,并于 1926 年获得硕士学位。1922 年,她开始在美国杂志上发表有关中国人生活的文章。她的第一部小说《东风,西风》(*East Wind, West Wind*)是在一艘驶往美国的船上写的。

1931 年,赛珍珠出版了《大地》(*The Good Earth*),小说讲述了以王龙和他的妻子阿兰为代表的中国农民生活的辛酸故事,甫一出版立即成为畅销书。这本书获得了 1932 年的普利策奖,奠定了赛珍珠中西方文化大使的身份,并被改编为舞台剧和电影。《大地》之后，赛珍珠还写了两本续集《儿子》（*Sons*）和《分家》（*A House Divided*）；三部曲被合并出版为《大地之家》（1935）。

1935 年起，赛珍珠定居美国。除了文学创作，她也投身社会运动，还收养了许多孩子。1949 年，为了帮助美国军人在亚洲养育的混血儿，她和其他人成立了一个收养机构名为“欢迎之家”（Welcome House）。她还成立了另一个儿童赞助机构——赛珍珠基金会，她将超过 700 万美元的收入都捐给了这个机构。

赛珍珠回到美国后转向传记写作，创作了很多关于她家人的传记，比如写她父亲的《流亡者》（*The Exile*）和写她母亲的《搏斗的天使》（*Fighting Angle*）。她后期的小说还包括《龙种》（*Dragon Seed*）和《帝国女性》（*Imperial Woman*）。她还发表了短篇小说，如《结发妻子与其他故事》（*The First Wife and Other Stories*），关于她智障女儿卡罗尔的一部非虚构作品《永不长大的孩子》（*The Child Who Never Grew*）。她还创作了一本自传《我的几个世界》（*My Several Worlds*）以及一些儿童读物。

赛珍珠于 1938 年获得诺贝尔文学奖，因为“她对中国农民生活的丰富而真实的史诗性描述，以及她杰出的传记作品”（“for her rich and truly epic descriptions of peasant life in China and for her biographical masterpieces”）。赛珍珠的写作风格受到传统中国小说的影响，她认为小说应该为人民服务，反映特定的历史背景，小说采取的语言也应该是人民能接受的通俗易懂的语言，小说的主要内容应该是和读者相关的、关于普通民众的生活。赛珍珠认为最好的小说家不应该卖弄技法，而应当是自然的，他/她应充分利用手头的素材，不偏不倚地讲述故事。作家的责任就是要在万千线索中理出头绪，发现真实。虽然有一些学者认为赛珍珠的文笔不够“文学”，甚至有些落伍，但是正如她所言，她的目的不在于追求文字的艺术，而在于为人民写作。赛珍珠最伟大的贡献就在于她给西方读者带去了一个尽可能真实的中国形象。20 世纪 30 年代大部分西方小说中的中国人形象还停留在挂着金钱鼠尾辫、干着偷鸡摸狗的营生的负面形象，赛珍珠的小说让西方读者首次接触到了勤劳、勇敢的广大中国劳动人民。

Ⅱ. 内容提要

《大地》讲述了王龙从一个贫苦农民到最终成为一个富裕地主的一生。在此期间,他的妻子阿兰陪伴在他身边,两人共同努力,辛勤劳作。赛珍珠通过王龙和阿兰展现了中国农民的婚姻、亲子关系和复杂人性,折射出那个年代中国人的特定生活方式,以及土地在中国农民心中的分量。

故事从王龙结婚那天开始。他从镇上一个黄姓地主家买了一个女仆阿兰,婚后,王龙辛勤劳动,阿兰也很吃苦耐劳,慢慢地他们攒钱从黄家买了一块又一块的地。阿兰接连生了一个儿子和两个女儿,第一个女儿因饥荒造成严重营养不良而智障,第二个女儿刚出生就被阿兰杀死,因为贫穷的生活难以为继。在大饥荒和干旱期间,王龙心狠手辣的叔叔想要敲诈一笔,用低价买走王龙的田产,王龙拒绝了,一家逃到南方的一个大城市。

在城里,阿兰和孩子们乞讨,王龙拉黄包车。他们发现乡村外的世界,整个国家是如此的不同。王龙时时刻刻想着回到自己的土地上,但是军队到了城里,他只能在晚上才敢出去干活。不久一场暴乱爆发,王龙被一伙暴徒席卷,他们正在抢劫一个富人的房子,并把这个人逼到角落里,这个人担心自己的生命安全,把所有的钱都给了王龙。与此同时,阿兰在另一所房子里发现了珠宝,并偷偷藏了起来。

王龙一家拿着富人给的这笔钱回到乡下,买了一头新牛和农具,还雇了佣人为他干活。不久,阿兰又生了三个孩子,一对双胞胎儿子和女儿。后来王龙发现了阿兰偷偷藏起的珠宝,用它们买下了黄家的剩余土地。王龙成了地主,将两个大儿子送去上学,想让小儿子继承他的田产。随着王龙越来越富裕,他买了一个叫莲花的小妾。阿兰默默忍受着丈夫的背叛,直到王龙拿走了她唯一要留给自己的珠宝——两颗珍珠,并把它们做成耳环送给莲花。阿兰郁郁寡欢,最终去世了,王龙在悼念她的逝去时,终于认识到了她在自己生命中的地位。

王龙一家搬进城,租了黄家的老房子。王龙现在已经是老人了,他希望一家人齐齐整整,但是争端不断,儿子妯娌之间总是吵架,小儿子离家出走去当兵。小说结尾,王龙无意中听到儿子们打算卖地,并试图劝阻他们。儿子们表面答应,却会心一笑。

本书选取的片段是小说的前四章,小说首先详细描写了王龙在娶妻之前的准备和心理活动,他去黄家路上的所见所闻,以及在王龙和阿兰结婚之后,他们的生产生活和相处模式,非常真实地反映了中国农民的家庭生活、社会组织结构和对土地的信仰。

Ⅲ. 作品:《大地》第 1-4 章

1

IT WAS Wang Lung's marriage day. At first, opening his eyes in the blackness of the curtains about his bed, he could not think why the dawn seemed different from any other. The house was still except for the faint, **gasp**①ing cough of his old father, whose room was opposite to his own across the middle room. Every morning the old man's cough was the first sound to be heard. Wang Lung usually lay listening to it and moved only when he heard it approaching nearer and when he heard the door of his father's room squeak upon its wooden hinges.

But this morning he did not wait. He sprang up and pushed aside the curtains of his bed. It was a dark, ruddy dawn, and through a small square hole of a window, where the **tattered**② paper fluttered, a glimpse of bronze sky gleamed. He went to the hole and tore the paper away.

"It is spring and I do not need this," he muttered.

He was ashamed to say aloud that he wished the house to look neat on this day. The hole was barely large enough to admit his hand and he thrust it out to feel of the air. A small soft wind blew gently from the east, a wind mild and murmurous and full of rain. It was a good **omen**③. The fields needed rain for fruition. There would be no rain this day, but within a few days, if this wind continued, there would be water. It was good. Yesterday he had said to his father that if this brazen, glittering sunshine continued, the wheat could not fill in the ear. Now it was as if Heaven had chosen this day to wish him well. Earth would bear fruit.

He hurried out into the middle room, drawing on his blue outer trousers as he went, and knotting about the fullness at his waist his **girdle**④ of blue cotton cloth. He left his upper body bare until he had heated water to bathe himself. He went into the shed which was the kitchen, leaning against the house, and out of its dusk an ox twisted its head from behind the corner next the door and lowed at him deeply. The kitchen was made of earthen

① 喘息。
② 破烂的。
③ 兆头。
④ 腰带。

bricks as the house was, great squares of earth dug from their own fields, and thatched with straw from their own wheat. Out of their own earth had his grandfather in his youth fashioned also the oven, baked and black with many years of meal preparing. On top of this earthen structure stood a deep, round, iron cauldron.

This cauldron he filled partly full of water, dipping it with a half gourd from an earthen jar that stood near, but he dipped cautiously, for water was precious. Then, after a hesitation, he suddenly lifted the jar and emptied all the water into the cauldron. This day he would bathe his whole body. Not since he was a child upon his mother's knee had anyone looked upon his body. Today one would, and he would have it clean.

He went around the oven to the **rear**①, and selecting a handful of the dry grass and stalks standing in the corner of the kitchen, he arranged it delicately in the mouth of the oven, making the most of every leaf. Then from an old flint and iron he caught a flame and thrust it into the straw and there was a blaze.

This was the last morning he would have to light the fire. He had lit it every morning since his mother died six years before. He had lit the fire, boiled water, and poured the water into a bowl and taken it into the room where his father sat upon his bed, coughing and **fumbling**② for his shoes upon the floor. Every morning for these six years the old man had waited for his son to bring in hot water to ease him of his morning coughing. Now father and son could rest. There was a woman coming to the house. Never again would Wang Lung have to rise summer and winter at dawn to light the fire. He could lie in his bed and wait, and he also would have a bowl of water brought to him, and if the earth were fruitful there would be tea leaves in the water. Once in some years it was so.

And if the woman wearied, there would be her children to light the fire, the many children she would bear to Wang Lung. Wang Lung stopped, struck by the thought of children running in and out of their three rooms. Three rooms had always seemed much to them, a house half empty since his mother died. They were always having to resist relatives who were more crowded...his uncle, with his endless brood of children, **coax**③ing.

"Now, how can two lone men need so much room? Cannot father and son sleep together? The warmth of the young one's body will comfort the old one's cough."

But the father always replied, "I am saving my bed for my grandson. He will warm my

① 后面。
② 乱摸。
③ 诱骗。

bones in my age."

Now the grandsons were coming, grandsons upon grandsons! They would have to put beds along the walls and in the middle room. The house would be full of beds. The blaze in the oven died down while Wang Lung thought of all the beds there would be in the half empty house, and the water began to chill in the cauldron. The shadowy figure of the old man appeared in the doorway, holding his unbuttoned garments about him. He was coughing and spitting and he gasped.

"How is it that there is not water yet to heat my lungs?"

Wang Lung stared and recalled himself and was ashamed.

"This fuel is damp," he muttered from behind the stove. "The damp wind..."

The old man continued to cough perseveringly and would not cease until the water boiled. Wang Lung dipped some into a bowl, and then, after a moment, he opened a glazed jar that stood upon a **ledge**① of the stove and took from it a dozen or so of the curled dried leaves and sprinkled them upon the surface of the water. The old man's eyes opened greedily and immediately he began to complain.

"Why are you wasteful? Tea is like eating silver."

"It is the day," replied Wang Lung with a short laugh. "Eat and be comforted."

The old man grasped the bowl in his **shriveled**②, knotty fingers, muttering, uttering little grunts. He watched the leaves uncurl and spread upon the surface of the water, unable to bear drinking the precious stuff.

"It will be cold," said Wang Lung.

"True...true..." said the old man in alarm, and he began to take great gulps of the hot tea. He passed into an animal satisfaction, like a child fixed upon its feeding. But he was not too forgetful to see Wang Lung dipping the water **recklessly**③ from the cauldron into a deep wooden tub. He lifted his head and stared at his son.

"Now there is water enough to bring a crop to fruit," he said suddenly.

Wang Lung continued to dip the water to the last drop. He did not answer.

"Now then!" cried his father loudly.

"I have not washed my body all at once since the New Year," said Wang Lung in a low voice.

---

① 壁架。

② 干瘪的,萎缩的。

③ 满不在乎地。

He was ashamed to say to his father that he wished his body to be clean for a woman to see. He hurried out, carrying the tub to his own room. The door was hung loosely upon a **warped**①wooden frame and it did not shut closely, and the old man tottered into the middle room and put his mouth to the opening and **bawl**②ed,

"It will be ill if we start the woman like this... tea in the morning water and all this washing!"

"It is only one day," shouted Wang Lung. And then he added, "I will throw the water on the earth when I am finished and it is not all waste."

The old man was silent at this, and Wang Lung unfastened his girdle and stepped out of his clothing. In the light that streamed in a square block from the hole he **wrung**③ a small towel from the steaming water and he scrubbed his dark slender body vigorously. Warm though he had thought the air, when his flesh was wet he was cold, and he moved quickly, passing the towel in and out of the water until from his whole body there went up a delicate cloud of steam. Then he went to a box that had been his mother's and drew from it a fresh suit of blue cotton cloth. He might be a little cold this day without the **wadding**④ of the winter garments, but he suddenly could not bear to put them on against his clean flesh. The covering of them was torn and filthy and the wadding stuck out of the holes, grey and **sodden**⑤. He did not want this woman to see him for the first time with the wadding sticking out of his clothes. Later she would have to wash and mend, but not the first day. He drew over the blue cotton coat and trousers a long robe made of the same material... his one long robe, which he wore on feast days only, ten days or so in the year, all told. Then with swift fingers he unplaited the long braid of hair that hung down his back, and taking a wooden comb from the drawer of the small, unsteady table, he began to comb out his hair.

His father drew near again and put his mouth to the crack of the door.

"Am I to have nothing to eat this day?" he complained. "At my age the bones are water in the morning until food is given them."

"I am coming," said Wang Lung, braiding his hair quickly and smoothly and weaving

---

① 弯曲的,扭曲的。
② 咆哮。
③ wring 的过去式,扭,拧。
④ 填塞物。
⑤ 发潮的,泡胀的。

into the strands a tasseled, black silk cord.

Then after a moment he removed his long gown and wound his braid about his head and went out, carrying the tub of water. He had quite forgotten the breakfast. He would stir a little water into corn meal and give it to his father. For himself he could not eat. He staggered with the tub to the threshold and poured the water upon the earth nearest the door, and as he did so he remembered he had used all the water in the cauldron for his bathing and he would have to start the fire again. A wave of anger passed over him at his father.

"That old head thinks of nothing except his eating and his drinking," he muttered into the mouth of the oven; but aloud he said nothing. It was the last morning he would have to prepare food for the old man. He put a very little water into the cauldron, drawing it in a bucket from the well near the door, and it boiled quickly and he stirred meal together and took it to the old man.

"We will have rice this night, my father," he said. "Meanwhile, here is corn."

"There is only a little rice left in the basket," said the old man, seating himself at the table in the middle room and stirring with his chopsticks the thick yellow gruel.

"We will eat a little less then at the spring festival," said Wang Lung. But the old man did not hear. He was supping loudly at his bowl.

Wang Lung went into his own room then, and drew about him again the long blue robe and let down the braid of his hair. He passed his hand over his shaven brow and over his cheeks. Perhaps he had better be newly shaven? It was scarcely sunrise yet. He could pass through the Street of the Barbers and be shaved before he went to the house where the woman waited for him. If he had the money he would do it.

He took from his girdle a small greasy pouch of grey cloth and counted the money in it. There were six silver dollars and a double handful of copper coins. He had not yet told his father he had asked friends to sup that night. He had asked his male cousin, the young son of his uncle, and his uncle for his father's sake, and three neighboring farmers who lived in the village with him. He had planned to bring back from the town that morning pork, a small pond fish, and a handful of chestnuts. He might even buy a few of the bamboo sprouts from the south and a little beef to stew with the cabbage he had raised in his own garden. But this only if there were any money left after the bean oil and the soybean sauce had been bought. If he shaved his head he could not, perhaps, buy the beef. Well, he would shave his head, he decided suddenly.

He left the old man without speech and went out into the early morning. In spite of the dark red dawn the sun was mounting the horizon clouds and sparkled upon the dew on the rising wheat and barley. The farmer in Wang Lung was **divert**①ed for an instant and he stooped to examine the budding heads. They were empty as yet and waiting for the rain. He smelled the air and looked anxiously at the sky. Rain was there, dark in the clouds, heavy upon the wind. He would buy a stick of incense and place it in the little temple to the Earth God. On a day like this he would do it.

He wound his way in among the fields upon the narrow path. In the near distance the grey city wall arose. Within that gate in the wall through which he would pass stood the great house where the woman had been a slave girl since her childhood, the House of Hwang. There were those who said, "It is better to live alone than to marry a woman who has been slave in a great house." But when he had said to his father, "Am I never to have a woman?" his father replied, "With weddings costing as they do in these evil days and every woman wanting gold rings and silk clothes before she will take a man, there remain only slaves to be had for the poor."

His father had stirred himself, then, and gone to the House of Hwang and asked if there were a slave to spare.

"Not a slave too young, and above all, not a pretty one," he had said.

Wang Lung had suffered that she must not be pretty. It would be something to have a pretty wife that other men would congratulate him upon having. His father, seeing his **mutinous**② face, had cried out at him,

"And what will we do with a pretty woman? We must have a woman who will tend the house and bear children as she works in the fields, and will a pretty woman do these things? She will be forever thinking about clothes to go with her face! No, not a pretty woman in our house. We are farmers. Moreover, who has heard of a pretty slave who was virgin in a wealthy house? All the young lords have had their fill of her. It is better to be first with an ugly woman than the hundredth with a beauty. Do you imagine a pretty woman will think your farmer's hands as pleasing as the soft hands of a rich man's son, and your sunblack face as beautiful as the golden skin of the others who have had her for their pleasure?"

Wang Lung knew his father spoke well. Nevertheless, he had to struggle with his flesh

---

① 转移,转向。

② 反抗的。

before he could answer. And then be said violently,

"At least, I will not have a woman who is **pock-marked**[①], or who has a split upper lip."

"We will have to see what is to be had," his father replied.

Well, the woman was not pock-marked nor had she a split upper lip. This much he knew, but nothing more. He and his father had bought two silver rings, washed with gold, and silver earrings, and these his father had taken to the woman's owner in acknowledgment of **betrothal**[②]. Beyond this, he knew nothing of the woman who was to be his, except that on this day he could go and get her.

He walked into the cool darkness of the city gate. Water carriers, just outside, their **barrows**[③] laden with great tubs of water, passed to and fro all day, the water splashing out of the tubs upon the stones. It was always wet and cool in the tunnel of the gate under the thick wall of earth and brick; cool even upon a summer's day, so that the melon vendors spread their fruits upon the stones, melons split open to drink in the moist coolness. There were none yet, for the season was too early, but baskets of small hard green peaches stood along the walls, and the vendor cried out,

"The first peaches of spring...the first peaches! Buy, eat, **purge**[④] your bowels of the poisons of winter!"

Wang Lung said to himself,

"If she likes them, I will buy her a handful when we return." He could not realize that when he walked back through the gate there would be a woman walking behind him.

He turned to the right within the gate and after a moment was in the Street of Barbers. There were few before him so early, only some farmers who had carried their produce into the town the night before in order that they might sell their vegetables at the dawn markets and return for the day's work in the fields. They had slept shivering and crouching over their baskets, the baskets now empty at their feet. Wang Lung avoided them lest some recognize him, for he wanted none of their joking on this day. All down the street in a long line the barbers stood behind their small stalls, and Wang Lung went to the furthest one and sat down upon the stool and motioned to the barber who stood chattering to his neigh-

① 痘疤印的。
② 订婚。
③ 独轮车。
④ 清除。

bor. The barber came at once and began quickly to pour hot water, from a kettle on his pot of charcoal, into his brass basin.

"Shave everything?" he said in a professional tone.

"My head and my face," replied Wang Lung.

"Ears and nostrils cleaned?" asked the barber.

"How much will that cost extra?" asked Wang Lung cautiously.

"Four pence," said the barber, beginning to pass a black cloth in and out of the hot water.

"I will give you two," said Wang Lung.

"Then I will clean one ear and one nostril," rejoined the barber promptly. "On which side of the face do you wish it done?" He grimaced at the next barber as he spoke and the other burst into a **guffaw**①. Wang Lung perceived that he had fallen into the hands of a joker, and feeling inferior in some unaccountable way, as he always did, to these town dwellers, even though they were only barbers and the lowest of persons, he said quickly,

"As you will...as you will..."

Then he submitted himself to the barber's soaping and rubbing and shaving, and being after all a generous fellow enough, the barber gave him without extra charge a series of skillful **poundings**② upon his shoulders and back to loosen his muscles. He commented upon Wang Lung as he shaved his upper forehead,

"This would not be a bad-looking farmer if he would cut off his hair. The new fashion is to take off the braid."

His razor **hover**③ed so near the circle of hair upon Wang Lung's crown that Wang Lung cried out,

"I cannot cut it off without asking my father!" And the barber laughed and skirted the round spot of hair.

When it was finished and the money counted into the barber's wrinkled, water-soaked hand, Wang Lung had a moment of horror. So much money! But walking down the street again with the wind fresh upon his shaven skin, he said to himself,

"It is only once."

---

① 哄笑,大笑。

② 敲击。

③ 盘旋。

He went to the market, then, and bought two pounds of pork and watched the butcher as he wrapped it in a dried lotus leaf, and then, hesitating, he bought also six ounces of beef. When all had been bought, even to fresh squares of beancurd, shivering in a jelly upon its leaf, he went to a candlemaker's shop and there he bought a pair of incense sticks. Then he turned his steps with great shyness toward the House of Hwang.

Once at the gate of the house he was seized with terror. How had he come alone? He should have asked his father... his uncle... even his nearest neighbor, Ching... anyone to come with him. He had never been in a great house before. How could he go in with his wedding feast on his arm, and say, "I have come for a woman?"

He stood at the gate for a long time, looking at it. It was closed fast, two great wooden gates, painted black and bound and studded with iron, closed upon each other. Two lions made of stone stood on guard, one at either side. There was no one else. He turned away. It was impossible.

He felt suddenly **faint**①. He would go first and buy a little food. He had eaten nothing... had forgotten food. He went into a small street restaurant, and putting two pence upon the table, he sat down. A dirty waiting boy with a shiny black apron came near and he called out to him, "Two bowls of noodles!" And when they were come, he ate them down greedily, pushing them into his mouth with his bamboo chopsticks, while the boy stood and spun the coppers between his black thumb and forefinger.

"Will you have more?" asked the boy indifferently.

Wang Lung shook his head. He sat up and looked about. There was no one he knew in the small, dark, crowded room full of tables. Only a few men sat eating or drinking tea. It was a place for poor men, and among them he looked neat and clean and almost well-to-do, so that a beggar, passing, whined at him,

"Have a good heart, teacher, and give me a small cash... I starve!"

Wang Lung had never had a beggar ask of him before, nor had any ever called him teacher. He was pleased and he threw into the beggar's bowl two small cash, which are one fifth of a penny, and the beggar pulled back with swiftness his black claw of a hand, and grasping the cash, fumbled them within his rags.

Wang Lung sat and the sun climbed upwards. The waiting boy **lounge**②d about impatiently. "If you are buying nothing more," he said at last with much impudence, "you will

① 眩晕。
② 闲逛。

have to pay rent for the stool."

Wang Lung was incensed at such impudence and he would have risen except that when he thought of going into the great House of Hwang and of asking there for a woman, sweat broke out over his whole body as though he were working in a field.

"Bring me tea," he said weakly to the boy. Before he could turn it was there and the small boy demanded sharply,

"Where is the penny?"

And Wang Lung, to his horror, found there was nothing to do but to produce from his girdle yet another penny.

"It is robbery," he muttered, unwilling. Then he saw entering the shop his neighbor whom he had invited to the feast, and he put the penny hastily upon the table and drank the tea at a **gulp**① and went out quickly by the side door and was once more upon the street.

"It is to be done," he said to himself desperately, and slowly he turned his way to the great gates.

This time, since it was after high noon, the gates were ajar and the keeper of the gate idled upon the threshold, picking his teeth with a bamboo **sliver**② after his meal. He was a tall fellow with a large mole upon his left cheek, and from the mole hung three long black hairs which had never been cut. When Wang Lung appeared he shouted roughly, thinking from the basket that he had come to sell something.

"Now then, what?"

With great difficulty Wang Lung replied,

"I am Wang Lung, the farmer."

"Well, and Wang Lung, the farmer, what?" **retort**③ed the gateman, who was polite to none except the rich friends of his master and mistress.

"I am come...I am come..." faltered Wang Lung.

"That I see," said the gateman with elaborate patience, twisting the long hairs of his mole.

"There is a woman," said Wang Lung, his voice sinking helplessly to a whisper. In the sunshine his face was wet.

---

① 狼吞虎咽。

② 长条。

③ 回嘴，反驳。

The gateman gave a great laugh.

"So you are he!" he **roar**①ed. "I was told to expect a bridegroom today. But I did not recognize you with a basket on your arm."

"It is only a few meats," said Wang Lung apologetically, waiting for the gateman to lead him within. But the gateman did not move. At last Wang Lung said with anxiety,

"Shall I go alone?"

The gateman affected a start of horror. "The Old Lord would kill you!"

Then seeing that Wang Lung was too innocent he said, "A little silver is a good key."

Wang Lung saw at last that the man wanted money of him.

"I am a poor man," he said **pleadingly**②.

"Let me see what you have in your girdle," said the gateman.

And he grinned when Wang Lung in his simplicity actually put his basket upon the stones and lifting his robe took out the small bag from his girdle and shook into his left hand what money was left after his purchases. There was one silver piece and fourteen copper pence.

"I will take the silver," said the gateman coolly, and before Wang Lung could protest the man had the silver in his sleeve and was striding through the gate, **bawl**③ing loudly,

"The bridegroom, the bridegroom!"

Wang Lung, in spite of anger at what had just happened and horror at this loud announcing of his coming, could do nothing but follow, and this he did, picking up his basket and looking neither to the right nor left.

Afterwards, although it was the first time he had ever been in a great family's house, he could remember nothing. With his face burning and his head bowed, he walked through court after court, hearing that voice roaring ahead of him, hearing tinkles of laughter on every side. Then suddenly when it seemed to him he had gone through a hundred courts, the gateman fell silent and pushed him into a small waiting room. There he stood alone while the gateman went into some inner place, returning in a moment to say,

"The Old Mistress says you are to appear before her."

Wang Lung started forward, but the gateman stopped him, crying in disgust,

"You cannot appear before a great lady with a basket on your arm...a basket of pork

---

① 咆哮。
② 恳求的。
③ 大叫,咆哮。

and beancurd! How will you bow?"

"True...true..." said Wang Lung in agitation. But he did not dare to put the basket down because he was afraid something might be stolen from it. It did not occur to him that all the world might not desire such **delicacies**① as two pounds of pork and six ounces of beef and a small pond fish. The gateman saw his fear and cried out in great **contempt**②,

"In a house like this we feed these meats to the dogs!" and seizing the basket he **thrust**③ it behind the door and pushed Wang Lung ahead of him.

Down a long narrow veranda they went, the roofs supported by delicate carven posts, and into a hall the like of which Wang Lung had never seen. A score of houses such as his whole house could have been put into it and have disappeared, so wide were the spaces, so high the roofs. Lifting his head in wonder to see the great carven and painted beams above him he **stumble**④d upon the high threshold of the door and would have fallen except that the gateman caught his arm and cried out,

"Now will you be so polite as to fall on your face like this before the Old Mistress?"

And collecting himself in great shame Wang Lung looked ahead of him, and upon a **dais**⑤ in the center of the room he saw a very old lady, her small fine body clothed in **lustrous**⑥, pearly grey satin, and upon the low bench beside her a pipe of opium stood, burning over its little lamp. She looked at him out of small, sharp, black eyes, as sunken and sharp as a monkey's eyes in her thin and wrinkled face. The skin of her hand that held the pipe's end was stretched over her little bones as smooth and as yellow as the gilt upon an idol. Wang Lung fell to his knees and knocked his head on the tiled floor.

"Raise him," said the old lady gravely to the gateman, "these **obeisances**⑦ are not necessary. Has he come for the woman?"

"Yes, Ancient One," replied the gateman.

"Why does he not speak for himself?" asked the old lady.

"Because he is a fool, Ancient One," said the gateman, twirling the hairs of his mole.

---

① 精致的东西。
② 鄙视。
③ 猛推。
④ 绊倒。
⑤ 高台,上座。
⑥ 有光泽的,光辉的。
⑦ 敬礼。

This roused Wang Lung and he looked with **indignation**[①] at the gateman.

"I am only a coarse person, Great and Ancient Lady," he said. "I do not know what words to use in such a presence."

The old lady looked at him carefully and with perfect **gravity**[②] and made as though she would have spoken, except that her hand closed upon the pipe which a slave had been tending for her and at once she seemed to forget him. She bent and sucked greedily at the pipe for a moment and the sharpness passed from her eyes and a film of forgetfulness came over them. Wang Lung remained standing before her until in passing her eyes caught his figure.

"What is this man doing here?" she asked with sudden anger. It was as though she had forgotten everything. The gateman's face was immovable. He said nothing.

"I am waiting for the woman, Great Lady," said Wang Lung in much astonishment.

"The woman? What woman? ..." the old lady began, but the slave girl at her side stooped and whispered and the lady recovered herself. "Ah, yes, I forgot for the moment... a small affair...you have come for the slave called O-lan. I remember we promised her to some farmer in marriage. You are that farmer?"

"I am he," replied Wang Lung.

"Call O-lan quickly," said the old lady to her slave. It was as though she was suddenly impatient to be done with all this and to be left alone in the stillness of the great room with her opium pipe.

And in an instant the slave appeared leading by the hand a square, rather tall figure, clothed in clean blue cotton coat and trousers. Wang Lung glanced once and then away, his heart beating. This was his woman.

"Come here, slave," said the old lady carelessly. "This man has come for you."

The woman went before the lady and stood with bowed head and hands clasped.

"Are you ready?" asked the lady.

The woman answered slowly as an echo, "Ready."

Wang Lung, hearing her voice for the first time, looked at her back as she stood before him. It was a good enough voice, not loud, not soft, plain, and not ill-tempered. The woman's hair was neat and smooth and her coat clean. He saw with an instant's disap-

---

① 愤怒。

② 严肃,庄重。

pointment that her feet were not bound. But this he could not dwell upon, for the old lady was saying to the gateman,

"Carry her box out to the gate and let them begone." And then she called Wang Lung and said, "Stand beside her while I speak." And when Wang had come forward she said to him, "This woman came into our house when she was a child of ten and here she has lived until now, when she is twenty years old. I bought her in a year of famine when her parents came south because they had nothing to eat. They were from the north in Shantung and there they returned, and I know nothing further of them. You see she has the strong body and the square cheeks of her kind. She will work well for you in the field and drawing water and all else that you wish. She is not beautiful but that you do not need. Only men of leisure have the need for beautiful women to divert them. Neither is she clever. But she does well what she is told to do and she has a good temper. So far as I know she is virgin. She has not beauty enough to tempt my sons and grandsons even if she had not been in the kitchen. If there has been anything it has been only a serving man. But with the **innumerable**① and pretty slaves running freely about the courts, I doubt if there has been anyone. Take her and use her well. She is a good slave, although somewhat slow and stupid, and had I not wished to acquire merit at the temple for my future existence by bringing more life into the world I should have kept her, for she is good enough for the kitchen. But I marry my slaves off if any will have them and the lords do not want them."

And to the woman she said,

"Obey him and bear him sons and yet more sons. Bring the first child to me to see."

"Yes, Ancient Mistress," said the woman **submissively**②.

They stood hesitating, and Wang Lung was greatly embarrassed, not knowing whether he should speak or what.

"Well, go, will you!" said the old lady in irritation, and Wang Lung, bowing hastily, turned and went out, the woman after him, and after her the gateman, carrying on his shoulder the box. This box he dropped down in the room where Wang Lung returned to find his basket and would carry it no further, and indeed he disappeared without another word.

Then Wang Lung turned to the woman and looked at her for the first time. She had a square, honest face, a short, broad nose with large black nostrils, and her mouth was wide

---

① 数不清的。
② 顺从的。

as a **gash**① in her face. Her eyes were small and of a dull black in color, and were filled with some sadness that was not clearly expressed. It was a face that seemed habitually silent and unspeaking, as though it could not speak if it would. She bore patiently Wang Lung's look, without embarrassment or response, simply waiting until he had seen her. He saw that it was true there was not beauty of any kind in her face... a brown, common, patient face. But there were no pock-marks on her dark skin, nor was her lip split. In her ears he saw his rings hanging, the gold-washed rings he had bought, and on her hands were the rings he had given her. He turned away with secret **exultation**②. Well, he had his woman!

"Here is this box and this basket," he said **gruffly**③.

Without a word she bent over and picking up one end of the box she placed it upon her shoulder and, **stagger**④ing under its weight, tried to rise. He watched her at this and suddenly he said,

"I will take the box. Here is the basket."

And he shifted the box to his own back, regardless of the best robe he wore, and she, still speechless, took the handle of the basket. He thought of the hundred courts he had come through and of his figure, absurd under its burden.

"If there were a side gate..." he muttered, and she nodded after a little thought, as though she did not understand too quickly what he said. Then she led the way through a small unused court that was grown up with weed, its pool choked, and there under a bent pine tree was an old round gate that she pulled loose from its bar, and they went through and into the street.

Once or twice he looked back at her. She **plod**⑤ded along steadily on her big feet as though she had walked there all her life, her wide face expressionless. In the gate of the wall he stopped uncertainly and fumbled in his girdle with one hand for the pennies he had left, holding the box steady on his shoulder with the other hand. He took out two pence and with these he bought six small green peaches.

"Take these and eat them for yourself," he said gruffly.

---

① 裂缝。
② 狂喜。
③ 态度生硬的,粗暴的。
④ 摇晃。
⑤ 沉重地走。

She clutched them greedily as a child might and held them in her hand without speech. When next he looked at her as they walked along the margin of the wheat fields she was nibbling one cautiously, but when she saw him looking at her she covered it again with her hand and kept her jaws motionless.

And thus they went until they reached the western field where stood the temple to the earth. This temple was a small structure, not higher in all than a man's shoulder and made of grey bricks and roofed with tile. Wang Lung's grandfather, who had farmed the very fields upon which Wang Lung now spent his life, had built it, hauling the bricks from the town upon his wheelbarrow. The walls were covered with plaster on the outside and a village artist had been hired in a good year once to paint upon the white plaster a scene of hills and bamboo. But the rain of generations had poured upon this painting until now there was only a faint feathery shadow of bamboos left, and the hills were almost wholly gone.

Within the temple **snug**[①]ly under the roof sat two small, solemn figures, earthen, for they were formed from the earth of the fields about the temple. These were the god himself and his lady. They wore robes of red and gilt paper, and the god had a scant, drooping moustache of real hair. Each year at the New Year Wang Lung's father bought sheets of red paper and carefully cut and pasted new robes for the pair. And each year rain and snow beat in and the sun of summer shone in and spoiled their robes.

At this moment, however, the robes were still new, since the year was but well begun, and Wang Lung was proud of their spruce appearance. He took the basket from the woman's arm and carefully he looked about under the pork for the sticks of incense he had bought. He was anxious lest they were broken and thus make an evil omen, but they were whole, and when he had found them he stuck them side by side in the ashes of other sticks of incense that were heaped before the gods, for the whole neighborhood worshipped these two small figures. Then fumbling for his flint and iron he caught, with a dried leaf for tinder, a flame to light the incense.

Together this man and this woman stood before the gods of their fields. The woman watched the ends of the incense redden and turn grey. When the ash grew heavy she leaned over and with her forefinger she pushed the head of ash away. Then as though fearful for what she had done, she looked quickly at Wang Lung, her eyes dumb. But there was

① 舒服的。

something he liked in her movement. It was as though she felt that the incense belonged to them both; it was a moment of marriage. They stood there in complete silence, side by side, while the incense **smoulder**[①]ed into ashes; and then because the sun was sinking, Wang Lung shouldered the box and they went home.

At the door of the house the old man stood to catch the last rays of the sun upon him. He made no movement as Wang Lung approached with the woman. It would have been beneath him to notice her. Instead he feigned great interest in the clouds and he cried,

"That cloud which hangs upon the left horn of the new moon speaks of rain. It will come not later than tomorrow night." And then as he saw Wang Lung take the basket from the woman he cried again, "And have you spent money?"

Wang Lung set the basket on the table. "There will be guests tonight," he said briefly, and he carried the box into the room where he slept and set it down beside the box where his own clothes were. He looked at it strangely. But the old man came to the door and said **volubly**[②],

"There is no end to the money spent in this house!"

Secretly he was pleased that his son had invited guests, but he felt it would not do to give out anything but complaints before his new daughter-in-law lest she be set from the first in ways of extravagance. Wang Lung said nothing, but he went out and took the basket into the kitchen and the woman followed him there. He took the food piece by piece from the basket and laid it upon the ledge of the cold stove and he said to her,

"Here is pork and here beef and fish. There are seven to eat. Can you prepare food?"

He did not look at the woman as he spoke. It would not have been seemly. The woman answered in her plain voice,

"I have been kitchen slave since I went into the House of Hwang. There were meats at every meal."

Wang Lung nodded and left her and did not see her again until the guests came crowding in, his uncle **jovial**[③] and **sly**[④] and hungry, his uncle's son an **impudent**[⑤] lad of fif-

① 慢慢烧。
② 滔滔不绝的。
③ 欢乐的。
④ 狡猾的。
⑤ 厚颜无耻的，冒失的。

teen, and the farmers clumsy and grinning with shyness. Two were men from the village with whom Wang Lung exchanged seed and labor at harvest time, and one was his next door neighbor, Ching, a small, quiet man, ever unwilling to speak unless he were compelled to it. After they had been seated about the middle room with **demurring**① and unwillingness to take seats, for politeness, Wang Lung went into the kitchen to bid the woman serve. Then he was pleased when she said to him,

"I will hand you the bowls if you will place them upon the table. I do not like to come out before men."

Wang Lung felt in him a great pride that this woman was his and did not fear to appear before him, but would not before other men. He took the bowls from her hands at the kitchen door and he set them upon the table in the middle room and called loudly,

"Eat, my uncle and my brothers." And when the uncle, who was fond of jokes, said, "Are we not to see the moth-browed bride?" Wang Lung replied firmly, "We are not yet one. It is not meet that other men see her until the marriage is **consummate**②d."

And he urged them to eat and they ate heartily of the good fare, heartily and in silence, and this one praised the brown sauce on the fish and that one the well-done pork, and Wang Lung said over and over in reply,

"It is poor stuff...it is badly prepared."

But in his heart he was proud of the dishes, for with what meats she had the woman had combined sugar and vinegar and a little wine and soy sauce and she had skillfully brought forth all the force of the meat itself, so that Wang Lung himself had never tasted such dishes upon the tables of his friends.

That night after the guests had **tarried**③ long over their tea and had done with their jokes, the woman still lingered behind the stove, and when Wang Lung had seen the last guest away he went in and she cowered there in the straw piles asleep beside the ox. There was straw in her hair when he roused her, and when he called her she put up her arm suddenly in her sleep as though to defend herself from a blow. When she opened her eyes at last, she looked at him with her strange speechless gaze, and he felt as though he faced a child. He took her by the hand and led her into the room where that morning he had bathed himself for her, and he lit a red candle upon the table. In this light he was suddenly

① 迟疑。

② 完成。

③ Tarry,逗留。

shy when he found himself alone with the woman and he was compelled to remind himself,

"There is this woman of mine. The thing is to be done."

And he began to undress himself doggedly. As for the woman, she crept around the corner of the curtain and began without a sound to prepare for the bed. Wang Lung said gruffly,

"When you lie down, put the light out first."

Then he lay down and drew the thick quilt about his shoulders and pretended to sleep. But he was not sleeping. He lay quivering, every nerve of his flesh awake. And when, after a long time, the room went dark, and there was the slow, silent, creeping movement of the woman beside him, an exultation filled him fit to break his body. He gave a hoarse laugh into the darkness and seized her.

2

THERE WAS this luxury of living. The next morning he lay upon his bed and watched the woman who was now wholly his own. She rose and drew about her loosened garments and fastened them closely about her throat and waist, fitting them to her body with a slow writhe and twist. Then she put her feet into her cloth shoes and drew them on by the straps hanging at the back. The light from the small hole shone on her in a bar and he saw her face dimly. It looked unchanged. This was an astonishment to Wang Lung. He felt as though the night must have changed him; yet here was this woman rising from his bed as though she had risen every day of her life. The old man's cough rose **querulously**① out of the dusky dawn and he said to her,

"Take to my father first a bowl of hot water for his lungs."

She asked, her voice exactly as it had been yesterday when she spoke, "Are there to be tea leaves in it?"

This simple question troubled Wang Lung. He would have liked to say, "Certainly there must be tea leaves. Do you think we are beggars?" He would have liked the woman to think that they made nothing of tea leaves in this house. In the House of Hwang, of course, every bowl of water was green with leaves. Even a slave, there, perhaps, would not drink only water. But he knew his father would be angry if on the first day the woman served tea to him instead of water. Besides, they really were not rich. He replied negligently, therefore,

---

① 爱发牢骚地。

"Tea? No...no...it makes his cough worse."

And then he lay in his bed warm and satisfied while in the kitchen the woman fed the fire and boiled the water. He would like to have slept, now that he could, but his foolish body, which he had made to arise every morning so early for all these years, would not sleep although it could, and so he lay there, tasting and savoring in his mind and in his flesh his luxury of **idleness**①.

He was still half ashamed to think of this woman of his. Part of the time he thought of his fields and of the grains of the wheat and of what his harvest would be if the rains came and of the white turnip seed he wished to buy from his neighbor Ching if they could agree upon a price. But between all these thoughts which were in his mind every day there ran weaving and interweaving the new thought of what his life now was, and it occurred to him, suddenly, thinking of the night, to wonder if she liked him. This was a new wonder. He had questioned only of whether he would like her and whether or not she would be satisfactory in his bed and in his house. Plain though her face was and rough the skin upon her hands the flesh of her big body was soft and untouched and he laughed when he thought of it...the short hard laugh he had thrown out into the darkness the night before. The young lords had not seen, then, beyond that plain face of the kitchen slave. Her body was beautiful, spare and big boned yet rounded and soft. He desired suddenly that she should like him as her husband and then he was ashamed.

The door opened and in her silent way she came in bearing in both hands a steaming bowl to him. He sat up in bed and took it. There were tea leaves floating upon the surface of the water. He looked up at her quickly. She was at once afraid and she said,

"I took no tea to the Old One...I did as you said...but to you I..."

Wang Lung saw that she was afraid of him and he was pleased and he answered before she finished, "I like it...I like it," and he drew his tea into his mouth with loud sups of pleasure.

In himself there was this new exultation which he was ashamed to make articulate even to his own heart, "This woman of mine likes me well enough!"

IT SEEMED to him that during these next months he did nothing except watch this woman of his. In reality he worked as he always had. He put his **hoe**② upon his shoulder and he walked to his plots of land and he cultivated the rows of grain, and he yoked the ox

① 闲来无事。

② 锄头。

to the **plow**① and he ploughed the western field for garlic and onions. But the work was luxury, for when the sun struck the **zenith**② he could go to his house and food would be there ready for him to eat, and the dust wiped from the table, and the bowls and the chopsticks placed neatly upon it. Hitherto he had had to prepare the meals when he came in, tired though he was, unless the old man grew hungry out of time and stirred up a little meal or baked a piece of flat, **unleavened**③ bread to roll about a stem of garlic.

Now whatever there was, was ready for him, and he could seat himself upon the bench by the table and eat at once. The earthen floor was swept and the fuel pile replenished. The woman, when he had gone in the morning, took the bamboo rake and a length of rope and with these she roamed the countryside, reaping here a bit of grass and there a twig or a handful of leaves, returning at noon with enough to cook the dinner. It pleased the man that they need buy no more fuel.

In the afternoon she took a hoe and a basket and with these upon her shoulder she went to the main road leading into the city where mules and donkeys and horses carried burdens to and fro, and there she picked the droppings from the animals and carried it home and piled the manure in the dooryard for fertilizer for the fields. These things she did without a word and without being commanded to do them. And when the end of the day came she did not rest herself until the ox had been fed in the kitchen and until she had dipped water to hold to its **muzzle**④ to let it drink what it would.

And she took their ragged clothes and with thread she herself spun on a bamboo spindle from a wad of cotton she mended and contrived to cover the rents in their winter clothes. Their bedding she took into the sun on the threshold and ripped the coverings from the quilts and washed them and hung them upon a bamboo to dry, and the cotton in the quilts that had grown hard and grey from years she picked over, killing the **vermin**⑤ that had flourished in the hidden folds, and sunning it all. Day after day she did one thing after another, until the three rooms seemed clean and almost **prosperous**⑥. The old man's cough grew better and he sat in the sun by the southern wall of the house, always half-a-

① 犁地。
② 顶点。
③ 未发酵的。
④ 动物的嘴。
⑤ 寄生虫。
⑥ 繁荣的,兴隆的。

sleep and warm and content.

But she never talked, this woman, except for the brief necessities of life. Wang Lung, watching her move steadily and slowly about the rooms on her big feet, watching secretly the stolid, square face, the unexpressed, half-fearful look of her eyes, made nothing of her. At night he knew the soft firmness of her body. But in the day her clothes, her plain blue cotton coat and trousers, covered all that he knew, and she was like a faithful, speechless serving maid, who is only a serving maid and nothing more. And it was not meet that he should say to her, "Why do you not speak?" It should be enough that she fulfilled her duty.

Sometimes, working over the clods in the fields, he would fall to **ponder**①ing about her. What had she seen in those hundred courts? What had been her life, that life she never shared with him? He could make nothing of it. And then he was ashamed of his own curiosity and of his interest in her. She was, after all, only a woman.

BUT THERE is not that about three rooms and two meals a day to keep busy a woman who has been a slave in a great house and who has worked from dawn until midnight. One day when Wang Lung was hard pressed with the swelling wheat and was cultivating it with his hoe, day after day, until his back throbbed with weariness, her shadow fell across the furrow over which he bent himself, and there she stood, with a hoe across her shoulder.

"There is nothing in the house until nightfall," she said briefly, and without speech she took the furrow to the left of him and fell into steady hoeing.

The sun beat down upon them, for it was early summer, and her face was soon dripping with her sweat. Wang Lung had his coat off and his back bare, but she worked with her thin garment covering her shoulders and it grew wet and clung to her like skin. Moving together in a perfect **rhythm**②, without a word, hour after hour, he fell into a union with her which took the pain from his labor. He had no articulate thought of anything; there was only this perfect **sympathy**③ of movement, of turning this earth of theirs over and over to the sun, this earth which formed their home and fed their bodies and made their gods. The earth lay rich and dark, and fell apart lightly under the points of their hoes. Sometimes they turned up a bit of brick, a splinter of wood. It was nothing. Some time, in some age, bodies of men and women had been buried there, houses had stood there, had fallen, and

① 仔细考虑,默想。

② 节奏。

③ 一致,协调。

gone back into the earth. So would also their house, some time, return into the earth, their bodies also. Each had his turn at this earth. They worked on, moving together...together...producing the fruit of this earth...speechless in their movement together.

When the sun had set he straightened his back slowly and looked at the woman. Her face was wet and streaked with the earth. She was as brown as the very soil itself. Her wet, dark garments clung to her square body. She smoothed a last furrow slowly. Then in her usual plain way she said, straight out, her voice flat and more than usually plain in the silent evening air,

"I am with child."

Wang Lung stood still. What was there to say to this thing, then! She stooped to pick up a bit of broken brick and threw it out of the furrow. It was as though she had said, "I have brought you tea," or as though she had said, "We can eat." It seemed as ordinary as that to her! But to him...he could not say what it was to him. His heart swelled and stopped as though it met sudden confines. Well, it was their turn at this earth!

He took the hoe suddenly from her hand and he said, his voice thick in his throat, "Let be for now. It is a day's end. We will tell the old man."

They walked home, then, she half a dozen paces behind him as befitted a woman. The old man stood at the door, hungry for his evening's food, which, now that the woman was in the house, he would never prepare for himself. He was impatient and he called out,

"I am too old to wait for my food like this!"

But Wang Lung, passing him into the room, said,

"She is with child already."

He tried to say it easily as one might say, "I have planted the seeds in the western field today," but he could not. Although he spoke in a low voice it was to him as though he had shouted the words out louder than he would.

The old man blinked for a moment and then comprehended, and **cackle**①d with laughter.

"Heh-heh-heh..." he called out to his daughter-in-law as she came, "so the harvest is in sight!"

Her face he could not see in the dusk, but she answered evenly,

"I shall prepare food now."

---

① 尖声笑。

"Yes...yes...food..." said the old man eagerly, following her into the kitchen like a child. Just as the thought of a grandson had made him forget his meal, so now the thought of food freshly before him made him forget the child.

But Wang Lung sat upon a bench by the table in the darkness and put his head upon his folded arms. Out of this body of his, out of his own loins, life!

3

WHEN THE HOUR for birth drew near he said to the woman,

"We must have someone to help at the time...some woman."

But she shook her head. She was clearing away the bowls after the evening food. The old man had gone to his bed and the two of them were alone in the night, with only the light that fell upon them from the **flickering**① flame of a small tin lamp filled with bean oil, in which a twist of cotton floated for a **wick**②.

"No woman?" he asked in **consternation**③. He was beginning now to be accustomed to these conversations with her in which her part was little more than a movement of head or hand, or at most an occasional word dropped unwillingly from her wide mouth. He had even come to feel no lack in such conversing. "But it will be odd with only two men in the house!" he continued. "My mother had a woman from the village. I know nothing of these affairs. Is there none in the great house, no old slave with whom you were friends, who could come?"

It was the first time he had mentioned the house from which she came. She turned on him as he had never seen her, her narrow eyes widened, her face stirred with dull anger.

"None in that house!" she cried out at him.

He dropped his pipe which he was filling and stared at her. But her face was suddenly as usual and she was collecting the chopsticks as though she had not spoken.

"Well, here is a thing!" he said in astonishment. But she said nothing. Then he continued in argument, "We two men, we have no ability in childbirth. For my father it is not fitting to enter your room...for myself, I have never even seen a cow give birth. My clumsy hands might mar the child. Someone from the great house, now, where the slaves are always giving birth..."

---

① 闪烁的。
② 灯芯。
③ 惊愕。

She had placed the chopsticks carefully down in an orderly heap upon the table and she looked at him, and after a moment's looking she said,

"When I return to that house it will be with my son in my arms. I shall have a red coat on him and red-flowered trousers and on his head a hat with a small **gilded**① Buddha sewn on the front and on his feet tiger-faced shoes. And I will wear new shoes and a new coat of black sateen and I will go into the kitchen where I spent my days and I will go into the great hall where the Old One sits with her opium, and I will show myself and my son to all of them."

He had never heard so many words from her before. They came forth steadily and without break, albeit slowly, and he realized that she had planned this whole thing out for herself. When she had been working in the fields beside him she had been planning all this out! How astonishing she was! He would have said that she had scarcely thought of the child, so stilly had she gone about her work, day in and day out. And instead she saw this child, born and fully clothed, and herself as his mother, in a new coat! He was for once without words himself, and he pressed the tobacco diligently into a ball between his thumb and forefinger, and picking up his pipe he fitted the tobacco into the bowl.

"I suppose you will need some money," he said at last with apparent gruffness.

"If you will give me three silver pieces..." she said fearfully. "It is a great deal, but I have counted carefully and I will waste no penny of it. I shall make the cloth dealer give me the last inch to the foot."

Wang Lung fumbled in his girdle. The day before he had sold a load and a half of reeds from the pond in the western field to the town market and he had in his girdle a little more than she wished. He put the three silver dollars upon the table. Then, after a little hesitation, he added a fourth piece which he had long kept by him on the chance of his wanting to gamble a little some morning at the tea house. But he never did more than linger about the tables and look at the dice as they clattered upon the table, fearful lest he lose if he played. He usually ended by spending his spare hours in the town at the storyteller's **booth**②, where one may listen to an old tale and pay no more than a penny into his bowl when it was passed about.

"You had better take the other piece," he said, lighting his pipe between the words, blowing quickly at the paper spill to set it aflame. "You may as well make his coat of a

① 镀金的。
② 小店。

small remnant of silk. After all, he is the first."

She did not at once take the money, but she stood looking at it, her face motionless. Then she said in a half-whisper,

"It is the first time I have had silver money in my hand."

Suddenly she took it and clenched it in her hand and hurried into the bedroom.

Wang Lung sat smoking, thinking of the silver as it had lain upon the table. It had come out of the earth, this silver, out of his earth that he ploughed and turned and spent himself upon. He took his life from this earth; drop by drop by his sweat he wrung food from it and from the food, silver. Each time before this that he had taken the silver out to give to anyone, it had been like taking a piece of his life and giving it to someone carelessly. But now for the first time such giving was not pain. He saw, not the silver in the alien hand of a merchant in the town; he saw the silver transmuted into something worth even more than itself... clothes upon the body of his son. And this strange woman of his, who worked about, saying nothing, seeming to see nothing, she had first seen the child thus clothed!

4

SHE WOULD have no one with her when the hour came. It came one night, early, when the sun was scarcely set. She was working beside him in the harvest field. The wheat had borne and been cut and the field flooded and the young rice set, and now the rice bore harvest, and the ears were ripe and full after the summer rains and the warm ripening sun of early autumn. Together they cut the **sheaves**① all day, bending and cutting with short-handled **scythes**②. She had **stoop**③ed stiffly, because of the burden she bore, and she moved more slowly than he, so that they cut unevenly, his row ahead, and hers behind. She began to cut more and more slowly as noon wore on to afternoon and evening, and he turned to look at her with impatience. She stopped and stood up then, her scythe dropped. On her face was a new sweat, the sweat of a new **agony**④.

"It is come," she said. "I will go into the house. Do not come into the room until I call. Only bring me a newly peeled reed, and slit it, that I may cut the child's life from

---

① 谷子。

② 镰刀。

③ 弯腰。

④ 痛苦。

mine."

She went across the fields toward the house as though there were nothing to come, and after he had watched her he went to the edge of the pond in the outer field and chose a slim green reed and peeled it carefully and slit it on the edge of his scythe. The quick autumn darkness was falling then and he shouldered his scythe and went home.

When he reached the house he found his supper hot on the table and the old man eating. She had stopped in her labor to prepare them food! He said to himself that she was a woman such as is not commonly found. Then he went to the door of their room and he called out,

"Here is the reed!"

He waited, expecting that she would call out to him to bring it in to her. But she did not. She came to the door and through the crack her hand reached out and took the reed. She said no word, but he heard her **pant**①ing as an animal pants which has run for a long way.

The old man looked up from his bowl to say, "Eat, or all will be cold." And then he said, "Do not trouble yourself yet...it will be a long time. I remember well when the first was born to me it was dawn before it was over. Ah me, to think that out of all the children I begot and your mother bore, one after the other...a score or so...I forget...only you have lived! You see why a woman must bear and bear." And then he said again, as though he had just thought of it newly, "By this time tomorrow I may be grandfather to a man child!" He began to laugh suddenly and he stopped his eating and sat chuckling for a long time in the dusk of the room.

But Wang Lung stood listening at the door to those heavy animal pants. A smell of hot blood came through the crack, a sickening smell that frightened him. The panting of the woman within became quick and loud, like whispered screams, but she made no sound aloud. When he could bear no more and was about to break into the room, a thin, fierce cry came out and he forgot everything.

"Is it a man?" he cried importunately, forgetting the woman. The thin cry burst out again, **wiry**②, insistent. "Is it a man?" he cried again, "tell me at least this...is it a man?"

And the voice of the woman answered as faintly as an echo, "A man!"

---

① 喘气。
② 坚韧的。

He went and sat down at the table then. How quick it had all been! The food was long cold and the old man was asleep on his bench, but how quick it had all been! He shook the old man's shoulder.

"It is a man child!" he called triumphantly. "You are grandfather and I am father!"

The old man woke suddenly and began to laugh as he had been laughing when he fell asleep.

"Yes...yes...of course," he cackled, "a grandfather...a grandfather..." and he rose and went to his bed, still laughing.

Wang Lung took up the bowl of cold rice and began to eat. He was very hungry all at once and he could not get the food into his mouth quickly enough. In the room he could hear the woman dragging herself about and the cry of the child was incessant and piercing.

"I suppose we shall have no more peace in this house now," he said to himself proudly.

When he had eaten all that he wished he went to the door again and she called to him to come in and he went in. The odor of spilt blood still hung hot upon the air, but there was no trace of it except in the wooden tub. But into this she had poured water and had pushed it under the bed so that he could hardly see it. The red candle was lit and she was lying neatly covered upon the bed. Beside her, wrapped in a pair of his old trousers, as the custom was in this part, lay his son.

He went up and for the moment there were no words in his mouth. His heart crowded up into his breast and he leaned over the child to look at it. It had a round wrinkled face that looked very dark and upon its head the hair was long and damp and black. It had ceased crying and lay with its eyes tightly shut.

He looked at his wife and she looked back at him. Her hair was still wet with her agony and her narrow eyes were sunken. Beyond this, she was as she always was. But to him she was touching, lying there. His heart rushed out to these two and he said, not knowing what else there was that could be said,

"Tomorrow I will go into the city and buy a pound of red sugar and stir it into boiling water for you to drink."

And then looking at the child again, this burst forth from him suddenly as though he had just thought of it, "We shall have to buy a good basketful of eggs and **dye**① them all

---

① 染色。

red for the village. Thus will everyone know I have a son!"

Ⅳ. 思考题

1. The title of this novel is *The Good Earth*. What do you think are the symbolic meanings of the earth?
2. What are some of the features of the Chinese society depicted in the excerpts?
3. How do you like Buck's depiction of other minor characters, such as Wang Lung's uncle, the barber, the vendors, the waiter, and the beggar? Do you think these characters are authentic or stereotypical?
4. Who do you think are Buck's target audience?

Ⅴ. 文学批评

东方主义

There are controversies about whether Buck has depicted an authentic China. Even her friend such as Lin Yutang is upset why Buck chooses to focus on the countryside. Some Chinese scholars even claim that since Buck is an American, she does not have the right to write about China and the whole project to depict the rural China is an orientalist approach.

Orientalism is best known in Edward W. Said's groundbreaking book, *Orientalism* (1978), which he defines as the acceptance in the West of "the basic distinction between East and West as the starting point for elaborate theories, epics, novels, social descriptions, and political accounts concerning the Orient, its people, customs, 'mind,' destiny and so on." In Said's concept, orientalism is a way that imagines, emphasizes, exaggerates and distorts differences of Arab peoples and cultures as compared to that of Europe and the U. S. It often involves seeing Arab culture as exotic, backward, uncivilized, and at times dangerous.

According to Said, Orientalism dates from the period of European Enlightenment and colonization of the Arab World. Orientalism provided a rationalization for European colonialism based on a self-serving history in which "the West" constructed "the East" as extremely different and inferior, and therefore in need of Western intervention or "rescue".

Examples of early Orientalism can be seen in European paintings and photographs and also in images from the World's Fair in the U. S. in the 19th and early 20th centuries. The process of orientalism initiated from the imperialist and colonial project and was consolidated through literary and artistic representations, institutionalized knowledge of such representations, and finally a popularization of the fixed and stereotypical concepts/images of the East.

The application of Orientalism now is not confined to the study of representation of the Arabic culture per se. it is more about the imbalanced power structures between the West and the East in a broad sense. When used in this sense, it implies old-fashioned and prejudiced outsider interpretations of Eastern cultures and peoples, allowing frequent misunderstanding of their cultural, ethical, and religious beliefs.

Ⅵ. 拓展阅读

Edward W Said's *Orientalism* (Vintage, 1979).

Karen J Leong's *The China Mystique: Pearl S. Buck, Anna May Wong, Mayling Soong, and the Transformation of American Orientalism* (U of California P, 2005).

Ⅶ. 参考文献

Buck, Pearl S. *The Good Earth*. Washington Square Press, 2004.

Editors of Encyclopaedia Britannica, "Pearl S. Buck." Retrieved June 7th, 2020, https://www.britannica.com/biography/Pearl-S-Buck.

Chapter 5 William Faulkner and the American South

Ⅰ. 作者简介

威廉·福克纳 William Faulkner(1897—1962)是美国南方密西西比州北部一个庄园主的后裔。他对地主家庭盛极而衰过程中的种种变化十分熟悉。在第一次世界大战期间,他曾在加拿大和英国空军服役。战后曾在密西西比大学学习,肄业一年。他曾在纽约的一家书店和新奥尔良的一家报社工作过,并在好莱坞做过短暂的编剧,他一生的大部分时间都在密西西比州的牛津镇上创作小说。

1925 年福克纳在新奥尔良结识了著名小说家舍伍德·安德森,在他的帮助下出版了第一部小说《士兵的报酬》(*Soldier's Pay*, 1926)。第二部小说题为《蚊群》(*Mosquitoes*, 1927)。1929 年出版第三部小说《沙特里斯》(*Sartoris*)。这是以虚构的约克纳帕塔法县为背景的第一部小说,写南方贵族地主的精神遗产对子孙的不良影响。这部小说被称为"站在门槛上"的书,通过它可以看出福克纳今后的重要作品中将要出现的主调、题材、情绪与艺术手法。福克纳自称从此开始,他发现他的“家乡那块邮票般小小的地方倒也值得一写,只怕一辈子也写不完”。他一共写了 19 部长篇小说和 70 多篇短篇小说,其中绝大多数以约克纳帕塔法县作为故事发生的地点,人们称他的作品为“约克纳帕塔法世系”。这部世系主要写这个县及杰弗逊镇属于不同社会阶层的若干家族的几代人的故事,时间从美国独立之前直到第二次世界大战以后,出场的人物有 600 多人,其中主要的人物在他的长篇小说与短篇小说中交替出现。小说中的故事互相都有一些关系,每一部书既是一个独立的故事,又是整个“世系”中的一个组成部分。福克纳写第一部作品时,似乎对约克纳帕塔法县里所有的人和事,大致上已有轮廓。

1929 年出版的《喧哗与骚动》(*The Sound and the Fury*)是福克纳最有代表性的作品。1929 至 1936 年是福克纳创作力最为旺盛的时期,除了《喧哗与骚动》,还写了长篇小说《我弥留之际》(*As I Lay Dying*,1930)、《八月之光》(*Light in August*,1932)、《押沙龙,押沙龙!》(*Absalom*,*Absalom*!,1936)。福克纳后期最重要的作品是《村子》(*The Hamlet*,1940)、《小镇》(*The Town*,1957)与《大宅》(*The Mansion*,1959)。《寓言》(*A Fable*,1954)是福克纳晚年的一部重要长篇小说,它的主题是反对帝国主义战争。

20 世纪 30 年代初,福克纳的几部重要作品已经出版,但收入不丰,还得经常为好莱坞写电影脚本维持生计。1946 年《袖珍本福克纳选集》出版之后,他的作品逐渐受到推崇。他于 1949 年获得诺贝尔文学奖,理由是“他对当代美国小说作出了强有力的和艺术上无与伦比的贡献”(“for his powerful and artistically unique contribution to the modern American novel”)。1951 年福克纳获得美国全国图书奖,1955、1963 年两次获普利策奖。1962 年 7 月 6 日因病于家乡牛津镇逝世。

福克纳在小说中描绘了一幅复杂的美国南方社会的图景,表现了两百年来美国南方社会的变迁。各阶级人物的浮沉起落、各种人物的命运与精神面貌,都在这幅图景里得到反映——尽管有时是扭曲的、主观色彩很浓重的反映。他一方面描写南方,同时也在作品中展现了 20 世纪“现代人”所关切的重大问题。如个人与社会的关系、如何面对历史负担、金钱与工业化带来的问题等。福克纳的作品反映了一个知识分子对时代问题的细致探讨。福克纳在小说的写法上进行了大胆的试验与创新,他对现代主义小说创作有不可磨灭的贡献。他喜欢在小说中运用“意识流”手法，以更深刻地发掘人物的内心活动。他也运用“多角度叙述”的手法，给小说叙事增加层次感和立体感。此外，他还运用“时序颠倒”“象征”等手法使作品更能反映现代生活的复杂性。

Ⅱ. 内容提要

《献给艾米丽的一朵玫瑰花》发表在 1930 年 4 月 30 号的《论坛》杂志上，是福克纳第一篇发表在知名杂志上的短篇小说。故事的背景是福克纳虚构的约克纳帕塔法县。福克纳采用了非线性叙事结构讲述了女主人公——南方落没贵族艾米丽·格里尔森——的生平。艾米丽在独居了很长一段时间与世隔绝后，于 74 岁去世，她的生活和死因在小镇上一直是一个谜。小说开始于她的葬礼。一群好奇的小镇居民来到艾米丽的葬礼，并回顾了他们所知道的一些有关艾米丽的故事。其中最为核心的事件是艾米丽与一个叫荷马·巴伦的北方劳工的恋情。这篇短篇小说常常被解读为是一个关于旧南方抵抗现代化的寓言，艾米丽是旧南方的代表，荷马和镇上的新兴阶层则是北方新文化的代表。

Ⅲ. 作品

I

WHEN Miss Emily Grierson died, our whole town went to her funeral: the men through a sort of respectful affection for a fallen **monument**①, the women mostly out of curiosity to see the inside of her house, which no one **save**② an old man-servant—a combined gardener and cook—had seen in at least ten years.

It was a big, **squarish**③ frame house that had once been white, decorated with **cupolas**④ and **spires**⑤ and scrolled balconies in the heavily lightsome style of the seventies, set

① 丰碑，纪念碑。
② 除了。
③ 呈方形的。
④ 冲天炉。
⑤ 尖顶。

on what had once been our most select street. But **garages**① and cotton **gins**② had **encroached**③ and **obliterated**④ even the **august**⑤ names of that neighborhood; only Miss Emily's house was left, lifting its stubborn and coquettish decay above the cotton wagons and the gasoline pumps—an **eyesore**⑥ among eyesores. And now Miss Emily had gone to join the representatives of those august names where they lay in the **cedar-bemused**⑦ **cemetery**⑧ among the ranked and anonymous graves of Union and Confederate soldiers who fell at the battle of Jefferson.

Alive, Miss Emily had been a tradition, a duty, and a care; a sort of **hereditary**⑨ obligation upon the town, dating from that day in 1894 when Colonel Sartoris, the mayor—he who fathered the **edict**⑩ that no Negro woman should appear on the streets without an apron—**remitted**⑪ her taxes, the **dispensation**⑫ dating from the death of her father on into **perpetuity**⑬. Not that Miss Emily would have accepted charity. Colonel Sartoris invented an involved tale to the effect that Miss Emily's father had loaned money to the town, which the town, as a matter of business, preferred this way of repaying. Only a man of Colonel Sartoris' generation and thought could have invented it, and only a woman could have believed it.

When the next generation, with its more modern ideas, became mayors and **aldermen**⑭, this arrangement created some little dissatisfaction. On the first of the year they mailed her a tax notice. February came, and there was no reply. They wrote her a formal letter, asking her to call at the sheriff's office at her convenience. A week later the mayor wrote her himself, offering to call or to send his car for her, and received in reply a note on

---

① 汽车间。
② 轧棉机。
③ 侵犯。
④ 消除,使忘却。
⑤ 令人敬畏的。
⑥ 碍眼的东西。
⑦ 雪松环绕着的。
⑧ 公墓。
⑨ 世袭的。
⑩ 法令。
⑪ 免除。
⑫ 豁免权,特赦。
⑬ 永久。
⑭ 市议员。

paper of an **archaic**[1] shape, in a thin, flowing calligraphy in faded ink, to the effect that she no longer went out at all. The tax notice was also enclosed, without comment.

They called a special meeting of the Board of Aldermen. A **deputation**[2] waited upon her, knocked at the door through which no visitor had passed since she ceased giving china-painting lessons eight or ten years earlier. They were admitted by the old Negro into a dim hall from which a stairway mounted into still more shadow. It smelled of dust and disuse—a close, dank smell. The Negro led them into the parlor. It was furnished in heavy, leather-covered furniture. When the Negro opened the blinds of one window, they could see that the leather was cracked; and when they sat down, a faint dust rose **sluggishly**[3] about their **thighs**[4], spinning with slow motes in the single sun-ray. On a **tarnished gilt easel**[5] before the fireplace stood a crayon portrait of Miss Emily's father.

They rose when she entered—a small, fat woman in black, with a thin gold chain **descending**[6] to her waist and vanishing into her belt, leaning on an **ebony cane**[7] with a tarnished gold head. Her skeleton was small and spare; perhaps that was why what would have been merely **plumpness**[8] in another was **obesity**[9] in her. She looked bloated, like a body long **submerged**[10] in motionless water, and of that **pallid**[11] **hue**[12]. Her eyes, lost in the fatty ridges of her face, looked like two small pieces of coal pressed into a lump of **dough**[13] as they moved from one face to another while the visitors stated their **errand**[14].

She did not ask them to sit. She just stood in the door and listened quietly until the spokesman came to a **stumbling**[15] halt. Then they could hear the invisible watch ticking at the end of the gold chain.

---

① 过时的,古旧的。
② 代表团。
③ 懒散地,缓慢地。
④ 大腿。
⑤ 已经失去金色光泽的画架。
⑥ 下降,垂落。
⑦ 乌木拐杖。
⑧ 丰满。
⑨ 肥胖。
⑩ 淹没、沉浸。
⑪ 苍白的、无生气的。
⑫ 色彩、色调。
⑬ 面团。
⑭ 差事、使命。
⑮ 结结巴巴的。

Her voice was dry and cold. "I have no taxes in Jefferson. Colonel Sartoris explained it to me. Perhaps one of you can gain access to the city records and satisfy yourselves."

"But we have. We are the city authorities, Miss Emily. Didn't you get a notice from the sheriff, signed by him?"

"I received a paper, yes," Miss Emily said. "Perhaps he considers himself the sheriff...I have no taxes in Jefferson."

"But there is nothing on the books to show that, you see We must go by the..."

"See Colonel Sartoris. I have no taxes in Jefferson."

"But, Miss Emily..."

"See Colonel Sartoris." (Colonel Sartoris had been dead almost ten years.) "I have no taxes in Jefferson. Tobe!" The Negro appeared. "Show these gentlemen out."

II

So SHE **vanquished**① them, **horse and foot**②, just as she had vanquished their fathers thirty years before about the smell. That was two years after her father's death and a short time after her sweetheart—the one we believed would marry her—had **deserted**③ her. After her father's death she went out very little; after her sweetheart went away, people hardly saw her at all. A few of the ladies had the **temerity**④ to call, but were not received, and the only sign of life about the place was the Negro man—a young man then—going in and out with a market basket.

"Just as if a man—any man—could keep a kitchen properly," the ladies said; so they were not surprised when the smell developed. It was another link between the **gross**⑤, **teeming**⑥ world and the high and mighty Griersons. A neighbor, a woman, complained to the mayor, Judge Stevens, eighty years old.

"But what will you have me do about it, madam?" he said.

"Why, send her word to stop it," the woman said. "Isn't there a law?"

"I'm sure that won't be necessary," Judge Stevens said. "It's probably just a snake or a rat that nigger of hers killed in the yard. I'll speak to him about it."

---

① 铲除,击败。

② 连人带马。

③ 抛弃。

④ 鲁莽、冒失。

⑤ 粗俗的。

⑥ 芸芸众生的。

The next day he received two more complaints, one from a man who came in **diffident**[①] **deprecation**[②]. "We really must do something about it, Judge. I'd be the last one in the world to bother Miss Emily, but we've got to do something." That night the Board of Aldermen met—three graybeards and one younger man, a member of the rising generation.

"It's simple enough," he said. "Send her word to have her place cleaned up. Give her a certain time to do it in, and if she don't..."

"Dammit, sir," Judge Stevens said, "will you accuse a lady to her face of smelling bad?"

So the next night, after midnight, four men crossed Miss Emily's lawn and **slunk**[③] about the house like burglars, sniffing along the base of the brickwork and at the **cellar**[④] openings while one of them performed a regular sowing motion with his hand out of a sack slung from his shoulder. They broke open the cellar door and **sprinkled**[⑤] **lime**[⑥] there, and in all the outbuildings. As they recrossed the lawn, a window that had been dark was lighted and Miss Emily sat in it, the light behind her, and her upright torso motionless as that of an idol. They crept quietly across the lawn and into the shadow of the locusts that lined the street. After a week or two the smell went away.

That was when people had begun to feel really sorry for her. People in our town, remembering how old lady Wyatt, her great-aunt, had gone completely crazy at last, believed that the Griersons held themselves a little too high for what they really were. None of the young men were quite good enough for Miss Emily and such. We had long thought of them as a **tableau**[⑦], Miss Emily a slender figure in white in the background, her father a **spraddled**[⑧] **silhouette**[⑨] in the **foreground**[⑩], his back to her and clutching a horsewhip, the two of them framed by the back-flung front door. So when she got to be thirty and was still sin-

---

① 羞怯的。
② 反对。
③ slink 的过去式,偷偷钻进。
④ 地下室。
⑤ 播撒。
⑥ 石灰。
⑦ 生动的场景。
⑧ 双脚叉开站立。
⑨ 轮廓,剪影。
⑩ 前景。

gle, we were not pleased exactly, but **vindicated**[1]; even with insanity in the family she wouldn't have turned down all of her chances if they had really materialized.

When her father died, it got about that the house was all that was left to her; and in a way, people were glad. At last they could pity Miss Emily. Being left alone, and a **pauper**[2], she had become humanized. Now she too would know the old thrill and the old despair of a penny more or less.

The day after his death all the ladies prepared to call at the house and offer **condolence**[3] and aid, as is our custom Miss Emily met them at the door, dressed as usual and with no trace of grief on her face. She told them that her father was not dead. She did that for three days, with the ministers calling on her, and the doctors, trying to persuade her to let them **dispose**[4] of the body. Just as they were about to resort to law and force, she broke down, and they buried her father quickly.

We did not say she was crazy then. We believed she had to do that. We remembered all the young men her father had driven away, and we knew that with nothing left, she would have to cling to that which had robbed her, as people will.

Ⅲ

SHE WAS SICK for a long time. When we saw her again, her hair was cut short, making her look like a girl, with a vague resemblance to those angels in colored church windows—sort of tragic and **serene**[5].

The town had just let the contracts for paving the sidewalks, and in the summer after her father's death they began the work. The construction company came with **riggers**[6] and **mules**[7] and machinery, and a **foreman**[8] named Homer Barron, a **Yankee**[9]—a big, dark, ready man, with a big voice and eyes lighter than his face. The little boys would follow in groups to hear him cuss the riggers, and the riggers singing in time to the rise and

---

① 证明是正确的。
② 贫民。
③ 吊唁。
④ 处置。
⑤ 宁静的,安详的。
⑥ 脚手架。
⑦ 骡子。
⑧ 工头。
⑨ 北方佬。

fall of picks. Pretty soon he knew everybody in town. Whenever you heard a lot of laughing anywhere about the square, Homer Barron would be in the center of the group. Presently we began to see him and Miss Emily on Sunday afternoons driving in the yellow-wheeled **buggy**① and the matched team of bays from the livery stable.

At first we were glad that Miss Emily would have an interest, because the ladies all said, "Of course a Grierson would not think seriously of a Northerner, a day laborer." But there were still others, older people, who said that even grief could not cause a real lady to forget *noblesse oblige*—without calling it *noblesse oblige*. They just said, "Poor Emily. Her **kinsfolk**② should come to her." She had some kin in Alabama; but years ago her father had fallen out with them over the estate of old lady Wyatt, the crazy woman, and there was no communication between the two families. They had not even been represented at the funeral.

And as soon as the old people said, "Poor Emily," the whispering began. "Do you suppose it's really so?" they said to one another. "Of course it is. What else could..." This behind their hands; rustling of craned silk and satin behind jalousies closed upon the sun of Sunday afternoon as the thin, swift clop-clop-clop of the matched team passed: "Poor Emily."

She carried her head high enough—even when we believed that she was fallen. It was as if she demanded more than ever the recognition of her dignity as the last Grierson; as if it had wanted that touch of earthiness to reaffirm her **imperviousness**③. Like when she bought the rat poison, the **arsenic**④. That was over a year after they had begun to say "Poor Emily," and while the two female cousins were visiting her.

"I want some poison," she said to the druggist. She was over thirty then, still a slight woman, though thinner than usual, with cold, **haughty**⑤ black eyes in a face the flesh of which was strained across the **temples**⑥ and about the **eyesockets**⑦ as you imagine a lighthouse-keeper's face ought to look. "I want some poison," she said.

"Yes, Miss Emily. What kind? For rats and such? I'd recom—"

---

① 小机动车。
② 亲戚。
③ 无动于衷,不受干扰。
④ 砒霜。
⑤ 傲慢的,目中无人的。
⑥ 太阳穴。
⑦ 眼袋。

"I want the best you have. I don't care what kind."

The druggist named several. "They'll kill anything up to an elephant. But what you want is..."

"**Arsenic**①," Miss Emily said. "Is that a good one?"

"Is... arsenic? Yes, ma'am. But what you want..."

"I want arsenic."

The druggist looked down at her. She looked back at him, **erect**②, her face like a strained flag. "Why, of course," the druggist said. "If that's what you want. But the law requires you to tell what you are going to use it for."

Miss Emily just stared at him, her head tilted back in order to look him eye for eye, until he looked away and went and got the arsenic and wrapped it up. The Negro delivery boy brought her the package; the druggist didn't come back. When she opened the package at home there was written on the box, under the skull and bones: "For rats."

IV

So THE NEXT day we all said, "She will kill herself"; and we said it would be the best thing. When she had first begun to be seen with Homer Barron, we had said, "She will marry him." Then we said, "She will persuade him yet," because Homer himself had remarked—he liked men, and it was known that he drank with the younger men in the Elks' Club—that he was not a marrying man. Later we said, "Poor Emily" behind the jalousies as they passed on Sunday afternoon in the glittering buggy, Miss Emily with her head high and Homer Barron with his hat cocked and a cigar in his teeth, reins and whip in a yellow glove.

Then some of the ladies began to say that it was a **disgrace**③ to the town and a bad example to the young people. The men did not want to **interfere**④, but at last the ladies forced the **Baptist minister**⑤—Miss Emily's people were **Episcopal**⑥—to call upon her. He would never **divulge**⑦ what happened during that interview, but he refused to go back

---

① 砷,砒霜。

② 身姿笔直的。

③ 耻辱。

④ 插手,干预。

⑤ 浸礼会牧师。

⑥ 圣公会,基督教的一个教派。

⑦ 泄露。

again. The next Sunday they again drove about the streets, and the following day the minister's wife wrote to Miss Emily's relations in Alabama.

So she had **blood-kin**① under her roof again and we sat back to watch developments. At first nothing happened. Then we were sure that they were to be married. We learned that Miss Emily had been to the jeweler's and ordered a man's toilet set in silver, with the letters H. B. on each piece. Two days later we learned that she had bought a complete **outfit**② of men's clothing, including a nightshirt, and we said, "They are married." We were really glad. We were glad because the two female cousins were even more Grierson than Miss Emily had ever been.

So we were not surprised when Homer Barron—the streets had been finished some time since—was gone. We were a little disappointed that there was not a public **blowing-off**③, but we believed that he had gone on to prepare for Miss Emily's coming, or to give her a chance to get rid of the cousins. (By that time it was a **cabal**④, and we were all Miss Emily's allies to help **circumvent**⑤ the cousins.) Sure enough, after another week they departed. And, as we had expected all along, within three days Homer Barron was back in town. A neighbor saw the Negro man admit him at the kitchen door at **dusk**⑥ one evening.

And that was the last we saw of Homer Barron. And of Miss Emily for some time. The Negro man went in and out with the market basket, but the front door remained closed. Now and then we would see her at a window for a moment, as the men did that night when they sprinkled the lime, but for almost six months she did not appear on the streets. Then we knew that this was to be expected too; as if that quality of her father which had **thwarted**⑦ her woman's life so many times had been too **virulent**⑧ and too furious to die.

When we next saw Miss Emily, she had grown fat and her hair was turning gray. During the next few years it grew grayer and grayer until it attained an even pepper-and-salt iron-gray, when it ceased turning. Up to the day of her death at seventy-four it was still that vigorous iron-gray, like the hair of an active man. From that time on her front door re-

---

① 血缘亲戚。
② 套装。
③ 送行告别的热闹。
④ 阴谋。
⑤ 规避。
⑥ 黄昏。
⑦ 挫败,阻挠。
⑧ 恶毒的,致命的。

mained closed, save for a period of six or seven years, when she was about forty, during which she gave lessons in china-painting. She fitted up a studio in one of the downstairs rooms, where the daughters and granddaughters of Colonel Sartoris' contemporaries were sent to her with the same regularity and in the same spirit that they were sent to church on Sundays with a twenty-five-cent piece for the collection plate. Meanwhile her taxes had been remitted.

Then the newer generation became the **backbone**① and the spirit of the town, and the painting pupils grew up and fell away and did not send their children to her with boxes of color and tedious brushes and pictures cut from the ladies' magazines. The front door closed upon the last one and remained closed for good. When the town got free postal delivery, Miss Emily alone refused to let them fasten the metal numbers above her door and attach a mailbox to it. She would not listen to them.

Daily, monthly, yearly we watched the Negro grow grayer and more **stooped**②, going in and out with the market basket. Each December we sent her a tax notice, which would be returned by the post office a week later, unclaimed. Now and then we would see her in one of the downstairs windows—she had evidently shut up the top floor of the house—like the carven torso of an idol in a niche, looking or not looking at us, we could never tell which. Thus she passed from generation to generation—dear, inescapable, impervious, **tranquil**③, and **perverse**④. And so she died. Fell ill in the house filled with dust and shadows, with only a **doddering**⑤ Negro man to wait on her. We did not even know she was sick; we had long since given up trying to get any information from the Negro. He talked to no one, probably not even to her, for his voice had grown harsh and rusty, as if from disuse.

She died in one of the downstairs rooms, in a heavy walnut bed with a curtain, her gray head propped on a pillow yellow and **moldy**⑥ with age and lack of sunlight.

V

THE NEGRO met the first of the ladies at the front door and let them in, with their

---

① 支柱。
② 弯腰驼背的。
③ 安静的。
④ 倔强的,违反常情的。
⑤ 蹒跚而行的,衰老的。
⑥ 发霉的,陈腐的。

hushed①, **sibilant**② voices and their quick, curious glances, and then he disappeared. He walked right through the house and out the back and was not seen again.

The two female cousins came at once. They held the funeral on the second day, with the town coming to look at Miss Emily beneath a mass of bought flowers, with the crayon face of her father musing profoundly above the **bier**③ and the ladies sibilant and **macabre**④; and the very old men —some in their brushed Confederate uniforms—on the porch and the lawn, talking of Miss Emily as if she had been a contemporary of theirs, believing that they had danced with her and courted her perhaps, confusing time with its mathematical progression, as the old do, to whom all the past is not a diminishing road but, instead, a huge **meadow**⑤ which no winter ever quite touches, divided from them now by the narrow bottle-neck of the most recent decade of years.

Already we knew that there was one room in that region above stairs which no one had seen in forty years, and which would have to be forced. They waited until Miss Emily was decently in the ground before they opened it. The violence of breaking down the door seemed to fill this room with pervading dust. A thin, **acrid**⑥ **pall**⑦ as of the tomb seemed to lie everywhere upon this room decked and furnished as for a bridal: upon the valance curtains of faded rose color, upon the rose-shaded lights, upon the dressing table, upon the delicate array of crystal and the man's toilet things backed with tarnished silver, silver so tarnished that the **monogram**⑧ was obscured. Among them lay a collar and tie, as if they had just been removed, which, lifted, left upon the surface a pale **crescent**⑨ in the dust. Upon a chair hung the suit, carefully folded; beneath it the two mute shoes and the discarded socks. The man himself lay in the bed.

For a long while we just stood there, looking down at the profound and fleshless grin. The body had apparently once lain in the attitude of an embrace, but now the long sleep

---

① 低声的。
② 发咝咝声的。
③ 棺材。
④ 恐怖的。
⑤ 草地。
⑥ 刺鼻的。
⑦ 棺罩。
⑧ 由姓名首字母组成的图案。
⑨ 新月。

that outlasts love, that conquers even the **grimace**① of love, had **cuckolded**② him. What was left of him, rotted beneath what was left of the nightshirt, had become inextricable from the bed in which he lay; and upon him and upon the pillow beside him lay that even coating of the patient and biding dust.

Then we noticed that in the second pillow was the **indentation**③ of a head. One of us lifted something from it, and leaning forward, that faint and invisible dust dry and acrid in the nostrils, we saw a long strand of iron-gray hair.

Ⅳ. 思考题

1. Try to reorder the events told in the story as they would have happened.
2. This is a story of horror. Has this sense of horror been conjured up for its own sake? If not, then why has the author intentionally inserted so much of the monstrous into the story? Is the horror meaningful?
3. What is Miss Emily like? What are the mainsprings of her character?
4. The story is told by one of the townspeople. And in the story, there is a constant reference to what the community thought of Miss Emily. Why does the author choose this narrative point of view?

Ⅴ. 文学批评

南方哥特小说

The Southern Gothic movement in literature brings the atmosphere and sensibilities of the Gothic, a genre originating in late 18th century England, to the American South. As early Gothic writers used the genre in part to criticize what they saw as the moral blindness of the medieval era, so Southern Gothic writers deal with their own past through Gothic tropes. This genre is unusual as a genre in that it is significantly limited to a certain geographical space. Many of the most notable American authors of the 20th century wrote in

---

① 痛苦。
② 使某人戴绿帽子,这里指驯服。
③ 压痕。

this tradition, and the genre can be seen in music and film as well.

Southern Gothic literature builds on the traditions of the larger Gothic genre, typically including supernatural elements, mental disease, and the grotesque. Much literature in this genre, however, eschews the supernatural and deals instead with disturbed personalities. It is known for its damaged and delusional characters, such as the heroines of Tennessee Williams' plays. Instead of perpetuating romanticized stereotypes of the Antebellum South, Southern Gothic literature often brings the stock characters of melodrama and Gothic novels to a Southern context in order to make a point about Southern mores.

Southern Gothic literature often deals with the plight of those who are ostracized or oppressed by traditional Southern culture—blacks, women, and gays, for example. Harper Lee's *To Kill a Mockingbird* (1960) deals with a clearly innocent black man who is convicted of rape and murdered simply because of his race. Tennessee William's *A Streetcar Named Desire* (1948) reinvents the Southern belle as a pretentious, mentally unstable woman, and his *Cat on a Hot Tin Roof* (1955) portrays the favorite son of a Southern dynasty as a repressed homosexual whose alcoholism threatens his marriage. William Faulkner's frequently anthologized "A Rose for Emily" (1930) brings the recurrent Gothic theme of unrequited love leading to madness to a Southern town in which the disapproving residents narrate in a single voice. Other notable writers in the tradition include Flannery O'Connor, Carson McCullers, Eudora Welty, and Truman Capote.

Ⅵ. 拓展阅读

Richard Gray's "Inside the Dark House: William Faulkner, *Absalom, Absalom*! and Southern Gothic." (*The Palgrave Handbook of the Southern Gothic*. Eds. Susan Castillo Street & Charles L. Crow. Palgrave Macmillan, 2016: 21-40.)

William Faulkner's speech at the Nobel Banquet at the City Hall in Stockholm, December 10, 1950.

Ⅶ. 参考文献

"What is the Southern Gothic Movement in Literature?" Retrieved June 7th, 2020, https://www.wisegeek.com/what-is-the-southern-gothic-movement-in-literature.htm.

Chapter 6　Winston Churchill and the Power of Speech

Ⅰ. 作者简介

温斯顿·伦纳德·斯宾塞·丘吉尔爵士 The Right Honourable Sir Winston Leonard Spencer Churchill(1874—1965)的父亲是兰道夫·丘吉尔勋爵,母亲是美国人珍妮·杰罗姆,他曾在哈罗和桑德赫斯特接受教育。他曾经历过短暂的军队生涯,于 1900 年成为保守党议员。在 20 世纪的头三十年里,他在自由和保守政府中担任过许多高级职务。在第二次世界大战爆发时,他被任命为海军部的第一任司令,这个职位他在 1911 年至 1915 年曾经担任过。1940 年 5 月,他成为首相兼国防部长,一直任职到 1945 年。他在 1951 年保守党的胜利中再次接任首相职位,并于 1955 年卸任。在 1964 年大选前,他一直是国会议员,虽然他没有寻求连任。1953 年,伊丽莎白二世女王授予丘吉尔爵士爵位,并授予他嘉德勋章。

丘吉尔的文学生涯始于竞选报告:《马拉坎德远征史》(*The Story of the Mala-*

kand Field Force）和《河上战争》（*The River War*）分别讲述了苏丹的战役和乌姆杜尔曼战役。1900年，他出版了他唯一的小说《萨弗罗拉》（*Savrola*）。6年后，他出版了他的第一部重要著作，即关于他父亲的传记。他另一本著名传记是关于他的祖先马尔伯勒公爵的一生，在1933年至1938年间陆续出版了四卷。丘吉尔关于第一次世界大战历史的记述以《世界危机》（*The World Crisis*）为题分为四卷，于1923—1929年间出版；他的《第二次世界大战回忆录》（*The Second World War*）共六卷，于1948-1954年间出版。丘吉尔退休后写了一部《英语民族史》（*History of the English-speaking Peoples*），讲述了主要英语国家的历史。他出色的演讲稿保留了十余卷，其中包括《不屈不挠的斗争》（*The Unrelenting Struggle*）、《解放的曙光》（*The Dawn of Liberation*）和《胜利》（*Victory*）。

丘吉尔获得了1953年的诺贝尔文学奖，因为"他精湛的历史书写和传记创作，以及他杰出的演讲能力，捍卫了人类崇高的价值"（"for his mastery of historical and biographical description as well as for brilliant oratory in defending exalted human values"）。虽然后世对于丘吉尔的演讲才能倍加推崇，但是他并非天赋异禀，事实上，他是不断克服了生理缺陷、不断学习打磨才成就了后来的演讲能力。他从古希腊、古罗马的著作中学习修辞术，并且坚持练习四十余年。在丘吉尔的演讲中，比较常见的有两种技巧：一是与观众直接交流，征求他们的观点，这样的问句形式促使听众与他一道进到他渲染的世界；二是首语重复，即不断重复句首的核心词汇，辅以一个接一个的生动意象，渲染堆积感情。丘吉尔认为演说家是大众激情的具身化。要能以情感染大众，他自己先须情不可遏；要能激起大众的怒火，他自己先须怒火填膺；若能让大众感动流泪，他自己先须涕泗横流；要说服大众，他自己先须坚信不疑。对丘吉尔来说，英语在战时成了一个重要的工具，借助它，他将他首相的意志传达下去，他的话也伴随着相应的行动，在黑暗时期激发了来自世界各地数百万人的希望和信心。

Ⅱ.内容提要

温斯顿·丘吉尔于1940年5月被任命为首相，当时纳粹对法国、荷兰、比利时和卢森堡发动了第一次严重的攻击。在这样的历史背景下，他第一次在议会发表演讲，即著名的"Blood，Toil，Tears，and Sweat"。5月13日，丘吉尔会见内阁成员时,告诉他们“我除了热血、辛劳、眼泪和汗水,什么都没有”(“I have nothing to offer but blood,toil,tears and sweat”)。当天晚些时候,当他要求下议院对他组阁的新政府进行信任投票时,他重复了这句话。工党的反应很正面,保守党的反应则是暧昧的,他们仍然非常希望走张伯伦的绥靖路线。丘吉尔为激励英国人与看似不可战胜的敌人纳粹德国作战发表了许多鼓舞士气的演讲,这个演讲是其中的第一个。

到 1940 年 6 月 4 日,德国已经控制了法国。大约 20 万英军、法军用一队小船从敦刻尔克撤离。随着法军的溃败,英国似乎对德国人也几乎毫无防备,德国人希望他们也能谈判投降条件。丘吉尔则决意继续抵抗,用他的决心和民族自豪感鼓舞着这个国家。1940 年 6 月 4 日丘吉尔发表的“我们将在海滩上战斗”(“Fight them on the Beaches”)的演讲是对英国在第二次世界大战中的努力的颂扬。尽管敦刻尔克撤退成功,但随着法国的沦陷,英国已成为德国攻击的目标。在这次演讲中,丘吉尔的目的是提醒公众不要沉迷在敦刻尔克的成功撤离。正如丘吉尔在演讲中著名的警告:“我们必须非常小心,敦刻尔克的成功撤退不是胜利。撤军不会赢得战争”(“We must be very careful not to assign to this deliverance the attributes of a victory. Wars are not won by evacuations”)。这种情况要求丘吉尔在讲话中平衡两个微妙的方面:既要渲染纳粹入侵迫在眉睫的危险,又要鼓舞士气,为战争胜利争取必要的公众支持。在撤离后,尽管英国士兵的归来使紧张气氛得到了极大的缓解,但据《群众观察》报道,许多英国地区的士气都非常低落。

丘吉尔在这两篇著名的演讲中展现了高超的语言能力,并多次运用了重复、隐喻和排比等修辞手法,两篇演讲均名留青史。

Ⅲ. 作品

“Blood,Toil,Tears,and Sweat”

To the House of Commons,13 May,1940

I beg to move,that this House welcomes the formation of a Government representing the united and inflexible **resolve**① of the nation to **prosecute**② the war with Germany to a victorious conclusion.

On Friday evening last I received His Majesty's commission to form a new Administration. It as the evident wish and will of Parliament and the nation that this should be conceived on the broadest possible basis and that it should include all parties, both those who supported the late Government and also the parties of the Opposition. I have completed the most important part of this task. A War **Cabinet**③ has been formed of five Members, representing, with the Opposition Liberals, the unity of the nation. The three party Leaders have agreed to serve, either in the War Cabinet or in high executive office. The three Fighting Services have been filled. It was necessary that this should be done in one single day, on account of the extreme urgency and rigour of events. A number of other positions, key positions, were filled yesterday, and I am submitting a further list to His Majesty to-night. I hope to complete the appointment of the principal Ministers during to-morrow. The appointment of the other Ministers usually takes a little longer, but I trust that, when Parliament meets again, this part of my task will be completed, and that the administration will be complete in all respects.

I considered it in the public interest to suggest that the House should be **summoned**④ to meet today. Mr. Speaker agreed, and took the necessary steps, in accordance with the powers **conferred**⑤ upon him by the Resolution of the House. At the end of the proceedings today, the **Adjournment**⑥ of the House will be proposed until Tuesday, 21st May, with, of course, provision for earlier meeting, if need be. The business to be considered during that week will be notified to Members at the earliest opportunity. I now invite the House, by the Motion which stands in my name, to record its approval of the steps taken and to declare its confidence in the new Government.

To form an Administration of this scale and complexity is a serious undertaking in itself, but it must be remembered that we are in the preliminary stage of one of the greatest battles in history, that we are in action at many other points in Norway and in Holland, that we have to be prepared in the Mediterranean, that the air battle is continuous and that man-

---

① 决心。
② 坚决执行。
③ 内阁。
④ 召集。
⑤ 授予。
⑥ 延期。

y preparations, such as have been indicated by my hon. Friend below the Gangway, have to be made here at home. In this crisis I hope I may be pardoned if I do not address the House at any length today. I hope that any of my friends and colleagues, or former colleagues, who are affected by the political reconstruction, will make **allowance**[①], all allowance, for any lack of ceremony with which it has been necessary to act. I would say to the House, as I said to those who have joined this government: "I have nothing to offer but blood, toil, tears and sweat."

We have before us an **ordeal**[②] of the most grievous kind. We have before us many, many long months of struggle and of suffering. You ask, what is our policy? I can say: It is to **wage**[③] war, by sea, land and air, with all our might and with all the strength that God can give us; to wage war against a monstrous tyranny, never surpassed in the dark, **lamentable**[④] catalogue of human crime. That is our policy. You ask, what is our aim?

I can answer in one word: It is victory, victory at all costs, victory in spite of all terror, victory, however long and hard the road may be; for without victory, there is no survival. Let that be realised; no survival for the British Empire, no survival for all that the British Empire has stood for, no survival for the urge and impulse of the ages, that mankind will move forward towards its goal. But I take up my task with buoyancy and hope. I feel sure that our cause will not be suffered to fail among men. At this time I feel entitled to claim the aid of all, and I say, "come then, let us go forward together with our united strength."

"Fight them on the Beaches"

To the House of Commons, 4 June, 1940.

"I have, myself, full confidence that if all do their duty, if nothing is neglected, and if the best arrangements are made, as they are being made, we shall prove ourselves once again able to defend our Island home, to ride out the storm of war, and to outlive the **menace**[⑤] of tyranny, if necessary for years, if necessary alone.

At any rate, that is what we are going to try to do. That is the resolve of His Majesty's Government—every man of them. That is the will of Parliament and the nation.

---

① 容许。

② 艰难,试炼。

③ 实行,展开。

④ 可悲的。

⑤ 威胁。

The British Empire and the French Republic, linked together in their cause and in their need, will defend to the death their native soil, aiding each other like good comrades to the utmost of their strength.

Even though large **tracts**[1] of Europe and many old and famous States have fallen or may fall into the **grip**[2] of the Gestapo and all the **odious**[3] apparatus of Nazi rule, we shall not flag or fail.

We shall go on to the end, we shall fight in France,
we shall fight on the seas and oceans,
we shall fight with growing confidence and growing strength in the air, we shall defend our Island, whatever the cost may be,
we shall fight on the beaches,
we shall fight on the landing grounds,
we shall fight in the fields and in the streets,
we shall fight in the hills;
we shall never surrender, and even if, which I do not for a moment believe, this Island or a large part of it were **subjugated**[4] and starving, then our Empire beyond the seas, armed and guarded by the British Fleet, would carry on the struggle, until, in God's good time, the New World, with all its power and might, steps forth to the rescue and the liberation of the old."

Ⅳ. 思考题

1. How does Churchill show his resolution to fight in these two speeches?
2. After reading these two speeches, are you motivated as well? If so, what contribute to the success of these two speeches?

---

① 广阔地面。
② 紧握,控制。
③ 可憎的。
④ 镇压。

V. 文学批评

修辞三要素

The structure of a great oral argument has been passed down through the ages, starting with Aristotle. Not only is it an incredibly valuable skill to have, it's important to know how you're being persuaded when you're a part of the audience. So using Sam Leith's *Words like Loaded Pistols* as our guide, **let's discuss Aristotle's three modes of persuasion: Ethos, Logos, and Pathos.**

But before we get into the specifics of the three modes, we need to decide on the structure of our argument itself. How? By doing the work required to have an opinion.

This phase is referred to as *invention*, but it's not about making something up; it's more about the information gathering or research phase of your work. Invention is doing your homework: thinking up in advance exactly what arguments can be made both for and against a given proposition, selecting the best on your own side, and finding counterarguments to those on the other.

This research phase should not be limited to the subject matter, it should also include your audience. **If there is one theme that resonates throughout Leith's book, it's that you must know your audience; their interests, prejudices and expectations**. Without that grounding, you're already setting yourself up for failure.

Ethos is about establishing your authority to speak on the subject, *logos* is your logical argument for your point and *pathos* is your attempt to sway an audience emotionally. Leith has a great example for summarizing what the three look like.

Ethos

The first part of ethos is establishing your credentials to be speaking to the audience on the specific subject matter. It's the verbal equivalent of all those degrees hanging up in your doctor's office. And once you've established why you are an authority on the subject, you need to build rapport. Ethos, when everything is stripped away, is about trust.

Your audience needs to know (or to believe) that you are trustworthy, that you have a locus standi to talk on the subject, and that you speak in good faith. You need your audience to believe that you are, in the well-known words, 'A pretty straight kind of guy.'

So if you're a politician and you're speaking about reforming the legal system, it's great to be a lawyer or a judge, but it's even better to be a lawyer or a judge who comes from the same community as your audience. **Between two speakers with identical credentials, the more closely relatable one will win the audience.**

You'll even see a *reverse ethos* appeal at times, an attack on an opponent which questions their credentials and trustworthiness and serves to alienate them from the audience. To head that off, it's best to establish your ethos early on, both to give your attackers more of a challenge and to create a hook for your logos to hang on.

Logos

Here's how Leith describes *logos*, the next link in the chain: If ethos is the ground on which your argument stands, logos is what drives it forward: it is the stuff of your arguments, the way one point proceeds to another, as if to show that the conclusion to which you are aiming is not only the right one, but so necessary and reasonable as to be more or less the only one.

Think of this as the logic behind your argument. You want your points to seem so straightforward and commanding that your audience can't conceive of an alternative.

Aristotle had a tip here: He found that the most effective use of *logos* is to encourage your audience to reach the conclusion to your argument on their own, just moments before your big reveal. They will relish in the fact that they were clever enough to figure it out, and the reveal will be that much more satisfying.

Another *logos* trick used often is the much abused syllogism. The syllogism is a way of combining two premises and drawing a fresh conclusion that follows logically from them. The classic instance you always hear quoted is the following: All men are mortal. Socrates is a man. Therefore, Socrates is mortal.

While you need to take care with the syllogisms you use — false syllogisms can lead to obvious logical fallacies — they can be a powerful tool for helping your audience draw certain conclusions.

Aristotle also advocated the use 'commonplaces', or accepted premises shared with the audience. The best arguments are soaked in them. A commonplace is a piece of shared wisdom: a tribal assumption. In the use of commonplaces, you can see where logos and ethos intersect. Commonplaces are culturally specific, but they will tend to be so deep-rooted in their appeal that they pass for universal truths. They are, in digested form, the appeal to 'common sense.' You get nowhere appealing to commonplaces alien to your audience.

The wise persuader starts from one or two commonplaces he knows he has in common with his audience—and, where possible, arrives at one too. Your use of commonplaces is also a good point to interject *pathos*, as many of these common beliefs can illicit an emotional response. Let's dig into *pathos*.

Pathos

Your logical argument will be that much more persuasive if it's wrapped up with a good dose of emotion. Because of the way we use the word *pathos* in the modern world, you may be thinking of something dramatic and sad. But *pathos* is more nuanced than that; it can be humor, love, patriotism, or any emotional response.

The key here once again is to **know your audience**. You can even invoke pathos by admitting a wrong. (*We all make mistakes*…) This can be a clever way to put your opponent off balance. This is the figure, called paromologia in the Greek, where you concede, or appear to concede, part of your opponent's point. It turns what is often necessity to advantage, because it makes you look honest and scrupulous, takes the wind out of your opponent's sails, and allows you to shift the emphasis of the argument in a way finally favorable to you. It's the equivalent of a tactical retreat, or of the judo fighter using an opponent's momentum against him.

Another tool you can use with pathos is something the ancients called aposiopesis. Aposiopesis—a sudden breaking off as if at a loss for words—can be intended to stir pathos. And even where something appears merely decorative—a run of alliteration or a mellifluously turned sentence—it serves to commend the speech more easily to memory, and to give pleasure to the audience. Delight is an end, as well as a means.

And we can't forget joy and laughter. A well received joke can help you both connect with the audience (ethos) and bring home the pathos appeal.

Ultimately, the three modes of persuasion are interconnected. It's helpful not to think of them in a linear way but more like three overlapping circles. If you can create something with ethos, logos, and pathos peppered throughout, and tie it all into your audience's belief system, you will have a very strong argument.

Ⅵ. 拓展阅读

Henry Hardwicke's *History of Oratory and Orators* (The Knickerbocker Press, 1896).

Maurice Ashley's *Churchill as Historian* (Secker & Warburg, 1968).

"Words Like Loaded Pistols: Wartime Rhetoric" (Retrieved June 7th, 2020, https://fs.blog/2016/11/words-like-loaded-pistols-wartime-rhetoric/).

Ⅶ. 参考文献

Churchill, Winston and Robert Rhodes James. *Winston S. Churchill, His Complete Speeches*. Chelsea house/bowker, 1974.

Leith, Sam. *Words like Loaded Pistols: Rhetoric from Aristotle to Obama*. Basic Books, 2012.

"Ethos, Logos and Pathos: The Structure of a Great Speech." Retrieved June 7th, 2020, https://fs.blog/2016/11/ethos-logos-pathos/.

Chapter 7 Earnest Hemingway and the Simplicity of Language

Ⅰ. 作者简介

欧内斯特·海明威 Earnest Hemingway（1899—1961），美国小说家。1899年7月21日，海明威出生在美国伊利诺伊州芝加哥郊外橡树园镇一个医生的家庭。他的父亲酷爱打猎、钓鱼等户外活动，他的母亲喜爱文学，这一切都对海明威日后的生活和创作产生了不小的影响。中学毕业后，海明威在美国西南的堪萨斯《星报》当了6个月的实习记者。这家报馆要求新闻报道简捷明快。海明威在《星报》受到了良好的写作训练，这对他日后的文风产生了很大影响。

第一次世界大战爆发后，海明威怀着要亲临战场领略感受战争的热切愿望，加入美国红十字会战场服务队，投身意大利战场。大战结束后，海明威被意大利政府授予十字军功奖章、银质奖章和勇敢奖章，获得中尉军衔。伴随荣誉的是他身上237处的伤痕和赶不走的恶魔般的战争记忆。

康复后海明威作为加拿大多伦多《星报》的记者常驻巴黎。他对创作怀着浓厚的兴趣,一面当记者,一面写小说。他的创作得到当时著名美国作家格特鲁德·斯泰因(Gertrude Stein)的鼓励和指点。在近10年的时间里他出版了许多作品,其中最有名的是1926年发表的《太阳照常升起》(*The Sun Also Rises*),写的是像海明威一样流落在法国的一群美国年轻人。他们在第一次世界大战后迷失了前进的方向,空虚、苦恼和忧郁,只能在沉沦中度日,斯泰因由此称他们为“迷惘的一代”。这部小说是海明威自己生活道路和世界观的真实写照,而海明威和他所代表的一个文学流派因而也被人称为“迷惘的一代”。1928年,海明威离开了巴黎,居住在美国的佛罗里达州和古巴,过着宁静的田园生活。但随着第二次世界大战爆发,海明威以战地记者的身份奔波于西班牙内战前线,并于1940年发表了以西班牙内战为背景的反法西斯主义的长篇小说《丧钟为谁而鸣》(*For Whom the Bell Tolls*)。作品描写了主人公美国青年乔顿,他志愿参加西班牙人民的反法西斯斗争,奉命在一支山区游击队的配合下,在指定时间炸毁一座具有战略意义的桥梁。乔顿炸毁了桥梁,在身负重伤的情况下独自狙击敌人,等待他的是死亡。

1952年,海明威发表了中篇小说《老人与海》(*The Old Man and the Sea*),并因此于1954年获得诺贝尔文学奖,获奖理由是:因为他精通叙事艺术,突出地表现在他的近著《老人与海》中,同时也由于他在当代风格中所发挥的影响(“for his mastery of the art of narrative, most recently demonstrated in *The Old Man and the Sea*, and for the influence that he has exerted on contemporary style”)。

获奖后的海明威患有多种疾病,给他身心造成极大的痛苦,没能再创作出有影响的作品,最终他以自杀的方式解脱了自己。但是海明威笔下的主人公则几乎都是完美人的象征:坚强、宽厚、仁慈、充满爱心,即使在人生的角斗场上失败了,面对不可逆转的命运,他们仍然是精神上的强者,是不折不扣的“硬汉”。海明威的生命哲学并不在于战胜命运,在他看来命运是不可能被战胜的,但是人生的终极奥义就在于持续不断地斗争,并通过这些斗争来确定人存在的意义。

除了鲜明的人物刻画以外,海明威的写作风格也独树一帜。受到他多年记者生涯的影响,海明威的写作风格简练直观、语言朴实。海明威喜欢用短句和简洁的段落表达,少用形容词、抽象名词、复杂语法结构。海明威也很少直接对事件做出评论和解释,而只是通过客观的叙述,让读者自行感受和理解。他著名的

"冰山理论"认为,好的作者仅需给出八分之一的内容,正如冰山海面上的八分之一,其他部分让读者自己感受和理解。

海明威认为孤独是一个作家创作的最好状态。但是当一个作家越有名,他就需要花更大的力气去摆脱孤独感。然而,对于一个真正的作家来说,每一本书都应该是一个新的开始,是一种新的尝试。可以说海明威自己的写作生涯也在践行他所奉行的生存哲学。

Ⅱ.内容提要

《士兵之家》收录于小说集《我们的时代》(*In Our Time*),首次出版于1925年。1917年,克莱波斯入伍参加了海军陆战队,直到1919年夏天他才回到美国。他回来太晚了,家乡对于有关战争暴行的故事听得太多,已经厌烦了,那种向凯旋英雄致敬的热潮已经过去了。为了引起人们的兴趣,他总是说谎,把战争中发生过的事情归到自己身上,或把一些无稽之谈说成是事实。但是说谎所引起的感受令他恶心。他已经失去了士兵时代的坦率,处于病态的恐惧之中。为了消磨时间,他每天看书、散步、打弹子,家里人都顺着他。参军以前,家里的汽车从来不许他驾驶。回家后,一天早晨,妈妈竟来告诉他,可以把汽车开出去,并且希望他能带个姑娘出去玩。对于女朋友他模模糊糊地觉得需要找,但又不想为了交朋友多费精神,他只希望与世无争地生活着。

"士兵之家"原为20世纪初在美国某些小城镇上存在的优抚性机构,供参加过内战甚或美西战争而又孤鳏无依的退伍及残废老兵居住。这些老兵平日默默无闻,遇到重大节日则穿上旧日军服,佩戴全副勋章,以示荣耀。海明威选取这个名字为题目,某种程度上是在暗示像克莱波斯这样参加过第一次世界大战归来的老兵与那些老兵一样,他们不再是鲜活的个体,而是成了爱国精神的象征,是活古董一样的存在。小说没有花哨的语言,没有生动的情节,主要通过对话揭示人物心理,简而又简。这种自然凝练、引而不发的文体风格充分体现了海明威文学创作的"冰山理论"。

Ⅲ.作品

"Soldier's Home"

Krebs went to the war from a Methodist college in Kansas. There is a picture which shows him among his **fraternity**① brothers, all of them wearing exactly the same height and style collar. He **enlisted**② in the Marines in 1917 and did not return to the United States until the second division returned from the **Rhine**③ in the summer of 1919.

There is a picture which shows him on the Rhine with two German girls and another **corporal**④. Krebs and the corporal look too big for their uniforms. The German girls are not beautiful. The Rhine does not show in the picture.

By the time Krebs returned to his home town in Oklahoma the greeting of heroes was over. He came back much too late. The men from the town who had been drafted had all been welcomed elaborately on their return. There had been a great deal of **hysteria**⑤. Now the reaction had set in. People seemed to think it was rather ridiculous for Krebs to be getting back so late, years after the war was over.

At first Krebs, who had been at Belleau Wood, Soissons, the Champagne, St. Mihiel and in the Argonne did not want to talk about the war at all. Later he felt the need to talk but no one wanted to hear about it. His town had heard too many **atrocity**⑥ stories to be thrilled by actualities. Krebs found that to be listened to at all he had to lie, and after he had done this twice he, too, had a reaction against the war and against talking about it. A distaste for everything that had happened to him in the war set in because of the lies he had told. All of the times that had been able to make him feel cool and clear inside himself when he thought of them; the times so long back when he had done the one thing, the only thing for a man to do, easily and naturally, when he might have done something else, now lost their cool, valuable quality and then were lost themselves.

---

① 兄弟会,大学联谊会。
② 入伍,参军。
③ 莱茵河,德国最长的河流。
④ 下士,班长。
⑤ 歇斯底里,狂热情绪。
⑥ 暴行。

His lies were quite unimportant lies and consisted in attributing to himself things other men had seen, done or heard of, and stating as facts certain **apocryphal**① incidents familiar to all soldiers. Even his lies were not sensational at the **pool room**②. His acquaintances, who had heard detailed accounts of German women found chained to machine guns in the Argonne forest and who could not comprehend, or were barred by their patriotism from interest in, any German machine gunners who were not chained, were not thrilled by his stories.

Krebs acquired the **nausea**③ in regard to experience that is the result of untruth or exaggeration, and when he occasionally met another man who had really been a soldier and they talked a few minutes in the dressing room at a dance he fell into the easy pose of the old soldier among other soldiers: that he had been badly, sickeningly frightened all the time. In this way he lost everything.

During this time, it was late summer, he was sleeping late in bed, getting up to walk down town to the library to get a book, eating lunch at home, reading on the front porch until he became bored and then walking down through the town to spend the hottest hours of the day in the cool dark of the pool room. He loved to play pool.

In the evening he practiced on his **clarinet**④, strolled down town, read and went to bed. He was still a hero to his two young sisters. His mother would have given him breakfast in bed if he had wanted it. She often came in when he was in bed and asked him to tell her about the war, but her attention always wandered. His father was **non-committal**⑤.

Before Krebs went away to the war he had never been allowed to drive the family motor car. His father was in the **real estate**⑥ business and always wanted the car to be at his command when he required it to take clients out into the country to show them a piece of farm property. The car always stood outside the First National Bank building where his father had an office on the second floor. Now, after the war, it was still the same car.

Nothing was changed in the town except that the young girls had grown up. But they

---

① 伪造的,杜撰的。
② 台球室。
③ 恶心。
④ 单簧管。
⑤ 不表态的。
⑥ 房地产。

lived in such a complicated world of already defined alliances and shifting **feuds**① that Krebs did not feel the energy or the courage to break into it. He liked to look at them, though. There were so many good-looking young girls. Most of them had their hair cut short. When he went away only little girls wore their hair like that or girls that were fast. They all wore sweaters and shirt waists with round Dutch collars. It was a pattern. He liked to look at them from the front porch as they walked on the other side of the street. He liked to watch them walking under the shade of the trees. He liked the round Dutch collars above their sweaters. He liked their silk stockings and flat shoes. He liked their bobbed hair and the way they walked.

When he was in town their appeal to him was not very strong. He did not like them when he saw them in the Greek's ice cream parlor. He did not want them themselves really. They were too complicated. There was something else. Vaguely he wanted a girl but he did not want to have to work to get her. He would have liked to have a girl but he did not want to have to spend a long time getting her. He did not want to get into the **intrigue**② and the politics. He did not want to have to do any courting. He did not want to tell any more lies. It wasn't worth it.

He did not want any consequences. He did not want any consequences ever again. He wanted to live along without consequences. Besides he did not really need a girl. The army had taught him that. It was all right to pose as though you had to have a girl. Nearly everybody did that. But it wasn't true. You did not need a girl. That was the funny thing. First a fellow **boasted**③ how girls mean nothing to him, that he never thought of them, that they could not touch him. Then a fellow boasted that he could not get along without girls, that he had to have them all the time, that he could not go to sleep without them.

That was all a lie. It was all a lie both ways. You did not need a girl unless you thought about them. He learned that in the army. Then sooner or later you always got one. When you were really ripe for a girl you always got one. You did not have to think about it. Sooner or later it would come. He had learned that in the army.

Now he would have liked a girl if she had come to him and not wanted to talk. But here at home it was all too complicated. He knew he could never get through it all again.

---

① 长期不和,积怨。

② 阴谋、钩心斗角。此处意为调情。

③ 炫耀、自夸。

It was not worth the trouble. That was the thing about French girls and German girls. There was not all this talking. You couldn't talk much and you did not need to talk. It was simple and you were friends. He thought about France and then he began to think about Germany. On the whole he had liked Germany better. He did not want to leave Germany. He did not want to come home. Still, he had come home. He sat on the front porch.

He liked the girls that were walking along the other side of the street. He liked the look of them much better than the French girls or the German girls. But the world they were in was not the world he was in. He would like to have one of them. But it was not worth it. They were such a nice pattern. He liked the pattern. It was exciting. But he would not go through all the talking. He did not want one badly enough. He liked to look at them all, though. It was not worth it. Not now when things were getting good again.

He sat there on the porch reading a book on the war. It was a history and he was reading about all the engagements he had been in. It was the most interesting reading he had ever done. He wished there were more maps. He looked forward with a good feeling to reading all the really good histories when they would come out with good detail maps. Now he was really learning about the war. He had been a good soldier. That made a difference.

One morning after he had been home about a month his mother came into his bedroom and sat on the bed. She smoothed her **apron**①.

"I had a talk with your father last night, Harold," she said, "and he is willing for you to take the car out in the evenings."

"Yeah?" said Krebs, who was not fully awake. "Take the car out? Yeah?"

"Yes. Your father has felt for some time that you should be able to take the car out in the evenings whenever you wished but we only talked it over last night."

"I'll bet you made him," Krebs said.

"No. It was your father's suggestion that we talk the matter over."

"Yeah. I'll bet you made him," Krebs sat up in bed.

"Will you come down to breakfast, Harold?" his mother said.

"As soon as I get my clothes on," Krebs said.

His mother went out of the room and he could hear her frying something downstairs while he washed, shaved and dressed to go down into the dining-room for breakfast. While

① 围裙。

he was eating breakfast his sister brought in the mail.

"Well, Hare," she said. "You old sleepy-head. What do you ever get up for?"

Krebs looked at her. He liked her. She was his best sister.

"Have you got the paper?" he asked.

She handed him The Kansas City Star and he shucked off its brown wrapper and opened it to the sporting page. He folded The Star open and **propped**① it against the **water pitcher**② with his cereal dish to steady it, so he could read while he ate.

"Harold," his mother stood in the kitchen doorway, "Harold, please don't **muss up**③ the paper. Your father can't read his Star if it's been mussed."

"I won't muss it," Krebs said.

His sister sat down at the table and watched him while he read.

"We're playing **indoor**④ over at school this afternoon," she said. "I'm going to **pitch**⑤."

"Good," said Krebs. "**How's the old wing**⑥?"

"I can pitch better than lots of the boys. I tell them all you taught me. The other girls aren't much good."

"Yeah?" said Krebs.

"I tell them all you're my **beau**⑦. Aren't you my beau, Hare?"

"You bet."

"Couldn't your brother really be your beau just because he's your brother?"

"I don't know."

"Sure you know. Couldn't you be my beau, Hare, if I was old enough and if you wanted to?"

"Sure. You're my girl now."

"Am I really your girl?"

"Sure."

"Do you love me?"

---

① 支撑,使倚靠在某物上。
② 水壶。
③ 弄脏,弄乱。
④ 指室内垒球。
⑤ 当投手。
⑥ 意为"胳膊如何?还有劲吗?"。
⑦ 情人。

"Uh, huh."

"Will you love me always?"

"Sure."

"Will you come over and watch me play indoor?"

"Maybe."

"Aw, Hare, you don't love me. If you loved me, you'd want to come over and watch me play indoor."

Krebs's mother came into the dining-room from the kitchen. She carried a plate with two fried eggs and some crisp bacon on it and a plate of **buckwheat**① cakes.

"You run along, Helen," she said. "I want to talk to Harold."

She put the eggs and bacon down in front of him and brought in a jug of maple syrup for the buckwheat cakes. Then she sat down across the table from Krebs.

"I wish you'd put down the paper a minute, Harold," she said.

Krebs took down the paper and folded it.

"Have you decided what you are going to do yet, Harold?" his mother said, taking off her glasses.

"No," said Krebs.

"Don't you think it's about time?" His mother did not say this in a mean way. She seemed worried.

"I hadn't thought about it," Krebs said.

"God has some work for every one to do," his mother said. "There can be no **idle**② hands in His Kingdom."

"I'm not in His Kingdom," Krebs said.

"We are all of us in His Kingdom."

Krebs felt embarrassed and **resentful**③ as always.

"I've worried about you so much, Harold," his mother went on. "I know the temptations you must have been exposed to. I know how weak men are. I know what your own dear grandfather, my own father, told us about the Civil War and I have prayed for you. I pray for you all day long, Harold."

Krebs looked at the bacon fat hardening on his plate.

---

① 荞麦。

② 空闲的。

③ 厌恶的,感到愤恨的。

"Your father is worried, too," his mother went on. "He thinks you have lost your ambition, that you haven't got a definite aim in life. Charley Simmons, who is just your age, has a good job and is going to be married. The boys are all settling down; they're all determined to get somewhere; you can see that boys like Charley Simmons are on their way to being really a credit to the community."

Krebs said nothing.

"Don't look that way, Harold," his mother said. "You know we love you and I want to tell you for your own good how matters stand. Your father does not want to **hamper**① your freedom. He thinks you should be allowed to drive the car. If you want to take some of the nice girls out riding with you, we are only too pleased. We want you to enjoy yourself. But you are going to have to settle down to work, Harold. Your father doesn't care what you start in at. All work is honorable as he says. But you've got to make a start at something. He asked me to speak to you this morning and then you can stop in and see him at his office."

"Is that all?" Krebs said.

"Yes. Don't you love your mother, dear boy?"

"No," Krebs said.

His mother looked at him across the table. Her eyes were shiny. She started crying.

"I don't love anybody," Krebs said.

It wasn't any good. He couldn't tell her, he couldn't make her see it. It was silly to have said it. He had only hurt her. He went over and took hold of her arm. She was crying with her head in her hands.

"I didn't mean it," he said. "I was just angry at something. I didn't mean I didn't love you."

His mother went on crying. Krebs put his arm on her shoulder.

"Can't you believe me, mother?"

His mother shook her head.

"Please, please, mother. Please believe me."

"All right," his mother said **chokily**②. She looked up at him. "I believe you, Harold."

Krebs kissed her hair. She put her face up to him.

---

① 阻碍。

② 哽咽地，抽泣地。

"I'm your mother," she said. "I held you next to my heart when you were a tiny baby."

Krebs felt sick and vaguely nauseated.

"I know, Mummy," he said. "I'll try and be a good boy for you."

"Would you kneel and pray with me, Harold?" his mother asked.

They knelt down beside the dining-room table and Krebs's mother prayed.

"Now, you pray, Harold," she said.

"I can't," Krebs said.

"Try, Harold."

"I can't."

"Do you want me to pray for you?"

"Yes."

So his mother prayed for him and then they stood up and Krebs kissed his mother and went out of the house. He had tried so to keep his life from being complicated. Still, none of it had touched him. He had felt sorry for his mother and she had made him lie. He would go to Kansas City and get a job and she would feel all right about it. There would be one more scene maybe before he got away. He would not go down to his father's office. He would miss that one. He wanted his life to go smoothly. It had just gotten going that way. Well, that was all over now, anyway. He would go over to the schoolyard and watch Helen play indoor baseball.

Ⅳ. 思考题

1. How is the war represented in this story?
2. What are some features of Hemingway's language?
3. How do you understand Hemingway's philosophy about human existence?

Ⅴ. 文学批评

海明威的冰山理论

The iceberg theory or theory of omission is a writing technique coined by American writer Ernest Hemingway. As a young journalist, Hemingway had to focus his newspaper reports on immediate events, with very little context or interpretation. When he became a writer of short stories, he retained this minimalistic style, focusing on surface elements without explicitly discussing underlying themes. Hemingway believed the deeper meaning of a story should not be evident on the surface, but should shine through implicitly.

In 1923, Hemingway conceived of the idea of a new theory of writing after finishing his short story "Out of Season". In A *Moveable Feast*, he explains: "I omitted the real end [of "Out of Season"] which was that the old man hanged himself. This was omitted on my new theory that you could omit anything ... and the omitted part would strengthen the story." In chapter sixteen of *Death in the Afternoon* he compares his theory about writing to an iceberg: "If a writer of prose knows enough of what he is writing about he may omit things that he knows and the reader, if the writer is writing truly enough, will have a feeling of those things as strongly as though the writer had stated them. The dignity of movement of an ice-berg is due to only one-eighth of it being above water. A writer who omits things because he does not know them only makes hollow places in his writing."

Ⅵ. 拓展阅读

Kenneth G. Johnston's *The Tip of the Iceberg: Hemingway and the Short Story* (Penkevill Publishing Company, 1987).

Ⅶ. 参考文献

Johnston, Kenneth G. *The Tip of the Iceberg: Hemingway and the Short Story*. Penkevill Publishing Company, 1987.

Lamb, Robert Paul. "The love song of Harold Krebs: Form, Argument, and Meaning in Hemingway's 'Soldier's Home'." *The Hemingway Review* 14.2 (1995): 18-37.

Chapter 8　Albert Camus and the Philosophy of Absurdity

Ⅰ. 作者简介

阿尔贝·加缪 Albert Camus（1913—1960）1913 年 11 月 7 日生于阿尔及利亚的蒙多维。加缪父亲在 1914 年第一次世界大战阵亡后，他随母亲移居阿尔及尔贫民区外祖母家，生活极为艰难。加缪由做佣人的母亲抚养长大，从小就在阿尔及利亚的贝尔库（Belcourt）平民区尝尽了生活艰辛。

1932 年，加缪在《南方》杂志上第一次发表随笔作品。1933 年，他进入阿尔及尔大学攻读哲学和古典文学。加缪 1935 年开始从事戏剧活动，曾创办过剧团，写过剧本，当过演员。戏剧在他一生的创作中占有重要地位。

1937 年，加缪出版了随笔集《反与正》（*The Wrong Side and the Right Side*），第一次表现出思想的锋芒。1940 年，加缪来到法国首都巴黎，和志同道合的朋友一起，在《巴黎晚报》从事编辑工作。这一年的 6 月 14 日，希特勒军队的铁蹄就踏进了巴黎市区，很快，由纳粹扶植起来的法国傀儡政权维希政府开始运作。

这年的冬天,加缪带着妻子离开沦陷的巴黎,来到了阿尔及利亚的奥兰城教书,在这里一共住了 18 个月,正是这一段生活,使他酝酿出了之后的《鼠疫》。1942 年,加缪离开阿尔及利亚前往巴黎,为《巴黎晚报》工作,然后在伽里马出版社做编辑,秘密地活跃于抵抗运动中,主编地下刊物《战斗报》。同年,加缪创作小说《局外人》(*The Stranger*)。随后,他又开始写作哲学随笔《西西弗的神话》(*The Myth of Sisyphus*)。1943 年 4 月,加缪结识了萨特和波伏娃,在哲学和戏剧等方面的共同爱好使他们成了非常亲密的朋友。

1945 年,戏剧《卡里古拉》(*Caligula*)首次演出。1947 年出版长篇小说《鼠疫》(*The Plague*)并获法国批评奖,进一步确立了他在西方当代文学中的重要地位。1951 年加缪发表了哲学论文《反抗者》(*The Rebel*)之后,遭到了左派知识分子阵营的攻击,并引起一场与萨特等人长达一年之久的论战,最后与萨特决裂。

1957 年 10 月,瑞典文学院宣布加缪获得该年的诺贝尔文学奖,加缪因此成为这个奖项历史上最年轻的获奖者,获奖理由是"他的重要文学作品透彻认真地阐明了当代人的良心所面临的问题"("for his important literary production, which with clear-sighted earnestness illuminates the problems of the human conscience in our times")。这一年的 12 月,他在瑞典乌普萨尔大学做了一场题为《艺术家及其时代》的演讲,他说:"一个人常常因为感到自己与众不同才选择了艺术家的命运,但他很快就明白,他只有承认他与众人相像,才能给予他的艺术、他的不同之处以营养。真正的艺术家什么都不蔑视,他们迫使自己去理解,而不是去评判。"

1960 年 1 月 4 日,加缪搭朋友的顺风车从普罗旺斯去巴黎,途中发生车祸,加缪当场死亡,年仅 47 岁。

Ⅱ. 内容提要

《局外人》全书分为两个部分,第一部分从莫尔索的母亲去世开始,到他在海滩上杀死阿拉伯人为止。小说叙述毫无抒情的意味,通篇都是莫尔索内心自发意识的流露,而他叙述的接二连三的事件、对话、姿势和感觉之间似乎也没有必然的联系,给人一种不连贯的荒谬之感。别人的姿势和语言在莫尔索看来都是没有意义的,是不可理解的;在他眼中有意义的事物似乎只有大海、阳光,但是阳光使他莫名其妙地杀了人。在第二部分里,牢房代替了大海,社会意识代替了莫尔索自发的意识。司法机构以其固有的逻辑,利用被告过去偶然发生的一些事件把莫尔索描绘成一个他自己都认不出来的形象,即把始终认为自己无罪、对一切都毫不在乎的莫尔索硬说成是一个冷酷无情、蓄意杀人的魔鬼。整个审讯几乎从未调查杀人案件,而是千方百计把杀人和他母亲之死及他和玛丽的关系联系在一起。

阿尔贝·加缪的《局外人》塑造了莫尔索这个行为惊世骇俗、言谈离经叛道的"局外人"形象,是文学史上的经典人物形象,这部作品是加缪"荒诞"哲学思想的完美文学阐释。

Ⅲ. 作品

Part One

I

Mother died today. Or, maybe, yesterday; I can't be sure. The telegram from the Home says: YOUR MOTHER PASSED AWAY. FUNERAL TOMORROW. DEEP SYMPATHY. Which leaves the matter doubtful; it could have been yesterday.

The Home for Aged Persons is at Marengo, some fifty miles from Algiers. With the two o'clock bus I should get there well before nightfall. Then I can spend the night there, keeping the usual **vigil**① beside the body, and be back here by tomorrow evening. I have fixed up with my employer for two days' leave; obviously, under the circumstances, he couldn't refuse. Still, I had an idea he looked annoyed, and I said, without thinking: "Sorry, sir, but it's not my fault, you know."

Afterwards it struck me I needn't have said that. I had no reason to excuse myself; it was up to him to express his sympathy and so forth. Probably he will do so the day after tomorrow, when he sees me in black. For the present, it's almost as if Mother weren't really dead. The funeral will bring it home to me, put an official seal on it, so to speak...

I took the two-o'clock bus. It was a **blazing**② hot afternoon. I'd lunched, as usual, at Céleste's restaurant. Everyone was most kind, and Céleste said to me, "There's no one

---

① 守夜祈祷。

② 酷热的。

like a mother." When I left they came with me to the door. It was something of a rush, getting away, as at the last moment I had to call in at Emmanuel's place to borrow his black tie and mourning band. He lost his uncle a few months ago.

I had to run to catch the bus. I suppose it was my hurrying like that, what with the **glare**① off the road and from the sky, the **reek**② of gasoline, and the **jolts**③, that made me feel so **drowsy**④. Anyhow, I slept most of the way. When I woke I was leaning against a soldier; he grinned and asked me if I'd come from a long way off, and I just nodded, to cut things short. I wasn't in a mood for talking.

The Home is a little over a mile from the village. I went there on foot. I asked to be allowed to see Mother at once, but the doorkeeper told me I must see the **warden**⑤ first. He wasn't free, and I had to wait a bit. The doorkeeper chatted with me while I waited; then he led me to the office. The warden was a very small man, with gray hair, and a Legion of Honor **rosette**⑥ in his buttonhole. He gave me a long look with his watery blue eyes. Then we shook hands, and he held mine so long that I began to feel embarrassed. After that he consulted a register on his table, and said:

"Madame Meursault entered the Home three years ago. She had no private means and depended entirely on you."

I had a feeling he was blaming me for something, and started to explain. But he cut me short.

"There's no need to excuse yourself, my boy. I've looked up the record and obviously you weren't in a position to see that she was properly cared for. She needed someone to be with her all the time, and young men in jobs like yours don't get too much pay. In any case, she was much happier in the Home."

I said, "Yes, sir; I'm sure of that."

Then he added: "She had good friends here, you know, old folks like herself, and one gets on better with people of one's own generation. You're much too young; you couldn't have been much of a companion to her."

That was so. When we lived together, Mother was always watching me, but we hardly

---

① 刺眼的光。
② 难闻的气味。
③ 颠簸、摇晃。
④ 昏昏欲睡的。
⑤ 管理员。
⑥ 玫瑰形装饰物。

ever talked. During her first few weeks at the Home she used to cry a good deal. But that was only because she hadn't settled down. After a month or two she'd have cried if she'd been told to leave the Home. Because this, too, would have been a wrench. That was why, during the last year, I seldom went to see her. Also, it would have meant losing my Sunday—not to mention the trouble of going to the bus, getting my ticket, and spending two hours on the journey each way.

The warden went on talking, but I didn't pay much attention. Finally he said:

"Now, I suppose you'd like to see your mother?"

I rose without replying, and he led the way to the door. As we were going down the stairs he explained:

"I've had the body moved to our little **mortuary**① —so as not to upset the other old people, you understand. Every time there's a death here, they're in a nervous state for two or three days. Which means, of course, extra work and worry for our staff."

We crossed a courtyard where there were a number of old men, talking amongst themselves in little groups. They fell silent as we came up with them. Then, behind our backs, the chattering began again. Their voices reminded me of parakeets in a cage, only the sound wasn't quite so shrill. The warden stopped outside the entrance of a small, low building.

"So here I leave you, Monsieur Meursault. If you want me for anything, you'll find me in my office. We propose to have the funeral tomorrow morning. That will enable you to spend the night beside your mother's coffin, as no doubt you would wish to do. Just one more thing; I gathered from your mother's friends that she wished to be buried with the rites of the Church. I've made arrangements for this; but I thought I should let you know."

I thanked him. So far as I knew, my mother, though not a professed **atheist**②, had never given a thought to religion in her life.

I entered the mortuary. It was a bright, spotlessly clean room, with whitewashed walls and a big skylight. The furniture consisted of some chairs and **trestles**③. Two of the latter stood open in the center of the room and the coffin rested on them. The lid was in place, but the screws had been given only a few turns and their nickeled heads stuck out above

---

① 停尸房。
② 无神论者。
③ 条凳。

the wood, which was stained dark walnut. An Arab woman—a nurse, I supposed—was sitting beside the bier; she was wearing a blue smock and had a rather gaudy scarf wound round her hair.

Just then the keeper came up behind me. He'd evidently been running, as he was a little out of breath.

"We put the lid on, but I was told to unscrew it when you came, so that you could see her."

While he was going up to the coffin I told him not to trouble.

"Eh? What's that?" he exclaimed. "You don't want me to ...?"

"No," I said.

He put back the screwdriver in his pocket and stared at me. I realized then that I shouldn't have said, "No," and it made me rather embarrassed. After eying me for some moments he asked:

"Why not?" But he didn't sound reproachful; he simply wanted to know.

"Well, really I couldn't say," I answered.

He began twiddling his white mustache; then, without looking at me, said gently:

"I understand."

He was a pleasant-looking man, with blue eyes and ruddy cheeks. He drew up a chair for me near the coffin, and seated himself just behind. The nurse got up and moved toward the door. As she was going by, the keeper whispered in my ear:

"It's a tumor she has, poor thing."

I looked at her more carefully and I noticed that she had a bandage round her head, just below her eyes. It lay quite flat across the bridge of her nose, and one saw hardly anything of her face except that strip of whiteness.

As soon as she had gone, the keeper rose.

"Now I'll leave you to yourself."

I don't know whether I made some gesture, but instead of going he halted behind my chair. The sensation of someone posted at my back made me uncomfortable. The sun was getting low and the whole room was flooded with a pleasant, mellow light. Two **hornets**① were buzzing overhead, against the skylight. I was so sleepy I could hardly keep my eyes open. Without looking round, I asked the keeper how long he'd been at the Home. "Five

① 大黄蜂。

years." The answer came so **pat**[①] that one could have thought he'd been expecting my question.

That started him off, and he became quite chatty. If anyone had told him ten years ago that he'd end his days as doorkeeper at a home at Marengo, he'd never have believed it. He was sixty-four, he said, and hailed from Paris.

When he said that, I broke in. "Ah, you don't come from here?"

I remembered then that, before taking me to the warden, he'd told me something about Mother. He had said she'd have to be buried mighty quickly because of the heat in these parts, especially down in the plain. "At Paris they keep the body for three days, sometimes four." After that he had mentioned that he'd spent the best part of his life in Paris, and could never manage to forget it. "Here," he had said, "things have to go with a rush, like. You've hardly time to get used to the idea that someone's dead, before you're hauled off to the funeral." "That's enough," his wife had put in. "You didn't ought to say such things to the poor young gentleman." The old fellow had blushed and begun to apologize. I told him it was quite all right. As a matter of fact, I found it rather interesting, what he'd been telling me; I hadn't thought of that before.

Now he went on to say that he'd entered the Home as an ordinary inmate. But he was still quite hale and hearty, and when the keeper's job fell vacant, he offered to take it on.

I pointed out that, even so, he was really an inmate like the others, but he wouldn't hear of it. He was "an official, like." I'd been struck before by his habit of saying "they" or, less often, "them old folks," when referring to inmates no older than himself. Still, I could see his point of view. As doorkeeper he had a certain standing, and some authority over the rest of them.

Just then the nurse returned. Night had fallen very quickly; all of a sudden, it seemed, the sky went black above the skylight. The keeper switched on the lamps, and I was almost blinded by the blaze of light.

He suggested I should go to the refectory for dinner, but I wasn't hungry. Then he proposed bringing me a mug of café au lait. As I am very partial to café au lait I said, "Thanks," and a few minutes later he came back with a tray. I drank the coffee, and then I wanted a cigarette. But I wasn't sure if I should smoke, under the circumstances—in Mother's presence. I thought it over; really, it didn't seem to matter, so I offered the

---

① 过于轻易的,敷衍的。

keeper a cigarette, and we both smoked.

After a while he started talking again.

"You know, your mother's friends will be coming soon, to keep vigil with you beside the body. We always have a 'vigil' here, when anyone dies. I'd better go and get some chairs and a pot of black coffee."

The glare off the white walls was making my eyes smart, and I asked him if he couldn't turn off one of the lamps. "Nothing doing," he said. They'd arranged the lights like that; either one had them all on or none at all. After that I didn't pay much more attention to him. He went out, brought some chairs, and set them out round the coffin. On one he placed a coffeepot and ten or a dozen cups. Then he sat down facing me, on the far side of Mother. The nurse was at the other end of the room, with her back to me. I couldn't see what she was doing, but by the way her arms moved I guessed that she was knitting. I was feeling very comfortable; the coffee had warmed me up, and through the open door came scents of flowers and breaths of cool night air. I think I dozed off for a while.

I was wakened by an odd **rustling**① in my ears. After having had my eyes closed, I had a feeling that the light had grown even stronger than before. There wasn't a trace of shadow anywhere, and every object, each curve or angle, seemed to score its outline on one's eyes. The old people, Mother's friends, were coming in. I counted ten in all, gliding almost soundlessly through the bleak white glare. None of the chairs **creaked**② when they sat down. Never in my life had I seen anyone so clearly as I saw these people; not a detail of their clothes or features escaped me. And yet I couldn't hear them, and it was hard to believe they really existed.

Nearly all the women wore aprons, and the strings drawn tight round their waists made their big stomachs bulge still more. I'd never yet noticed what big paunches old women usually have. Most of the men, however, were as thin as rakes, and they all carried sticks. What struck me most about their faces was that one couldn't see their eyes, only a dull glow in a sort of nest of wrinkles.

On sitting down, they looked at me, and **wagged**③ their heads awkwardly, their lips sucked in between their toothless gums. I couldn't decide if they were greeting me and

---

① 沙沙声。

② 嘎吱作响。

③ 摇摆、摆动。

trying to say something, or if it was due to some **infirmity**① of age. I inclined to think that they were greeting me, after their fashion, but it had a queer effect, seeing all those old fellows grouped round the keeper, solemnly eyeing me and dandling their heads from side to side. For a moment I had an absurd impression that they had come to sit in judgment on me.

A few minutes later one of the women started weeping. She was in the second row and I couldn't see her face because of another woman in front. At regular intervals she emitted a little choking sob; one had a feeling she would never stop. The others didn't seem to notice. They sat in silence, **slumped**② in their chairs, staring at the coffin or at their walking sticks or any object just in front of them, and never took their eyes off it. And still the woman sobbed. I was rather surprised, as I didn't know who she was. I wanted her to stop crying, but dared not speak to her. After a while the keeper bent toward her and whispered in her ear; but she merely shook her head, mumbled something I couldn't catch, and went on sobbing as steadily as before.

The keeper got up and moved his chair beside mine. At first he kept silent; then, without looking at me, he explained.

"She was devoted to your mother. She says your mother was her only friend in the world, and now she's all alone."

I had nothing to say, and the silence lasted quite a while. Presently the woman's sighs and sobs became less frequent, and, after blowing her nose and snuffling for some minutes, she, too, fell silent.

I'd ceased feeling sleepy, but I was very tired and my legs were aching badly. And now I realized that the silence of these people was telling on my nerves. The only sound was a rather queer one; it came only now and then, and at first I was puzzled by it. However, after listening attentively, I guessed what it was; the old men were sucking at the insides of their cheeks, and this caused the odd, wheezing noises that had mystified me. They were so much absorbed in their thoughts that they didn't know what they were up to. I even had an impression that the dead body in their midst meant nothing at all to them. But now I suspect that I was mistaken about this.

We all drank the coffee, which the keeper handed round. After that, I can't remem-

---

① 体弱、生病。

② 重重地坐、倒下。

ber much; somehow the night went by. I can recall only one moment; I had opened my eyes and I saw the old men sleeping **hunched**① up on their chairs, with one exception. Resting his chin on his hands clasped round his stick, he was staring hard at me, as if he had been waiting for me to wake. Then I fell asleep again. I woke up after a bit, because the ache in my legs had developed into a sort of cramp.

There was a glimmer of dawn above the skylight. A minute or two later one of the old men woke up and coughed repeatedly. He spat into a big check handkerchief, and each time he spat it sounded as if he were retching. This woke the others, and the keeper told them it was time to make a move. They all got up at once. Their faces were **ashen**② gray after the long, uneasy vigil. To my surprise each of them shook hands with me, as though this night together, in which we hadn't exchanged a word, had created a kind of intimacy between us.

I was quite done in. The keeper took me to his room, and I tidied myself up a bit. He gave me some more "white" coffee, and it seemed to do me good. When I went out, the sun was up and the sky mottled red above the hills between Marengo and the sea. A morning breeze was blowing and it had a pleasant salty tang. There was the promise of a very fine day. I hadn't been in the country for ages, and I caught myself thinking what an agreeable walk I could have had, if it hadn't been for Mother.

As it was, I waited in the courtyard, under a plane tree. I sniffed the smells of the cool earth and found I wasn't sleepy any more. Then I thought of the other fellows in the office. At this hour they'd be getting up, preparing to go to work; for me this was always the worst hour of the day. I went on thinking, like this, for ten minutes or so; then the sound of a bell inside the building attracted my attention. I could see movements behind the windows; then all was calm again. The sun had risen a little higher and was beginning to warm my feet. The keeper came across the yard and said the warden wished to see me. I went to his office and he got me to sign some document. I noticed that he was in black, with pin-stripe trousers. He picked up the telephone receiver and looked at me.

"The undertaker's men arrived some moments ago, and they will be going to the mortuary to screw down the coffin. Shall I tell them to wait, for you to have a last glimpse of your mother?"

"No," I said.

---

① 弓背,耸肩。

② 面色苍白的,没有血色的。

He spoke into the receiver, lowering his voice. "That's all right, Figeac. Tell the men to go there now."

He then informed me that he was going to attend the funeral, and I thanked him. Sitting down behind his desk, he crossed his short legs and leaned back. Besides the nurse on duty, he told me, he and I would be the only mourners at the funeral. It was a rule of the Home that inmates shouldn't attend funerals, though there was no objection to letting some of them sit up beside the coffin, the night before.

"It's for their own sakes," he explained, "to spare their feelings. But in this particular instance I've given permission to an old friend of your mother to come with us. His name is Thomas Pérez." The warden smiled. "It's a rather touching little story in its way. He and your mother had become almost inseparable. The other old people used to tease Pérez about having a fiancée. 'When are you going to marry her?' they'd ask. He'd turn it with a laugh. It was a standing joke, in fact. So, as you can guess, he feels very badly about your mother's death. I thought I couldn't decently refuse him permission to attend the funeral. But, on our medical officer's advice, I forbade him to sit up beside the body last night."

For some time we sat there without speaking. Then the warden got up and went to the window. Presently he said:

"Ah, there's the padre from Marengo. He's a bit ahead of time."

He warned me that it would take us a good three quarters of an hour, walking to the church, which was in the village. Then we went downstairs.

The priest was waiting just outside the mortuary door. With him were two acolytes, one of whom had a censer. The priest was stooping over him, adjusting the length of the silver chain on which it hung. When he saw us he straightened up and said a few words to me, addressing me as, "My son." Then he led the way into the mortuary.

I noticed at once that four men in black were standing behind the coffin and the screws in the lid had now been driven home. At the same moment I heard the warden remark that the **hearse**① had arrived, and the priest starting his prayers. Then everybody made a move. Holding a strip of black cloth, the four men approached the coffin, while the priest, the boys, and myself filed out. A lady I hadn't seen before was standing by the door. "This is Monsieur Meursault," the warden said to her. I didn't catch her name, but

① 灵车。

I gathered she was a nursing sister attached to the Home. When I was introduced, she bowed, without the trace of a smile on her long, gaunt face. We stood aside from the doorway to let the coffin by; then, following the bearers down a corridor, we came to the front entrance, where a hearse was waiting. **Oblong**①, **glossy**②, **varnished**③ black all over, it vaguely reminded me of the pen trays in the office.

Beside the hearse stood a quaintly dressed little-man, whose duty it was, I understood, to supervise the funeral, as a sort of master of ceremonies. Near him, looking constrained, almost bashful, was old M. Pérez, my mother's special friend. He wore a soft felt hat with a pudding-basin crown and a very wide brim—he **whisked**④ it off the moment the coffin emerged from the doorway—trousers that **concertinaed**⑤ on his shoes, a black tie much too small for his high white double collar. Under a bulbous, pimply nose, his lips were trembling. But what caught my attention most was his ears; pendulous, scarlet ears that showed up like blobs of sealing wax on the pallor of his cheeks and were framed in wisps of silky white hair.

The undertaker's **factotum**⑥ shepherded us to our places, with the priest in front of the hearse, and the four men in black on each side of it. The warden and myself came next, and, bringing up the rear, old Pérez and the nurse.

The sky was already a blaze of light, and the air stoking up rapidly. I felt the first waves of heat lapping my back, and my dark suit made things worse. I couldn't imagine why we waited so long for getting under way. Old Pérez, who had put on his hat, took it off again. I had turned slightly in his direction and was looking at him when the warden started telling me more about him. I remember his saying that old Pérez and my mother used often to have a longish stroll together in the cool of the evening; sometimes they went as far as the village, accompanied by a nurse, of course.

I looked at the countryside, at the long lines of **cypresses**⑦ sloping up toward the skyline and the hills, the hot red soil **dappled**⑧ with vivid green, and here and there a lonely

---

① 长椭圆形的。
② 有光泽的。
③ 给…上清漆。
④ 匆匆带走。
⑤ 像六角风琴一样折叠。
⑥ 勤杂工。
⑦ 柏树。
⑧ 使(某物)有斑点。

house sharply outlined against the light—and I could understand Mother's feelings. Evenings in these parts must be a sort of mournful **solace**①. Now, in the full glare of the morning sun, with everything shimmering in the heat haze, there was something inhuman, discouraging, about this landscape.

At last we made a move. Only then I noticed that Pérez had a slight limp. The old chap steadily lost ground as the hearse gained speed. One of the men beside it, too, fell back and drew level with me. I was surprised to see how quickly the sun was climbing up the sky, and just then it struck me that for quite a while the air had been throbbing with the hum of insects and the rustle of grass warming up. Sweat was running down my face. As I had no hat I tried to fan myself with my handkerchief.

The undertaker's man turned to me and said something that I didn't catch. At that same time he wiped the crown of his head with a handkerchief that he held in his left hand, while with his right he tilted up his hat. I asked him what he'd said. He pointed upward.

"Sun's pretty bad today, ain't it?"

"Yes," I said.

After a while he asked: "Is it your mother we're burying?"

"Yes," I said again.

"What was her age?"

"Well, she was getting on." As a matter of fact, I didn't know exactly how old she was.

After that he kept silent. Looking back, I saw Pérez limping along some fifty yards behind. He was swinging his big felt hat at arm's length, trying to make the pace. I also had a look at the warden. He was walking with carefully measured steps, economizing every gesture. **Beads**② of perspiration **glistened**③ on his forehead, but he didn't wipe them off.

I had an impression that our little procession was moving slightly faster. Wherever I looked I saw the same sun-drenched countryside, and the sky was so dazzling that I dared not raise my eyes. Presently we struck a patch of freshly **tarred**④ road. A shimmer of heat

---

① 安慰。
② 珠子,液体的小滴。
③ 闪光、闪亮。
④ 涂了沥青的。

played over it and one's feet **squelched**① at each step, leaving bright black **gashes**②. In front, the coachman's glossy black hat looked like a lump of the same sticky substance, poised above the hearse. It gave one a queer, dreamlike impression, that blue-white glare overhead and all this blackness round one: the sleek black of the hearse, the dull black of the men's clothes, and the silvery-black gashes in the road. And then there were the smells, smells of hot leather and horse **dung**③ from the hearse, veined with whiffs of incense smoke. What with these and the hangover from a poor night's sleep, I found my eyes and thoughts growing blurred.

I looked back again. Pérez seemed very far away now, almost hidden by the heat haze; then, abruptly, he disappeared altogether. After puzzling over it for a bit, I guessed that he had turned off the road into the fields. Then I noticed that there was a bend of the road a little way ahead. Obviously Pérez, who knew the district well, had taken a short cut, so as to catch up with us. He rejoined us soon after we were round the bend; then began to lose ground again. He took another short cut and met us again farther on; in fact, this happened several times during the next half-hour. But soon I lost interest in his movements; my temples were throbbing and I could hardly drag myself along.

After that everything went with a rush; and also with such precision and matter-of-factness that I remember hardly any details. Except that when we were on the outskirts of the village the nurse said something to me. Her voice took me by surprise; it didn't match her face at all; it was musical and slightly **tremulous**④. What she said was: "If you go too slowly there's the risk of a heatstroke. But, if you go too fast, you perspire, and the cold air in the church gives you a chill." I saw her point; either way one was in for it.

Some other memories of the funeral have stuck in my mind. The old boy's face, for instance, when he caught up with us for the last time, just outside the village. His eyes were streaming with tears, of exhaustion or distress, or both together. But because of the wrinkles they couldn't flow down. They spread out, crisscrossed, and formed a smooth gloss on the old, worn face.

And I can remember the look of the church, the villagers in the street, the red **gerani-**

---

① (如在泥泞中走时)发出啪唧声。
② 伤口、切口。
③ 粪。
④ 颤抖的。

ums① on the graves, Pérez's fainting fit—he crumpled up like a rag doll—the **tawny**②-red earth pattering on Mother's coffin, the bits of white roots mixed up with it; then more people, voices, the wait outside a café for the bus, the **rumble**③ of the engine, and my little thrill of pleasure when we entered the first brightly lit streets of Algiers, and I pictured myself going straight to bed and sleeping twelve hours at a stretch.

Ⅱ

ON WAKING I understood why my employer had looked rather cross when I asked for my two days off; it's a Saturday today. I hadn't thought of this at the time; it only struck me when I was getting out of bed. Obviously he had seen that it would mean my getting four days' holiday straight off, and one couldn't expect him to like that. Still, for one thing, it wasn't my fault if Mother was buried yesterday and not today; and then, again, I'd have had my Saturday and Sunday off in any case. But naturally this didn't prevent me from seeing my employer's point.

Getting up was an effort, as I'd been really exhausted by the previous day's experiences. While shaving, I wondered how to spend the morning, and decided that a swim would do me good. So I caught the streetcar that goes down to the harbor.

It was quite like old times; a lot of young people were in the swimming pool, amongst them Marie Cardona, who used to be a typist at the office. I was rather keen on her in those days, and I fancy she liked me, too. But she was with us so short a time that nothing came of it.

While I was helping her to climb on to a raft, I let my hand stray over her breasts. Then she lay flat on the raft, while I trod water. After a moment she turned and looked at me. Her hair was over her eyes and she was laughing. I clambered up on to the raft, beside her. The air was pleasantly warm, and, half jokingly, I let my head sink back upon her lap. She didn't seem to mind, so I let it stay there. I had the sky full in my eyes, all blue and gold, and I could feel Marie's stomach rising and falling gently under my head. We must have stayed a good half-hour on the raft, both of us half asleep. When the sun got too hot she dived off and I followed. I caught up with her, put my arm round her waist, and we swam side by side. She was still laughing.

---

① 天竺葵。

② 黄褐色的。

③ 持续而低沉的声音。

While we were drying ourselves on the edge of the swimming pool she said: "I'm browner than you." I asked her if she'd come to the movies with me that evening. She laughed again and said, "Yes," if I'd take her to the comedy everybody was talking about, the one with Fernandel in it.

When we had dressed, she stared at my black tie and asked if I was in mourning. I explained that my mother had died. "When?" she asked, and I said, "Yesterday." She made no remark, though I thought she shrank away a little. I was just going to explain to her that it wasn't my fault, but I checked myself, as I remembered having said the same thing to my employer, and realizing then it sounded rather foolish. Still, foolish or not, somehow one can't help feeling a bit guilty, I suppose.

Anyhow, by evening Marie had forgotten all about it. The film was funny in parts, but some of it was downright stupid. She pressed her leg against mine while we were in the picture house, and I was fondling her breast. Toward the end of the show I kissed her, but rather clumsily. Afterward she came back with me to my place.

When I woke up, Marie had gone. She'd told me her aunt expected her first thing in the morning. I remembered it was a Sunday, and that put me off; I've never cared for Sundays. So I turned my head and lazily sniffed the smell of brine that Marie's head had left on the pillow. I slept until ten. After that I stayed in bed until noon, smoking cigarettes. I decided not to lunch at Céleste's restaurant as I usually did; they'd be sure to pester me with questions, and I dislike being questioned. So I fried some eggs and ate them off the pan. I did without bread as there wasn't any left, and I couldn't be bothered going down to buy it.

After lunch I felt at loose ends and roamed about the little flat. It suited us well enough when Mother was with me, but now that I was by myself it was too large and I'd moved the dining table into my bedroom. That was now the only room I used; it had all the furniture I needed: a brass bedstead, a dressing table, some cane chairs whose seats had more or less caved in, a wardrobe with a tarnished mirror. The rest of the flat was never used, so I didn't trouble to look after it.

A bit later, for want of anything better to do, I picked up an old newspaper that was lying on the floor and read it. There was an advertisement of Kruschen Salts and I cut it out and pasted in into an album where I keep things that amuse me in the papers. Then I washed my hands and, as a last resource, went out on to the balcony.

My bedroom overlooks the main street of our district. Though it was a fine afternoon, the paving blocks were black and glistening. What few people were about seemed in an absurd hurry. First of all there came a family, going for their Sunday-afternoon walk; two small boys in sailor suits, with short trousers hardly down to their knees, and looking rather uneasy in their Sunday best; then a little girl with a big pink bow and black patent-leather shoes. Behind them was their mother, an enormously fat woman in a brown silk dress, and their father, a dapper little man, whom I knew by sight. He had a straw hat, a walking stick, and a butterfly tie. Seeing him beside his wife, I understood why people said he came of a good family and had married beneath him.

Next came a group of young fellows, the local "bloods," with sleek oiled hair, red ties, coats cut very tight at the waist, braided pockets, and square-toed shoes. I guessed they were going to one of the big theaters in the center of the town. That was why they had started out so early and were hurrying to the streetcar stop, laughing and talking at the top of their voices.

After they had passed, the street gradually emptied. By this time all the matinees must have begun. Only a few shopkeepers and cats remained about. Above the **sycamores**[①] bordering the road the sky was cloudless, but the light was soft. The tobacconist on the other side of the street brought a chair out on to the pavement in front of his door and sat astride it, resting his arms on the back. The streetcars which a few minutes before had been crowded were now almost empty. In the little café, Chez Pierrot, beside the tobacconist's, the waiter was sweeping up the sawdust in the empty restaurant. A typical Sunday afternoon...

I turned my chair round and seated myself like the tobacconist, as it was more comfortable that way. After smoking a couple of cigarettes, I went back to the room, got a tablet of chocolate, and returned to the window to eat it. Soon after, the sky clouded over, and I thought a summer storm was coming. However, the clouds gradually lifted. All the same, they had left in the street a sort of threat of rain, which made it darker. I stayed watching the sky for quite a while.

At five there was a loud clanging of streetcars. They were coming from the stadium in our suburb where there had been a football match. Even the back platforms were crowded and people were standing on the steps. Then another streetcar brought back the teams. I knew they were the players by the little suitcase each man carried. They were bawling out

---

① 无花果树。

their team song, "Keep the ball rolling, boys." One of them looked up at me and shouted, "We licked them!" I waved my hand and called back, "Good work!" From now on there was a steady stream of private cars.

The sky had changed again; a reddish glow was spreading up beyond the housetops. As dusk set in, the street grew more crowded. People were returning from their walks, and I noticed the dapper little man with the fat wife amongst the passers-by. Children were **whimpering**① and trailing wearily after their parents. After some minutes the local picture houses **disgorged**② their audiences. I noticed that the young fellows coming from them were taking longer strides and gesturing more vigorously than at ordinary times; doubtless the picture they'd been seeing was of the wild-West variety. Those who had been to the picture houses in the middle of the town came a little later, and looked more sedate, though a few were still laughing. On the whole, however, they seemed languid and exhausted. Some of them remained loitering in the street under my window. A group of girls came by, walking arm in arm. The young men under my window swerved so as to brush against them, and shouted humorous remarks, which made the girls turn their heads and giggle. I recognized them as girls from my part of the town, and two or three of them, whom I knew, looked up and waved to me.

Just then the street lamps came on, all together, and they made the stars that were beginning to glimmer in the night sky paler still. I felt my eyes getting tired, what with the lights and all the movement I'd been watching in the street. There were little pools of brightness under the lamps, and now and then a streetcar passed, lighting up a girl's hair, or a smile, or a silver bangle.

Soon after this, as the streetcars became fewer and the sky showed velvety black above the trees and lamps, the street grew emptier, almost **imperceptibly**③, until a time came when there was nobody to be seen and a cat, the first of the evening, crossed, unhurrying, the deserted street.

It struck me that I'd better see about some dinner. I had been leaning so long on the back of my chair, looking down, that my neck hurt when I straightened myself up. I went down, bought some bread and spaghetti, did my cooking, and ate my meal standing. I'd intended to smoke another cigarette at my window, but the night had turned rather chilly and

---

① 抽泣、呜咽。
② 大量涌出。
③ 察觉不出地。

I decided against it. As I was coming back, after shutting the window, I glanced at the mirror and saw reflected in it a corner of my table with my spirit lamp and some bits of bread beside it. It occurred to me that somehow I'd got through another Sunday, that Mother now was buried, and tomorrow I'd be going back to work as usual. Really, nothing in my life had changed.

Ⅲ

I HAD a busy morning in the office. My employer was in a good humor. He even inquired if I wasn't too tired, and followed it up by asking what Mother's age was. I thought a bit, then answered, "Round about sixty," as I didn't want to make a blunder. At which he looked relieved—why, I can't imagine—and seemed to think that closed the matter.

There was a pile of bills of lading waiting on my desk, and I had to go through them all. Before leaving for lunch I washed my hands. I always enjoyed doing this at midday. In the evening it was less pleasant, as the roller towel, after being used by so many people, was sopping wet. I once brought this to my employer's notice. It was regrettable, he agreed—but, to his mind, a mere detail. I left the office building a little later than usual, at half-past twelve, with Emmanuel, who works in the Forwarding Department. Our building overlooks the sea, and we paused for a moment on the steps to look at the shipping in the harbor. The sun was scorching hot. Just then a big truck came up, with a din of chains and backfires from the engine, and Emmanuel suggested we should try to jump it. I started to run. The truck was well away, and we had to chase it for quite a distance. What with the heat and the noise from the engine, I felt half **dazed**①. All I was conscious of was our mad rush along the water front, amongst cranes and winches, with dark hulls of ships alongside and masts swaying in the offing. I was the first to catch up with the truck. I took a flying jump, landed safely, and helped Emmanuel to scramble in beside me. We were both of us out of breath, and the bumps of the truck on the roughly laid cobbles made things worse. Emmanuel chuckled, and panted in my ear, "We've made it!"

By the time we reached Céleste's restaurant we were dripping with sweat. Céleste was at his usual place beside the entrance, with his apron bulging on his paunch, his white mustache well to the fore. When he saw me he was sympathetic and "hoped I wasn't feeling too badly." I said, "No," but I was extremely hungry. I ate very quickly and had some coffee to finish up. Then I went to my place and took a short nap, as I'd drunk a

① 茫然的,神志不清的。

glass of wine too many.

When I woke I smoked a cigarette before getting off my bed. I was a bit late and had to run for the streetcar. The office was stifling, and I was kept hard at it all the afternoon. So it came as a relief when we closed down and I was strolling slowly along the wharves in the coolness. The sky was green, and it was pleasant to be out-of-doors after the stuffy office. However, I went straight home, as I had to put some potatoes on to boil.

The hall was dark and, when I was starting up the stairs, I almost bumped into old Salamano, who lived on the same floor as I. As usual, he had his dog with him. For eight years the two had been inseparable. Salamano's spaniel is an ugly brute, afflicted with some skin disease—mange, I suspect; anyhow, it has lost all its hair and its body is covered with brown scabs. Perhaps through living in one small room, cooped up with his dog, Salamano has come to resemble it. His towy hair has gone very thin, and he has reddish **blotches**① on his face. And the dog has developed something of its master's queer hunched-up **gait**②; it always has its **muzzle**③ stretched far forward and its nose to the ground. But, oddly enough, though so much alike, they **detest**④ each other.

Twice a day, at eleven and six, the old fellow takes his dog for a walk, and for eight years that walk has never varied. You can see them in the rue de Lyon, the dog pulling his master along as hard as he can, till finally the old chap misses a step and nearly falls. Then he beats his dog and calls it names. The dog cowers and lags behind, and it's his master's turn to drag him along. Presently the dog forgets, starts tugging at the **leash**⑤ again, gets another hiding and more abuse. Then they halt on the pavement, the pair of them, and glare at each other; the dog with terror and the man with hatred in his eyes. Every time they're out, this happens. When the dog wants to stop at a lamppost, the old boy won't let him, and drags him on, and the wretched spaniel leaves behind him a trail of little drops. But, if he does it in the room, it means another hiding.

It's been going on like this for eight years, and Céleste always says it's a "crying shame," and something should be done about it; but really one can't be sure. When I met him in the hall, Salamano was bawling at his dog, calling him a bastard, a lousy mon-

---

① 斑点。
② 步态。
③ 口鼻。
④ 厌恶。
⑤ 拴狗绳。

grel, and so forth, and the dog was whining. I said, "Good evening," but the old fellow took no notice and went on cursing. So I thought I'd ask him what the dog had done. Again, he didn't answer, but went on shouting, "You bloody cur!" and the rest of it. I couldn't see very clearly, but he seemed to be fixing something on the dog's collar. I raised my voice a little. Without looking round, he mumbled in a sort of suppressed fury: "He's always in the way, blast him!" Then he started up the stairs, but the dog tried to resist and flattened itself out on the floor, so he had to haul it up on the leash, step by step.

Just then another man who lives on my floor came in from the street. The general idea hereabouts is that he's a pimp. But if you ask him what his job is, he says he's a warehouseman. One thing's sure: he isn't popular in our street. Still, he often has a word for me, and drops in sometimes for a short talk in my room, because I listen to him. As a matter of fact, I find what he says quite interesting. So, really I've no reason for freezing him off. His name is Sintès; Raymond Sintès. He's short and thick-set, has a nose like a boxer's, and always dresses very sprucely. He, too, once said to me, referring to Salamano, that it was "a damned shame," and asked me if I wasn't disgusted by the way the old man served his dog. I answered: "No."

We went up the stairs together, Sintès and I, and when I was turning in at my door, he said:

"Look here! How about having some grub with me? I've a black pudding and some wine."

It struck me that this would save my having to cook my dinner, so I said, "Thanks very much."

He, too, has only one room, and a little kitchen without a window. I saw a pink-and-white plaster angel above his bed, and some photos of sporting champions and naked girls pinned to the opposite wall. The bed hadn't been made and the room was dirty. He began by lighting a paraffin lamp; then fumbled in his pocket and produced a rather grimy bandage, which he wrapped round his right hand. I asked him what the trouble was. He told me he'd been having a roughhouse with a fellow who'd annoyed him.

"I'm not one who looks for trouble," he explained, "only I'm a bit short-tempered. That fellow said to me, challenging-like, 'Come down off that streetcar, if you're a man.' I says, 'You keep quiet, I ain't done nothing to you.' Then he said I hadn't any guts. Well, that settled it. I got down off the streetcar and I said to him, 'You better keep your mouth shut, or I'll shut it for you.' 'I'd like to see you try!' says he. Then I gave him one across the face, and laid him out good and proper. After a bit I started to help him get up, but all he did was to kick at me from where he lay. So I gave him one with my knee and a couple more swipes. He was bleeding like a pig when I'd done with him. I asked him if he'd had enough, and he said, 'Yes.'"

Sintès was busy fixing his bandage while he talked, and I was sitting on the bed.

"So you see," he said, "it wasn't my fault; he was asking for it, wasn't he?"

I nodded, and he added:

"As a matter of fact, I rather want to ask your advice about something; it's connected with this business. You've knocked about the world a bit, and I daresay you can help me. And then I'll be your pal for life; I never forget anyone who does me a good turn."

When I made no comment, he asked me if I'd like us to be pals. I replied that I had no objection, and that appeared to satisfy him. He got out the black pudding, cooked it in a frying pan, then laid the table, putting out two bottles of wine. While he was doing this he didn't speak.

We started dinner, and then he began telling me the whole story, hesitating a bit at first.

"There's a girl behind it—as usual. We slept together pretty regular. I was keeping her, as a matter of fact, and she cost me a tidy sum. That fellow I knocked down is her brother."

Noticing that I said nothing, he added that he knew what the neighbors said about him, but it was a filthy lie. He had his principles like everybody else, and a job in a warehouse.

"Well," he said, "to go on with my story ... I found out one day that she was letting me down." He gave her enough money to keep her going, without extravagance, though; he paid the rent of her room and twenty francs a day for food. "Three hundred francs for rent, and six hundred for her grub, with a little present thrown in now and then, a pair of stockings or whatnot. Say, a thousand francs a month. But that wasn't enough for my fine lady; she was always grumbling that she couldn't make both ends meet with what I gave her. So one day I says to her, 'Look here, why not get a job for a few hours a day? That'd make things easier for me, too. I bought you a new dress this month, I pay your rent and give you twenty francs a day. But you go and waste your money at the café with a pack of girls. You give them coffee and sugar. And, of course, the money comes out of my pocket. I treat you on the square, and that's how you pay me back.' But she wouldn't hear of working, though she kept on saying she couldn't make do with what I gave her. And then one day I found out she was doing me dirt."

He went on to explain that he'd found a lottery ticket in her bag, and, when he asked where the money'd come from to buy it, she wouldn't tell him. Then, another time, he'd found a pawn ticket for two bracelets that he'd never set eyes on.

"So I knew there was dirty work going on, and I told her I'd have nothing more to do with her. But, first, I gave her a good hiding, and I told her some home truths. I said that there was only one thing interested her and that was getting into bed with men whenever she'd the chance. And I warned her straight, 'You'll be sorry one day, my girl, and wish you'd got me back. All the girls in the street, they're jealous of your luck in having me to keep you.' "

He'd beaten her till the blood came. Before that he'd never beaten her. "Well, not hard, anyhow; only affectionately-like. She'd howl a bit, and I had to shut the window. Then, of course, it ended as per usual. But this time I'm done with her. Only, to my mind, I ain't punished her enough. See what I mean?"

He explained that it was about this he wanted my advice. The lamp was smoking, and he stopped pacing up and down the room, to lower the wick. I just listened, without speaking. I'd had a whole bottle of wine to myself and my head was buzzing. As I'd used up my cigarettes I was smoking Raymond's. Some late streetcars passed, and the last noises of the street died off with them. Raymond went on talking. What bored him was that he had "a sort of lech on her" as he called it. But he was quite determined to teach her a lesson.

His first idea, he said, had been to take her to a hotel, and then call in the special police. He'd persuade them to put her on the register as a "common prostitute," and that would make her wild. Then he'd looked up some friends of his in the underworld, fellows who kept tarts for what they could make out of them, but they had practically nothing to suggest. Still, as he pointed out, that sort of thing should have been right up their street; what's the good of being in that line if you don't know how to treat a girl who's let you down? When he told them that, they suggested he should "brand" her. But that wasn't what he wanted, either. It would need a lot of thinking out. ... But, first, he'd like to ask me something. Before he asked it, though, he'd like to have my opinion of the story he'd been telling, in a general way.

I said I hadn't any, but I'd found it interesting.

Did I think she really had done him dirt?

I had to admit it looked like that. Then he asked me if I didn't think she should be punished and what I'd do if I were in his shoes. I told him one could never be quite sure how to act in such cases, but I quite understood his wanting her to suffer for it.

I drank some more wine, while Raymond lit another cigarette and began explaining what he proposed to do. He wanted to write her a letter, "a real stinker, that'll get her on the raw," and at the same time make her repent of what she'd done. Then, when she came back, he'd go to bed with her and, just when she was "properly primed up," he'd spit in her face and throw her out of the room. I agreed it wasn't a bad plan; it would punish her, all right.

But, Raymond told me, he didn't feel up to writing the kind of letter that was needed, and that was where I could help. When I didn't say anything, he asked me if I'd mind doing it right away, and I said, "No," I'd have a shot at it.

He drank off a glass of wine and stood up. Then he pushed aside the plates and the bit of cold pudding that was left, to make room on the table. After carefully wiping the oilcloth, he got a sheet of squared paper from the drawer of his bedside table; after that, an envelope, a small red wooden penholder, and a square inkpot with purple ink in it. The moment he mentioned the girl's name I knew she was a **Moor**①.

I wrote the letter. I didn't take much trouble over it, but I wanted to satisfy Raymond, as I'd no reason not to satisfy him. Then I read out what I'd written. Puffing at his cigarette, he listened, nodding now and then. "Read it again, please," he said. He seemed delighted. "That's the stuff," he chuckled. "I could tell you was a brainy sort, old boy, and you know what's what."

At first I hardly noticed that "old boy." It came back to me when he slapped me on the shoulder and said, "So now we're pals, ain't we?" I kept silence and he said it again. I didn't care one way or the other, but as he seemed so set on it, I nodded and said, "Yes."

He put the letter into the envelope and we finished off the wine. Then both of us smoked for some minutes, without speaking. The street was quite quiet, except when now and again a car passed. Finally, I remarked that it was getting late, and Raymond agreed. "Time's gone mighty fast this evening," he added, and in a way that was true. I wanted

---

① 摩尔人(居住在非洲西北部的穆斯林)。

to be in bed, only it was such an effort making a move. I must have looked tired, for Raymond said to me, "You mustn't let things get you down." At first I didn't catch his meaning. Then he explained that he had heard of my mother's death; anyhow, he said, that was something bound to happen one day or another. I appreciated that, and told him so.

When I rose, Raymond shook hands very warmly, remarking that men always understood each other. After closing the door behind me I lingered for some moments on the landing. The whole building was as quiet as the grave, a dank, dark smell rising from the well hole of the stairs. I could hear nothing but the blood throbbing in my ears, and for a while I stood still, listening to it. Then the dog began to moan in old Salamano's room, and through the sleep-bound house the little plaintive sound rose slowly, like a flower growing out of the silence and the darkness.

Ⅳ

I HAD a busy time in the office throughout the week. Raymond dropped in once to tell me he'd sent off the letter. I went to the pictures twice with Emmanuel, who doesn't always understand what's happening on the screen and asks me to explain it. Yesterday was Saturday, and Marie came as we'd arranged. She had a very pretty dress, with red and white stripes, and leather sandals, and I couldn't take my eyes off her. One could see the outline of her firm little breasts, and her sun-tanned face was like a velvety brown flower. We took the bus and went to a beach I know, some miles out of Algiers. It's just a strip of sand between two rocky spurs, with a line of rushes at the back, along the tide line. At four o'clock the sun wasn't too hot, but the water was pleasantly **tepid**①, and small, **languid**② ripples were creeping up the sand.

Marie taught me a new game. The idea was, while one swam, to suck in the spray off the waves and, when one's mouth was full of foam, to lie on one's back and spout it out against the sky. It made a sort of **frothy**③ **haze**④ that melted into the air or fell back in a warm shower on one's cheeks. But very soon my mouth was smarting with all the salt I'd drawn in; then Marie came up and hugged me in the water, and pressed her mouth to

① 不冷不热的,温吞的。
② 慵懒的,慢悠悠的。
③ 有泡沫的。
④ 烟雾。

mine. Her tongue cooled my lips, and we let the waves roll us about for a minute or two before swimming back to the beach.

When we had finished dressing, Marie looked hard at me. Her eyes were sparkling. I kissed her; after that neither of us spoke for quite a while. I pressed her to my side as we scrambled up the foreshore. Both of us were in a hurry to catch the bus, get back to my place, and tumble on to the bed. I'd left my window open, and it was pleasant to feel the cool night air flowing over our sunburned bodies.

Marie said she was free next morning, so I proposed she should have luncheon with me. She agreed, and I went down to buy some meat. On my way back I heard a woman's voice in Raymond's room. A little later old Salamano started **grumbling**① at his dog and presently there was a sound of boots and paws on the wooden stairs; then, "**Filthy**② brute! Get on, you cur!" and the two of them went out into the street. I told Marie about the old man's habits, and it made her laugh. She was wearing one of my pajama suits, and had the sleeves rolled up. When she laughed I wanted her again. A moment later she asked me if I loved her. I said that sort of question had no meaning, really; but I supposed I didn't. She looked sad for a bit, but when we were getting our lunch ready she brightened up and started laughing, and when she laughs I always want to kiss her. It was just then that the row started in Raymond's room.

First we heard a woman saying something in a high-pitched voice; then Raymond **bawling**③ at her, "You let me down, you bitch! I'll learn you to let me down!" There came some thuds, then a piercing scream—it made one's blood run cold—and in a moment there was a crowd of people on the landing. Marie and I went out to see. The woman was still screaming and Raymond still knocking her about. Marie said, wasn't it horrible! I didn't answer anything. Then she asked me to go and fetch a policeman, but I told her I didn't like policemen. However, one turned up presently; the lodger on the second floor, a plumber, came up, with him. When he banged on the door the noise stopped inside the room. He knocked again, and, after a moment, the woman started crying, and Raymond opened the door. He had a cigarette dangling from his underlip and a rather sickly smile.

"Your name?" Raymond gave his name. "Take that cigarette out of your mouth when you're talking to me," the policeman said gruffly. Raymond hesitated, glanced at me, and

---

① 嘟囔,发牢骚。

② 肮脏的,下流的。

③ 怒吼。

kept the cigarette in his mouth. The policeman promptly swung his arm and gave him a good hard **smack**① on the left cheek. The cigarette shot from his lips and dropped a yard away. Raymond made a **wry**② face, but said nothing for a moment. Then in a humble tone he asked if he mightn't pick up his cigarette.

The officer said, "Yes," and added: "But don't you forget next time that we don't stand for any nonsense, not from guys like you."

Meanwhile the girl went on sobbing and repeating: "He hit me, the coward. He's a **pimp**③."

"Excuse me, officer," Raymond put in, "but is that in order, calling a man a pimp in the presence of witnesses?"

The policeman told him to shut his trap.

Raymond then turned to the girl. "Don't you worry, my pet. We'll meet again."

"That's enough," the policeman said, and told the girl to go away. Raymond was to stay in his room till summoned to the police station. "You ought to be ashamed of yourself," the policeman added, "getting so tight you can't stand steady. Why, you're shaking all over!"

"I'm not tight," Raymond explained. "Only when I see you standing there and looking at me, I can't help trembling. That's only natural."

Then he closed his door, and we all went away. Marie and I finished getting our lunch ready. But she hadn't any appetite, and I ate nearly all. She left at one, and then I had a nap.

Toward three there was a knock at my door and Raymond came in. He sat down on the edge of my bed and for a minute or two said nothing. I asked him how it had gone off. He said it had all gone quite smoothly at first, as per program; only then she'd **slapped**④ his face and he'd seen red, and started **thrashing**⑤ her. As for what happened after that, he needn't tell me, as I was there.

"Well," I said, "you taught her a lesson, all right, and that's what you wanted, isn't it?"

---

① 打巴掌，掴。

② 挖苦的，揶揄的。

③ 皮条客。

④ 打，掴。

⑤ 连续击打。

He agreed, and pointed out that whatever the police did, that wouldn't change the fact she'd had her punishment. As for the police, he knew exactly how to handle them. But he'd like to know if I'd expected him to return the blow when the policeman hit him.

I told him I hadn't expected anything whatsoever and, anyhow, I had no use for the police. Raymond seemed pleased and asked if I'd like to come out for a stroll with him. I got up from the bed and started brushing my hair. Then Raymond said that what he really wanted was for me to act as his witness. I told him I had no objection; only I didn't know what he expected me to say.

"It's quite simple," he replied. "You've only got to tell them that the girl had let me down."

So I agreed to be his witness.

We went out together, and Raymond stood me a brandy in a café. Then we had a game of billiards; it was a close game and I lost by only a few points. After that he proposed going to a brothel, but I refused; I didn't feel like it. As we were walking slowly back he told me how pleased he was at having paid out his mistress so satisfactorily. He made himself extremely amiable to me, and I quite enjoyed our walk.

When we were nearly home I saw old Salamano on the doorstep; he seemed very excited. I noticed that his dog wasn't with him. He was turning like a teetotum, looking in all directions, and sometimes peering into the darkness of the hall with his little bloodshot eyes. Then he'd mutter something to himself and start gazing up and down the street again.

Raymond asked him what was wrong, but he didn't answer at once. Then I heard him grunt, "The bastard! The filthy cur!" When I asked him where his dog was, he scowled at me and snapped out, "Gone!" A moment later, all of a sudden, he launched out into it.

"I'd taken him to the Parade Ground as usual. There was a fair on, and you could hardly move for the crowd. I stopped at one of the booths to look at the Handcuff King. When I turned to go, the dog was gone. I'd been meaning to get a smaller collar, but I never thought the brute could slip it and get away like that."

Raymond assured him the dog would find its way home, and told him stories of dogs that had traveled miles and miles to get back to their masters. But this seemed to make the old fellow even more worried than before.

"Don't you understand, they'll do away with him; the police, I mean. It's not likely anyone will take him in and look after him; with all those scabs he puts everybody off."

I told him that there was a pound at the police station, where stray dogs are taken. His dog was certain to be there and he could get it back on payment of a small charge. He asked me how much the charge was, but there I couldn't help him. Then he flew into a rage again.

"Is it likely I'd give money for a mutt like that? No damned fear! They can kill him, for all I care." And he went on calling his dog the usual names.

Raymond gave a laugh and turned into the hall. I followed him upstairs, and we parted on the landing. A minute or two later I heard Salamano's footsteps and a knock on my door.

When I opened it, he halted for a moment in the doorway.

"Excuse me ... I hope I'm not disturbing you."

I asked him in, but he shook his head. He was staring at his toe caps, and the gnarled old hands were trembling. Without meeting my eyes, he started talking.

"They won't really take him from me, will they, Monsieur Meursault? Surely they wouldn't do a thing like that. If they do—I don't know what will become of me."

I told him that, so far as I knew, they kept stray dogs in the pound for three days, waiting for their owners to call for them. After that they disposed of the dogs as they thought fit.

He stared at me in silence for a moment, then said, "Good evening." After that I heard him pacing up and down his room for quite a while. Then his bed creaked. Through the wall there came to me a little wheezing sound, and I guessed that he was weeping. For some reason, I don't know what, I began thinking of Mother. But I had to get up early next day; so, as I wasn't feeling hungry, I did without supper, and went straight to bed.

V

RAYMOND rang me up at the office. He said that a friend of his—to whom he'd spoken about me—invited me to spend next Sunday at his little seaside **bungalow**① just outside Algiers. I told him I'd have been delighted; only I had promised to spend Sunday with a girl. Raymond promptly replied that she could come, too. In fact, his friend's wife would be very pleased not to be the only woman in a party of men.

I'd have liked to hang up at once, as my employer doesn't approve of my using the office phone for private calls. But Raymond asked me to hold on; he had something else to

① 平房,独座房屋。

tell me, and that was why he'd rung me up, though he could have waited till the evening to pass on the invitation.

"It's like this," he said. "I've been shadowed all the morning by some Arabs. One of them's the brother of that girl I had the row with. If you see him hanging round the house when you come back, pass me the word."

I promised to do so.

Just then my employer sent for me. For a moment I felt uneasy, as I expected he was going to tell me to stick to my work and not waste time chattering with friends over the phone. However, it was nothing of the kind. He wanted to discuss a project he had in view, though so far he'd come to no decision. It was to open a branch at Paris, so as to be able to deal with the big companies on the spot, without postal delays, and he wanted to know if I'd like a post there.

"You're a young man," he said, "and I'm pretty sure you'd enjoy living in Paris. And, of course, you could travel about France for some months in the year."

I told him I was quite prepared to go; but really I didn't care much one way or the other.

He then asked if a "change of life," as he called it, didn't appeal to me, and I answered that one never changed his way of life; one life was as good as another, and my present one suited me quite well.

At this he looked rather hurt, and told me that I always **shilly-shallied**①, and that I lacked ambition—a grave defect, to his mind, when one was in business.

I returned to my work. I'd have preferred not to vex him, but I saw no reason for "changing my life." By and large it wasn't an unpleasant one. As a student I'd had plenty of ambition of the kind he meant. But, when I had to drop my studies, I very soon realized all that was pretty futile.

Marie came that evening and asked me if I'd marry her. I said I didn't mind; if she was keen on it, we'd get married.

Then she asked me again if I loved her. I replied, much as before, that her question meant nothing or next to nothing—but I supposed I didn't.

"If that's how you feel," she said, "why marry me?"

I explained that it had no importance really, but, if it would give her pleasure, we

---

① 优郁、踌躇。

could get married right away. I pointed out that, anyhow, the suggestion came from her; as for me, I'd merely said, "Yes."

Then she remarked that marriage was a serious matter.

To which I answered: "No."

She kept silent after that, staring at me in a curious way. Then she asked:

"Suppose another girl had asked you to marry her—I mean, a girl you liked in the same way as you like me—would you have said 'Yes' to her, too?"

"Naturally."

Then she said she wondered if she really loved me or not. I, of course, couldn't enlighten her as to that. And, after another silence, she murmured something about my being "a queer fellow." "And I daresay that's why I love you," she added. "But maybe that's why one day I'll come to hate you."

To which I had nothing to say, so I said nothing.

She thought for a bit, then started smiling and, taking my arm, repeated that she was in earnest; she really wanted to marry me.

"All right," I answered. "We'll get married whenever you like." I then mentioned the proposal made by my employer, and Marie said she'd love to go to Paris.

When I told her I'd lived in Paris for a while, she asked me what it was like.

"A dingy sort of town, to my mind. Masses of pigeons and dark courtyards. And the people have washed-out, white faces."

Then we went for a walk all the way across the town by the main streets. The women were good-lookers, and I asked Marie if she, too, noticed this. She said, "Yes," and that she saw what I meant. After that we said nothing for some minutes. However, as I didn't want her to leave me, I suggested we should dine together at Céleste's. She'd have loved to dine with me, she said, only she was booked up for the evening. We were near my place, and I said, "Au revoir, then."

She looked me in the eyes.

"Don't you want to know what I'm doing this evening?"

I did want to know, but I hadn't thought of asking her, and I guessed she was making a grievance of it. I must have looked embarrassed, for suddenly she started laughing and bent toward me, pouting her lips for a kiss.

I went by myself to Céleste's. When I had just started my dinner an odd-looking little woman came in and asked if she might sit at my table. Of course she might. She had a chubby face like a ripe apple, bright eyes, and moved in a curiously jerky way, as if she were on wires. After taking off her closefitting jacket she sat down and started studying the bill of fare with a sort of rapt attention. Then she called Céleste and gave her order, very fast but quite distinctly; one didn't lose a word. While waiting for the hors d'oeuvre she opened her bag, took out a slip of paper and a pencil, and added up the bill in advance. Diving into her bag again, she produced a purse and took from it the exact sum, plus a small tip, and placed it on the cloth in front of her.

Just then the waiter brought the hors d'oeuvre, which she proceeded to wolf down voraciously. While waiting for the next course, she produced another pencil, this time a blue one, from her bag, and the radio magazine for the coming week, and started making ticks against almost all the items of the daily programs. There were a dozen pages in the magazine, and she continued studying them closely throughout the meal. When I'd finished mine she was still ticking off items with the same meticulous attention. Then she rose, put on her jacket again with the same abrupt, robot-like gestures, and walked briskly out of the restaurant.

Having nothing better to do, I followed her for a short distance. Keeping on the curb of the pavement, she walked straight ahead, never swerving or looking back, and it was extraordinary how fast she covered the ground, considering her smallness. In fact, the pace was too much for me, and I soon lost sight of her and turned back homeward. For a moment the "little robot" (as I thought of her) had much impressed me, but I soon forgot about her.

As I was turning in at my door I ran into old Salamano. I asked him into my room, and he informed me that his dog was definitely lost. He'd been to the pound to inquire, but it wasn't there, and the staff told him it had probably been run over. When he asked them whether it was any use inquiring about it at the police station, they said the police had more important things to attend to than keeping records of stray dogs run over in the streets. I suggested he should get another dog, but, reasonably enough, he pointed out that he'd become used to this one, and it wouldn't be the same thing.

I was seated on my bed, with my legs up, and Salamano on a chair beside the table, facing me, his hands spread on his knees. He had kept on his battered felt hat and was mumbling away behind his draggled yellowish mustache. I found him rather boring, but I had nothing to do and didn't feel sleepy. So, to keep the conversation going, I asked some questions about his dog—how long he had had it and so forth. He told me he had got it soon after his wife's death. He'd married rather late in life. When a young man, he wanted to go on the stage; during his military service he'd often played in the regimental theatricals and acted rather well, so everybody said. However, finally, he had taken a job in the railway, and he didn't regret it, as now he had a small **pension**①. He and his wife had never hit it off very well, but they'd got used to each other, and when she died he felt lonely. One of his mates on the railway whose bitch had just had pups had offered him one, and he had taken it, as a companion. He'd had to feed it from the bottle at first. But, as a dog's life is shorter than a man's, they'd grown old together, so to speak.

"He was a cantankerous brute," Salamano said. "Now and then we had some proper set-tos, he and I. But he was a good mutt all the same."

I said he looked well bred, and that evidently pleased the old man.

"Ah, but you should have seen him before his illness!" he said. "He had a wonderful coat; in fact, that was his best point, really. I tried hard to cure him; every mortal night after he got that skin disease I rubbed an ointment in. But his real trouble was old age, and there's no curing that."

Just then I yawned, and the old man said he'd better make a move. I told him he could stay, and that I was sorry about what had happened to his dog. He thanked me, and mentioned that my mother had been very fond of his dog. He referred to her as "your poor mother," and was afraid I must be feeling her death terribly. When I said nothing he added hastily and with a rather embarrassed air that some of the people in the street said nasty things about me because I'd sent my mother to the Home. But he, of course, knew better; he knew how devoted to my mother I had always been.

I answered—why, I still don't know—that it surprised me to learn I'd produced such a bad impression. As I couldn't afford to keep her here, it seemed the obvious thing to do, to send her to a home. "In any case," I added, "for years she'd never had a word to say to me, and I could see she was moping, with no one to talk to."

"Yes," he said, "and at a home one makes friends, anyhow."

He got up, saying it was high time for him to be in bed, and added that life was going to be a bit of a problem for him, under the new conditions. For the first time since I'd known him he held out his hand to me—rather shyly, I thought—and I could feel the scales on his skin. Just as he was going out of the door, he turned and, smiling a little,

① 退休金。

said:

"Let's hope the dogs won't bark again tonight. I always think it's mine I hear..."

Ⅵ

IT was an effort waking up that Sunday morning; Marie had to jog my shoulders and shout my name. As we wanted to get into the water early, we didn't trouble about breakfast. My head was aching slightly and my first cigarette had a bitter taste. Marie told me I looked like a mourner at a funeral, and I certainly did feel very **limp**①. She was wearing a white dress and had her hair loose. I told her she looked quite **ravishing**② like that, and she laughed happily.

On our way out we banged on Raymond's door, and he shouted that he'd be with us in a **jiffy**③. We went down to the street and, because of my being rather under the weather and our having kept the blind down in my room, the glare of the morning sun hit me in the eyes like a clenched fist.

Marie, however, was almost dancing with delight, and kept repeating, "What a heavenly day!" After a few minutes I was feeling better, and noticed that I was hungry. I mentioned this to Marie, but she paid no attention. She was carrying an oilcloth bag in which she had stowed our bathing kit and a towel. Presently we heard Raymond shutting his door. He was wearing blue trousers, a short-sleeved white shirt, and a straw hat. I noticed that his forearms were rather hairy, but the skin was very white beneath. The straw hat made Marie giggle. Personally, I was rather put off by his getup. He seemed in high spirits and was whistling as he came down the stairs. He greeted me with, "Hello, old boy!" and addressed Marie as "Mademoiselle."

On the previous evening we had visited the police station, where I gave evidence for Raymond—about the girl's having been false to him. So they let him off with a warning. They didn't check my statement.

After some talk on the doorstep we decided to take the bus. The beach was within easy walking distance, but the sooner we got there the better. Just as we were starting for the bus stop, Raymond plucked my sleeve and told me to look across the street. I saw some Arabs lounging against the tobacconist's window. They were staring at us silently, in the

---

① 无力的,无生气的。

② 非常美丽的。

③ 瞬间。

special way these people have—as if we were blocks of stone or dead trees. Raymond whispered that the second Arab from the left was "his man," and I thought he looked rather worried However, he assured me that all that was ancient history. Marie, who hadn't followed his remarks, asked, "What is it?"

I explained that those Arabs across the way had a grudge against Raymond. She insisted on our going at once. Then Raymond laughed, and squared his shoulders. The young lady was quite right, he said. There was no point in hanging about here. Halfway to the bus stop he glanced back over his shoulder and said the Arabs weren't following. I, too, looked back. They were exactly as before, gazing in the same vague way at the spot where we had been.

When we were in the bus, Raymond, who now seemed quite at ease, kept making jokes to amuse Marie. I could see he was attracted by her, but she had hardly a word for him. Now and again she would catch my eye and smile.

We alighted just outside Algiers. The beach is not far from the bus stop; one has only to cross a patch of highland, a sort of **plateau**①, which overlooks the sea and shelves down steeply to the sands. The ground here was covered with yellowish pebbles and wild lilies that showed snow-white against the blue of the sky, which had already the hard, metallic **glint**② it gets on very hot days. Marie amused herself swishing her bag against the flowers and sending the petals showering in all directions. Then we walked between two rows of little houses with wooden balconies and green or white **palings**③. Some of them were half hidden in clumps of **tamarisks**④; others rose naked from the stony plateau. Before we came to the end of it, the sea was in full view; it lay smooth as a mirror, and in the distance a big headland jutted out over its black reflection. Through the still air came the faint buzz of a motor engine and we saw a fishing boat very far out, gliding almost imperceptibly across the dazzling smoothness.

Marie picked some rock irises. Going down the steep path leading to the sea, we saw some bathers already on the sands.

Raymond's friend owned a small wooden bungalow at the near end of the beach. Its back rested against the cliffside, while the front stood on piles, which the water was already

① 小高原。
② 闪亮。
③ 尖木桩,围栏。
④ (多见于地中海地区的)怪柳。

lapping. Raymond introduced us to his friend, whose name was Masson. He was tall, broad-shouldered, and thick-set; his wife was a plump, cheerful little woman who spoke with a Paris accent.

Masson promptly told us to make ourselves at home. He had gone out fishing, he said, first thing in the morning, and there would be fried fish for lunch. I congratulated him on his little bungalow, and he said he always spent his week ends and holidays here. "With the missus, needless to say," he added. I glanced at her, and noticed that she and Marie seemed to be getting on well together; laughing and chattering away. For the first time, perhaps, I seriously considered the possibility of my marrying her.

Masson wanted to have a swim at once, but his wife and Raymond were disinclined to move. So only the three of us, Marie, Masson, and myself, went down to the beach. Marie promptly plunged in, but Masson and I waited for a bit. He was rather slow of speech and had, I noticed, a habit of saying "and what's more" between his phrases—even when the second added nothing really to the first. Talking of Marie, he said: "She's an awfully pretty girl, and what's more, charming."

But I soon ceased paying attention to this trick of his; I was basking in the sunlight, which, I noticed, was making me feel much better. The sand was beginning to stoke up underfoot and, though I was eager for a **dip**①, I postponed it for a minute or two more. At last I said to Masson: "Shall we go in now?" and plunged. Masson walked in gingerly and only began to swim when he was out of his depth. He swam hand over hand and made slow headway, so I left him behind and caught up with Marie. The water was cold and I felt all the better for it. We swam a long way out, Marie and I, side by side, and it was pleasant feeling how our movements matched, hers and mine, and how we were both in the same mood, enjoying every moment.

Once we were out in the open, we lay on our backs and, as I gazed up at the sky, I could feel the sun drawing up the film of salt water on my lips and cheeks. We saw Masson swim back to the beach and slump down on the sand under the sun. In the distance he looked enormous, like a stranded whale. Then Marie proposed that we should swim tandem. She went ahead and I put my arms round her waist, from behind, and while she drew me forward with her arm strokes, I kicked out behind to help us on.

That sound of little splashes had been in my ears for so long that I began to feel I'd

① 游泳、泡水。

had enough of it. So I let go of Marie and swam back at an easy pace, taking long, deep breaths. When I made the beach I stretched myself belly downward beside Masson, resting my face on the sand. I told him "it was fine" here, and he agreed. Presently Marie came back. I raised my head to watch her approach. She was glistening with brine and holding her hair back. Then she lay down beside me, and what with the combined warmth of our bodies and the sun, I felt myself dropping off to sleep.

After a while Marie tugged my arm. and said Masson had gone to his place; it must be nearly lunchtime. I rose at once, as I was feeling hungry, but Marie told me I hadn't kissed her once since the early morning. That was so—though I'd wanted to, several times. "Let's go into the water again," she said, and we ran into the sea and lay flat amongst the ripples for a moment. Then we swam a few strokes, and when we were almost out of our depth she flung her arms round me and hugged me. I felt her legs twining round mine, and my senses tingled.

When we got back, Masson was on the steps of his bungalow, shouting to us to come. I told him I was ravenously hungry, and he promptly turned to his wife and said he'd taken quite a fancy to me. The bread was excellent, and I had my full share of the fish. Then came some steak and potato chips. None of us spoke while eating. Masson drank a lot of wine and kept refilling my glass the moment it was empty. By the time coffee was handed round I was feeling slightly muzzy, and I started smoking one cigarette after another. Masson, Raymond, and I discussed a plan of spending the whole of August on the beach together, sharing expenses.

Suddenly Marie exclaimed: "I say! Do you know the time? It's only half-past eleven!"

We were all surprised at that, and Masson remarked that we'd had a very early lunch, but really lunch was a movable feast, you had it when you felt like it.

This set Marie laughing, I don't know why. I suspect she'd drunk a bit too much.

Then Masson asked if I'd like to come with him for a stroll on the beach.

"My wife always has a nap after lunch," he said. "Personally I find it doesn't agree with me; what I need is a short walk. I'm always telling her it's much better for the health. But, of course, she's entitled to her own opinion."

Marie proposed to stay and help with the washing up. Mme Masson smiled and said that, in that case, the first thing was to get the men out of the way. So we went out together, the three of us.

The light was almost **vertical**① and the glare from the water **seared**② one's eyes. The beach was quite deserted now. One could hear a faint **tinkle**③ of knives and forks and **crockery**④ in the shacks and bungalows lining the foreshore. Heat was welling up from the rocks, and one could hardly breathe.

At first Raymond and Masson talked of things and people I didn't know. I gathered that they'd been acquainted for some time and had even lived together for a while. We went down to the water's edge and walked along it; now and then a longer wave wet our canvas shoes. I wasn't thinking of anything, as all that sunlight beating down on my bare head made me feel half asleep.

Just then Raymond said something to Masson that I didn't quite catch. But at the same moment I noticed two Arabs in blue dungarees a long way down the beach, coming in our direction. I gave Raymond a look and he nodded, saying, "That's him." We walked steadily on. Masson wondered how they'd managed to track us here. My impression was that they had seen us taking the bus and noticed Marie's oilcloth bathing bag; but I didn't say anything.

Though the Arabs walked quite slowly, they were much nearer already. We didn't change our pace, but Raymond said:

"Listen! If there's a **roughhouse**⑤, you, Masson, take on the second one. I'll tackle the fellow who's after me. And you, Meursault, stand by to help if another one comes up, and lay him out."

I said, "Right," and Masson put his hands in his pockets.

The sand was as hot as fire, and I could have sworn it was glowing red. The distance between us and the Arabs was steadily decreasing. When we were only a few steps away the Arabs halted. Masson and I slowed down, while Raymond went straight up to his man. I couldn't hear what he said, but I saw the native lowering his head, as if to butt him in the chest. Raymond lashed out promptly and shouted to Masson to come. Masson went up to the man he had been marking and struck him twice with all his might. The fellow fell flat into the water and stayed there some seconds with bubbles coming up to the surface

---

① 垂直的。
② 烧灼,灼伤。
③ 丁零声,当啷响。
④ 餐具。
⑤ 打斗。

round his head. Meanwhile Raymond had been slogging the other man, whose face was streaming with blood. He glanced at me over his shoulder and shouted:

"Just you watch! I ain't finished with him yet!"

"Look out!" I cried. "He's got a knife."

I spoke too late. The man had gashed Raymond's arm and his mouth as well.

Masson sprang forward. The other Arab got up from the water and placed himself behind the fellow with the knife. We didn't dare to move. The two natives backed away slowly, keeping us at bay with the knife and never taking their eyes off us. When they were at a safe distance they swung round and took to their heels. We stood stock-still, with the sunlight beating down on us. Blood was dripping from Raymond's wounded arm, which he was squeezing hard above the elbow.

Masson remarked that there was a doctor who always spent his Sundays here, and Raymond said: "Good. Let's go to him at once." He could hardly get the words out, as the blood from his other wound made bubbles in his mouth.

We each gave him an arm and helped him back to the bungalow. Once we were there he told us the wounds weren't so very deep and he could walk to where the doctor was. Marie had gone quite pale, and Mme Masson was in tears.

Masson and Raymond went off to the doctor's while I was left behind at the bungalow to explain matters to the women. I didn't much relish the task and soon dried up and started smoking, staring at the sea.

Raymond came back at about half-past one, accompanied by Masson. He had his arm bandaged and a strip of sticking plaster on the corner of his mouth. The doctor had assured him it was nothing serious, but he was looking very glum. Masson tried to make him laugh, but without success.

Presently Raymond said he was going for a stroll on the beach. I asked him where he proposed to go, and he mumbled something about "wanting to take the air." We—Masson and I—then said we'd go with him, but he flew into a rage and told us to mind our own business. Masson said we mustn't insist, seeing the state he was in. However, when he went out, I followed him.

It was like a **furnace**① outside, with the sunlight **splintering**② into flakes of fire on the sand and sea. We walked for quite a while, and I had an idea that Raymond had a def-

① 熔炉。

② 使裂成碎片。

inite idea where he was going; but probably I was mistaken about this.

At the end of the beach we came to a small stream that had cut a channel in the sand, after coming out from behind a biggish rock. There we found our two Arabs again, lying on the sand in their blue **dungarees**①. They looked harmless enough, as if they didn't bear any **malice**②, and neither made any move when we approached. The man who had slashed Raymond stared at him without speaking. The other man was blowing down a little **reed**③ and extracting from it three notes of the scale, which he played over and over again, while he watched us from the corner of an eye.

For a while nobody moved; it was all sunlight and silence except for the tinkle of the stream and those three little lonely sounds. Then Raymond put his hand to his **revolver**④ pocket, but the Arabs still didn't move. I noticed the man playing on the reed had his big toes splayed out almost at right angles to his feet.

Still keeping his eyes on his man, Raymond said to me: "Shall I plug him one?"

I thought quickly. If I told him not to, considering the mood he was in, he might very well fly into a temper and use his gun. So I said the first thing that came into my head.

"He hasn't spoken to you yet. It would be a **lowdown**⑤ trick to shoot him like that, in cold blood."

Again, for some moments one heard nothing but the tinkle of the stream and the flute notes weaving through the hot, still air.

"Well," Raymond said at last, "if that's how you feel, I'd better say something insulting, and if he answers back I'll loose off."

"Right," I said. "Only, if he doesn't get out his knife you've no business to fire."

Raymond was beginning to fidget. The Arab with the reed went on playing, and both of them watched all our movements.

"Listen," I said to Raymond. "You take on the fellow on the right, and give me your revolver. If the other one starts making trouble or gets out his knife, I'll shoot."

The sun glinted on Raymond's revolver as he handed it to me. But nobody made a move yet; it was just as if everything had closed in on us so that we couldn't stir. We

---

① 粗棉布工装裤。

② 恶意。

③ 簧片。

④ 左轮手枪。

⑤ 卑鄙的,下流的。

could only watch each other, never lowering our eyes; the whole world seemed to have come to a standstill on this little strip of sand between the sunlight and the sea, the twofold silence of the reed and stream. And just then it crossed my mind that one might fire, or not fire—and it would come to absolutely the same thing.

Then, all of a sudden, the Arabs vanished; they'd slipped like lizards under cover of the rock. So Raymond and I turned and walked back. He seemed happier, and began talking about the bus to catch for our return.

When we reached the bungalow Raymond promptly went up the wooden steps, but I halted on the bottom one. The light seemed **thudding**① in my head and I couldn't face the effort needed to go up the steps and make myself amiable to the women. But the heat was so great that it was just as bad staying where I was, under that flood of blinding light falling from the sky. To stay, or to make a move—it came to much the same. After a moment I returned to the beach, and started walking.

There was the same red glare as far as eye could reach, and small waves were lapping the hot sand in little, flurried gasps. As I slowly walked toward the **boulders**② at the end of the beach I could feel my **temples**③ swelling under the impact of the light. It pressed itself on me, trying to check my progress. And each time I felt a hot blast strike my forehead, I gritted my teeth, I clenched my fists in my trouser pockets and keyed up every nerve to fend off the sun and the dark **befuddlement**④ it was pouring into me. Whenever a blade of vivid light shot upward from a bit of shell or broken glass lying on the sand, my jaws set hard. I wasn't going to be beaten, and I walked steadily on.

The small black hump of rock came into view far down the beach. It was rimmed by a dazzling sheen of light and feathery spray, but I was thinking of the cold, clear stream behind it, and longing to hear again the tinkle of running water. Anything to be rid of the glare, the sight of women in tears, the strain and effort—and to retrieve the pool of shadow by the rock and its cool silence!

But when I came nearer I saw that Raymond's Arab had returned. He was by himself this time, lying on his back, his hands behind his head, his face shaded by the rock while the sun beat on the rest of his body. One could see his dungarees steaming in the heat. I

---

① 有力跳动。

② 巨石。

③ 太阳穴。

④ 迷糊、迷惑。

was rather taken aback; my impression had been that the incident was closed, and I hadn't given a thought to it on my way here.

On seeing me, the Arab raised himself a little, and his hand went to his pocket. Naturally, I gripped Raymond's revolver in the pocket of my coat. Then the Arab let himself sink back again, but without taking his hand from his pocket. I was some distance off, at least ten yards, and most of the time I saw him as a blurred dark form wobbling in the heat haze. Sometimes, however, I had glimpses of his eyes glowing between the half-closed lids. The sound of the waves was even lazier, feebler, than at noon. But the light hadn't changed; it was pounding as fiercely as ever on the long stretch of sand that ended at the rock. For two hours the sun seemed to have made no progress; becalmed in a sea of **molten**① steel. Far out on the horizon a steamer was passing; I could just make out from the corner of an eye the small black moving patch, while I kept my gaze fixed on the Arab.

It struck me that all I had to do was to turn, walk away, and think no more about it. But the whole beach, pulsing with heat, was pressing on my back. I took some steps toward the stream. The Arab didn't move. After all, there was still some distance between us. Perhaps because of the shadow on his face, he seemed to be grinning at me.

I waited. The heat was beginning to **scorch**② my cheeks; beads of sweat were gathering in my eyebrows. It was just the same sort of heat as at my mother's funeral, and I had the same disagreeable sensations—especially in my forehead, where all the veins seemed to be **bursting**③ through the skin. I couldn't stand it any longer, and took another step forward. I knew it was a fool thing to do; I wouldn't get out of the sun by moving on a yard or so. But I took that step, just one step, forward. And then the Arab drew his knife and held it up toward me, athwart the sunlight.

A shaft of light shot upward from the steel, and I felt as if a long, thin blade transfixed my forehead. At the same moment all the sweat that had accumulated in my eyebrows splashed down on my eyelids, covering them with a warm film of moisture. Beneath a veil of **brine**④ and tears my eyes were blinded; I was conscious only of the **cymbals**⑤ of the sun clashing on my skull, and, less distinctly, of the keen blade of light flashing up from the

---

① 熔化的。
② 炙烤。
③ 爆裂、涨满。
④ 盐水。
⑤ 钹(一种打击乐器)。

knife, scarring my eyelashes, and **gouging**① into my eyeballs.

Then everything began to **reel**② before my eyes, a fiery **gust**③ came from the sea, while the sky cracked in two, from end to end, and a great sheet of flame poured down through the rift. Every nerve in my body was a steel spring, and my grip closed on the revolver. The trigger gave, and the smooth underbelly of the butt **jogged**④ my palm. And so, with that crisp, **whipcrack**⑤ sound, it all began. I shook off my sweat and the clinging veil of light. I knew I'd shattered the balance of the day, the spacious calm of this beach on which I had been happy. But I fired four shots more into the **inert**⑥ body, on which they left no visible trace. And each successive shot was another loud, fateful rap on the door of my undoing.

Ⅳ. 思考题

1. Meursault is a stranger to whom? In what way is he a stranger or outsider?
2. Note that the novel opens with the death and burial of the mother, and it closes on the eve of Meursault's public execution—for a murder committed at the center of the book. Is death an important motif of the novel? What does the author imply by making this arrangement?
3. The narrator Meursault's account reads more like a diary which contains many elements that are irrelevant to the events leading up to the murder, elements that pertain to the ordinary routines of his everyday life. Also, rarely can we find any causal relation in his account: Meursault's favorite conjunction is "and"—never "since", "because", or "therefore". How do these narrative techniques contribute to the general tone of the novel? And does the narrative tone serve any purpose in relation to the theme of the story?
4. Does the story strike a resonance in your mind? Is it significant for contemporary society?

---

① 凿。
② 旋转、摇晃。
③ 一阵强风。
④ 轻触、轻击。
⑤ 抽鞭声。
⑥ 无行动力的。

V. 文学批评

荒诞哲学

Not without reason, the term "absurd" rarely now makes an appearance in academic discourse, even academic discourse on existentialist philosophy, with which the term is usually associated. However, the importance of the concept to Camus's intellectual trajectory cannot be overstated, and a detailed account of what he means by the absurd would be necessary for any serious discussion of his ideas.

For reasons such as these, it is important to examine Camus's ideas regarding the absurd carefully, and in order to understand his conception of the absurd accurately it is necessary to examine his essay *The Myth of Sisyphus* (1942). Here Camus claims that the absurd arises out of the "confrontation between human need and the unreasonable silence of the world" (MS 32). Human beings are naturally inclined to want and expect the world to be intelligible "in the full and familiar ways that religious and philosophical systems have portrayed it". This kind of intelligibility purports to be comprehensive, to explain the world as a whole, and crucially, it purports to explain the world "in terms that human beings care about", in ways that make sense "with respect to human values". In Camus's view, neither human existence nor the world are themselves absurd. Instead the absurd arises because the world is resistant to this kind of intelligibility: "we want the world to make sense, but it does not make sense. To see this conflict is to see the absurd" (Kamber 52). "If there is an absurd," Camus says at one point, "it is in man's universe" (MS 38). What normally brings the individual into confrontation with his absurd condition, suggests Camus, is the awareness not of human mortality per se, but of his own personal mortality. In the case of Camus himself, this awareness came with his first attack of tuberculosis, in 1930 or 1931, at the age of seventeen. For someone whose juvenile writing displayed a profound bond with the natural world, the sudden visceral awareness of his own mortality, the imperviousness of nature to the private traumas of humankind, the feeling of dying slowly from the inside, the painfully asphyxiating experience of the pneumothorax treatments that denied him even the pantheistic prayer of uninhibited respiration, left clear fissures in the latent pantheism of his earliest, mainly lyrical, writing. However, this is not to say that the absurd is born of an irrational response to the realization of human mortality. While feelings of the absurd may thus be awoken, awareness of the absurd, Camus insists, is specifically a rational, intellectual discovery, deduced from the recognition of the division between our expectations of the world and the world itself, unresponsive to those expectations (MS 26).

"The mind's deepest desire", he says, "is an insistence upon familiarity, an appetite for clarity. Understanding the world for a man is reducing it to the human, stamping it with his seal" (MS: 22–3; E: 110). It is Camus's contention that ordinary human existence tends to take this level of perfect coherence for granted, but that occasionally, or perhaps inevitably, "the stage-sets collapse", and one is wrenched from one's ontological complacency and forced to confront the radical incoherence perceived to be at the heart of the relation between the self and the world, that sense of absurdity which a recent critic has characterized as "the feeling of radical divorce, of living in a once familiar but now suddenly radically alien homeland, of being adrift between past and future and unable to rely on either to give meaning to the present, of being a stranger to the world and to oneself" (Carroll 56–7).

Despite this view, Camus's absurd is not a prelude to nihilism. He asserts repeatedly that it is the implications of the absurd that interest him: "I was looking for a method and not a doctrine. I was practicing methodical doubt. I was trying to make a tabula rasa, on the basis of which it would be possible to construct something." The absurd, then, as conceived by Camus is fundamentally an epistemological claim addressing an ontological need; that is, a claim regarding the knowledge we can have of the world.

Having posited and accepted the absurd as an epistemic principle, Camus quickly poses what he considers to be the most important and urgent philosophical question to emerge from it: is life worth living? Or more accurately, if human existence is governed by the absurd, does the absurd dictate that we respond in one way or in another? Although it might seem that the absurdity of life is sufficient reason to deem it unworthy of effort, on the other hand, assuming that there is as little perfect coherence in death as there is in life, there is no clear choice between the two. Camus argues that we should keep the absurd alive rather than attempt to suppress it through philosophical suicide, or destroy it through physical suicide. He explains his reasoning as follows: Living an experience, a particular fate, is accepting it fully. Now, no one will live this fate, knowing it to be absurd, unless he does everything to keep before him that absurd brought to life by consciousness. Negating one of the terms of the opposition on which he lives amounts to escaping it. To abolish conscious revolt is to elude the problem. The theme of permanent revolution is thus carried into individual experience. Living is keeping the absurd alive. Keeping it alive is above all contemplating it. One of the only coherent philosophical positions is thus revolt. It is a constant confrontation between man and his own obscurity. Just as danger provided man with the unique opportunity of seizing awareness, so metaphysical revolt extends awareness to the whole experience. It is that constant presence of man in his own eyes. It is not aspiration, for it is devoid of hope. That revolt is the certainty of a crushing fate, without the resignation that ought to accompany it. (MS: 53-4) Suicide, he says, is a "repudiation", an acquiescence to the absurd, while Camus would have us accept it without acquiescing to it. Suicide is not, therefore, for Camus an ultimate act of hubris, but is in fact a renunciation of all human values and indeed the possibility of human values. For Camus the absurd describes "a tension, born of a discrepancy between external reality and the human desire for familiarity", but this does not discount such things as the existence of beauty, friendship, health, satisfying work and creativity. While these values are contingent, a relative happiness remains possible, and "to commit suicide because of their relativity is to surrender all that is possible... The doxa of life are a weave of beauty and ugliness, friendship and understanding, health and sickness, insight and opacity. It is a question of living with the mix and not succumbing to the temptation" to make an absolute value out of either hope or despair.

The absurd has meaning, he says, "only in so far as it is not agreed to". Already, Camus appears to be advocating a form of revolt in the face of the condition that seems to render life meaningless. Revolt here is an acceptance of the fact of the absurd (this, after all, is only to acknowledge the character of the human condition), but it is not a meek acceptance. Instead it is an acceptance filled with scorn, defiance and suffering. The incarnation of these responses is the mythical Sisyphus, condemned by the gods to "ceaselessly rolling a rock to the top of a mountain, whence the stone would fall back of its own weight": "Sisyphus, proletarian of the gods, powerless and rebellious, knows the whole extent of his wretched condition... the lucidity that was to constitute his torture at the same time crowns his victory. There is no fate that cannot be surmounted by scorn." It is in the context of this "absurd joy" derived from lucidity that we should consider the paradoxical statement with which *The Myth of Sisyphus* concludes, that "one must imagine Sisyphus happy". Although Camus tells us that Sisyphus's scorn of the gods and his fruitless task accomplish "nothing", "the 'nothing' he accomplishes each time he pushes his rock up to the very top of the hill", suggests Carroll, "is in fact the 'something' of art". This determination to reject suicide, to hold jealously to the absurd condition, to imagine Sisyphus happy, may seem to have brought us to the conclusion of our investigation of the absurd. It has, after all, answered the question with which The Myth of Sisyphus was ostensibly concerned – "does the absurd dictate death?" –by positing the "absurd hero" of a smiling Sisyphus filled with scorn for the gods, and committed to his fate.

Ⅵ. 拓展阅读

Jean-Paul Sartre's "An Explication of *The Stranger*." (*Bloom's Modern Critical Interpretations: Albert Camus' The Stranger*, Ed. Harold Bloom. Infobase Publishing, 2001).

Ⅶ. 参考文献

Foley, John. *Albert Camus: from Absurd to Revolt*. Acumen Publishing, 2008.

Chapter 9 Toni Morrison and the Deconstruction of Cultural Myth

Ⅰ.作者简介

托妮·莫里森 Toni Morrison(1931—2019)出生于俄亥俄州的钢铁小城洛林,父亲是船厂的焊接工,母亲则在白人家里做帮佣。为了逃避种族歧视和贫穷,她的父母从俄亥俄州(美国中西部)迁徙到美国南方,又为了工作迁移到北方。由于莫里森出生于大萧条时期,她的家境一度非常艰辛。

莫里森的父母为黑人文化感到骄傲,莫里森从小在家里就学会了无数的黑人歌曲,听过许多南方黑人的民间传说。她读遍与黑人文化相关的书籍,同时也为简·奥斯汀、理查德·赖特、马克·吐温等人的经典作品深深着迷。年幼的莫里森便对文学产生了兴趣。

1949 年,莫里森以优异成绩高中毕业,并考上了专门为黑人开办的霍华德大学,攻读英语和古典文学,继续追求她对文学的兴趣。在大学里,她跟随哈莱姆文艺复兴的代表人物艾伦·洛克学习人文学科,并加入了学校的戏剧团队。

从霍华德大学毕业后，莫里森到康奈尔大学深造，专门研究福克纳和伍尔夫的小说，并以此为题完成论文，于1955年获得硕士学位。完成学业后，莫里森回到得克萨斯州，并在得克萨斯南方大学和霍华德大学任教。在霍华德大学，莫里森遇到了建筑师哈罗德·莫里森，他们于1958年结婚，生育了两个孩子，最终在1964年离婚。

离婚后，莫里森带着两个孩子定居纽约，并进入出版行业。1966年，她在纽约兰登书屋担任高级编辑，成为兰登书屋有史以来第一位黑人女性高级编辑。在出版社工作期间，她曾为拳王穆罕默德·阿里的自传和一些青年黑人作家作品的出版竭尽全力，努力将黑人文学纳入主流。她所主编的《黑人之书》记叙了美国黑人300年的历史，被称为美国黑人史的百科全书。1970年，莫里森的处女作《最蓝的眼睛》发表，彼时她已经39岁了。这部写了整整5年的长篇小说，部分章节是在纽约拥挤的通勤路上所写就的。莫里森小时候并没有幻想成为作家，在开始写作的很长时间里，她依旧过着朝九晚五的生活，并独立抚养两个孩子。她开始写作是因为感到有些东西非说不可，有些答案必须要去寻找。

莫里森最为知名的小说包括《宠儿》(*Beloved*)、《所罗门之歌》(*Song of Solomon*)、《爵士乐》(*Jazz*)、《柏油娃娃》(*Tar Baby*)等。莫里森曾获得美国国家图书奖、美国国家书评人协会奖、普利策奖等荣誉。1993年莫里森获诺贝尔文学奖，瑞典文学院给她的评价是："在小说中以丰富的想象力和富有诗意的表达方式使美国现实的一个极其重要方面充满活力"("who in novels characterized by visionary force and poetic import, gives life to an essential aspect of American reality")。作为20世纪第一位获得此奖的美国黑人女作家和第八位获得此奖的女作家，莫里森克服了性别和种族的双重障碍，为记录非裔美国人的声音做出了巨大贡献。

成名后的莫里森一直活跃在公共领域，她出现在电视节目"脱口秀女王"及演讲、读书俱乐部等活动中，也经常接受采访对政治时事发表评论。正如美国脱口秀主持人奥普拉回忆莫里森时说的那样："我们的良知，我们的先知，说真话的人。她是一位语言的魔术师，她明白话语的力量。"

莫里森认为小说应该具有政治意义，她认为小说应该是美的、有力的，但同时也应发挥作用。小说应有启迪性，应能开启一扇门、指出一条路。作品必须具有政治意义，作品的力量必须在此。同莫里森小说的政治色彩一样鲜明的，还有她的语言风格。莫里森的小说成功吸取和发扬了黑人文化传统中独特的魅力，把从黑奴时代起就开始流传的民间口头文学传统运用到自己的创作中。

2019 年 8 月 5 日，莫里森在纽约安详去世，《观察家》报评论："当她开口讲话，整个美国都洗耳恭听。"美国前总统奥巴马更新推特状态，称莫里森是"民族的宝藏"，并称"能和她在同一片天空下呼吸，哪怕只是一会儿，也是上天赐予的礼物"。

Ⅱ. 内容提要

《最蓝的眼睛》讲述的是发生在 1941 年俄亥俄州洛林市某个黑人社区一个 11 岁的黑人小姑娘皮科拉的悲剧生活。故事源于作者童年时代的一位女友，她整天向上帝祈祷，请求赐她一双像白人姑娘那样的蓝眼睛。小说的故事情节并不复杂。中心人物是一个名叫皮科拉 · 布里德洛瓦的黑人女孩，她整天憧憬一双蓝眼睛。因为在幼小的她看来，如果她有了像白人女孩一样的眼睛，她的生活就会变得不一样：父亲不会再酗酒、殴打母亲保琳，母亲保琳不会再嫌她丑而冷落她、虐待她，哥哥也不会频频离家出走，学校的老师与同学也不会再鄙视她、嘲笑她。为此，她整夜祈求，可等待她的，却是一桩无人能够料想的悲剧……到头来母亲的殴打，周围人们的鄙视和嘲讽，终于令小皮科拉精神崩溃，神智失常，完全沉浸在自己虚构的世界里，坚信自己已经拥有了一双美丽的蓝眼睛。

莫里森在 2019 年上映的纪录片《托妮 · 莫里森：我的作品》中说道，"我的一生都在写作中努力摆脱'白人凝视'"。这本小说刚出版时印了 2 000 本，评价并不高。莫里森也只拿到很低的报酬。直到她获得诺贝尔文学奖，该书再版。她在后记里写道：对这本书的接受程度与她的主要人物在世界上受到的待遇是一样的，"被解雇，被轻视，被误读"，"赢回它的发表尊严，足足花了 25 年"。

Ⅲ. 作品

Here is the house. It is green and white. It has a red door. It is very pretty. Here is the family. Mother, Father, Dick, and Jane live in the green-and-white house. They are very happy. See Jane. She has a red dress She wants to play. Who will play with

Jane? See the cat. It goes meow-meow. Come and play. Come play with Jane. The kitten will not play. See Mother. Mother is very nice. Mother, will you play with Jane? Mother laughs. Laugh, Mother, laugh. See Father. He is big and strong. Father, will you play with Jane? Father is smiling. Smile, Father, smile. See the dog. Bowwow goes the dog. Do you want to play with Jane? See the dog run. Run, dog, run. Look, look. Here comes a friend. The friend will play with Jane. They will play a good game. Play, Jane, play.

Here is the house it is green and white it has a red door it is very pretty here is the family mother father dick and jane live in the green-and-white house they are very happy see jane she has a red dress she wants to play who will play with jane see the cat it goes meow-meow come and play come play with jane the kitten will not play see mother mother is very nice mother will you play with jane mother laughs laugh mother laugh see father he is big and strong father will you play with jane father is smiling smile father smile see the dog bowwow goes the dog do you want to play do you want to play with jane see the dog run run dog run look look here comes a friend the friend will play with jane they will play a good game play jane play

Hereisthehouseitisgreenandwhiteithasareddooritisveryprettyhereisthefa
milymotherfatherdickandjaneliveinthegreenandwhitehousetheyareveryh
appyseejaneshehasareddressshewantstoplaywhowillplaywithjaneseetheca
titgoesmeowmeowcomeandplaycomeplaywithjanethekittenwillnotplays
eemothermotherisverynicemotherwillyouplaywithjanemotherlaughslau
ghmotherlaughseefatherheisbigandstrongfatherwillyouplaywithjanefatherissmilin
gsmilefathersmileseethedogbowwowgoesthedogdoyouwantto
playdoyouwanttoplaywithjaneseethedogrunrundogrunlooklookherecom
Esafriendthefriendwillplaywithjanetheywillplayagoodgameplayjaneplay

Autmn

Quiet as it's kept, there were no **marigolds**① *in the fall* 1941. *We thought, at the time, that it was because Pecola was having her father's baby that the marigolds did not grow. A little examination and much less melancholy would have proved to us that our seeds were not the only ones that did not sprout; nobody's did. Not even the gardens fronting the lake showed marigolds that year. But so deeply concerned were we with the health and safe delivery of Pecola's baby we could think of nothing but our own magic: if we planted the seeds, and said the right words over them, they would blossom, and everything would be all right.*

It was a long time before my sister and I admitted to ourselves that no green was going to spring from our seeds. Once we knew, our guilt was relieved only by fights and mutual accusations about who was to blame. For years I thought my sister was right: it was my fault. I had planted them too far down in the earth. It never occurred to either of us that the earth itself might have been unyielding. We had dropped our seeds in our own little plot of black dirt just as Pecola's father had dropped his seeds in his own plot of black dirt. Our innocence and faith were no more productive than his lust or despair. What is clear now is that of all of that hope, fear, lust, love, and grief, nothing remains but Pecola and the unyielding earth. Cholly Breedlove is dead; our innocence too. The seeds shriveled and died; her baby too.

There is really nothing more to say—except why. But since why is difficult to handle, one must take refuge in how.

Nuns② go by as quiet as lust, and drunken men with sober eyes sing in the lobby of the Greek hotel. Rosemary Villanucci, our next-door friend who lives above her father's cafe, sits in a 1939 Buick eating bread and butter. She rolls down the window to tell my sister Frieda and me that we can't come in. We stare at her, wanting her bread, but more than that wanting to poke the arrogance out of her eyes and smash the pride of ownership

① 金盏花。
② 修女。

that curls her chewing mouth. When she comes out of the car we will beat her up, make red marks on her white skin, and she will cry and ask us do we want her to pull her pants down. We will say no. We don't know what we should feel or do if she does, but whenever she asks us, we know she is offering us something precious and that our own pride must be asserted by refusing to accept.

School has started, and Frieda and I get new brown stockings and cod-liver oil. Grown-ups talk in tired, edgy voices about Zick's Coal Company and take us along in the evening to the railroad tracks where we fill burlap sacks with the tiny pieces of coal lying about. Later we walk home, glancing back to see the great carloads of slag being dumped, red hot and smoking, into the ravine that skirts the steel mill. The dying fire lights the sky with a dull orange glow. Frieda and I lag behind, staring at the patch of color surrounded by black. It is impossible not to feel a shiver when our feet leave the gravel path and sink into the dead grass in the field.

Our house is old, cold, and green. At night a **kerosene lamp**① lights one large room. The others are braced in darkness, peopled by **roaches**② and mice. Adults do not talk to us—they give us directions. They issue orders without providing information. When we trip and fall down they glance at us; if we cut or bruise ourselves, they ask us are we crazy. When we catch colds, they shake their heads in disgust at our lack of consideration. How, they ask us, do you expect anybody to get anything done if you all are sick? We cannot answer them. Our illness is treated with contempt, **foul**③ **Black Draught**④, and **castor oil**⑤ that **blunts**⑥ our minds.

When, on a day after a trip to collect coal, I cough once, loudly, through **bronchial tubes**⑦ already packed tight with **phlegm**⑧, my mother frowns. "Great Jesus. Get on in that bed. How many times do I have to tell you to wear something on your head? You must be the biggest fool in this town. Frieda? Get some rags and stuff that window."

---

① 煤油灯。
② 大麻卷烟的烟蒂。
③ 难闻的。
④ 一种泻药。
⑤ 蓖麻油。
⑥ 使变钝。
⑦ 支气管。
⑧ 痰。

Frieda restuffs the window. I **trudge**[①] off to bed, full of guilt and self-pity. I lie down in my underwear, the metal in my black garters hurts my legs, but I do not take them off, for it is too cold to lie stockingless. It takes a long time for my body to heat its place in the bed. Once I have generated a **silhouette**[②] of warmth, I dare not move, for there is a cold place one-half inch in any direction. No one speaks to me or asks how I feel. In an hour or two my mother comes. Her hands are large and rough, and when she rubs the Vicks **salve**[③] on my chest, I am rigid with pain. She takes two fingers' full of it at a time, and massages my chest until I am faint. Just when I think I will tip over into a scream, she scoops out a little of the salve on her forefinger and puts it in my mouth, telling me to swallow. A hot flannel is wrapped about my neck and chest. I am covered up with heavy quilts and ordered to sweat, which I do—promptly.

Later I throw up, and my mother says, "What did you puke on the bed clothes for? Don't you have sense enough to hold your head out the bed? Now, look what you did. You think I got time for nothing but washing up your puke?"

The puke swaddles down the pillow onto the sheet—green-gray, with flecks of orange. It moves like the insides of an uncooked egg. Stubbornly clinging to its own mass, refusing to break up and be removed. How, I wonder, can it be so neat and nasty at the same time?

My mother's voice drones on. She is not talking to me. She is talking to the puke, but she is calling it my name: Claudia. She wipes it up as best she can and puts a scratchy towel over the large wet place. I lie down again. The rags have fallen from the window crack, and the air is cold. I dare not call her back and am reluctant to leave my warmth. My mother's anger humiliates me; her words chafe my cheeks, and I am crying. I do not know that she is not angry at me, but at my sickness. I believe she despises my weakness for letting the sickness "take holt." By and by I will not get sick; I will refuse to. But for now I am crying. I know I am making more snot, but I can't stop.

My sister comes in. Her eyes are full of sorrow. She sings to me: "When the deep purple falls over sleepy garden walls, someone thinks of me...." I doze, thinking of plums, walls, and "someone."

But was it really like that? As painful as I remember? Only mildly. Or rather, it was

---

① 缓慢地走,吃力地走。

② 轮廓,(事物的)形状。

③ 药膏,软膏。

a productive and **fructifying**① pain. Love, thick and dark as Alaga **syrup**②, eased up into that cracked window. I could smell it—taste it—sweet, musty, with an edge of wintergreen in its base—everywhere in that house. It stuck, along with my tongue, to the frosted windowpanes. It coated my chest, along with the salve, and when the flannel came undone in my sleep, the clear, sharp curves of air outlined its presence on my throat. And in the night, when my coughing was dry and tough, feet padded into the room, hands repinned the flannel, readjusted the quilt, and rested a moment on my forehead. So when I think of autumn, I think of somebody with hands who does not want me to die.

It was autumn too when Mr. Henry came. Our roomer. Our roomer. The words ballooned from the lips and hovered about our heads—silent, separate, and pleasantly mysterious. My mother was all ease and satisfaction in discussing his coming.

"You know him," she said to her friends. "Henry Washington. He's been living over there with Miss Delia Jones on Thirteenth Street. But she's too addled now to keep up. So he's looking for another place."

"Oh, yes." Her friends do not hide their curiosity. "I been wondering how long he was going to stay up there with her. They say she's real bad off. Don't know who he is half the time, and nobody else."

"Well, that old crazy nigger she married up with didn't help her head nonq."

"Did you hear what he told folks when he left her?" "Uh-uh. What?"

"Well, he run off with that trifling Peggy—from Elyria. You know."

"One of Old Slack Bessie's girls?"

"That's the one. Well, somebody asked him why he left a nice good church woman like Delia for that heifer. You know Delia always did keep a good house. And he said the honest-to-God real reason was he couldn't take no more of that violet water Delia Jones used. Said he wanted a woman to smell like a woman. Said Delia was just too clean for him."

"Old dog. Ain't that nasty!"

"You telling me. What kind of reasoning is that?"

"No kind. Some men just dogs."

"Is that what give her them strokes?"

---

① 有成果的,结果实的。

② 枫糖浆。

"Must have helped. But you know, none of them girls wasn't too bright. Remember that grinning Hattie? She wasn't never right. And their Auntie Julia is still trotting up and down Sixteenth Street talking to herself."

"Didn't she get put away?"

"Naw. County wouldn't take her. Said she wasn't harming anybody."

"Well, she's harming me. You want something to scare the living shit out of you, you get up at five-thirty in the morning like I do and see that old hag floating by in that bonnet. Have mercy!"

They laugh.

Frieda and I are washing Mason jars. We do not hear their words, but with grown-ups we listen to and watch out for their voices.

"Well, I hope don't nobody let me roam around like that when I get senile. It's a shame." "What they going to do about Delia? Don't she have no people?"

"A sister's coming up from North Carolina to look after her. I expect she wants to get a holt of Delia's house."

"Oh, come on. That's a evil thought, if ever I heard one."

"What you want to bet? Henry Washington said that sister ain't seen Delia in fifteen years."

"I kind of thought Henry would marry her one of these days."

"That old woman?"

"Well, Henry ain't no chicken."

"No, but he ain't no buzzard, either."

"He ever been married to anybody?"

"No." "How come? Somebody cut it off?"

"He's just picky."

"He ain't picky. You see anything around here you'd marry?"

"Well ... no."

"He's just sensible. A steady worker with quiet ways. I hope it works out all right."

"It will. How much you charging?"

"Five dollars every two weeks."

"That'll be a big help to you."

"I'll say."

Their conversation is like a gently **wicked**① dance: sound meets sound, **curtsies**②, **shimmies**③, and retires. Another sound enters but is **upstaged**④ by still another: the two circle each other and stop. Sometimes their words move in lofty spirals; other times they take **strident**⑤ leaps, and all of it is **punctuated**⑥ with warm-pulsed laughter—like the **throb**⑦ of a heart made of **jelly**⑧. The edge, the curl, the thrust of their emotions is always clear to Frieda and me. We do not, cannot, know the meanings of all their words, for we are nine and ten years old. So we watch their faces, their hands, their feet, and listen for truth in **timbre**⑨.

So when Mr. Henry arrived on a Saturday night, we smelled him. He smelled wonderful. Like trees and lemon vanishing cream, and Nu Nile Hair Oil and flecks of Sen Sen. He smiled a lot, showing small even teeth with a friendly gap in the middle. Frieda and I were not introduced to him—merely pointed out. Like, here is the bathroom; the clothes closet is here; and these are my kids, Frieda and Claudia; watch out for this window; it don't open all the way.

We looked sideways at him, saying nothing and expecting him to say nothing. Just to nod, as he had done at the clothes closet, acknowledging our existence. To our surprise, he spoke to us.

"Hello there. You must be Greta Garbo, and you must be Ginger Rogers."

We giggled. Even my father was startled into a smile.

"Want a penny?" He held out a shiny coin to us. Frieda lowered her head, too pleased to answer. I reached for it. He snapped his thumb and forefinger, and the penny disappeared. Our shock was laced with delight. We searched all over him, poking our fingers into his socks, looking up the inside back of his coat. If happiness is anticipation with certainty, we were happy. And while we waited for the coin to reappear, we knew we were amusing Mama and Daddy. Daddy was smiling, and Mama's eyes went soft as they fol-

---

① 淘气的，调皮的。
② （女子）行屈膝礼。
③ 挑希米舞，一种抖动肩膀和臀部的舞蹈；一摇一摆地走。
④ 抢镜头，抢风头。
⑤ 坚定的。
⑥ 不时打断。
⑦ 跳动。
⑧ 果冻。
⑨ 音质、音色。

lowed our hands wandering over Mr. Henry's body.

We loved him. Even after what came later, there was no bitterness in our memory of him.

She slept in the bed with us. Frieda on the outside because she is brave—it never occurs to her that if in her sleep her hand hangs over the edge of the bed "something" will crawl out from under it and bite her fingers off. I sleep near the wall because that thought has occurred to me. Pecola, therefore, had to sleep in the middle.

Mama had told us two days earlier that a "case" was coming—a girl who had no place to go. The county had placed her in our house for a few days until they could decide what to do, or, more precisely, until the family was reunited. We were to be nice to her and not fight. Mama didn't know "what got into people," but that old Dog Breedlove had burned up his house, gone upside his wife's head, and everybody, as a result, was outdoors.

Outdoors, we knew, was the real terror of life. The threat of being outdoors surfaced frequently in those days. Every possibility of excess was curtailed with it. If somebody ate too much, he could end up outdoors. If somebody used too much coal, he could end up outdoors. People could gamble themselves outdoors, drink themselves outdoors. Sometimes mothers put their sons outdoors, and when that happened, regardless of what the son had done, all sympathy was with him. He was outdoors, and his own flesh had done it. To be put outdoors by a landlord was one thing—unfortunate, but an aspect of life over which you had no control, since you could not control your income. But to be slack enough to put oneself outdoors, or heartless enough to put one's own kin outdoors—that was criminal.

There is a difference between being put out and being put outdoors. If you are put out, you go somewhere else; if you are outdoors, there is no place to go. The distinction was subtle but final. Outdoors was the end of something, an **irrevocable**①, physical fact, defining and complementing our metaphysical condition. Being a minority in both caste and class, we moved about anyway on the **hem**② of life, struggling to consolidate our weaknesses and hang on, or to creep singly up into the major folds of the **garment**③. Our **peripheral**④ existence, however, was something we had learned to deal with—probably be-

① 无法改变的。
② （衣服的）褶边，卷边。
③ （一件）衣服。
④ 边缘的。

cause it was abstract. But the concreteness of being outdoors was another matter—like the difference between the concept of death and being, in fact, dead. Dead doesn't change, and outdoors is here to stay.

Knowing that there was such a thing as outdoors bred in us a hunger for property, for ownership. The firm possession of a yard, a porch, a grape arbor. Propertied black people spent all their energies, all their love, on their nests. Like **frenzied**①, desperate birds, they overdecorated everything; fussed and fidgeted over their hard-won homes; canned, jellied, and preserved all summer to fill the cupboards and shelves; they painted, picked, and poked at every corner of their houses. And these houses loomed like hothouse sunflowers among the rows of weeds that were the rented houses. Renting blacks cast **furtive**② glances at these owned yards and porches, and made firmer commitments to buy themselves "some nice little old place." In the meantime, they saved, and scratched, and piled away what they could in the rented hovels, looking forward to the day of property.

Cholly Breedlove, then, a renting black, having put his family outdoors, had catapulted himself beyond the reaches of human consideration. He had joined the animals; was, indeed, an old dog, a snake, a ratty nigger. Mrs. Breedlove was staying with the woman she worked for; the boy, Sammy, was with some other family; and Pecola was to stay with us. Cholly was in jail.

She came with nothing. No little paper bag with the other dress, or a nightgown, or two pair of whitish cotton bloomers. She just appeared with a white woman and sat down.

We had fun in those few days Pecola was with us. Frieda and I stopped fighting each other and concentrated on our guest, trying hard to keep her from feeling outdoors.

When we discovered that she clearly did not want to dominate us, we liked her. She laughed when I clowned for her, and smiled and accepted gracefully the food gifts my sister gave her.

"Would you like some **graham crackers**③?"

"I don't care."

Frieda brought her four graham crackers on a saucer and some milk in a blue-and-white Shirley Temple cup. She was a long time with the milk, and gazed fondly at the silhouette of Shirley Temple's dimpled face. Frieda and she had a loving conversation about

---

① 疯狂的。

② 鬼鬼祟祟的,偷偷摸摸的。

③ 全麦饼干。

how cu-ute Shirley Temple was. I couldn't join them in their adoration because I hated Shirley. Not because she was cute, but because she danced with Bojangles, who was *my* friend, *my* uncle, *my* daddy, and who ought to have been soft-shoeing it and chuckling with me. Instead he was enjoying, sharing, giving a lovely dance thing with one of those little white girls whose socks never slid down under their heels. So I said, "I like Jane Withers."

They gave me a puzzled look, decided I was incomprehensible, and continued their reminiscing about old **squint-eyed**① Shirley.

Younger than both Frieda and Pecola, I had not yet arrived at the turning point in the development of my psyche which would allow me to love her. What I felt at that time was unsullied hatred. But before that I had felt a stranger, more frightening thing than hatred for all the Shirley Temples of the world.

It had begun with Christmas and the gift of dolls. The big, the special, the loving gift was always a big, blue-eyed Baby Doll. From the clucking sounds of adults I knew that the doll represented what they thought was my fondest wish. I was **bemused**② with the thing itself, and the way it looked. What was I supposed to do with it? Pretend I was its mother? I had no interest in babies or the concept of motherhood. I was interested only in humans my own age and size, and could not generate any enthusiasm at the prospect of being a mother. Motherhood was old age, and other remote possibilities. I learned quickly, however, what I was expected to do with the doll: rock it, fabricate storied situations around it, even sleep with it. Picture books were full of little girls sleeping with their dolls. Raggedy Ann dolls usually, but they were out of the question. I was physically revolted by and secretly frightened of those round **moronic**③ eyes, the pancake face, and orange worms hair.

The other dolls, which were supposed to bring me great pleasure, succeeded in doing quite the opposite. When I took it to bed, its hard unyielding limbs resisted my flesh—the **tapered**④ fingertips on those **dimpled**⑤ hands scratched. If, in sleep, I turned, the bone-cold head collided with my own. It was a most uncomfortable, patently aggressive sleeping

---

① 斜视的。
② 困惑的。
③ 愚蠢的，白痴的。
④ 逐渐变窄的，锥形的。
⑤ 有小坑的，有浅凹的。

companion. To hold it was no more rewarding. The **starched**① **gauze**② or lace on the cotton dress irritated any embrace. I had only one desire: to dismember it. To see of what it was made, to discover the dearness, to find the beauty, the desirability that had escaped me, but apparently only me. Adults, older girls, shops, magazines, newspapers, window signs—all the world had agreed that a blue-eyed, yellow-haired, pink-skinned doll was what every girl child treasured. "Here," they said, "this is beautiful, and if you are on this day 'worthy' you may have it." I fingered the face, wondering at the single-stroke eyebrows; picked at the pearly teeth stuck like two piano keys between red bowline lips. Traced the turned-up nose, poked the glassy blue eyeballs, twisted the yellow hair. I could not love it. But I could examine it to see what it was that all the world said was lovable. Break off the tiny fingers, bend the flat feet, loosen the hair, twist the head around, and the thing made one sound—a sound they said was the sweet and plaintive cry "Mama," but which sounded to me like the **bleat**③ of a dying lamb, or, more precisely, our icebox door opening on rusty hinges in July. Remove the cold and stupid eyeball, it would bleat still, "Ahhhhhh," take off the head, shake out the sawdust, crack the back against the brass bed rail, it would bleat still. The gauze back would split, and I could see the disk with six holes, the secret of the sound. A mere metal roundness.

Grown people frowned and fussed: "You don't know how to take care of nothing. I never had a baby doll in my whole life and used to cry my eyes out for them. Now you got one—a beautiful one and—you tear it up, what's the matter with you?"

How strong was their outrage. Tears threatened to erase the aloofness of their authority. The emotion of years of unfulfilled longing **preened**④ in their voices. I did not know why I destroyed those dolls. But I did know that nobody ever asked me what I wanted for Christmas. Had any adult with the power to fulfill my desires taken me seriously and asked me what I wanted, they would have known that I did not want to have anything to own, or to possess any object. I wanted rather to feel something on Christmas day. The real question would have been, "Dear Claudia, what experience would you like on Christmas?" I could have spoken up, "I want to sit on the low stool in Big Mama's kitchen with my lap full of

---

① 硬挺的。
② 网纱。
③ 咩咩叫,抱怨。
④ 得意扬扬,沾沾自喜。

lilacs[①] and listen to Big Papa play his violin for me alone." The lowness of the stool made for my body, the security and warmth of Big Mama's kitchen, the smell of the lilacs, the sound of the music, and, since it would be good to have all of my senses engaged, the taste of a peach, perhaps, afterward.

Instead I tasted and smelled the **acridness**[②] of **tin**[③] plates and cups designed for tea parties that bored me. Instead I looked with loathing on new dresses that required a hateful bath in a **galvanized**[④] zinc tub before wearing. Slipping around on the zinc, no time to play or soak, for the water chilled too fast, no time to enjoy one's nakedness, only time to make curtains of soapy water careen down between the legs. Then the scratchy towels and the dreadful and humiliating absence of dirt. The irritable, unimaginative cleanliness. Gone the ink marks from legs and face, all my creations and accumulations of the day gone, and replaced by **goose pimples**[⑤].

I destroyed white baby dolls.

But the dismembering of dolls was not the true horror. The truly horrifying thing was the transference of the same impulses to little white girls. The indifference with which I could have axed them was shaken only by my desire to do so. To discover what **eluded**[⑥] me: the secret of the magic they weaved on others. What made people look at them and say, "Awwwww," but not for me? The eye slide of black women as they approached them on the street, and the possessive gentleness of their touch as they handled them.

If I pinched them, their eyes—unlike the crazed glint of the baby doll's eyes—would fold in pain, and their cry would not be the sound of an icebox door, but a fascinating cry of pain. When I learned how **repulsive**[⑦] this disinterested violence was, that it was repulsive because it was disinterested, my shame **floundered**[⑧] about for refuge. The best hiding place was love. Thus the conversion from **pristine sadism**[⑨] to fabricated hatred, to **fraud-**

① 丁香花。
② 难闻的气味。
③ 锡,镀锡的。
④ 镀锌的。
⑤ 鸡皮疙瘩。
⑥ 躲避,使不理解。
⑦ 令人反感的。
⑧ 艰苦挣扎。
⑨ 施虐狂。

ulent① love. It was a small step to Shirley Temple. I learned much later to worship her, just as I learned to delight in cleanliness, knowing, even as I learned, that the change was adjustment without improvement.

"Three quarts of milk. That's what was in that icebox yesterday. Three whole quarts. Now they ain't none. Not a drop. I don't mind folks coming in and getting what they want, but three quarts of milk! What the devil does anybody need with three quarts of milk?"

The "folks" my mother was referring to was Pecola. The three of us, Pecola, Frieda, and I, listened to her downstairs in the kitchen fussing about the amount of milk Pecola had drunk. We knew she was fond of the Shirley Temple cup and took every opportunity to drink milk out of it just to handle and see sweet Shirley's face. My mother knew that Frieda and I hated milk and assumed Pecola drank it out of greediness. It was certainly not for us to "dispute" her. We didn't initiate talk with grown-ups; we answered their questions.

Ashamed of the insults that were being heaped on our friend, we just sat there: I picked toe jam, Frieda cleaned her fingernails with her teeth, and Pecola finger-traced some scars on her knee—her head cocked to one side. My mother's fussing soliloquies always irritated and depressed us. They were interminable, insulting, and although indirect (Mama never named anybody—just talked about folks and some people), extremely painful in their thrust. She would go on like that for hours, connecting one offense to another until all of the things that chagrined her were spewed out. Then, having told everybody and everything off, she would burst into song and sing the rest of the day. But it was such a long time before the singing part came. In the meantime, our stomachs jellying and our necks burning, we listened, avoided each other's eyes, and picked toe **jam**② or whatever.

"... I don't know what I'm supposed to be running here, a charity ward, I guess. Time for me to get out of the giving line and get in the getting line. I guess I ain't supposed to have nothing. I'm supposed to end up in the poorhouse. Look like nothing I do is going to keep me out of there. Folks just spend all their time trying to figure out ways to send me to the poorhouse. I got about as much business with another mouth to feed as a cat has with side pockets. As if I don't have trouble enough trying to feed my own and

---

① 欺骗的。
② 足垢。

keep out the poorhouse, now I got something else in here that's just going to drink me on in there. Well, naw, she ain't. Not long as I got strength in my body and a tongue in my head. There's a limit to everything. I ain't got nothing to just throw away. Don't nobody need three quarts of milk. Henry Ford don't need three quarts of milk. That's just down rightful. I'm willing to do what I can for folks. Can't nobody say I ain't. But this has got to stop, and I'm just the one to stop it. Bible say watch as well as pray. Folks just dump they children off on you and go on 'bout they business. Ain't nobody even peeped in here to see whether that child has a loaf of bread. Look like they would just peep in to see whether I had a loaf of bread to give her. But naw. That thought don't cross they mind. That old rifling Cholly been out of jail two whole days and ain't been here yet to see if his own child was 'live or dead. She could be dead for all he know. And that mama neither. What kind of something is that?"

When Mama got around to Henry Ford and all those people who didn't care whether she had a loaf of bread, it was time to go. We wanted to miss the part about Roosevelt and the CCC camps.

Frieda got up and started down the stairs. Pecola and I followed, making a wide arc to avoid the kitchen doorway. We sat on the steps of the porch, where my mother's words could reach us only in spurts.

It was a lonesome Saturday. The house smelled of Pels **Naphtha**① and the sharp odor of mustard greens cooking. Saturdays were lonesome, tossy, soapy days. Second in misery only to those tight, starchy, cough-drop Sundays, so full of "don'ts" and "set'cha self downs."

If my mother was in a singing mood, it wasn't so bad. She would sing about hard times, bad times, and somebody-done gone and left-me times. But her voice was so sweet and her singing-eyes so melty I found myself longing for those hard times, yearning to be grown without "a thin di-i-ime to my name." I looked forward to the delicious time when "my man" would leave me, when I would "hate to see that evening sun go down ..." cause then I would know "my man has left this town." Misery colored by the greens and blues in my mother's voice took all of the grief out of the words and left me with a conviction that pain was not only endurable, it was sweet.

But without song, those Saturdays sat on my head like a **coal scuttle**②, and if Mama

① 石脑油。
② 煤筐。

was fussing, as she was now, it was like somebody throwing stones at it.

"... and here I am poor as a bowl of yak-me. What do they think I am? Some kind of Sandy Claus? Well, they can just take they stocking down 'cause it ain't Christmas. ..."

We fidgeted.

"Let's do something," Frieda said.

"What do you want to do?" I asked.

"I don't know. Nothing."

Frieda stared at the tops of the trees. Pecola looked at her feet.

"You want to go up to Mr. Henry's room and look at his girlie magazines?"

Frieda made an ugly face. She didn't like to look at dirty pictures. "Well," I continued, "we could look at his Bible. That's pretty." Frieda sucked her teeth and made iphttt sound with her lips. "O. K., then. We could go thread needles for the half-blind lady. She'll give us a penny."

Frieda snorted. "Her eyes look like snot. I don't feel like looking at them. What you want to do Pecola?"

"I don't care," she said. "Anything you want."

I had another idea. "We could go up the alley and see what's in the trash cans."

"Too cold," said Frieda. She was bored and irritable.

"I know. We could make some **fudge**①."

"You kidding? With Mama in there fussing? When she starts fussing at the walls, you know she's gonna be at it all day. She wouldn't even let us."

"Well, let's go over to the Greek hotel and listen to them **cuss**②."

"Oh, who wants to do that? Besides, they say the same old words all the time."

My supply of ideas exhausted, I began to concentrate on the white spots on my fingernails. The total signified the number of boyfriends I would have. Seven.

Mama's soliloquy slid into the silence "... Bible say feed the hungry. That's fine. That's all right. But I ain't feeding no elephants.... Anybody need three quarts of milk to live need to get out of here. They in the wrong place. What is this? Some kind of dairy farm?"

Suddenly Pecola bolted straight up, her eyes wide with terror. A **whinnying**③ sound

① 软糖。
② 诅咒,咒骂。
③ 嘶叫。

came from her mouth.

"What's the matter with you?" Frieda stood up too.

Then we both looked where Pecola was staring. Blood was running down her legs. Some drops were on the steps. I leaped up. "Hey. You cut yourself? Look. It's all over your dress."

A brownish-red stain discolored the back of her dress. She kept whinnying, standing with her legs far apart.

Frieda said, "Oh. Lordy! I know. I know what that is!"

"What?" Pecola's fingers went to her mouth.

"That's '**ministratin**①'."

"What's that?"

"You know."

"Am I going to die?" she asked.

"Noooo. You won't die. It just means you can have a baby!"

"What?"

"How do you know?" I was sick and tired of Frieda knowing everything.

"Mildred told me, and Mama too."

"I don't believe it."

"You don't have to, dummy. Look. Wait here. Sit down, Pecola. Right here." Frieda was all authority and zest. "And you," she said to me, "you go get some water."

"Water?"

"Yes, stupid. Water. And be quiet, or Mama will hear you."

Pecola sat down again, a little less fear in her eyes. I went into the kitchen.

"What you want, girl?" Mama was rinsing curtains in the sink.

"Some water, ma'am."

"Right where I'm working, naturally. Well, get a glass. Not no clean one neither. Use that jar."

I got a Mason jar and filled it with water from the **faucet**②. It seemed a long time filling.

"Don't nobody never want nothing till they see me at the sink. Then everybody got to drink water...."

---

① 此处是 Frieda 在模仿"menstruating"的发音，menstruate：来月经。

② 水龙头。

When the jar was full, I moved to leave the room.

"Where you going?"

"Outside."

"Drink that water right here!"

"I ain't gonna break nothing."

"You don't know what you gonna do."

"Yes, ma'am. I do. Lemme take it out. I won't spill none."

"You bed' not."

I got to the porch and stood there with the Mason jar of water. Pecola was crying.

"What you crying for? Does it hurt?"

She shook her head.

"Then stop slinging snot."

Frieda opened the back door. She had something tucked in her blouse. She looked at me in amazement and pointed to the jar. "What's that supposed to do?"

"You told me. You said get some water."

"Not a little old jar full. Lots of water. To scrub the steps with, dumbbell!"

"How was I supposed to know?"

"Yeah. How was you. Come on." She pulled Pecola up by the arm. "Let's go back here." They headed for the side of the house where the bushes were thick.

"Hey. What about me? I want to go."

"Shut uuuup," Frieda stage-whispered. "Mama will hear you. You wash the steps."

They disappeared around the corner of the house.

I was going to miss something. Again. Here was something important, and I had to stay behind and not see any of it. I poured the water on the steps, sloshed it with my shoe, and ran to join them.

Frieda was on her knees; a white rectangle of cotton was near her on the ground. She was pulling Pecola's pants off. "Come on. Step out of them." She managed to get the soiled pants down and flung them at me. "Here."

"What am I supposed to do with these?"

"Bury them, moron."

Frieda told Pecola to hold the cotton thing between her legs.

"How she gonna walk like that?" I asked.

Frieda didn't answer. Instead she took two safety pins from the hem of her skirt and began to pin the ends of the napkin to Pecola's dress.

I picked up the pants with two fingers and looked about for something to dig a hole with. A rustling noise in the bushes startled me, and turning toward it, I saw a pair of fascinated eyes in a dough-white face. Rosemary was watching us. I grabbed for her face and succeeded in scratching her nose. She screamed and jumped back.

"Mrs. MacTeer! Mrs. MacTeer!" Rosemary hollered. "Frieda and Claudia are out here playing nasty! Mrs. MacTeer!"

Mama opened the window and looked down at us.

"What?"

"They're playing nasty, Mrs. MacTeer. Look. And Claudia hit me 'cause I seen them!"

Mama slammed the window shut and came running out the back door.

"What you all doing? Oh. Uh-huh. Uh-huh. Playing nasty, huh?" She reached into the bushes and pulled off a switch. "I'd rather raise pigs than some nasty girls. Least I can slaughter them!"

We began to shriek. "No, Mama. No, ma'am. We wasn't! She's a liar! No, ma'am, Mama! No, ma'am, Mama!"

Mama grabbed Frieda by the shoulder, turned her around, and gave her three or four stinging cuts on her legs. "Gonna be nasty, huh? Naw you ain't!"

Frieda was destroyed. Whippings wounded and insulted her.

Mama looked at Pecola. "You too!" she said. "Child of mine or not!" She grabbed Pecola and spun her around. The safety pin snapped open on one end of the napkin, and Mama saw it fall from under her dress. The switch hovered in the air while Mama blinked. "What the devil is going on here?"

Frieda was sobbing. I, next in line, began to explain. "She was bleeding. We was just trying to stop the blood!"

Mama looked at Frieda for verification. Frieda nodded. "She's ministratin'. We was just helping."

Mama released Pecola and stood looking at her. Then she pulled both of them toward her, their heads against her stomach. Her eyes were sorry. "All right, all right. Now, stop crying. I didn't know. Come on, now. Get on in the house. Go on home, Rosemary. The show is over."

We trooped in, Frieda sobbing quietly, Pecola carrying a white tail, me carrying the little-girl-gone-to-woman pants.

Mama led us to the bathroom. She **prodded**① Pecola inside, and taking the underwear from me, told us to stay out.

We could hear water running into the bathtub.

"You think she's going to drown her?"

"Oh, Claudia. You so dumb. She's just going to wash her clothes and all."

"Should we beat up Rosemary?"

"No. Leave her alone."

The water **gushed**②, and over its gushing we could hear the music of my mother's laughter.

That night, in bed, the three of us lay still. We were full of awe and respect for Pecola. Lying next to a real person who was really ministratin' was somehow sacred. She was different from us now—grown-up-like. She, herself, felt the distance, but refused to lord it over us.

After a long while she spoke very softly. "Is it true that I can have a baby now?"

"Sure," said Frieda drowsily. "Sure you can."

"But ... how?" Her voice was hollow with wonder.

"Oh," said Frieda, "somebody has to love you."

"Oh."

There was a long pause in which Pecola and I thought this over. It would involve, I supposed, "my man," who, before leaving me, would love me. But there weren't any babies in the songs my mother sang. Maybe that's why the women were sad: the men left before they could make a baby.

Then Pecola asked a question that had never entered my mind. "How do you do that? I mean, how do you get somebody to love you?" But Frieda was asleep. And I didn't know.

HEREISTHEHOUSEITISGREENANDWHITEITHASAREDDOORITISV
ERYPRETTYITISVERYPRETTYPRETTYPRETTYPRETTYP

There is an abandoned store on the southeast corner of Broadway and Thirty-fifth

① 戳,捅,督促。
② 大量涌出。

Street in Lorain, Ohio. It does not recede into its background of leaden sky, nor harmonize with the gray frame houses and black telephone poles around it. Rather, it foists itself on the eye of the passerby in a manner that is both irritating and melancholy. Visitors who drive to this tiny town wonder why it has not been torn down, while pedestrians, who are residents of the neighborhood, simply look away when they pass it.

At one time, when the building housed a pizza parlor, people saw only slow-footed teen-aged boys huddled about the corner. These young boys met there to feel their groins, smoke cigarettes, and plan mild outrages. The smoke from their cigarettes they **inhaled**① deeply, forcing it to fill their lungs, their hearts, their thighs, and keep at bay the shiveriness, the energy of their youth. They moved slowly, laughed slowly, but flicked the ashes from their cigarettes too quickly, too often, and exposed themselves, to those who were interested, as novices to the habit. But long before the sound of their lowing and the sight of their preening, the building was leased to a Hungarian baker, modestly famous for his **brioche**② and poppy-seed rolls. Earlier than that, there was a real-estate office there, and even before that, some gypsies used it as a base of operations. The gypsy family gave the large plate-glass window as much distinction and character as it ever had. The girls of the family took turns sitting between yards of velvet draperies and Oriental rugs hanging at the windows. They looked out and occasionally smiled, or winked, or beckoned—only occasionally. Mostly they looked, their elaborate dresses, long-sleeved and long-skirted, hiding the nakedness that stood in their eyes.

So fluid has the population in that area been, that probably no one remembers longer, longer ago, before the time of the gypsies and the time of the teen-agers when the Breedloves lived there, nestled together in the storefront. **Festering**③ together in the debris of a realtor's whim. They slipped in and out of the box of peeling gray, making no stir in the neighborhood, no sound in the labor force, and no wave in the mayor's office. Each member of the family in his own cell of consciousness, each making his own patchwork quilt of reality—collecting fragments of experience here, pieces of information there. From the tiny impressions gleaned from one another, they created a sense of belonging and tried to make do with the way they found each other.

The plan of the living quarters was as unimaginative as a first-generation Greek land-

---

① 吸入。

② 奶油面包卷。

③ 溃烂。

lord could contrive it to be. The large "store" area was **partitioned**① into two rooms by beaver board planks that did not reach to the ceiling. There was a living room, which the family called the front room, and the bedroom, where all the living was done. In the front room were two sofas, an upright piano, and a tiny artificial Christmas tree which had been there, decorated and dust-laden, for two years. The bedroom had three beds: an arrow iron bed for Sammy, fourteen years old, another for Pecola, eleven years old, and a double bed for Cholly and Mrs. Breedlove. In the center of the bedroom, for the even distribution of heat, stood a coal stove. Trunks, chairs, a small end table, and a cardboard "wardrobe" closet were placed around the walls. The kitchen was in the back of this apartment, a separate room. There were no bath facilities. Only a toilet bowl, inaccessible to the eye, if not the ear, of the **tenants**②.

There is nothing more to say about the furnishings. They were anything but describable, having been conceived, manufactured, shipped, and sold in various states of thoughtlessness, greed, and indifference. The furniture had aged without ever having become familiar. People had owned it, but never known it. No one had lost a penny or a brooch under the cushions of either sofa and remembered the place and time of the loss or the finding. No one had clucked and said, "But I had it just a minute ago. I was sitting right there talking to ..." or "Here it is. It must have slipped down while I was feeding the baby!" No one had given birth in one of the beds—or remembered with fondness the peeled paint places, because that's what the baby, when he learned to pull himself up, used to pick loose. No thrifty child had tucked a wad of gum under the table. No happy drunk—a friend of the family, with a fat neck, unmarried, you know, but God how he eats! — had sat at the piano and played "You Are My Sunshine." No young girl had stared at the tiny Christmas tree and remembered when she had decorated it, or wondered if that blue ball was going to hold, or if HE would ever come back to see it.

There were no memories among those pieces. Certainly no memories to be cherished. Occasionally an item provoked a physical reaction: an increase of acid irritation in the upper intestinal tract, a light flush of perspiration at the back of the neck as circumstances surrounding the piece of furniture were recalled. The sofa, for example. It had been purchased new, but the fabric had split straight across the back by the time it was delivered.

---

① 隔断。

② 租户。

The store would not take the responsibility.

"Looka here, buddy. It was O. K. when I put it on the truck. The store can't do anything about it once it's on the truck. ..." Listerine and Lucky Strike breath.

"But I don't want no tore couch if it's bought new." Pleading eyes and tightened testicles.

"Tough shit, buddy. Your tough shit..."

You could hate a sofa, of course—that is, if you could hate a sofa. But it didn't matter. You still had to get together $4.80 a month. If you had to pay $4.80 a month for a sofa that started off split, no good, and humiliating—you couldn't take any joy in owning it. And the joylessness stank, pervading everything. The stink of it kept you from painting the beaver board walls; from getting a matching piece of material for the chair; even from sewing up the split, which became a gash, which became a gaping chasm that exposed the cheap frame and cheaper upholstery. It withheld the refreshment in a sleep slept on it. It imposed a furtiveness on the loving done on it. Like a sore tooth that is not content to throb in isolation, but must diffuse its own pain to other parts of the body—making breathing difficult, vision limited, nerves unsettled, so a hated piece of furniture produces a **fretful**① **malaise**② that asserts itself throughout the house and limits the delight of things not related to it.

The only living thing in the Breedloves' house was the coal stove, which lived independently of everything and everyone, its fire being "out," "banked," or "up" at its own **discretion**③, in spite of the fact that the family fed it and knew all the details of its **regimen**④: sprinkle, do not dump, not too much.... The fire seemed to live, go down, or die according to its own **schemata**⑤. In the morning, however, it always saw fit to die.

HEREISTHEFAMILYMOTHERFATHERDICKANDJANETHEYLIVEINTHE
GREENANDWHITEHOUSETHEYAREVERYH

The Breedloves did not live in a storefront because they were having temporary difficulty adjusting to the cutbacks at the plant. They lived there because they were poor and

① 烦躁的。
② 莫名的不适。
③ 自行决定权。
④ 生活规则。
⑤ 纲要。

black, and they stayed there because they believed they were ugly. Although their poverty was traditional and **stultifying**①, it was not unique. But their ugliness was unique. No one could have convinced them that they were not **relentlessly**② and aggressively ugly. Except for the father, Cholly, whose ugliness (the result of despair, **dissipation**③, and violence directed toward petty things and weak people) was behavior, the rest of the family—Mrs. Breedlove, Sammy Breedlove, and Pecola Breedlove—wore their ugliness, put it on, so to speak, although it did not belong to them. The eyes, the small eyes set closely together under narrow foreheads. The low, irregular hairlines, which seemed even more irregular in contrast to the straight, heavy eyebrows which nearly met. Keen but **crooked**④ noses, with **insolent**⑤ nostrils. They had high cheekbones, and their ears turned forward. **Shapely**⑥ lips which called attention not to themselves but to the rest of the face. You looked at them and wondered why they were so ugly; you looked closely and could not find the source. Then you realized that it came from conviction, their conviction. It was as though some mysterious all-knowing master had given each one a **cloak**⑦ of ugliness to wear, and they had each accepted it without question. The master had said, "You are ugly people." They had looked about themselves and saw nothing to contradict the statement; saw, in fact, support for it leaning at them from every billboard, every movie, every glance. "Yes," they had said. "You are right." And they took the ugliness in their hands, threw it as a **mantle**⑧ over them, and went about the world with it. Dealing with it each according to his way. Mrs. Breedlove handled hers as an actor does a **prop**⑨: for the articulation of character, for support of a role she frequently imagined was hers—**martyrdom**⑩. Sammy used his as a weapon to cause others pain. He adjusted his behavior to it, chose his companions on the basis of it: people who could be fascinated, even intimidated by it. And Pecola. She hid behind hers. Concealed, veiled, eclipsed—peeping out from behind the **shroud**⑪

---

① 一成不变的。
② 不停地,不减弱地。
③ 放荡。
④ 不直的,弯曲的。
⑤ 粗野的,傲慢的。
⑥ 有曲线的。
⑦ 披风,斗篷。
⑧ (旧时的)披风、斗篷,职责,责任。
⑨ 道具。
⑩ 受难、殉道。
⑪ 裹尸布。

very seldom, and then only to yearn for the return of her mask.

This family, on a Saturday morning in October, began, one by one, to stir out of their dreams of affluence and vengeance into the anonymous misery of their storefront.

Mrs. Breedlove slipped noiselessly out of bed, put a sweater on over her nightgown (which was an old day dress), and walked toward the kitchen. Her one good foot made hard, bony sounds; the twisted one whispered on the linoleum. In the kitchen she made noises with doors, faucets, and pans. The noises were hollow, but the threats they implied were not. Pecola opened her eyes and lay staring at the dead coal stove. Cholly mumbled, thrashed about in the bed for a minute, and then was quiet.

Even from where Pecola lay, she could smell Cholly's whiskey. The noises in the kitchen became louder and less hollow. There was direction and purpose in Mrs. Breedlove's movements that had nothing to do with the preparation of breakfast. This awareness, supported by ample evidence from the past, made Pecola tighten her stomach muscles and ration her breath.

Cholly had come home drunk. Unfortunately he had been too drunk to quarrel, so the whole business would have to erupt this morning. Because it had not taken place immediately, the oncoming fight would lack spontaneity; it would be calculated, uninspired, and deadly.

Mrs. Breedlove came swiftly into the room and stood at the foot of the bed where Cholly lay.

"I need some coal in this house."

Cholly did not move.

"Hear me?" Mrs. Breedlove jabbed Cholly's foot.

Cholly opened his eyes slowly. They were red and **menacing**①. With no exception, Cholly had the meanest eyes in town.

"Awwwwww, woman!"

"I said I need some coal. It's as cold as a witch's tit in this house. Your whiskey ass wouldn't feel hell fire, but I'm cold. I got to do a lot of things, but I ain't got to freeze."

"Leave me lone."

"Not until you get me some coal. If working like a **mule**② don't give me the right to

---

① 威胁的，恐吓的。
② 骡子。

be warm, what am I doing it for? You sure ain't bringing in nothing. If it was left up to you, we'd all be dead...." Her voice was like an earache in the brain. "... If you think I'm going to wade out in the cold and get it myself, you'd better think again."

"I don't give a shit how you get it." A bubble of violence burst in his throat.

"You going to get your drunk self out of that bed and get me some coal or not?"

Silence.

"Cholly!"

Silence.

"Don't try me this morning, man. You say one more word, and I'll split you open!"

Silence.

"All right. All right. But if I sneeze once, just once, God help your butt!"

Sammy was awake now too, but pretending to be asleep. Pecola still held her stomach muscles **taut**① and conserved her breath. They all knew that Mrs. Breedlove could have, would have, and had, gotten coal from the shed, or that Sammy or Pecola could be directed to get it. But the unquarreled evening hung like the first note of a **dirge**② in sullenly expectant air. An escapade of drunkenness, no matter how routine, had its own ceremonial close. The tiny, undistinguished days that Mrs. Breedlove lived were identified, grouped, and classed by these quarrels. They gave substance to the minutes and hours otherwise dim and unrecalled. They relieved the tiresomeness of poverty, gave grandeur to the dead rooms. In these violent break sin routine that were themselves routine, she could display the style and imagination of what she believed to be her own true self. To deprive her of these fights was to deprive her of all the zest and reasonableness of life. Cholly, by his habitual drunkenness and **orneriness**③, provided them both with the material they needed to make their lives tolerable. Mrs. Breedlove considered herself an upright and Christian woman, burdened with a no-count man, whom God wanted her to punish. (Cholly was beyond redemption, of course, and redemption was hardly the point—could be heard discoursing with Jesus about Cholly, pleading with Him to help her "strike the bastard down from his pea-knuckle of pride." And once when a drunken gesture catapulted Cholly into the red-hot stove, she screamed, "Get him, Jesus! Get him!" If Cholly had stopped drinking, she would never have forgiven Jesus. She needed Cholly's sins desperately. The lower he

---

① 绷紧的。

② 哀歌。

③ 脾气暴躁。

sank, the wilder and more irresponsible he became, the more splendid she and her task became. In the name of Jesus.

No less did Cholly need her. She was one of the few things **abhorrent**① to him that he could touch and therefore hurt. He poured out on her the sum of all his inarticulate fury and aborted desires. Hating her, he could leave himself intact. When he was still very young, Cholly had been surprised in some bushes by two white men while he was newly but earnestly engaged in eliciting sexual pleasure from a little country girl. The men had shone a flashlight right on his behind. He had stopped, terrified. They chuckled. The beam of the flashlight did not move. "Go on," they said. "Go on and finish. And, nigger! make it good." The flashlight did not move. For some reason Cholly had not hated the white men; he hated, despised, the girl. Even a half-remembrance of this episode, along with **myriad**② other humiliations, defeats, and **emasculations**③, could stir him into flights of depravity that surprised himself—but only himself. Somehow he could not **astound**④. He could only be astounded. So he gave that up, too.

Cholly and Mrs. Breedlove fought each other with a darkly brutal formalism that was paralleled only by their lovemaking. **Tacitly**⑤ they had agreed not to kill each other. He fought her the way a coward fights a man—with feet, the palms of his hands, and teeth. She, in turn, fought back in a purely feminine way—with frying pans and pokers, and occasionally a flat iron would sail toward his head. They did not talk, groan, or curse during these beatings. There was only the muted sound of falling things, and flesh on unsurprised flesh.

There was a difference in the reaction of the children to these battles. Sammy cursed for a while, or left the house, or threw himself into the fray. He was known, by the time he was fourteen, to have run away from home no less than twenty-seven times. Once he got to Buffalo and stayed three months. His returns, whether by force or circumstance, were sullen. Pecola, on the other hand, restricted by youth and sex, experimented with methods of endurance. Though the methods varied, the pain was as consistent as it was deep. She struggled between an overwhelming desire that one would kill the other, and a profound wish

① 令人憎恨的。
② 无数的,各种各样的。
③ 阉割。
④ 使震惊。
⑤ 心照不宣地。

that she herself could die. Now she was whispering, "Don't, Mrs. Breedlove. Don't." Pecola, like Sammy and Cholly, always called her mother Mrs. Breedlove.

"Don't, Mrs. Breedlove. Don't."

But Mrs. Breedlove did.

By the grace, no doubt, of God, Mrs. Breedlove sneezed. Just once.

She ran into the bedroom with a dishpan full of cold water and threw it in Cholly's face. He sat up, choking and spitting. Naked and **ashen**①, he leaped from the bed, and with a flying tackle, grabbed his wife around the waist, and they hit the floor. Cholly picked her up and knocked her down with the back of his hand. She fell in a sitting position, her back supported by Sammy's bed frame. She had not let go of the dishpan, and began to hit at Cholly's thighs and groin with it. He put his foot in her chest, and she dropped the pan. Dropping to his knee, he struck her several times in the face, and she might have **succumbed**② early had he not hit his hand against the metal bed frame when his wife ducked. Mrs. Breedlove took advantage of this momentary suspension of blows and slipped out of his reach. Sammy, who had watched in silence their struggling at his bedside, suddenly began to hit his father about the head with both fists, shouting "You naked fuck!" over and over and over. Mrs. Breedlove, having snatched up the round, flat stove lid, ran tippy-toe to Cholly as he was pulling himself up from his knees, and struck him two blows, knocking him right back into the senselessness out of which she had provoked him. Panting, she threw a quilt over him and let him lie.

Sammy screamed, "Kill him! Kill him!"

Mrs. Breedlove looked at Sammy with surprise. "Cut out that noise, boy." She put the stove lid back in place, and walked toward the kitchen. At the doorway she paused long enough to say to her son, "Get up from there anyhow. I need some coal."

Letting herself breathe easy now, Pecola covered her head with the quilt. The sick feeling, which she had tried to prevent by holding in her stomach, came quickly in spite of her precaution. There surged in her the desire to heave, but as always, she knew she would not.

"Please, God," she whispered into the palm of her hand. "Please make me disappear." She squeezed her eyes shut. Little parts of her body faded away. Now slowly, now with a rush. Slowly again. Her fingers went, one by one; then her arms disappeared all the

---

① 面色苍白的。
② 屈服、投降。

way to the elbow. Her feet now. Yes, that was good. The legs all at once. It was hardest above the thighs. She had to be real still and pull. Her stomach would not go. But finally it, too, went away. Then her chest, her neck. The face was hard, too. Almost done, almost. Only her tight, tight eyes were left. They were always left.

Try as she might, she could never get her eyes to disappear. So what was the point? They were everything. Everything was there, in them. All of those pictures, all of those faces. She had long ago given up the idea of running away to see new pictures, new faces, as Sammy had so often done. He never took her, and he never thought about his going ahead of time, so it was never planned. It wouldn't have worked anyway. As long as she looked the way she did, as long as she was ugly, she would have to stay with these people. Somehow she belonged to them. Long hours she sat looking in the mirror, trying to discover the secret of the ugliness, the ugliness that made her ignored or despised at school, by teachers and classmates alike. She was the only member of her class who sat alone at a double desk. The first letter of her last name forced her to sit in the front of the room always. But what about Marie Appolonaire? Marie was in front of her, but she shared a desk with Luke Angelino. Her teachers had always treated her this way. They tried never to glance at her, and called on her only when everyone was required to respond. She also knew that when one of the girls at school wanted to be particularly insulting to a boy, or wanted to get an immediate response from him, she could say, "Bobby loves Pecola Breedlove! Bobby loves Pecola Breedlove!" and never fail to get peals of laughter from those in earshot, and mock anger from the accused.

It had occurred to Pecola some time ago that if her eyes, those eyes that held the pictures, and knew the sights—if those eyes of hers were different, that is to say, beautiful, she herself would be different. Her teeth were good, and at least her nose was not big and flat like some of those who were thought so cute. If she looked different, beautiful, maybe Cholly would be different, and Mrs. Breedlove too. Maybe they'd say, "Why, look at pretty-eyed Pecola. We mustn't do bad things in front of those pretty eyes." Pretty eyes. Pretty blue eyes. Big blue pretty eyes.

Run, Jip, run. Jip runs, Alice runs. Alice has blue eyes. Jerry has blue eyes. Jerry runs. Alice runs. They run with their blue eyes. Four blue eyes. Four pretty blue eyes. Blue-sky eyes. Blue—like Mrs. Forrest's blue blouse eyes. Morning-glory blue-eyes. Alice and Jerry blue story book-eyes.

Each night, without fail, she prayed for blue eyes. **Fervently**①, for a year she had prayed. Although somewhat discouraged, she was not without hope. To have something as wonderful as that happen would take a long, long time.

Thrown, in this way, into the binding conviction that only a miracle could relieve her, she would never know her beauty. She would see only what there was to see: the eyes of other people.

She walks down Garden Avenue to a small grocery store which sells penny candy. Three pennies are in her shoe—slipping back and forth between the sock and the inner-sole. With each step she feels the painful press of the coins against her foot. A sweet, endurable, even cherished irritation, full of promise and delicate security. There is plenty of time to consider what to buy. Now, however, she moves down an avenue gently buffeted by the familiar and therefore loved images. The **dandelions**② at the base of the telephone pole. Why, she wonders, do people call them weeds? She thought they were pretty. But grownups say, "Miss Dunion keeps her yard so nice. Not a dandelion anywhere." Hunkie women in black **babushkas**③ go into the fields with baskets to pull them up. But they do not want the yellow heads—only the jagged leaves. They make dandelion soup. Dandelion wine. Nobody loves the head of a dandelion. Maybe because they are so many, strong, and soon.

There was the sidewalk crack shaped like a Y, and the other one that lifted the concrete up from the dirt floor. Frequently her **sloughing**④ step had made her trip over that one. Skates would go well over this sidewalk—old it was, and smooth; it made the wheels glide evenly, with a mild whirr. The newly paved walks were bumpy and uncomfortable, and the sound of skate wheels on new walks was grating.

These and other inanimate things she saw and experienced. They were real to her. She knew them. They were the codes and touchstones of the world, capable of translation and possession. She owned the crack that made her stumble; she owned the clumps of dandelions whose white heads, last fall, she had blown away; whose yellow heads, this fall, she peered into. And owning them made her part of the world, and the world a part of her.

She climbs four wooden steps to the door of Yacobowski's Fresh Veg. Meat and Sun-

---

① 热切地。

② 蒲公英。

③ 老婆婆头巾。

④ 拖拉的。

dries Store. A bell tinkles as she opens it. Standing before the counter, she looks at the array of candies. All Mary Janes, she decides. Three for a penny. The resistant sweetness that breaks open at last to deliver peanut butter—the oil and salt which complement the sweet pull of **caramel**①. A peal of anticipation unsettles her stomach.

She pulls off her shoe and takes out the three pennies. The gray head of Mr. Yacobowski looms up over the counter. He urges his eyes out of his thoughts to encounter her. Blue eyes. Blear-dropped. Slowly, like Indian summer moving **imperceptibly**② toward fall, he looks toward her. Somewhere between **retina**③ and object, between vision and view, his eyes draw back, hesitate, and hover. At some fixed point in time and space he senses that he need not waste the effort of a glance. He does not see her, because for him there is nothing to see. How can a fifty-two-year-old white immigrant storekeeper with the taste of potatoes and beer in his mouth, his mind honed on the doe-eyed Virgin Mary, his sensibilities blunted by a permanent awareness of loss, see a little black girl? Nothing in his life even suggested that the feat was possible, not to say desirable or necessary.

"Yeah?"

She looks up at him and sees the **vacuum**④ where curiosity ought to lodge. And something more. The total absence of human recognition—the glazed separateness. She does not know what keeps his glance suspended. Perhaps because he is grown, or a man, and she a little girl. But she has seen interest, disgust, even anger in grown male eyes. Yet this vacuum is not new to her. It has an edge; somewhere in the bottom lid is the distaste. She has seen it lurking in the eyes of all white people. So. The distaste must be for her, her blackness. All things in her are flux and anticipation. But her blackness is static and dread. And it is the blackness that accounts for, that creates, the vacuum edged with distaste in white eyes.

She points her finger at the Mary Janes—a little black shaft of finger, its tip pressed on the display window. The quietly in offensive assertion of a black child's attempt to communicate with a white adult.

"Them." The word is more sigh than sense.

"What? These? These?" Phlegm and impatience mingle in his voice.

---

① 焦糖。
② 细微地,察觉不到地。
③ 视网膜。
④ 真空,空白。

She shakes her head, her fingertip fixed on the spot which, in her view, at any rate, identifies the Mary Janes. He cannot see her view—the angle of his vision, the slant of her finger, makes it incomprehensible to him. His **lumpy**① red hand plops around in the glass casing like the agitated head of a chicken outraged by the loss of its body.

"Christ. Kantcha talk?"

His fingers brush the Mary Janes.

She nods.

"Well, why'nt you say so? One? How many?"

Pecola unfolds her fist, showing the three pennies. He scoots three Mary Janes toward her—three yellow rectangles in each packet. She holds the money toward him. He hesitates, not wanting to touch her hand. She does not know how to move the finger of her right hand from the display counter or how to get the coins out of her left hand. Finally he reaches over and takes the pennies from her hand. His nails **graze**② her damp palm.

Outside, Pecola feels the inexplicable shame ebb.

Dandelions. A dart of affection leaps out from her to them. But they do not look at her and do not send love back. She thinks, "They are ugly. They are weeds." Preoccupied with that revelation, she trips on the sidewalk crack. Anger stirs and wakes in her; it opens its mouth, and like a **hot-mouthed**③ puppy, **laps up**④ the **dredges**⑤ of her shame.

Anger is better. There is a sense of being in anger. A reality and presence. An awareness of worth. It is a lovely surging. Her thoughts fall back to Mr. Yacobowski's eyes, his phlegmy voice. The anger will not hold; the puppy is too easily **surfeited**⑥. Its thirst too quickly quenched, it sleeps. The shame wells up again, its muddy **rivulets**⑦ seeping into her eyes. What to do before the tears come. She remembers the Mary Janes.

Each pale yellow wrapper has a picture on it. A picture of little Mary Jane, for whom the candy is named. Smiling white face. Blond hair in gentle disarray, blue eyes looking at her out of a world of clean comfort. The eyes are petulant, mischievous. To Pecola they are simply pretty. She eats the candy, and its sweetness is good. To eat the candy is somehow

---

① 凹凸不平的,块状的。
② 轻擦,轻触。
③ 贪婪的。
④ 舔食,欣然接受。
⑤ 残渣。
⑥ 吃得过多。
⑦ 小河、小溪。

to eat the eyes, eat Mary Jane. Love Mary Jane. Be Mary Jane.

Three pennies had bought her nine lovely orgasms with Mary Jane. Lovely Mary Jane, for whom a candy is named.

Winter

My daddy's face is a **study**①. Winter moves into it and presides there. His eyes become a cliff of snow threatening to **avalanche**②; his eyebrows bend like black limbs of leafless trees. His skin takes on the pale, cheerless yellow of winter sun; for a jaw he has the edges of a snowbound field dotted with **stubble**③; his high forehead is the frozen sweep of the **Erie**④, hiding currents of **gelid**⑤ thoughts that eddy in darkness. Wolf killer turned **hawk**⑥ fighter, he worked night and day to keep one from the door and the other from under the windowsills. A **Vulcan**⑦ guarding the flames, he gives us instructions about which doors to keep closed or opened for proper distribution of heat, lays kindling by, discusses qualities of coal, and teaches us how to **rake**⑧, feed, and bank the fire. And he will not unrazor his lips until spring.

Winter tightened our heads with a band of cold and melted our eyes. We put pepper in the feet of our stockings, Vaseline on our faces, and stared through dark icebox mornings at four stewed **prunes**⑨, slippery lumps of **oatmeal**⑩, and cocoa with a roof of skin.

But mostly we waited for spring, when there could be gardens.

By the time this winter had stiffened itself into a hateful knot that nothing could loosen, something did loosen it, or rather someone. A someone who splintered the knot into silver threads that tangled us, netted us, made us long for the dull **chafe**⑪ of the previous boredom.

This disrupter of seasons was a new girl in school named Maureen Peal. A high-

① 绘画草稿。
② 雪崩,崩塌。
③ 庄稼茬。
④ 伊利湖,北美五大湖之一。
⑤ 冰冷的,冻结的。
⑥ 鹰。
⑦ 主司火的神灵。
⑧ 铲煤。
⑨ 西梅干。
⑩ 麦片粥。
⑪ 烦恼。

yellow dream child with long brown hair braided into two lynch ropes that hung down her back. She was rich, at least by our standards, as rich as the richest of the white girls, swaddled in comfort and care. The quality of her clothes threatened to derange Frieda and me. Patent-leather shoes with buckles, a cheaper version of which we got only at Easter and which had disintegrated by the end of May. Fluffy sweaters the color of lemon drops tucked into skirts with pleats so orderly they astounded us. Brightly colored knee socks with white borders, a brown velvet coat trimmed in white rabbit fur, and a matching muff. There was a hint of spring in her sloe **green**① eyes, something summery in her complexion, and a rich autumn ripeness in her walk.

She enchanted the entire school. When teachers called on her, they smiled encouragingly. Black boys didn't trip her in the halls; white boys didn't stone her, white girls didn't suck their teeth when she was assigned to be their work partners; black girls stepped aside when she wanted to use the sink in the girls' toilet, and their eyes genuflected under sliding lids. She never had to search for anybody to eat with in the cafeteria—they flocked to the table of her choice, where she opened fastidious lunches, shaming our jelly-stained bread with egg-salad sandwiches cut into four dainty squares, pink-frosted cupcakes, sticks of celery and carrots, proud, dark apples. She even bought and liked white milk.

Frieda and I were bemused, irritated, and fascinated by her. We looked hard for flaws to restore our **equilibrium**②, but had to be content at first with uglying up her name, changing Maureen Peal to **Meringue Pie**③. Later a minor epiphany was ours when we discovered that she had a dog tooth—a charming one to be sure—but a dog tooth nonetheless. And when we found out that she had been born with six fingers on each hand and that there was a little bump where each extra one had been removed, we smiled. They were small triumphs, but we took what we could get—snickering behind her back and calling her Six-finger-dog-tooth-meringue-pie. But we had to do it alone, for none of the other girls would cooperate with our hostility. They adored her.

When she was assigned a **locker**④ next to mine, I could indulge my jealousy four times a day. My sister and I both suspected that we were secretly prepared to be her

① 蓝绿色。
② 平衡。
③ 蛋白派。
④ 储物柜。

friend, if she would let us, but I knew it would be a dangerous friendship, for when my eye traced the white border patterns of those Kelly-green knee socks, and felt the pull and lack of my brown stockings, I wanted to kick her. And when I thought of the unearned **haughtiness**① in her eyes, I plotted accidental slammings of locker doors on her hand.

As locker friends, however, we got to know each other a little, and I was even able to hold a sensible conversation with her without visualizing her fall off a cliff, or giggling my way into what I thought was a clever insult.

One day, while I waited at the locker for Frieda, she joined me.

"Hi."

"Hi."

"Waiting for your sister?"

"Uh-huh."

"Which way do you go home?"

"Down Twenty-first Street to Broadway."

"Why don't you go down Twenty-second Street?"

"'Cause I live on Twenty-first Street."

"Oh. I can walk that way, I guess. Partly, anyway."

"Free country."

Frieda came toward us, her brown stockings straining at the knees because she had tucked the toe under to hide a hole in the foot.

"Maureen's gonna walk part way with us."

Frieda and I exchanged glances, her eyes begging my restraint, mine promising nothing.

It was a false spring day, which, like Maureen, had pierced the shell of a deadening winter. There were **puddles**②, mud, and an inviting warmth that deluded us. The kind of day on which we draped our coats over our heads, left our galoshes in school, and came down with croup the following day. We always responded to the slightest change in weather, the most minute shifts in time of day. Long before seeds were stirring, Frieda and I were scruffing and poking at the earth, swallowing air, drinking rain....

As we emerged from the school with Maureen, we began to **moult**③ immediately. We

---

① 傲慢。
② 水洼。
③ 脱衣服。

put our head scarves in our coat pockets, and our coats on our heads. I was wondering how to **maneuver**① Maureen's fur muff into a gutter when a **commotion**② in the playground distracted us. A group of boys was circling and holding at bay a victim, Pecola Breedlove.

Bay Boy, Woodrow Cain, Buddy Wilson, Junie Bug—like a necklace of semiprecious stones they surrounded her. Heady with the smell of their own musk, thrilled by the easy power of a majority, they gaily harassed her.

"**Black e mo**③. Black e mo. Ya dadd sleeps nekked. Black e mo black e mo ya dadd sleeps nekked. Black e mo ..."

They had **extemporized**④ a verse made up of two insults about matters over which the victim had no control; the color of her skin and speculations on the sleeping habits of an adult, wildly fitting in its incoherence. That they themselves were black, or that their own father had similarly relaxed habits was irrelevant. It was their contempt for their own blackness that gave the first insult its teeth. They seemed to have taken all of their smoothly cultivated ignorance, their exquisitely learned self-hatred, their elaborately designed hopelessness and sucked it all up into a fiery cone of scorn that had burned for ages in the hollows of their minds—cooled and spilled over lips of outrage, consuming whatever was in its path. They danced a **macabre**⑤ ballet around the victim, whom, for their own sake, they were prepared to sacrifice to the flaming pit.

Black e mo Black e mo Ya daddy sleeps nekked Stch ta ta stch tata stach ta ta ta ta ta

Pecola edged around the circle crying. She had dropped her notebook, and covered her eyes with her hands.

We watched, afraid they might notice us and turn their energies our way. Then Frieda, with set lips and Mama's eyes, snatched her coat from her head and threw it on the ground. She ran toward them and brought her books down on Woodrow Cain's head. The circle broke. Woodrow Cain grabbed his head.

"Hey, girl!"

"You cut that out, you hear?" I had never heard Frieda's voice so loud and clear.

Maybe because Frieda was taller than he was, maybe because he saw her eyes, maybe

---

① 移动。

② 喧闹、骚乱。

③ 小黑鬼。

④ 即兴胡诌。

⑤ 恐怖的,可怕的。

because he had lost interest in the game, or maybe because he had a crush on Frieda, in any case Woodrow looked frightened just long enough to give her more courage.

"Leave her 'lone, or I'm gone tell everybody what you did!"

Woodrow did not answer; he just walled his eyes.

Bay Boy piped up, "Go on, gal. Ain't nobody bothering you."

"You shut up, Bullet Head." I had found my tongue.

"Who you calling Bullet Head?"

"I'm calling you Bullet Head, Bullet Head."

Frieda took Pecola's hand.

"Come on." "You want a fat lip?" Bay Boy drew back his fist at me.

"Yeah. Gimme one of yours."

"You gone get one."

Maureen appeared at my elbow, and the boys seemed reluctant to continue under her springtime eyes so wide with interest. They buckled in confusion, not willing to beat up three girls under her watchful gaze. So they listened to a budding male instinct that told them to pretend we were unworthy of their attention.

"Come on, man."

"Yeah. Come on. We ain't got time to fool with them."

Grumbling a few disinterested epithets, they moved away.

I picked up Pecola's notebook and Frieda's coat, and the four of us left the playground.

"Old Bullet Head, he's always picking on girls." Frieda agreed with me.

"Miss Forrester said he was **incorrigival**①."

"Really?" I didn't know what that meant, but it had enough of a doom sound in it to be true of Bay Boy.

While Frieda and I clucked on about the near fight, Maureen, suddenly animated, put her velvet-sleeved arm through Pecola's and began to behave as though they were the closest of friends.

"I just moved here. My name is Maureen Peal. What's yours?"

"Pecola."

"Pecola? Wasn't that the name of the girl in *Imitation of Life*?"

---

① 屡教不改。

"I don't know. What is that?"

"The picture show, you know. Where this **mulatto**① girl hates her mother 'cause she is black and ugly but then cries at the funeral. It was real sad. Everybody cries in it. Claudette Colbert too."

"Oh." Pecola's voice was no more than a sigh.

"Anyway, her name was Pecola too. She was so pretty. When it comes back, I'm going to see it again. My mother has seen it four times."

Frieda and I walked behind them, surprised at Maureen's friendliness to Pecola, but pleased. Maybe she wasn't so bad, after all. Frieda had put her coat back on her head, and the two of us, so draped, trotted along enjoying the warm breeze and Frieda's heroics.

"You're in my gym class, aren't you?" Maureen asked Pecola.

"Yes."

"Miss Erkmeister's legs sure are bow. I bet she thinks they're cute. How come she gets to wear real shorts, and we have to wear those old bloomers? I want to die every time I put them on."

Pecola smiled but did not look at Maureen.

"Hey." Maureen stopped short. "There's an Isaley's. Want some ice cream? I have money."

She unzipped a hidden pocket in her muff and pulled out a multi-folded dollar bill. I forgave her those knee socks.

"My uncle sued Isaley's." Maureen said to the three of us. "He sued the Isaley's in Akron. They said he was disorderly and that that was why they wouldn't serve him, but a friend of his, a policemen, came in and beared the witness, so the suit went through."

"What's a suit?"

"It's when you can beat them up if you want to and won't anybody do nothing. Our family does it all the time. We believe in suits."

At the entrance to Isaley's Maureen turned to Frieda and me, asking, "You all going to buy some ice cream?"

We looked at each other. "No," Frieda said.

Maureen disappeared into the store with Pecola.

Frieda looked placidly down the street; I opened my mouth, but quickly closed it. It

① 混血的。

was extremely important that the world not know that I fully expected Maureen to buy us some ice cream, that for the past 120 seconds I had been selecting the flavor, that I had begun to like Maureen, and that neither of us had a penny.

We supposed Maureen was being nice to Pecola because of the boys, and were embarrassed to be caught—even by each other—thinking that she would treat us, or that we deserved it as much as Pecola did.

The girls came out. Pecola with two dips of orange-pineapple, Maureen with black raspberry.

"You should have got some," she said. "They had all kinds. Don't eat down to the tip of the cone," she advised Pecola.

"Why?"

"Because there's a fly in there."

"How you know?"

"Oh, not really. A girl told me she found one in the bottom of hers once, and ever since then she throws that part away."

"Oh."

We passed the Dreamland Theater, and **Betty Grable**① smiled down at us.

"Don't you just love her?" Maureen asked.

"Uh-huh," said Pecola.

I differed. "**Hedy Lamarr**② is better."

Maureen agreed. "Ooooo yes. My mother told me that a girl named Audrey, she went to the beauty parlor where we lived before, and asked the lady to fix her hair like Hedy Lamarr's, and the lady said, 'Yeah, when you grow some hair like Hedy Lamarr's." She laughed long and sweet.

"Sounds crazy," said Frieda.

"She sure is. Do you know she doesn't even menstruate yet, and she's sixteen. Do you, yet?"

"Yes." Pecola glanced at us.

"So do I." Maureen made no attempt to disguise her pride. "Two months ago I started. My girl friend in Toledo, where we lived before, said when she started she was scared to death. Thought she had killed herself."

① 贝蒂·格雷布尔,美国舞蹈家,歌手,演员。
② 海蒂·拉马尔,奥地利裔美国女演员。

"Do you know what it's for?" Pecola asked the question as though hoping to provide the answer herself.

"For babies." Maureen raised two pencil-stroke eyebrows at the obviousness of the question. "Babies need blood when they are inside you, and if you are having a baby, then you don't menstruate. But when you're not having a baby, then you don't have to save the blood, so it comes out."

"How do babies get the blood?" asked Pecola.

"Through the life-line. You know. Where your belly button is. That is where the life-line grows from and pumps the blood to the baby."

"Well, if the belly buttons are to grow like-lines to give the baby blood, and only girls have babies, how come boys have bellybuttons?"

Maureen hesitated. "I don't know," she admitted. "But boys have all sorts of things they don't need." Her tinkling laughter was somehow stronger than our nervous ones. She curled her tongue around the edge of the cone, scooping up a dollop of purple that made my eyes water. We were waiting for a stop light to change. Maureen kept scooping the ice cream from around the cone's edge with her tongue; she didn't bite the edge as I would have done. Her tongue circled the cone. Pecola had finished hers; Maureen evidently liked her things to last. While I was thinking about her ice cream, she must have been thinking about her last remark, for she said to Pecola, "Did you ever see a naked man?"

Pecola blinked, then looked away. "No. Where would I see a naked man?"

"I don't know. I just asked."

"I wouldn't even look at him, even if I did see him. That's dirty. Who wants to see a naked man?" Pecola was agitated. "Nobody's father would be naked in front of his own daughter. Not unless he was dirty too."

"I didn't say 'father'. I just said 'a naked man'."

"Well ..."

"How come you said 'father'?" Maureen wanted to know.

"Who else would she see, dog tooth?" I was glad to have a chance to show anger. Not only because of the ice cream, but because we had seen our own father naked and didn't care to be reminded of it and feel the shame brought on by the absence of shame. He had been walking down the hall from the bathroom into his bedroom and passed the open door of our room. We had lain there wide-eyed. He stopped and looked in, trying to see in the dark room whether we were really asleep—or was it his imagination that opened eyes were looking at him? Apparently he convinced himself that we were sleeping. He moved away, confident that his little girls would not lie open-eyed like that, staring, staring. When he had moved on, the dark took only him away, not his nakedness. That stayed in the room with us. Friendly-like.

"I'm not talking to you," said Maureen. "Besides, I don't care if she sees her father naked. She can look at him all day if she wants to. Who cares?"

"You do," said Frieda. "That's all you talk about."

"It is not."

"It is so. Boys, babies, and somebody's naked daddy. You must be boy-crazy."

"You better be quiet."

"Who's gonna make me?" Frieda put her hand on her hip and jutted her face toward Maureen.

"You all ready made. Mammy made."

"You stop talking about my mama."

"Well, you stop talking about my daddy."

"Who said anything about your old daddy?"

"You did."

"Well, you started it."

"I wasn't even talking to you. I was talking to Pecola."

"Yeah. About seeing her naked daddy."

"So what if she did see him?"

Pecola shouted, "I never saw my daddy naked. Never."

"You did too," Maureen snapped. "Bay Boy said so."

"I did not."

"You did."

"I did not."

"Did Your own daddy, too!"

Pecola tucked her head in—a funny, sad, helpless movement. A kind of hunching of the shoulders, pulling in of the neck, as though she wanted to cover her ears.

"You stop talking about her daddy," I said.

"What do I care about her old black daddy?" asked Maureen.

"Black? Who you calling black?"

"You!"

"You think you so cute!" I swung at her and missed, hitting Pecola in the face. Furious at my clumsiness, I threw my notebook at her, but it caught her in the small of her velvet back, for she had turned and was flying across the street against traffic.

Safe on the other side, she screamed at us, "I am cute! And you ugly! Black and ugly black e mos. I am cute!"

She ran down the street, the green knee socks making her legs look like wild dandelion stems that had somehow lost their heads. The weight of her remark stunned us, and it was a second or two before Frieda and I collected ourselves enough to shout, "Six-finger-dog-tooth-meringue-pie!" We chanted this most powerful of our arsenal of insults as long as we could see the green stems and rabbit fur.

Grown people frowned at the three girls on the curbside, two with their coats draped over their heads, the collars framing the eyebrows like nuns' habits, black garters showing where they bit the tops of brown stockings that barely covered the knees, angry faces knotted like dark cauliflowers.

Pecola stood a little apart from us, her eyes hinged in the direction in which Maureen had fled. She seemed to fold into herself, like a **pleated**① wing. Her pain **antagonized**② me. I wanted to open her up, crisp her edges, **ram**③ a stick down that hunched and curving spine, force her to stand erect and spit the misery out on the streets. But she held it in where it could lap up into her eyes.

Frieda snatched her coat from her head. "Come on, Claudia. 'Bye, Pecola."

We walked quickly at first, and then slower, pausing every now and then to fasten garters, tie shoelaces, scratch, or examine old scars. We were sinking under the wisdom, accuracy, and relevance of Maureen's last words. If she was cute—and if anything could be believed, she was—then we were not. And what did that mean? We were lesser. Nicer, brighter, but still lesser. Dolls we could destroy, but we could not destroy the honey voices of parents and aunts, the obedience in the eyes of our peers, the slippery light in the eyes of our teachers when they encountered the Maureen Peals of the world. What was the secret? What did we lack? Why was it important? And so what? Guileless and without vanity, we were still in love with ourselves then. We felt comfortable in our skins, enjoyed the news

---

① 打褶的。
② 使愤怒。
③ 塞进。

that our senses released to us, admired our dirt, cultivated our scars, and could not comprehend this unworthiness. Jealousy we understood and thought natural—a desire to have what somebody else had; but envy was a strange, new feeling for us. And all the time we knew that Maureen Peal was not the Enemy and not worthy of such intense hatred. The Thing to fear was the Thing that made her beautiful, and not us.

Spring

SEEMOTHERMOTHERISVERYNICEMOTHERWILLYOUPRAYWITHJAN
EMOTHERLAUGHSLAUGHMOTHERLAUGHLA

The easiest thing to do would be to build a case out of her foot. That is what she herself did. But to find out the truth about how dreams die, one should never take the word of the dreamer. The end of her lovely beginning was probably the **cavity**① in one of her front teeth. She preferred, however, to think always of her foot. Although she was the ninth of eleven children and lived on a ridge of red Alabama clay seven miles from the nearest road, the complete indifference with which a rusty nail was met when it punched clear through her foot during her second year of life saved Pauline Williams from total anonymity. The wound left her with a crooked, archless foot that flopped when she walked—not a limp that would have eventually twisted her spine, but a way of lifting the bad foot as though she were extracting it from little whirlpools that threatened to pull it under. Slight as it was, this **deformity**② explained for her many things that would have been otherwise incomprehensible: why she alone of all the children had no nickname; why there were no funny jokes and anecdotes about funny things she had done; why no one ever remarked on her food preferences—no saving of the wing or neck for her—no cooking of the peas in a separate pot without rice because she did not like rice; why nobody teased her; why she never felt at home anywhere, or that she belonged anyplace. Her general feeling of separateness and unworthiness she blamed on her foot. Restricted, as a child, to this **cocoon**③ of her family's spinning, she cultivated quiet and private pleasures. She liked, most of all, to arrange things. To line things up in rows—jars on shelves at canning, peach pits on the

① (龋齿的)洞。
② 畸形。
③ 蚕茧。

step, sticks, stones, leaves—and the members of her family let these arrangements be. When by some accident somebody scattered her rows, they always stopped to retrieve them for her, and she was never angry, for it gave her a chance to rearrange them again. Whatever portable plurality she found, she organized into neat lines, according to their size, shape, or gradations of color. Just as she would never align a pine needle with the leaf of a cottonwood tree, she would never put the jars of tomatoes next to the green beans. During all of her four years of going to school, she was enchanted by numbers and depressed by words. She missed—without knowing what she missed—paints and crayons.

Near the beginning of World War I, the Williamses discovered, from returning neighbors and kin, the possibility of living better in another place. In shifts, lots, batches, mixed in with other families, they migrated, in six months and four journeys, to Kentucky, where there were mines and mill work.

"*When all us left from dawn home and was waiting down by the depot for the truck, it was nighttime. June bugs was shooting everywhere. They lighted up a tree leaf, and I seen a streak of green every now and again. That was the last time I seen real June bugs. These things up here ain't June bugs. They's something else. Folks here call them fireflies. Down home they was different. But I recollect that streak of green. I recollect it well.*"

In Kentucky they lived in a real town, ten to fifteen houses on a single street, with water piped right into the kitchen. Ada and Fowler Williams found a five-room frame house for their family. The yard was bounded by a once-white fence against which Pauline's mother planted flowers and within which they kept a few chickens. Some of her brothers joined the Army, one sister died, and two got married, increasing the living space and giving the entire Kentucky venture a feel of luxury. The relocation was especially comfortable to Pauline, who was old enough to leave school. Mrs. Williams got a job cleaning and cooking for a white minister on the other side of town, and Pauline, now the oldest girl at home, took over the care of the house. She kept the fence repair, pulling the pointed stakes erect, securing them with bits of wire, collected eggs, swept, cooked, washed, and minded the two younger children—a pair of twins called Chicken and Pie, who were still in school. She was not only good at housekeeping, she enjoyed it. After her parents left for work and the other children were at school or in mines, the house was quiet. The stillness and isolation both calmed and energized her. She could arrange and clean without interruption until two o'clock, when Chicken and Pie came home.

When the war ended and the twins were ten years old, they too left school to work. Pauline was fifteen, still keeping house, but with less enthusiasm. Fantasies about men and love and touching were drawing her mind and hands away from her work. Changes in weather began to affect her, as did certain sights and sounds. These feelings translated themselves to her in extreme melancholy. She thought of the death of new born things, lonely roads, and strangers who appear out of nowhere simply to hold one's hand, woods in which the sun was always setting. In church especially did these dreams grow. The songs caressed her, and while she tried to hold her mind on the wages of sin, her body trembled for redemption, salvation, a mysterious rebirth that would simply happen, with no effort on her part. In none of her fantasies was she ever aggressive; she was usually idling by the river bank, or gathering berries in a field when a someone appeared, with gentle and penetrating eyes, who—with no exchange of words—understood; and before whose glance her foot straightened and her eyes dropped. The someone had no face, no form, no voice, no odor. He was a simple Presence, an all-embracing tenderness with strength and a promise of rest. It did not matter that she had no idea of what to do or say to the Presence—after the wordless knowing and the soundless touching, her dreams disintegrated. But the Presence would know what to do. She had only to lay her head on his chest and he would lead her away to the sea, to the city, to the woods ... forever.

There was a woman named Ivy who seemed to hold in her mouth all of the sounds of Pauline's soul. Standing a little apart from the choir, Ivy sang the dark sweetness that Pauline could not name; she the death-defying death that Pauline yearned for; she sang of the Stranger who knew ...

Precious Lord take my hand
Lead me on, let me stand
I am tired, I am weak, I am worn.
Through the storms, through the night.
Lead me on to the light.
Take my hand, precious Lord, lead me on.

When my way grows **drear**①

---

① 阴沉的。

Precious Lord linger near,
When my life is almost gone
Hear my cry hear my call.
Hold my hand lest I fall
Take my hand, precious Lord, lead me on.

Thus it was that when the Stranger, the someone, did appear out of nowhere, Pauline was grateful but not surprised.

He came, **strutting**① right out of a Kentucky sun on the hottest day of the year. He came big, he came strong, he came with yellow eyes, flaring nostrils, and he came with his own music. Pauline was leaning idly on the fence, her arms resting on the cross rail between the pickets. She had just put down some biscuit dough and was cleaning the flour from under her nails. Behind her at some distance she heard whistling. One of these rapid, high-note riffs that black boys make up as they go while sweeping, shoveling, or just walking along. A kind of city-street music where laughter belies anxiety, and joy is as short and straight as the blade of a pocketknife. She listened carefully to the music and let it pull her lips into a smile. The whistling got louder, and still she did not turn around, for she wanted it to last. While smiling to herself and holding fast to the break in somber thoughts, she felt something **tickling**② her foot. She laughed aloud and turned to see. The whistler was bending down tickling her foot and kissing her leg. She could not stop her laughter—not until he looked up at her and she saw the Kentucky sun drenching the yellow, heavy-lidded eyes of Cholly Breedlove.

"*When I first seed Cholly, I want you to know it was like all the bits of color from that time down home when all us chil'ren went berry picking after a funeral and I put some in the pocket of my Sunday dress, and they mashed up and stained my hips. My whole dress was messed with purple, and it never did wash out. Not the dress nor me. I could feel that purple deep inside me. And that lemonade Mama used to make when Pap came in out the fields. It be cool and yellowish, with seeds floating near the bottom. And that streak of green them June bugs made on the trees the night we left from down home. All of them colors was in me. Just sitting there. So when Cholly come up and tickled my foot, it was like them ber-*

① 趾高气扬地走。
② 挠。

ries, that lemonade, them streaks of green the June bugs made, all come together. Cholly was thin then, with real light eyes. He used to whistle, and when I heerd him, **shivers**① *come on my skin.*"

Pauline and Cholly loved each other. He seemed to relish her company and even to enjoy her country ways and lack of knowledge about city things. He talked with her about her foot and asked, when they walked through the town or in the fields, if she were tired. Instead of ignoring her infirmity, pretending it was not there, he made it seem like something special and endearing. For the first time Pauline felt that her bad foot was an asset.

And he did touch her, firmly but gently, just as she had dreamed. But minus the gloom of setting suns and lonely river banks. She was secure and grateful; he was kind and lively. She had not known there was so much laughter in the world.

They agreed to marry and go 'way up north, where Cholly said steel mills were begging for workers. Young, loving, and full of energy, they came to Lorain, Ohio. Cholly found work in the steel mills right away, and Pauline started keeping house.

And then she lost her front tooth. But there must have been a **speck**②, a brown speck easily mistaken for food but which did not leave, which sat on the **enamel**③ for months, and grew, until it cut into the surface and then to the brown putty underneath, finally eating away to the root, but avoiding the nerves, so its presence was not noticeable or uncomfortable. Then the weakened roots, having grown accustomed to the poison, responded one day to severe pressure, and the tooth fell free, leaving a ragged stump behind. But even before the little brown speck, there must have been the conditions, the setting that would allow it to exist in the first place.

In that young and growing Ohio town whose side streets, even, were paved with concrete, which sat on the edge of a calm blue lake, which boasted an affinity with Oberlin, the underground railroad station, just thirteen miles away, this melting pot on the lip of America facing the cold but receptive Canada—What could go wrong?

"*Me and Cholly was getting along good then. We come up north; supposed to be more jobs and all. We moved into two rooms up over a furniture store, and I set about housekeep-*

---

① 战栗。
② 斑点。
③ 牙釉质。

ing. Cholly was working at the steel plant, and everything was looking good. I don't know what all happened. Everything changed. It was hard to get to know folks up here, and I missed my people. I weren't used to so much white folks. The ones I seed before was something hateful, but they didn't come around too much. I mean, we didn't have too much truck with them. Just now and then in the fields, or at the commissary. But they want all over us. Up north they was everywhere—next door, downstairs, all over the streets—and colored folks few and far between. Northern colored folk was different too. **Dicty-like**① *. No better than whites for meanness. They could make you feel just as* **no-count**② *, 'cept I didn't expect it from them. That was the lonesomest time of my life. I 'member looking out them front windows just waiting for Cholly to come home at three o'clock. I didn't even have a cat to talk to."*

In her loneliness, she turned to her husband for reassurance, entertainment, for things to fill the vacant places. Housework was not enough; there were only two rooms, and no yard to keep or move about in. The women in the town wore high-heeled shoes, and when Pauline tried to wear them, they **aggravated**③ her shuffle into a pronounced limp. Cholly was kindness still, but began to resist her total dependence on him. They were beginning to have less and less to say to each other. He had no problem finding other people and other things to occupy him—men were always climbing the stairs asking for him, and he was happy to accompany them, leaving her alone.

Pauline felt uncomfortable with the few black women she met. They were amused by her because she did not straighten her hair. When she tried to make up her face as they did, it came off rather badly. Their **goading**④ glances and private **snickers**⑤ at her way of talking (saying "chil'ren") and dressing developed in her a desire for new clothes. When Cholly began to quarrel about the money she wanted, she decided to go to work. Taking jobs as a day worker helped with the clothes, and even a few things for the apartment, but it did not help with Cholly. He was not pleased with her purchases and began to tell her so. Their marriage was shredded with quarrels. She was still no more than a girl, and still waiting for that plateau of happiness, that hand of a precious Lord who, when her

---

① 爱时髦的。
② 没价值的人。
③ 加重。
④ 刺激的。
⑤ 窃笑,暗笑。

way grew drear, would always linger near. Only now she had a clearer idea of what drear meant. Money became the focus of all their discussions, hers for clothes, his for drink. The sad thing was that Pauline did not really care for clothes and makeup. She merely wanted other women to cast favorable glances her way.

After several months of doing day work, she took a steady job in the home of a family of slender means and nervous, pretentious ways.

One winter Pauline discovered she was pregnant. When she told Cholly, he surprised her by being pleased. He began to drink less and come home more often. They eased back into a relationship more like the early days of their marriage, when he asked if she were tired or wanted him to bring her something from the store. In this state of ease, Pauline stopped doing day work and returned to her own housekeeping. But the loneliness in those two rooms had not gone away. When the winter sun hit the peeling green paint of the kitchen chairs, when the smoked **hocks**① were boiling in the pot, when all she could hear was the truck delivering furniture downstairs, she thought about back home, about how she had been all alone most of the time then too, but that this lonesomeness was different. Then she stopped staring at the green chairs, at the delivery truck; she went to the movies instead. There in the dark her memory was refreshed, and she succumbed to her earlier dreams. Along with the idea of romantic love, she was introduced to another—physical beauty. Probably the most destructive ideas in the history of human thought. Both originated in envy, thrived in insecurity, and ended in disillusion. In equating physical beauty with virtue, she stripped her mind, bound it, and collected self-contempt by the heap. She forgot lust and simple caring for. She regarded love as possessive mating, and romance as the goal of the spirit. It would be for her a well-spring from which she would draw the most destructive emotions, deceiving the lover and seeking to imprison the beloved, curtailing freedom in every way.

She was never able, after her education in the movies, to look at a face and not assign it some category in the **scale**② of absolute beauty, and the scale was one she absorbed in full from the silver screen. There at last were the darkened woods, the lonely roads, the river banks, the gentle knowing eyes. There the flawed became whole, the blind sighted, and the lame and halt threw away their crutches. There death was dead, and people made every gesture in a cloud of music. There the black-and-white images came together, making a

① 猪蹄。
② 标尺。

magnificent whole—all projected through the ray of light from above and behind.

It was really a simple pleasure, but she learned all there was to love and all there was to hate.

"*The onliest time I be happy seem like was when I was in the picture show. Every time I got, I went. I'd go early, before the show started. They'd cut off the lights, and everything be black. Then the screen would light up, and I'd move right on in them pictures. White men taking such good care of they women, and they all dressed up in big clean houses with the bathtubs right in the same room with the toilet. Them pictures gave me a lot of pleasure, but it made coming home hard, and looking at Cholly hard. I don't know. I 'member one time I went to see Clark Gable and Jean Harlow. I fixed my hair up like I'd seen hers on a magazine. A part on the side, with one little curl on my forehead. It looked just like her. Well, almost just like. Anyway, I sat in that show with my hair done up that way and had a good time. I thought I'd see it through to the end again, and I got up to get me some candy. I was sitting back in my seat, and I taken a big bite of that candy, and it pulled a tooth right out of my mouth. I could of cried. I had good teeth, not a rotten one in my head. I don't believe I ever did get over that. There I was, five months pregnant, trying to look like Jean Harlow, and a front tooth gone. Everything went then. Look like I just didn't care no more after that. I let my hair go back, plaited it up, and settled down to just being ugly. I still went to the pictures, though, but the meanness got worse. I wanted my tooth back. Cholly poked fun at me, and we started fighting again. I tried to kill him. He didn't hit me too hard, 'cause I were pregnant I guess, but the fights, once they got started up again, kept up. He begin to make me madder than anything I knowed, and I couldn't keep my hands off him. Well, I had that baby—a boy—and after that got pregnant again with another one. But it weren't like I thought it was gone be. I loved them and all, I guess, but maybe it was having no money, or maybe it was Cholly, but they sure worried the life out of me. Sometimes I'd catch myself* **hollering**① *at them and beating them, and I'd feel sorry for them, but I couldn't seem to stop. When I had the second one, a girl, I 'member I said I'd love it no matter what it looked like. She looked like a black ball of hair. I don't recollect trying to get pregnant that first time. But that second time, I actually tried to get pregnant. Maybe 'cause I'd had one already and wasn't scairt to do it. Anyway, I felt good, and wasn't thinking on the carrying, just the baby itself. I used to talk to it whilst it*

① 叫喊。

be still in the womb. Like good friends we was. You know. I be hanging wash and I knowed lifting weren't good for it. I'd say to it holt on now I gone hang up these few rags, don't get froggy; it be over soon. It wouldn't leap or nothing. Or I be mixing something in a bowl for the other chile and I'd talk to it then too. You know, just friendly talk. On up til the end I felted good about that baby. I went to the hospital when my time come. So I could be easeful. I didn't want to have it at home like I done with the boy. They put me in a big room with a whole mess of women. The pains was coming, but not too bad. A little old doctor come to examine me. He had all sorts of stuff. He gloved his hand and put some kind of jelly on it and rammed it up between my legs. When he left off some more doctors come. One old one and some young ones. The old one was learning the young ones about babies. Showing them how to do. When he got to me he said now these here women you don't have any trouble with. They deliver right away and with no pain. Just like horses. The young ones smiled it little. They looked at my stomach and between my legs. They never said nothing to me. Only one looked at me. Looked at my face, I mean. I looked right back at him. He dropped his eyes and turned red. He knowed, I reckon, that maybe I weren't no horse **foaling**[①]*. But them others. They didn't know. They went on. I seed them talking to them white women: 'How you feel? Gonna have twins?' Just shucking them, of course, but nice talk. Nice friendly talk. I got edgy, and when them pains got harder, I was glad. Glad to have something else to think about. I moaned something awful. The pains wasn't as bad as I let on, but I had to let them people know having a baby was more than a bowel movement. I hurt just like them white women. Just 'cause I wasn't* **hooping**[②] *and hollering before didn't mean I wasn't feeling pain. What'd they think? That just 'cause I knowed how to have a baby with no fuss that my behind wasn't pulling and aching like theirs? Besides, that doctor don't know what he talking about. He must never seed no mare foal. Who say they don't have no pain? Just 'cause she don't cry? 'Cause she can't say it, they think it ain't there? If they looks in her eyes and see them eyeballs lolling back, see the sorrowful look, they'd know. Anyways, the baby come. Big old healthy thing. She looked different from what I thought. Reckon I talked to it so much before I* **conjured up**[③] *a mind's eye view of it. So when I seed it, it was like looking at a picture of your mama when she was a girl. You knows who she is but she don't look the same. They give her to me for a nursing,*

---

① 产小马驹。

② 身体蜷曲。

③ 使想起,使浮现于脑海。

and she liked to pull my nipple off right away. She caught on fast. Not like Sammy, he was the hardest child to feed. But Pecola look like she knowed right off what to. A right smart baby she was. I used to like to watch her. You know they makes them greedy sounds. Eyes all soft and wet. A cross between a puppy and a dying man. But I knowed she was ugly. Head full of pretty hair, but Lord she was ugly. "

When Sammy and Pecola were still young Pauline had to go back to work. She was older now, with no time for dreams and movies. It was time to put all of the pieces together, make coherence where before there had been none. The children gave her this need; she herself was no longer a child. So she became, and her process of becoming was like most of ours: she developed a hatred for things that mystified or obstructed her; acquired virtues that were easy to maintain; assigned herself a role in the scheme of things; and harked back to simpler times for gratification.

She took on the full responsibility and recognition of breadwinner and returned to church. First, however, she moved out of the two rooms into a spacious first floor of a building that had been built as a store. She came into her own with the women who had despised her, by being more moral than they; she avenged herself on Cholly by forcing him to indulge in the weaknesses she despised. She joined a church where shouting was frowned upon, served on Stewardess Board No. 3, and became a member of Ladies Circle No. 1. At prayer meeting she moaned and sighed over Cholly's ways, and hoped God would help her keep the children from the sins of the father. She stopped saying "chil'ren" and said "childring" instead. She let another tooth fall, and was outraged by painted ladies who thought only of clothes and men. Holding Cholly as a model of sin and failure, she bore him like a crown of thorns, and her children like a cross.

It was her good fortune to find a permanent job in the home of a well-to-do family whose members were affectionate, appreciative, and generous. She looked at their houses, smelled their linen, touched their silk **draperies**①, and loved all of it. The child's pink **nightie**②, the stacks of white pillow slips edged with **embroidery**③, the sheets with top hems picked out with blue cornflowers. She became what is known as an ideal servant, for such a role filled practically all of her needs. When she bathed the little Fisher girl, it was

---

① 窗帘。
② 睡衣。
③ 绣花。

in a porcelain tub with silvery taps running infinite quantities of hot, clear water. She dried her in fluffy white towels and put her in cuddly nightclothes. Then she brushed the yellow hair, enjoying the roll and slip of it between her fingers. No zinc tub, no buckets of stove-heated water, no flaky, stiff, grayish towels washed in a kitchen sink, dried in a dusty back-yard, no tangled black puffs of rough wool to comb. Soon she stopped trying to keep her own house. The things she could afford to buy did not last, had no beauty or style, and were absorbed by the dingy storefront. More and more she neglected her house, her children, her man—they were like the afterthoughts one has just before sleep, the early-morning and late-evening edges of her day, the dark edges that made the daily life with the Fishers lighter, more delicate, more lovely. Here she could arrange things, clean things, line things up in neat rows. Here her foot flopped around on deep pile carpets, and there was no uneven sound. Here she found beauty, order, cleanliness, and praise. Mr. Fisher said, "I would rather sell her blueberry cobblers than real estate." She **reigned**① over cupboards stacked high with food that would not be eaten for weeks, even months; she was queen of canned vegetables bought by the case, special **fondants**② and ribbon candy curled up in tiny silver dishes. The creditors and service people who humiliated her when she went to them on her own behalf respected her, were even intimidated by her, when she spoke for the Fishers. She refused beef slightly dark or with edges not properly trimmed. The slightly **reeking**③ fish that she accepted for her own family she would all but throw in the fish man's face if he sent it to the Fisher house. Power, praise, and luxury were hers in this household. They even gave her what she had never had—a nickname—Polly. It was her pleasure to stand in her kitchen at the end of a day and survey her handiwork. Knowing there were soap bars by the dozen, bacon by the rasher, and reveling in her shiny pots and pans and polished floors. Hearing, "We'll never let her go. We could never find anybody like Polly. She will not leave the kitchen until everything is in order. Really, she is the ideal servant."

Pauline kept this order, this beauty, for herself, a private world, and never introduced it into her storefront, or to her children. Them she bent toward respectability, and in so doing taught them fear: fear of being clumsy, fear of being like their father, fear of not being loved by God, fear of madness like Cholly's mother's. Into her son she beat a loud desire

---

① 统治、为王。

② 软糖。

③ 散发臭气的。

to runaway, and into her daughter she beat a fear of growing up, fear of other people, fear of life.

All the meaningfulness of her life was in her work. For her virtues were **intact**①. She was an active church woman, did not drink, smoke, or **carouse**②, defended herself mightily against Cholly, rose above him in every way, and felt she was fulfilling a mother's role conscientiously when she pointed out their father's faults to keep them from having them, or punished them when they showed any **slovenliness**③, no matter how slight, when she worked twelve to sixteen hours a day to support them. And the world itself agreed with her.

It was only sometimes, sometimes, and then rarely, that she thought about the old days, or what her life had turned to. They were musings, idle thoughts, full sometimes of the old dreaminess, but not the kind of thing she cared to dwell on.

"*I started to leave him once, but something came up. Once, after he tried to set the house on fire, I was all set in my mind to go. I can't even 'member now what held me. He sure ain't give me much of a life. But it wasn't all bad. Sometimes things wasn't all bad. He used to come easing into bed sometimes, not too drunk. I make out like I'm asleep, 'cause it's late, and he taken three dollars out of my pocketbook that morning or something. I hear him breathing, but I don't look around. I can see in my mind's eye his black arms thrown back behind his head, the muscles like great big peach stones sanded down, with veins running like little swollen rivers down his arms. Without touching him I be feeling those ridges on the tips of my fingers. I sees the palms of his hands* **calloused**④ *to* **granite**⑤, *and the long fingers curled up and still. I think about the thick, knotty hair on his chest, and the two big swells his breast muscles make. I want to rub my face hard in his chest and feel the haircut my skin. I know just where the hair growth slacks out—just above his navel—and how it picks up again and spreads out. Maybe he'll shift a little, and his leg will touch me, or I feel his flank just graze my behind. I don't move even yet. Then he lift his head, turn over, and put his hand on my waist. If I don't move, he'll move his hand*

---

① 完好无损的,一尘不染的。
② 痛饮狂欢。
③ 懒散、邋遢。
④ 长老茧的。
⑤ 花岗岩。

over to pull and **knead**① *my stomach. Soft and slow-like. I still don't move, because I don't want him to stop. I want to pretend sleep and have him keep on rubbing my stomach. Then he will lean his head down and bite my tit. Then I don't want him to rub my stomach anymore. I want him to put his hand between my legs. I pretend to wake up, and turn to him, but not opening my legs. I want him to open them for me. He does, and I be soft and wet where his fingers are strong and hard. I be softer than I ever been before. All my strength in his hand. My brain curls up like wilted leaves. A funny, empty feeling is in my hands. I want to grab holt of something, so I hold his head. His mouth is under my chin. Then I don't want his hand between my legs no more, because I think I am softening away. I stretch my legs open, and he is on top of me. ... The bed springs sounds like them crickets used to back home. He puts his fingers in mine, and we stretches our arm outwise like Jesus on the cross. I hold on tight. My fingers and my feet hold on tight, because everything else is going, going. I know he wants me to come first. But I can't. Not until he does. Not until I feel him loving me. Just me. Sinking into me. Not until I know that my flesh is all that be on his mind. ...When he does, I feel a power. I be strong, I be pretty, I be young. And then I wait. He shivers and tosses his head. Now I be strong enough, pretty enough, and young enough to let him make me come. I take my fingers out of his and put my hands on his behind. My legs drop back onto the bed. I don't make no noise, because the chil'ren might hear. I begin to feel those little bits of color floating up into me—deep in me. That streak of green from the June-bug light, the purple from the berries trickling along my thighs, Mama's lemonade yellow runs sweet in me. Then I feel like I'm laughing between my legs, and the laughing gets all mixed up with the color, and I'm afraid I'll come, and afraid I won't. But I know I will. And I do. And it be rainbow all inside. And it lasts and lasts and lasts. I want to thank him, but don't know how, so I pat him like you do a baby. He asks me if I'm all right. I say yes. He gets off me and lies down to sleep. I want to say something, but I don't. I don't want to take my mind off the rainbow. I should get up and go to the toilet, but I don't. Besides, Cholly is asleep with his leg throwed over me. I can't move and don't want to.*

"But it ain't like that anymore. Most times he's thrashing away inside me before I'm woke, and through when I am. The rest of the time I can't even be next to his stinking drunk self. But I don't care 'bout it no more. My Maker will take care of me. I know He will. I

① 揉、捏。

know He will. Besides, it don't make no difference about this old earth. There is sure to be a glory. Only thing I miss sometimes is that rainbow. But like I say, I don't recollect it much anymore."

SEEFATHERHEISBIGANDSTRONGFATHERWILLYOUPLAYWITHJANEF ATHERISSMILINGSMILEFATHERSMILESMILE

When Cholly was four days old, his mother wrapped him in two blankets and one newspaper and placed him on a junk heap by the railroad. His Great Aunt Jimmy, who had seen her niece carrying a bundle out of the back door, rescued him. She beat his mother with a **razor strap**① and wouldn't let her near the baby after that. Aunt Jimmy raised Cholly herself, but took delight sometimes in telling him of how she had saved him. He gathered from her that his mother wasn't right in the head. But he never had a chance to find out, because she ran away shortly after the razor strap, and no one had heard of her since.

Cholly was grateful for having been saved. Except sometimes. Sometimes when he watched Aunt Jimmy eating **collards**② with her fingers, sucking her four gold teeth, or smelled her when she wore the **asafetida**③ bag around her neck, or when she made him sleep with her for warmth in winter and he could see her old, wrinkled breasts sagging in her nightgown—then he wondered whether it would have been just as well to have died there. Down in the rim of a tire under a soft black Georgia sky.

He had four years of school before he got courage enough to ask his aunt who and where his father was.

"That Fuller boy, I believe it was," his aunt said. "He was hanging around then, but he taken off pretty quick before you was born. I think he gone to Macon. Him or his brother. Maybe both. I hear old man Fuller say something bout it once."

"What name he have?" asked Cholly.

"Fuller, Foolish."

"I mean what his given name?"

"Oh." She closed her eyes to think, and sighed. "Can't recollect."

① 磨剃刀的皮带。

② 甘蓝菜。

③ 阿魏胶,一种药物。

It was in the spring, a very chilly spring, that Aunt Jimmy died of peach **cobbler**①. She went to a camp meeting that took place after a rainstorm, and the damp wood of the benches was bad for her. For four or five days afterward, she felt poorly. Friends came to see about her. Some made **camomile tea**②; others rubbed her with **liniment**③. Miss Alice, her closest friend, read the Bible to her. Still she was declining. Advice was prolific, if contradictory.

"Don't eat no whites of eggs."

"Drink new milk."

"Chew on this root."

Aunt Jimmy ignored all but Miss Alice's Bible reading. She nodded in drowsy appreciation as the words from First Corinthians droned over her. Sweet amens fell from her lips as she was chastised for all her sins. But her body would not respond.

Finally it was decided to fetch M'Dear. M'Dear was a quiet woman who lived in a shack near the woods. She was a competent midwife and decisive diagnostician. Few could remember when M'Dear was not around. In any illness that could not be handled by ordinary means—known cures, intuition, or endurance—the word was always, "Fetch M'Dear."

When she arrived at Aunt Jimmy's house, Cholly was amazed at the sight of her. He had always pictured her as shriveled and hunched over, for he knew she was very, very old. But M'Dear loomed taller than the preacher who accompanied her. She must have been over six feet tall. Four big white knots of hair gave power and authority to her soft black face. Standing straight as a poker, she seemed to need her hickory stick not for support but for communication. She tapped it lightly on the floor as she looked down at Aunt Jimmy's wrinkled face. She stroked the knob with the thumb of her right hand while she ran her left one over Aunt Jimmy's body. The backs of her long fingers she placed on the patient's cheek, then placed her palm on the forehead. She ran her fingers through the sick woman's hair, lightly scratching the scalp, and then looking at what the fingernails revealed. She lifted Aunt Jimmy's hand and looked closely at it—fingernails, back skin, the flesh of the palm she

---

① 酥皮水果馅饼。

② 甘菊茶。

③ 镇痛油。

pressed with three fingertips. Later she put her ear on Aunt Jimmy's chest and stomach to listen. At M'Dear's request, the women pulled the **slop jar**① from under the bed to show the stools. M'Dear tapped her stick while looking at them.

"Bury the slop jar and everything in it," she said to the women. To Aunt Jimmy she said, "You done caught cold in your womb. Drink pot liquor and nothing else."

"Will it pass?" asked Aunt Jimmy. "Is I'm gone be all right?"

"I reckon."

M'Dear turned and left the room. The preacher put her in his buggy to take her home. That evening the women brought bowls of pot liquor from black eyed peas, from mustards, from cabbage, from kale, from collards, from turnips, from beets, from green beans. Even the juice from a boiling hog jowl.

Two evenings later Aunt Jimmy had gained much strength. When Miss Alice and Mrs. Gaines stopped in to check on her, they remarked on her improvement. The three women sat talking about various miseries they had had, their cure or abatement, what had helped. Over and over again they returned to Aunt Jimmy's condition. Repeating its cause, what could have been done to prevent the misery from taking hold, and M'Dear's infallibility. Their voices blended into a **threnody**② of nostalgia about pain. Rising and falling, complex in harmony, uncertain in pitch, but constant in the recitative of pain. They hugged the memories of illnesses to their bosoms. They licked their lips and clucked their tongues in fond remembrance of pains they had endured—childbirth, **rheumatism**③, **croup**④, **sprains**⑤, backaches, **piles**⑥. All of the bruises they had collected from moving about the earth—harvesting, cleaning, **hoisting**⑦, **pitching**⑧, **stooping**⑨, kneeling, picking—always with young ones underfoot.

---

① 粪盆。

② 哀歌。

③ 风湿病。

④ 喉炎。

⑤ 扭伤。

⑥ 痔疮。

⑦ 抬高。

⑧ 跳跃。

⑨ 弯腰。

But they had been young once. The odor of their **armpits**[1] and **haunches**[2] had mingled into a lovely **musk**[3]; their eyes had been furtive, their lips relaxed, and the delicate turn of their heads on those slim black necks had been like nothing other than a **doe**[4]'s. Their laughter had been more touch than sound.

Then they had grown. Edging into life from the back door. Becoming. Everybody in the world was in a position to give them orders. White women said, "Do this." White children said, "Give me that." White men said, "Come here." Black men said, "Lay down." The only people they need not take orders from were black children and each other. But they took all of that and re-created it in their own image. They ran the houses of white people, and knew it. When white men beat their men, they cleaned up the blood and went home to receive abuse from the victim. They beat their children with one hand and stole for them with the other. The hands that felled trees also cut **umbilical cords**[5]; the hands that wrung the necks of chickens and butchered hogs also nudged African **violets**[6] into bloom; the arms that loaded sheaves, bales, and sacks rocked babies into sleep. They patted biscuits into flaky ovals of innocence—and shrouded the dead. They plowed all day and came home to nestle like **plums**[7] under the limbs of their men. The legs that straddled a mule's back were the same ones that straddled their men's hips. And the difference was all the difference there was.

Then they were old. Their bodies **honed**[8], their odor sour. **Squatting**[9] in a **cane**[10] field, stooping in a cotton field, kneeling by a river bank, they had carried a world on their heads. They had given over the lives of their own children and tendered their grandchildren. With relief they wrapped their heads in rags, and their

---

① 腋窝。
② 臀胯部。
③ 麝香味。
④ 母鹿。
⑤ 脐带。
⑥ 紫罗兰。
⑦ 李子,梅子。
⑧ 磨炼。
⑨ 蹲坐。
⑩ 甘蔗。

breasts in flannel; eased their feet into felt. They were through with lust and **lactation**[1], beyond tears and terror. They alone could walk the roads of Mississippi, the lanes of Georgia, the fields of Alabama **unmolested**[2]. They were old enough to be irritable when and where they chose, tired enough to look forward to death, disinterested enough to accept the idea of pain while ignoring the presence of pain. They were, in fact and at last, free. And the lives of these old black women were synthesized in their eyes—a **puree**[3] of tragedy and humor, wickedness and serenity, truth and fantasy.

They chattered far into the night. Cholly listened and grew sleepy. The lullaby of grief enveloped him, rocked him, and at last numbed him. In his sleep the foul odor of an old woman's stools turned into the healthy smell of horse shit, and the voices of the three women were muted into the pleasant notes of a mouth organ. He was aware, in his sleep, of being curled up in a chair, his hands tucked between his thighs.

On a wet Saturday night, before Aunt Jimmy felt strong enough to get out of the bed, Essie Foster brought her a peach cobbler. The old lady ate a piece, and the next morning when Cholly went to empty the slop jar, she was dead. Her mouth was a slackened O, and her hands, those long fingers with a man's hard nails, having done their laying by, could now be dainty on the sheet. One open eye looked at him as if to say, "Mind how you take holt of that jar, boy." Cholly stared back, unable to move, until a fly settled at the corner of her mouth. He fanned it away angrily, looked back at the eye, and did its bidding.

Aunt Jimmy's funeral was the first Cholly had ever attended. As a member of the family, one of the **bereaved**[4], he was the object of a great deal of attention. The ladies had cleaned the house, aired everything out, notified everybody, and stitched together what looked like a white wedding dress for Aunt Jimmy, a maiden lady, to wear when she met Jesus. They even produced a dark suit, white shirt, and tie for Cholly. The husband of one of them cut his hair. He was enclosed in fastidious tenderness. Nobody talked to him; that is, they treated him like the child he was, never engaging him in serious conversation; but they anticipated wishes he never had: meals ap-

---

① 泌乳。
② 不被骚扰。
③ 糊,酱。
④ 死者的亲友。

peared, hot water for the wooden tub, clothes laid out. At the wake he was allowed to fall asleep, and arms carried him to bed. Only on the third day after the death—the day of the funeral—did he have to share the spotlight. Aunt Jimmy's people came from nearby towns and farms. Her brother O. V., his children and wife, and lots of cousins. But Cholly was still the major figure, because he was "Jimmy's boy, the last thing she loved," and "the one who found her." The solicitude of the women the head pats of the men, pleased Cholly, and the creamy conversations fascinated him.

The funeral banquet was a peal of joy after the thunderous beauty of the funeral. It was like a street tragedy with spontaneity tucked softly into the corners of a highly formal structure. The deceased was the tragic hero, the survivors the innocent victims; there was the **omnipresence**① of the **deity**②, **strophe**③ and anti-strophe of the chorus of mourners led by the preacher. There was grief over the waste of Life; the stunned wonder at the ways of God, and the restoration of order in nature at the graveyard.

Thus the banquet was the **exultation**④, the harmony, the acceptance of physical frailty, joy in the termination of misery. Laughter, relief, a steep hunger for food.

Cholly had not yet fully realized his aunt was dead. Everything was so interesting. Even at the graveyard he felt nothing but curiosity, and when his turn had come to view the body at the church, he had put his hand out to touch the corpse to see if it were really ice cold like everybody said. But he drew his hand back quickly. Aunt Jimmy looked so private, and it seemed wrong somehow to disturb that privacy. He had trudged back to his pew dry-eyed amid tearful shrieks and shouts of others, wondering if he should try to cry.

Back in his house, he was free to join in the gaiety and enjoy what he really felt—a kind of carnival spirit. He ate greedily and felt good enough to try to get to know his cousins. There was some question, according to the adults, as to whether they were his real cousins or not, since Jimmy's brother O. V. was only a half-brother, and Cholly's mother had been the daughter of Jimmy's sister, but that sister was

---

① 无所不在。
② 上帝,天主。
③ 诗节。
④ 欢悦。

from the second marriage of Jimmy's father, and O. V. was from the first marriage.

One of these cousins interested Cholly in particular. He was about fifteen or sixteen years old. Cholly went outside and found the boy standing with some others near the tub where Aunt Jimmy used to boil her clothes.

He ventured a tentative "Hey." They responded with another. The fifteen-year-old named Jake offered Cholly a rolled-up cigarette. Cholly took it, but when he held the cigarette at arm's length and stuck the tip of it into the match flame, instead of putting it in his mouth and drawing on it, they laughed at him. Shamefaced, he threw the cigarette down. He felt it important to do something to reinstate himself with Jake. So when he asked Cholly if he knew any girls, Cholly said, "Sure."

All the girls Cholly knew were at the banquet, and he pointed to a cluster of them standing, hanging, draping on the back porch. Darlene too. Cholly hoped Jake wouldn't pick her.

"Let's get some and walk around," said Jake.

The two boys sauntered over to the porch. Cholly didn't know how to begin. Jake wrapped his legs around the rickety porch rail and just sat there staring off into space as though he had no interest in them at all. He was letting them look him over, and guardedly evaluating them in return.

The girls pretended they didn't see the boys and kept on chattering. Soon their talk got sharp; the gentle teasing they had been engaged in with each other changed to bitchiness, a serious kind of making fun. That was Jake's clue; the girls were reacting to him. They had gotten a whiff of his manhood and were shivering for a place in his attention.

Jake left the porch rail and walked right up to a girl named Suky, the one who had been most bitter in her making fun.

"Want to show me 'round?" He didn't even smile.

Cholly held his breath, waiting for Suky to shut Jake up. She was good at that, and well known for her sharp tongue. To his enormous surprise, she readily agreed, and even lowered her lashes. Taking courage, Cholly turned to Darlene and said, "Come on 'long. We just going down to the gully." He waited for her to screw up her face and say no, or what for, or some such thing. His feelings about her were mostly fear—fear that she would not like him, and fear that she would.

His second fear materialized. She smiled and jumped down the three waning steps to join him. Her eyes were full of compassion, and Cholly remembered that he was the bereaved.

"If you want to," she said, "but not too far. Mama said we got to leave early, and its getting dark."

The four of them moved away. Some of the other boys had come to the porch and were about to begin that partly hostile, partly indifferent, partly desperate mating dance. Suky, Jake, Darlene, and Cholly walked through several backyards until they came to an open field. They ran across it and came to a dry riverbed lined with green. The object of the walk was a wild **vineyard**[①] where the **muscadine**[②] grew. Too new, too tight to have much sugar, they were eaten anyway. None of them wanted—not then—the grape's easy **relinquishing**[③] of all its dark juice. The restraint, the holding off, the promise of sweetness that had yet to unfold, excited them more than full ripeness would have done. At last their teeth were on edge, and the boys diverted themselves by **pelting**[④] the girls with the grapes. Their slim black boy wrists made G **clefs**[⑤] in the air as they executed the tosses. The chase took Cholly and Darlene away from the lip of the gully, and when they paused for breath, Jake and Suky were nowhere in sight. Darlene's white cotton dress was stained with juice. Her big blue hair bow had come undone, and the sundown breeze was picking it up and fluttering it about her head. They were out of breath and sank down in the green-and-purple grass on the edge of the pine woods.

Cholly lay on his back **panting**[⑥]. His mouth full of the taste of muscadine, listening to the pine needles rustling loudly in their anticipation of rain. The smell of promised rain, pine, and muscadine made him **giddy**[⑦]. The sun had gone and pulled away its shreds of light. Turning his head to see where the moon was, Cholly caught sight of Darlene in moonlight behind him. She was huddled into a D—arms encircling

---

① 葡萄园。
② 圆叶葡萄。
③ 放弃,出让。
④ 向…投掷。
⑤ 谱号,G谱号就是我们熟知的高音谱号。
⑥ 喘气。
⑦ 头晕目眩。

drawn-up knees, on which she rested her head. Cholly could see her **bloomers**① and the muscles of her young thighs.

"We bed' get on back," he said.

"Yeah." She stretched her legs flat on the ground and began to retie her hair ribbon. "Mama gone whup me."

"Naw she ain't."

"Uh-huh. She told me she would if I get dirty."

"You ain't dirty."

"I am too. Looka that." She dropped her hands from the ribbon and smoothed out a place on her dress where the grape stains were heaviest.

Cholly felt sorry for her; it was just as much his fault. Suddenly he realized that Aunt Jimmy was dead, for he missed the fear of being whipped. There was nobody to do it except Uncle O. V., and he was the bereaved too.

"Let me," he said. He rose to his knees facing her and tried to tie her ribbon. Darlene put her hands under his open shirt and rubbed the damp tight skin. When he looked at her in surprise, she stopped and laughed. He smiled and continued knotting the bow. She put her hands back under his shirt.

"Hold still," he said. "How I gone get this?"

She tickled his ribs with her fingertips. He giggled and grabbed his rib cage. They were on top of each other in a moment. She corkscrewing her hands into his clothes. Here turning the play, digging into the neck of her dress, and then under her dress. When he got his hand in her bloomers, she suddenly stopped laughing and looked serious. Cholly, frightened, was about to take his hand away, but she held his wrist so he couldn't move it. He examined her then with his fingers, and she kissed his face and mouth. Cholly found her muscadine-lipped mouth distracting. Darlene released his head, shifted her body, and pulled down her pants. After some trouble with the buttons, Cholly dropped his pants down to his knees. Their bodies began to make sense to him, and it was not as difficult as he had thought it would be. She moaned a little, but the excitement collecting inside him made him close his eyes and regard her moans as no more than pine sighs over his head. Just as he felt an explo-

① 内裤。

sion threaten, Darlene froze and cried out. He thought he had hurt her, but when he looked at her face, she was staring wildly at something over his shoulder. He jerked around.

There stood two white men. One with a spirit **lamp**①, the other with a flashlight. There was no mistake about their being white; he could smell it. Cholly jumped, trying to kneel, stand, and get his pants up all in one motion. The men had long guns.

"Hee heehee heeeee." The snicker was a long asthmatic cough.

The other raced the flashlight all over Cholly and Darlene.

"Get on wid it, nigger," said the flashlight one.

"Sir?" said Cholly, trying to find a buttonhole.

"I said, get on wid it. An' make it good, nigger, make it good."

There was no place for Cholly's eyes to go. They slid about furtively searching for shelter, while his body remained paralyzed. The flashlight man lifted his gun down from his shoulder, and Cholly heard the clop of metal. He dropped back to his knees. Darlene had her head averted, her eyes staring out of the lamplight into the surrounding darkness and looking almost unconcerned, as though they had no part in the drama taking place around them. With a violence born of total helplessness, he pulled her dress up, lowered his trousers and underwear.

"Hee hee hee hee heeeeee."

Darlene put her hands over her face as Cholly began to simulate what had gone on before. He could do no more than make-believe. The flashlight made a moon on his behind.

"Hee hee hee hee heeee."

"Come on, coon. Faster. You ain't doing nothing for her."

"Hee hee hee hee heeee."

Cholly, moving faster, looked at Darlene. He hated her. He almost wished he could do it—hard, long, and painfully, he hated her so much. The flashlight wormed its way into his guts and turned the sweet taste of muscadine into rotten **fetid**② **bile**③. He stared at Darlene's hands covering her face in the moon and lamplight. They

---

① 酒精灯。

② 恶臭的。

③ 胆汁。

looked like baby claws.

"Hee hee hee hee heee."

Some dogs howled. "Thas them. Thas them. I know thas Old Honey."

"Yep," said the spirit lamp.

"Come on." The flashlight turned away, and one of them whistled to Honey.

"Wait," said the spirit lamp, "the coon ain't comed yet."

"Well, he have to come on his own time. Good luck, coon baby."

They crushed the pineneedles underfoot. Cholly could hear them whistling for a longtime, and then the dogs' answer no longer a howl, but warm excited yelps of recognition.

Cholly raised himself and in silence buttoned his trousers. Darlene did not move. Cholly wanted to strangle her, but instead he touched her leg with his foot. "We got to get, girl. Come on!"

She reached for her underwear with her eyes closed, and could not find them. The two of them patted about in the moonlight for the panties. When she found them, she put them on with the movements of an old woman. They walked away from the pine woods toward the road. He in front, she plopping along behind. It started to rain. "That's good," Cholly thought. "It will explain away our clothes."

When they got back to the house, some ten or twelve guests were still there. Jake was gone, Suky too. Some people had gone back for more helpings of food—potato pie, ribs. All were engrossed in early-night reminiscences about dreams, figures, **premonitions**①. Their stuffed comfort was **narcotic**② and had produced recollection sand fabrications of hallucinations.

Cholly and Darlene's entrance produced only a mild stir.

"Ya'll soaked, ain't you?"

Darlene's mother was only vaguely fussy. She had eaten and drunk too much. Her shoes were under her chair, and the side snaps of her dress were opened. "Girl. Come on in here. Thought I told you ..."

The next day was cleaning-out day, settling accounts, distributing Aunt Jimmy's goods. Mouths were set in downward crescents, eyes veiled, feet tentative.

---

① 预感。

② 致幻的,催眠的。

Cholly floated about aimlessly, doing chores as he was told. All the glamour and warmth the adults had given him on the previous day were replaced by a sharpness that agreed with his mood. He could think only of the flashlight, the muscadines, and Darlene's hands. And when he was not thinking of them, the vacancy in his head was like the space left by a newly pulled tooth still conscious of the rottenness that had once filled it. Afraid of running into Darlene, he would not go far from the house, but neither could he endure the atmosphere of his dead Aunt's house. The picking through her things, the comments on the "condition" of her goods. Sullen, irritable, he cultivated his hatred of Darlene. Never did he once consider directing his hatred toward the hunters. Such an emotion would have destroyed him. They were big, white, armed men. He was small, black, helpless. His subconscious knew what his conscious mind did not guess—that hating them would have consumed him, burned him up like a piece of soft coal, leaving only flakes of ash and a question mark of smoke. He was, in time, to discover that hatred of white men—but not now. Not in impotence but later, when the hatred could finds weet expression. For now, he hated the one who had created the situation, the one who bore witness to his failure, his impotence. The one whom he had not been able to protect, to spare, to cover from the round moon glow of the flashlight. The hee-hee-hee's. He recalled Darlene's dripping hair ribbon, flapping against her face as they walked back in silence in the rain. The loathing that galloped through him made him tremble.

The day Cholly's uncle was ready to leave, when everything was packed, when the quarrels about who gets what had seethed down to a sticking gravy on everybody's tongue, Cholly sat on the back porch waiting. It had occurred to him that Darlene might be pregnant. It was a wildly irrational, completely uninformed idea, but the fear it produced was complete enough.

He had to get away. Never mind the fact that he was leaving that very day. A town or two away was not far enough, especially since he did not like or trust his uncle, and Darlene's mother could surely find him, and Uncle O. V. would turn him over to her. Cholly knew it was wrong to run out on a pregnant girl, and recalled, with sympathy, that his father had done just that. Now he understood. He knew then what he must do—find his father. His father would understand. Aunt Jimmy said he had gone to Macon.

With no more thought than a chick leaving its shell, he stepped off the porch. He had gotten a little way when he remembered the treasure; Aunt Jimmy had left something, and he had forgotten all about it. In a stove flue no longer used, she had hidden a little meal bag which she called her treasure. He slipped into the house and found the room empty. Digging into the flue, he encountered webs and soot, and then the soft bag. He sorted the money; fourteen one-dollar bills, two two dollar bills, and lots of silver change ... twenty-three dollars in all. Surely that would be enough to get to Macon. What a good, strong sounding word, *Macon*.

Running away from home for a Georgia black boy was not a great problem. You just sneaked away and started walking. When night came you slept in a barn, if there were no dogs, a cane field, or an empty sawmill. You ate from the ground and bought root beer and licorice in little country stores. There was always an easy tale of woe to tell inquiring black adults, and whites didn't care, unless they were looking for sport.

When he was several days away, he could go to the back door of nice houses and tell the black cook or white mistress that he wanted a job weeding, plowing, picking, cleaning, and that he lived nearby. A week or more there, and he could take off. He lived this way through the turn of summer, and only the following October did he reach a town big enough to have a regular bus station. Dry-mouthed with excitement and apprehension, he went to the colored side of the counter to buy his ticket.

"How much to Macon, sir?"

"Eleven dollars. Five-fifty for children under twelve."

Cholly had twelve dollars and four cents.

"How old you be?"

"Just on twelve, sir, but my mama only give me ten dollars."

"You jest about the biggest twelve I ever seed."

"Please, sir, I got to get to Macon. My mama's sick."

"Thought you said you mama give you ten dollars."

"That's my play mama. My real mama is in Macon, sir."

"I reckon I knows a lying nigger when I sees one, but jest in case you ain't, jest in case one of them mammies is really dyin' and wants to see her little old smoke before she meets her maker, I gone do it."

Cholly heard nothing. The insults were part of the nuisances of life, like **lice**[①]. The bus wasn't leaving for four hours, and the minutes of those hours struggled like **gnats**[②] on fly paper—dying slow, exhausted with the fight to stay alive. Cholly was afraid to stir, even to relieve himself. The bus might leave while he was gone. Finally, rigid with constipation, he boarded the bus to Macon.

He found a window seat in the back all to himself, and all of Georgia slid before his eyes, until the sun shrugged out of sight. Even in the dark, he hungered to see, and only after the fiercest fight to keep his eyes open did he fall asleep. When he awoke it was very well into day, and a fat black lady was nudging him with a biscuit gashed with cold bacon. With the taste of bacon still in his teeth, they sidled into Macon.

At the end of the alley he could see men clustered like grapes. One large whooping voice spiraled over the heads of the bended forms. The kneeling forms, the leaning forms, all intent on one ground spot. As he came closer, he inhaled a rife and stimulating man smell. The men were gathered, just as the man in the pool hall had said, for and about dice and money. Each figure was decorated some way with the slight pieces of green. Some of them had separated their money, folded the bills around their fingers, clenched the fingers into fists, so the neat ends of the money stuck out in a blend of daintiness and violence. Others had stacked their bills, creased them down the middle, and held the wad as though they were about to deal cards. Still others had left their money in loosely crumpled balls. One man had money sticking out from under his cap. Another stroked his bills with a thumb and forefinger. There was more money in those black hands than Cholly had ever seen before. He shared their excitement, and the dry-mouthed apprehension on meeting his father gave way to the saliva flow of excitement. He glanced at the faces, looking for the one who might be his father. How would he know him? Would he look like a larger version of himself? At that moment Cholly could not remember what his own self looked like. He only knew he was fourteen years old, black, and already six feet tall. He searched the faces and saw only eyes, pleading eyes, cold eyes, eyes gone flat with malice, others laced with fear—all focused on the movement of a pair of dice that one man was throwing,

---

① 虱子。

② 小飞虫。

snatching up[①], and throwing again. Chanting a kind of **litany**[②] to which the others responded, rubbing the dice as though they were two hot coals, he whispered to them. Then with a whoop the cubes flew from his hand to a chorus of amazements and disappointments. Then the thrower scooped up money, and someone shouted, "Take it and crawl, you water dog, you, the best I know." There was some laughter, and a noticeable release of tension, during which some men exchanged money.

Cholly tapped an old white-haired man on the back.

"Can you tell me is Samson Fuller 'round here somewhere?"

"Fuller?" The name was familiar to the man's tongue. "I don't know, he here somewhere. They he is. In the brown jacket." The man pointed.

A man in a light-brown jacket stood at the far end of the group. He was gesturing in a quarrelsome, agitated manner with another man. Both of them had folded their faces in anger. Cholly edged around to where they stood, hardly believing he was at the end of his journey. There was his father, a man like any other man, but there indeed were his eyes, his mouth, his whole head. His shoulders lurked beneath that jacket, his voice, his hands—all real. They existed, really existed, somewhere. Right here. Cholly had always thought of his father as a giant of a man, so when he was very close it was with a shock that he discovered that he was taller than his father. In fact, he was staring at a balding spot on his father's head, which he suddenly wanted to stroke. While thus fascinated by the pitiable clean space **hedged around**[③] by neglected tufts of wool, the man turned a hard, belligerent face to him.

"What you want, boy?"

"Uh. I mean ... is you Samson Fuller?"

"Who sent you?"

"Huh?"

"You Melba's boy?"

No, sir, I'm ..." Cholly blinked. He could not remember his mother's name. Had he ever known it? What could he say? Whose boy was he? He couldn't say, "I'm your boy." That sounded disrespectful.

---

① 迅速拿起。
② 祷文。
③ 被包围。

The man was impatient. "Something wrong with your head? Who told you to come after me?"

"Nobody." Cholly's hands were sweating. The man's eyes frightened him. "I just thought ... I mean, I was just wandering around, and, uh, my name is Cholly...."

But Fuller had turned back to the game that was about to begin anew. He bent down to toss a bill on the ground, and waited for a throw. When it was gone, he stood up and in a **vexed**① and whiny voice shouted at Cholly, "Tell that bitch she get her money. Now, get the fuck outta my face!"

Cholly was a long time picking his foot up from the ground. He was trying to back up and walk away. Only with extreme effort could he get the first muscle to co-operate. When it did, he walked back up the alley, out of its shade, toward the blazing light of the street. As he emerged into the sun, he felt something in his legs give way. An orange **crate**② with a picture of clasping hands pasted on its side was upended on the sidewalk. Cholly sat down on it. The sunshine dropped like honey on his head. A horse-drawn fruit wagon went by, its driver singing: "Fresh from the vine, sweet as sugar, red as wine."

Noises seemed to increase in volume. The clic-cloc of the women's heels, the laughter of idling men in doorways. There was a street car somewhere. Cholly sat. He knew if he was very still he would be all right. But then the trace of pain edged his eyes, and he had to use everything to send it away. If he was very still, he thought, and kept his eyes on one thing, the tears would not come. So he sat in the dripping honey sun, pulling every nerve and muscle into service to stop the fall of water from his eyes. While straining in this way, focusing every **erg**③ of energy on his eyes, his **bowels**④ suddenly opened up, and before he could realize what he knew, liquid stools were running down his legs. At the mouth of the alley where his father was, on an orange crate in the sun, on a street full of grown men and women, he had **soiled**⑤ himself like a baby.

Evening came. The dark, the warmth, the quiet, enclosed Cholly like the skin

---

① 恼火的。
② 大木箱。
③ 尔格,能量的单位。
④ 肠。
⑤ 弄脏。

and flesh of an elder berry protecting its own seed.

Cholly stirred. The ache in his head was all he felt. Soon, like bright bits of glass, the events of that afternoon cut into him. At first he saw only money in black fingers, then he thought he was sitting on an uncomfortable chair, but when he looked, it turned out to be the head of a man, a head with a bald spot the size of an orange. When finally these bits merged into full memory, Cholly began to smell himself. He stood up and found himself weak, trembling, and dizzy. He leaned for a moment on the pier post, then took off his pants, underwear, socks, and shoes. He rubbed handfuls of dirt on his shoes; then he crawled to the river edge. He had to find the water's beginning with his hands, for he could not see it clearly. Slowly he swirled his clothes in the water and rubbed them until he thought they were clean. Back near his post, he took off his shirt and wrapped it around his waist, then spread his trousers and underwear on the ground. He squatted down and picked at the rotted wood of the pier. Suddenly he thought of his Aunt Jimmy, her asafetida bag, her four gold teeth, and the purple rag she wore around her head. With a longing that almost split him open, he thought of her handing him a bit of smoked hock out of her dish. He remembered just how she held it—clumsy-like, in three fingers, but with so much affection. No words, just picking up a bit of meat and holding it out to him. And then the tears rushed down his cheeks, to make a **bouquet**① under his chin.

Three women are leaning out of two windows. They see the long clean neck of a new young boy and call to him. He goes to where they are. Inside, it is dark and warm. They give him lemonade in a Mason jar. As he drinks, their eyes float up to him through the bottom of the jar, through the slick sweet water. They give him back his manhood, which he takes aimlessly.

The pieces of Cholly's life could become coherent only in the head of a musician. Only those who talk their talk through the gold of curved metal, or in the touch of black-and-white rectangles and taut skins and strings echoing from wooden corridors, could give true form to his life. Only a musician would sense, know, without even knowing that he knew, that Cholly was free. Dangerously free. Free to feel whatever he felt—fear, guilt, shame, love, grief, pity. Free to be tender or violent, to whistle or

---

① 花束。

weep. Free to sleep in doorways or between the white sheets of a singing woman. Free to take a job, free to leave it. He could go to jail and not feel imprisoned, for he had already seen the furtiveness in the eyes of his jailer, free to say, "No, suh," and smile, for he had already killed three white men. Free to take a woman's insults, for his body had already conquered hers. Free even to knock her in the head, for he had already cradled that head in his arms. Free to be gentle when she was sick, or mop her floor, for she knew what and where his maleness was. He was free to drink himself into a silly helplessness, for he had already been a gandy dancer, done thirty days on a chain gang, and picked a woman's bullet out of the calf of his leg. He was free to live his fantasies, and free even to die, the how and the when of which held no interest for him. In those days, Cholly was truly free. Abandoned in a junk heap by his mother, rejected for a crap game by his father, there was nothing more to lose. He was alone with his own perceptions and appetites, and they alone interested him.

It was in this godlike state that he met Pauline Williams. And it was Pauline, or rather marrying her, that did for him what the flashlight did not do. The constantness, variety lessness, the sheer weight of sameness drove him to despair and froze his imagination. To be required to sleep with the same woman forever was a curious and unnatural idea to him; to be expected to dredge up enthusiasms for old acts, and routine ploys; he wondered at the arrogance of the female. When he had met Pauline in Kentucky, she was hanging over a fence scratching herself with a broken foot. The neatness, the charm, the joy he awakened in her made him want to nest with her. He had yet to discover what destroyed that desire. But he did not dwell on it. He thought rather of whatever had happened to the curiosity he used to feel. Nothing, nothing, interested him now. Not himself, not other people. Only in drink was there some break, some floodlight, and when that closed, there was oblivion.

But the aspect of married life that dumbfounded him and rendered him totally disfunctional was the appearance of children. Having no idea of how to raise children, and having never watched any parent raise himself, he could not even comprehend what such a relationship should be. Had he been interested in the accumulation of things, he could have thought of them as his material heirs; had he needed to prove himself to some nameless "others", he could have wanted them to excel in his own image and for his own sake. He had not been alone in the world since he was thirteen, knowing only a dying old woman who felt responsible for him, but whose age, sex, and interests were sore mote from his own, he might have felt a stable connection between himself and the children. As it was, he reacted to them, and his reactions were based on what he felt at the moment.

So it was on a Saturday afternoon, in the thin light of spring, he staggered home **reeling**① drunk and saw his daughter in the kitchen.

She was washing dishes. Her small back hunched over the sink. Cholly saw her dimly and could not tell what he saw or what he felt. Then he became aware that he was uncomfortable; next he felt the discomfort dissolve into pleasure. The sequence of his emotions was revulsion, guilt, pity, then love. His revulsion was a reaction to her young, helpless, hopeless presence. Her back hunched that way; her head to one side as though crouching from a permanent and unrelieved blow. Why did she have to look so whipped? She was a child—unburdened—why wasn't she happy? The clear statement of her misery was an accusation. He wanted to break her neck—but tenderly. Guilt and impotence rose in a **bilious**② duet. What could he do for her—ever? What give her? What say to her? What could a burned-out black man say to the hunched back of his eleven-year-old daughter? If he looked into her face, he would see those haunted, loving eyes. The hauntedness would irritate him—he love would move him to fury. How dare she love him? Hadn't she any sense at all? What was he supposed to do about that? Return it? How? What could his calloused hands produce to make her smile? What of his knowledge of the world and of life could be useful to her? What could his heavy arms and **befuddled**③ brain accomplish that would earn him his own respect, that would in turn allow him to accept her love? His hatred of her slimed in his stomach and threatened to become vomit. But just before the puke moved from anticipation to sensation, she shifted her weight and stood on one foot scratching the back of her calf with her toe. It was a quiet and pitiful gesture. Her hands were going around and around a frying pan, scraping flecks of black into cold, greasy dishwater. The timid, tucked-in look of the scratching toe—that was what

---

① 踉跄，摇摇晃晃摆动。

② 狂暴的。

③ 糊涂的。

Pauline was doing the first time he saw her in Kentucky. Leaning over a fence staring at nothing in particular. The creamy toe of her bare foot scratching a velvet leg. It was such a small and simple gesture, but it filled him then with a wondering softness. Not the usual lust to part tight legs with his own, but a tenderness, a protectiveness. A desire to cover her foot with his hand and gently nibble away the itch from the calf with his teeth. He did it then, and startled Pauline into laughter. He did it now.

The tenderness welled up in him, and he sank to his knees, his eyes on the foot of his daughter. Crawling on all fours toward her, he raised his hand and caught the foot in an upward stroke. Pecola lost her balance and was about to **careen**① to the floor. Cholly raised his other hand to her hips to save her from falling. He put his head down and nibbled at the back of her leg. His mouth trembled at the firm sweetness of the flesh. He closed his eyes, letting his fingers dig into her waist. The rigidness of her shocked body, the silence of her stunned throat, was better than Pauline's easy laughter had been. The confused mixture of his memories of Pauline and the doing of a wild and forbidden thing excited him, and a bolt of desire ran down his genitals, giving it length, and softening the lips of his anus. Surrounding all of this lust was a border of politeness. He wanted to fuck her—tenderly. But the tenderness would not hold. The tightness of her vagina was more than he could bear. His soul seemed to slip down to his guts and fly out into her, and the gigantic thrust he made into her then provoked the only sound she made—a hollow suck of air in the back of her throat. Like the rapid loss of air from a circus balloon.

Following the disintegration—the falling away—of sexual desire, he was conscious of her wet, soapy hands on his wrists, the fingers clenching, but whether her grip was from a hopeless but stubborn struggle to be free, or from some other emotion, he could not tell.

She appeared to have fainted. Cholly stood up and could see only her grayish panties, so sad and limp around her ankles. Again the hatred mixed with tenderness. The hatred would not let him pick her up; the tenderness forced him to cover her.

So when the child regained consciousness, she was lying on the kitchen floor under a heavy quilt, trying to connect the pain between her legs with the face of her

① 倾斜。

mother looming over her.

Ⅳ. 思考题

1. The novel's epigraph is a "Dick and Jane" children's story and the story is repeated for three times with a monotonous rhythm. Why does Morrison make this arrangement? Also, each segment of the "Dick and Jane" story is used as a section "title" to introduce its counterpart in Pecola's family. What is the author's intention of doing this?
2. References to movies and movie stars punctuate the narrative and everyday consumer goods like the white baby dolls, Shirley Temple cups, Mary Jane Candies figure largely in the novel. What purposes do they serve?
3. Toni Morrison puts different narrative voices in the novel: she breaks the narrative into parts that have to be reassembled by the reader. Also, note that Pecola's voice is absent throughout the novel. We have no sense of what she thinks and what she has experienced. Why does Morrison choose to shift the point of view? What would the novel be like if it is narrated from an omniscient third-person point of view or first-person point of view?
4. Analyze the character Cholly Breedlove. Is he a tragic character? What motivate him to rape his daughter?
5. What is the standard of beauty in our society? Think about how it is constructed.

Ⅴ. 文学批评

非裔美国文学简介

To read African American novels is, nevertheless, to be confronted with difference. And one of the fundamental differences between the earlier periods of African American novel writing and the present is not only the range of voices that we hear but also the intensity and creativity with which African American writers transform their own and other literary traditions. James Olney notes that a remarkable quality of the early slave narrative—the predecessor to the novel—was not its unqualified uniqueness, but its sameness. Like the slave narrators, early African American novelists had to map a course for their fictional texts between an often-hostile audience and a demanding sponsor or publisher. This "triangular relationship of narrator, audience, and sponsors" continued to dictate the development of thematic and formal conventions in the novel well into the twentieth century. The burden of multiple allegiances evokes a Du Boisian "double consciousness" and has been reinterpreted by Bernard Bell as "socialized ambivalence… the network of understandings that defines black American culture and informs black American consciousness… resulting from systematic barriers of exclusions and discrimination… producing a residue of shared memories and frames of reference." While the social mission of the novel bears a special relationship to the history of African Americans, its aesthetic significance lies in the rhetorical strategies and metaphorical language the author uses to reenact if not resolve the novel's inherent tensions. At times these tensions appear in the form of conflicting literary traditions: sentimentalism and realism in Frances Harper and Jessie Fauset; or gothicism and naturalism in Richard Wright and Gayle Jones, for example. At other times the novelist creates dramatic tension by borrowing from African-derived oral forms or traditional Western literary forms. Charles Chesnutt turns to the folktale; Alice Walker, the epistolary novel and the female Bildungsroman; Charles Johnson and Sherley Anne Williams, the slave narrative; Margaret Walker, the folk novel; James Baldwin and Leon Forrest, the African American ser-mon; and Ralph Ellison and Albert Murray, the blues. The value placed on narrative closure differs markedly from novel to novel as well. Ernest Gaines wants us to see the lessons learned by the men and women who people his narratives; Toni Morrison emphasizes the internalization of those conflicts that shatter our sense of reality, making narrative closure difficult.

The African American novel maintains its reputation for linguistic and rhetorical innovation, through reinvention as a narrative construct and the intensity of its social meaning. Informed historical criticism with close textual analysis has brought more clarity to our understanding of what is meant by the African American novel today. Those critical perspectives that assumed the novel to be a unified text emerging from a logo-centric or writing-centered tradition are continually being revised. Thus, while scholars consider "the shortcomings of imposing structuralist, post-structuralist, psychoanalytic and feminist theories on black texts," the motivation to find more relevant theories or to produce an African American literary theory from within the texts has created a dynamic, provocative, and anesthetically complex interplay between the African American novelist, the reader, and critic. In the African American novel, the world may be real or imagined, history can continue to haunt and anger, and the reader must confront the terrible silences that have made us a nation with a shared history from which no one can escape. Even in the more popular novels-by Octavia Butler, J. California Cooper, or Walter Mosley, for example—the lives of black people are presented through a veil of humor or satiric displacement that defies simplistic analysis. The African American novelist is aware of a new relationship to the reader and critic, one that pleases and challenges, always testing the limits of our current critical understanding.

With the boundaries of critical theory still expanding and the recovery of history and texts an ongoing process for scholars and students, our best reading of the African American novel is an open one, which questions both the objective and subjective reality, recognizes both the discontinuities and continuities in traditions, and considers the relationships between oral and written forms of discourse. While these elements may be true of many novels, they apply with greater consistency to the novels written by African Americans who write against the very same establishment from which they need approval.

Of particular significance is the autobiographical impulse in the African American novel. The continuous need to explain and "inscribe the self" in a world which has historically denied the existence of that self gives both focus and intensity to the act of writing a story about black life. To examine the African American novel, then, is to understand its paradoxical nature: it grants the African American author the freedom to create a sustained vision in a world characterized by a series of counter-freedoms and conflicting visions; it allows for the humanistic formation of cultural memory, and it gives particularity to something that is often a fluctuating collection of perceptions and abstractions.

For many an African American author, the act of writing is part of a larger process of cultural revisionism, of redefining history and historical memory, and of confronting the past in innovative and provocative ways that are intentionally self-reflexive. To change the future is to give meaning to a common past in new ways. The common part of America lies in the experience of slavery, an experience that has much to teach us when treated narratively. As the only indigenous form of American writing, the slave narrative "belongs" to African American novelists as no other literary form does. Remembering that the African American novel, like the novel generally, has the capacity to alter the world by putting it into words, African American writers have reap-propriated the slave narrative as a principal means for looking more deeply into human consciousness as they alter that world for us. In the novels of Octavia Butler, Charles Johnson, Sherley Anne Williams, Ishmael Reed, and Toni Morrison, reclaiming and returning to slavery allows us to locate in that psychic wound those aspects of human identity which are part of all Americans, that cannot be forgotten, the site of America's most important triumph and failure.

Ⅵ. 拓展阅读

Donald Gibson's "Text and Countertext in Toni Morrison's *The Bluest Eye*." (*Bloom's Modern Critical Interpretations*: *Toni Morrison's The Bluest Eye*, Ed. Harold Bloom. Infobase Publishing, 2007).

Ⅶ. 参考文献

Graham, Maryemma. "Introduction." *Cambridge Companion to the African American Novel*. Ed. Maryemma Graham. Cambridge UP, 2004. 1-13.

Chapter 10　Wislawa Szymborska and Her Poetics of Daily Life

Ⅰ. 作者简介

维斯拉瓦·辛波斯卡（Wislawa Szymborska）（1923—2012）生于波兰小镇布宁。1931年举家迁往克拉科夫市并一直居住在此。1945—1948年辛波斯卡在杰格隆尼大学学习波兰文学和社会学。在大学期间，她接触到了克拉科夫的文学圈，遇见了波兰诗人米沃什，并深受其影响。1953年至1981年，她一直是克拉科夫《文学生活》杂志编辑，负责诗歌部，培养了大批年轻诗人。她没有生育，过着朴素的生活，尤其是在丈夫去世后的晚年。她喜欢抽烟，喜欢鲱鱼和伏特加。她的日常生活平淡无奇，这将为难任何试图为她写传记的人。阅读占据了辛波斯卡的大量时间，也呼应着了她平缓的生活节奏。1981年，《文学生活》停刊，辛波斯卡又为《选举报》陆续写过一些书评。她的书评行文不拘一格，随性展开，轻松幽默，短小精悍，深受波兰读者喜爱。她非常热爱阅读，甚至说过："我很老派，我认为阅读是人类迄今发明的最荣耀的事。"在一次访谈中，她说:“我无法想象诗人不去争取安闲和平静。不幸的是,诗歌并非诞生于喧闹、人群之中,也并非诞生于公共汽车上。所以,必须有四面墙,并且保证电话不会响起。这是写作所需要的一切。”

辛波斯卡擅长以幽默、诗意的口吻描述严肃主题和日常事物。她的诗风凝练、清澈,悠然从容,因而被誉为“诗界莫扎特”;她总能微妙地道破读者的小心思,让读者在读诗时会心一笑。这位女诗人活了 88 岁,写了 60 多年诗,一共只发表了不到 400 首,也即平均一年只写 7 首诗,但她却凭借数量极其有限的诗问鼎 1996 年的诺贝尔文学奖,足见其作品分量之重。瑞典文学院的颁奖词是“由于其在诗歌艺术中精辟精妙的反讽,挖掘出了人类一点一滴的现实生活背后历史更迭与生物演化的深意”(“for poetry that with ironic precision allows the historical and biological context to come to light in fragments of human reality”)。2001 年辛波斯卡成为美国文学艺术学院名誉会员,是美国授予杰出艺术家的最高荣誉。2012 年 2 月 1 日,辛波斯卡于克拉科夫安然逝世。

Ⅱ.内容提要

本章选取了辛波斯卡的 6 首诗。第一首《三个最奇怪的词》是一首充满哲思的小诗,辛波斯卡借助这首诗精妙地探讨了语言的本质和命名行为。第二首《未进行的喜马拉雅之旅》和第三首《种种可能》反映了诗人对人世和人世间每一个个体、每一件物品博大温柔的爱,从中我们可以窥见辛波斯卡的世界观。第四首《写履历表》是诗人对写履历表这件事的反思,充满反讽,诗人在这首诗中以小见大、举重若轻,在生活的琐碎和司空见惯中洞见人生的深意。第五首《越南》和第六首《结束与开始》可以视为是诗人的政治诗,《越南》直接处理战争主题,揭露出发问者和回答者权力的不对等以及战争的残酷;《结束与开始》相对而言间接一些,诗人不写战争本身的开始与结束,而是写战争结束,重建开始的困难,并且抛出了一个重要问题:安逸与遗忘是否会种下另一场战争的种子?

Ⅲ.作品

The Three Oddest Words

When I pronounce the word Future,
the first syllable already belongs to the past.
When I pronounce the word Silence,
I destroy it.
When I pronounce the word Nothing,
I make something no non-being can hold.

Notes from a Nonexistent Himalayan Expedition

So these are the Himalayas.
Mountains racing to the moon.
The moment of their start recorded
on the startling, ripped canvas of the sky.
Holes punched in a desert of clouds.
Thrust into nothing.
Echo—a white mute.
Quiet.

Yeti①, down there we've got Wednesday,
bread and alphabets.
Two times two is four.
Roses are red there,
and violets are blue.

Yeti, crime is not all
we're up to down there.
Yeti, not every sentence there
means death.

---

① 雪人(似人或似熊的巨大长毛动物,据传生活在喜马拉雅山)。

We've inherited hope—
the gift of forgetting.
You'll see how we give
birth among the ruins.

Yeti, we've got Shakespeare there.
Yeti, we play solitaire
and violin. At nightfall,
we turn lights on, Yeti.

Up here it's neither moon nor earth.
Tears freeze.
Oh Yeti, semi-moonman,
turn back, think again!

I called this to the Yeti
inside four walls of avalanche,
stomping my feet for warmth
on the everlasting
snow.

Possibilities

I prefer movies.
I prefer cats.
I prefer the **oaks**① along the **Warta**②.
I prefer Dickens to **Dostoyevsky**③.
I prefer myself liking people to myself loving mankind.
I prefer keeping a needle and thread on hand, just in case.
I prefer the color green.
I prefer not to maintain that reason is to blame for everything.
I prefer exceptions.

---

① 橡树。
② 瓦尔塔河,位于波兰。
③ 陀思妥耶夫斯基,俄国作家。

I prefer to leave early.
I prefer talking to doctors about something else.
I prefer the old **fine-lined**① illustrations.
I prefer the absurdity of writing poems to the absurdity of not writing poems.
I prefer, where love's concerned, non specific anniversaries that can be celebrated every day.
I prefer moralists who promise me nothing.
I prefer **cunning**② kindness to the over-trustful kind.
I prefer the earth in **civvies**③.
I prefer conquered to conquering countries.
I prefer having some reservations.
I prefer the hell of chaos to the hell of order.
I prefer **Grimms' fairy tales**④ to the newspapers' front pages.
I prefer leaves without flowers to flowers without leaves.
I prefer dogs with **uncropped**⑤ tails.
I prefer light eyes, since mine are dark. I prefer desk drawers.
I prefer many things that I haven't mentioned hereto many things I've also left unsaid.
I prefer zeroes **on the loose**⑥ to those lined up behind a cipher.
I prefer the time of insects to the time of stars.
I prefer to knock on wood. I prefer not to ask how much longer and when.
I prefer keeping in mind even the possibility that existence has its own reason for being.

Writing a Résumé

What needs to be done?
Fill out the application and enclose the resume.
Regardless of the length of life,
a resume is best kept short.

---

① 线条细致的。
② 可爱的。
③ 平民。
④ 格林童话。
⑤ 未被剪过的。
⑥ 散漫的。

Concise, well-chosen facts are **de rigor.** ①
Landscapes are replaced by addresses,
shaky memories give way to unshakable dates.
Of all your loves, mention only the marriage;
of all your children, only those who were born.
Who knows you matters more than whom you know.
Trips only if taken abroad.
Memberships in what but without why.
Honors, but not how they were earned.

Write as if you'd never talked to yourself
and always kept yourself at arm's length.
Pass over in silence your dogs, cats, birds,
dusty **keepsakes**②, friends, and dreams.

Price, not worth,
and title, not what's inside.
His shoe size, not where he's off to,
that one you pass off as yourself.

In addition, a photograph with one ear showing.
What matters is its shape, not what it hears.
What is there to hear, anyway?
The **clatter**③ of **paper shredders**④.

Vietnam

"Woman, what's your name?" "I don't know."
"How old are you? Where are you from?" "I don't know."
"Why did you dig that **burrow**⑤?" "I don't know."

① 必需的。
② 纪念品。
③ 咔嗒声。
④ 碎纸机。
⑤ 地洞。

"How long have you been hiding?" "I don't know."
"Why did you bite my finger?" "I don't know."
"Don't you know that we won't hurt you?" "I don't know."
"Whose side are you on?" "I don't know."
"This is war. You've got to choose." "I don't know."
"Does your village still exist?" "I don't know."
"Are those your children?" "Yes."

The End and the Beginning

After every war
someone's got to **tidy up**①.
Things won't
Pick themselves up, after all.

Someone's got to **shove**② the **rubble**③
to the roadsides
so the **carts**④ loaded with corpses
can get by.

Someone's got to **trudge**⑤
through **sludge**⑥ and ashes,
through the sofa springs,
the shards of glass,
the bloody rags.

Someone's got to **lug**⑦ the post
to **prop**⑧ the wall,

① 整理,清洁。
② 推。
③ 碎石。
④ 运货车。
⑤ 步履艰难地走。
⑥ 污泥。
⑦ 用力拉或拖。
⑧ 使倚靠在某物。

someone's got to **glaze**① the window,
set the door in its frame.

No sound bites,
no photo opportunities
and it takes years.
All the cameras have gone
to other wars.

The bridges need to be rebuilt,
the railroad stations, too.
Shirt sleeves will be rolled
to shreds.

Someone, **broom**② in hand,
still remembers how it was.
Someone else listens,
nodding his **unshattered**③ head.
But others are bound to be **bustling**④ nearby
who'll find all that a little boring.

From time to time
someone still must dig up a rusted argument
from underneath a bus hand
haul it **off**⑤ to the dump.

Those who knew
what this was all about
must make way for
those who know little.

---

① 上釉。
② 扫帚。
③ 未粉碎的。
④ 忙乱的。
⑤ 转向避开。

And less than that.
And at last nothing less than nothing.

Someone's got to lie
therein the grass
that covers up the causes and effects
with a **cornstalk** ①in his teeth, **gawking**② at clouds.

Ⅳ. 思考题

1. In her Nobel Prize acceptance speech, Szymborska said that "in more fortunate countries, where human dignity isn't assaulted so readily, poets yearn, of course, to be published, read, and understood, but they do little, if anything, to set themselves above the common **herd**③ and the **daily grind**④." How does Szymborska position herself as a poet? Are her poems above the common herd and daily grind?
2. Szymborska's poetry is famous for its "ironic precision". Try to locate and explain the "ironic precision" in *The Three Oddest Words*, *Writing a Résumé*, and *Golden Anniversary*.
3. *Vietnam* and *The End and the Beginning* are concerned with war. What are the specific things about war that the poet want to make comments? What is her attitude toward war implied in these two poems?

Ⅴ. 文学批评

诗歌要素

Poetry is often described as "literature in metrical form" or "compositions forming rhythmic lines". It has a set of specific features that differentiate it from other forms of literature. It is not necessary that all the elements should be employed in every poem that is

① 玉米秆。
② 呆呆地看。
③ 人群。
④ 单调的日常生活。

penned. However, the presence of at least two of these elements are noted in most poems. For example, a lot of poets choose to write "blank verses" which are poems that lack rhyme.

However, a blank verse does have a set rhythm and meter pattern that is followed. Now, a "free verse" will neither have rhyme or rhythm, but these verses are usually opulent in other elements like metaphors, symbols and spectacular word images.

Stanza

A stanza is to a poem as a paragraph is to a piece of prosaic writing—a fixed number of lines of verse forming a single unit of a poem. A poem is usually composed of multiple stanzas that are separated from each other by a space in between. Usually, all stanzas are made up of equal number of lines in a poem. However, there are many examples of poems where this approach has been largely deviated in form. A poem may have a combination of stanzas that have varying number of lines.

Based on the number of lines present in a stanza, they are assigned different names. They are:

- A "couplet" is a stanza that has only 2 lines.
- A "tercet" is composed of 3 lines.
- A "quatrain" consists of 4 lines.
- A "cinquain" has 5 lines.
- A "sestet" comprises 6 lines.
- A "sonnet" is an entire poem with exactly 14 lines.

Rhyme and Rhyme Scheme

Rhyming in poetry is one convention that makes this form of literature recognizably different from prose and drama. Even in this age when free verses are quite popular, rhyme in poesy is what makes it poetic. One of the unique qualities of rhyme in poetry is that it has the ability to provide a systematic flow to a bundle of thoughts that may seem absolutely chaotic if put together otherwise.

A rhyme smoothens out the rough edges and abrupt protrusions. This element can be simplistically defined from the similarity in the sounds of two or more lines. In poetry, this is generally achieved by using similar sounding words at the end of lines.

Example of a Rhyme:

Humpty Dumpty sat on a **wall**,
Humpty Dumpty had a great **fall.**
All the king's horses and all the king's **men**
Couldn't put Humpty together **again.**

Rhythm and Meter

The primary thing to keep in mind here is that "rhyme" and "rhythm" are not the same at all. Rhythm is basically the pattern in which a poet chooses to sequence the stressed and unstressed syllables in every line of a poem, for the creation of oral patterns.

The three factors that help to determine the rhythm in a poem are:

- The total number of syllables present in each line.
- The total count of accented (stressed) syllables in each line.
- The tally of recurring patterns of two or three syllables-stressed and unstressed-clubbed in every line.

Each recurring pattern is individually called a foot. And a number of feet, on identification, can tell us the systematic rhythm or the meter that a poem follows. There are various types of foot and they are named accordingly.

- One foot: Monometer
- Two feet: Dimeter
- Three feet: Trimeter
- Four feet: Tetrameter
- Five feet: Pentameter
- Six feet: Hexameter

And there are five different types of constant beat patterns that the feet can occur in:

- Iamb (Iambic)-One weak syllable followed by one accented syllable.
- Trochee (Trochaic)-One accented syllable followed by one weak syllable.
- Anapest (Anapestic)-Two weak syllables followed by one accented syllable.
- Dactyl (Dactylic)-One accented syllable followed by two weak syllables.
- Spondee (Spondaic)-Two consecutive accented syllables. This can usually be found at the end of a line.

Imagery

The figurative painting of a vivid picture in the mind of a reader with words is imagery. This element is used mostly in descriptive poem where the poet has the scope to use ornate adjectives, lofty language and an exquisitely elaborate canvas to give wings to his imagination. Of course, this scope is primarily offered by the dynamic nature of a descriptive poem.

Symbolism

The presentation of a tangible object that actually represents an abstract or intangible concept or idea is symbolism. A symbol can be presented to the readers in the form of a character, an object strategically placed in the narrative, a word or phrase, or even a place. A symbol is mostly subtle in nature or at least never blatantly explained.

Symbols are mostly multi-layered in nature and can be interpreted differently by different people. Over the years, owing to repeated usage of symbolism, some objects have acquired one particular value that is usually associated with them, like the apple is usually seen as a symbol of seduction and sensuality (the forbidden fruit association), the loss and regrowth of leaves in a tree has come to be seen as the circle of life, the raven is indicative of imminent death and so on.

However, none of these associations would be considered absolute truth by a reader as the presentation of these very objects can change massively depending on the context of poems.

Ⅵ. 拓展阅读

Jeffery Wainwright's *Poetry: The Basics* (Routledge, 2004).

Mary Oliver's *A Poetry Handbook* (Mariner Books, 1994).

Ⅶ. 参考文献

"A Beginner's Guide to the Basic Elements of Poetry" Retrieved June 7th, 2020, https://penlighten.com/basic-elements-of-poetry.

Chapter 11 Mo Yan and the Artistry of Language

Ⅰ. 作者简介

莫言(1955—),原名管谟业,1955 年 3 月 5 日出生于中国山东省高密市。莫言是中国当代知名小说家,以其丰富的想象力和人文主义关怀而闻名,莫言的小说于 20 世纪 80 年代开始风靡,他于 2012 年获诺贝尔文学奖。

莫言在家乡读小学至五年级时因为"文革"而辍学。之后他从事农活多年,到 1973 年才开始在一家工厂工作。他 1981 年开始用莫言的笔名写故事。1984 年至 1986 年,莫言在解放军艺术学院学习文学,其间曾发表过《透亮的红萝卜》等短篇小说。他的首部长篇小说《红高粱》发表于 1986 年,为他赢得了广泛的声誉,特别是在改编为同名电影《红高粱》(1987)上映之后。在随后的作品中,他采用了多种写作元素,从神话到现实主义,从讽刺到爱情故事,但他的故事总是带有一种热情洋溢的人文主义关怀。1989 年,他的小说《天堂蒜薹之歌》出版,1992 年《酒国》出版,1995 年《莫言文集》出版。

莫言1997年离开了解放军编制，当过报纸编辑，也继续小说创作，仍旧以农村老家为背景。他承认自己深受威廉·福克纳、詹姆斯·乔伊斯、加布里埃尔·加西亚·马尔克斯等众多作家的影响。他的其他作品包括《丰乳肥臀》(1995)、《檀香刑》(2001)、《生死疲劳》(2006)、《蛙》(2009)。莫言的作品体裁很广，创作了短篇小说、长篇小说，以及散文。他的叙述风格带有魔幻现实主义的色彩。莫言的写作常常以中国古老的文学和通俗的口述传统为出发点，将这些叙事模式与当代社会问题结合起来。

莫言于2012年获得诺贝尔文学奖，因为其小说“独特的魔幻现实主义兼容民间故事、历史和当下”(“with hallucinatory realism merges folk tales, history and the contemporary”)。莫言的小说聚焦芸芸众生中的小人物，通过他们的悲欢离合折射出宏观的历史变迁，挑战了一成不变的正统历史叙事。正如莫言在获奖演讲中说的那样，他聚焦小人物的历史时也曾被攻击，被认为是偏离正统革命文学而饱受批评。随着年龄的增长和对人性越来越深的理解，莫言希望他的写作能实现“高尚人格”的理想追求，而莫言作品中的众多人物无疑都是这些高尚人格的某个横截面。

莫言小说的语言也极具艺术性：首先，他的语言具有强烈的地域色彩，他采用高密的方言赋予了文字别样的力量，虽然有时显得粗俗，但是饱含情感。其次，莫言在小说中的用词极富感官性的冲击，同时有多重感觉的呈现，充满比喻、夸张、通感等手法，色彩鲜明，用词诡谲，意象纷呈。再次，莫言的语言极富创新精神，使其小说呈现出奇特的想象性与神奇感的色彩，思想和语言都是天马行空、不受拘束。

Ⅱ. 作品简介

1986年出版的《红高粱》是莫言魔幻现实主义小说的代表作。这部小说以20世纪20年代至70年代的中国为背景，以非线性的时间顺序讲述了抗日战争期间山东家族三代人从高粱酿酒师过渡到抗战士兵的故事。

在故事的开头，余占鳌司令和他的士兵准备攻击入侵的日军。然而，当他的妻子戴凤莲带着士兵们的食物穿过高粱地时，她被日本人开枪打死了。随着故事的发展，这位无名的叙述者(余司令的孙子)回忆起了他家族的历史和他们在战争中的参与。他的祖母被迫嫁给一个富有的酒厂老板的儿子,但是他的祖父余占鳌,一个强盗,已经爱上了她,他杀了酒厂老板的儿子,于是他的祖母接管了生意。

叙述者的记忆是模糊的,并且带有寓言的性质。整个故事在不同的时间段跳跃,但是不妨碍读者对于小说的理解。叙述者的叙事角度也常常切换,有时候甚至从某些动物的观点来叙述,这些记忆共同拼凑出来高密人民联合起来与日本人抗争的历史,同时也不讳言人民之间争夺武器、食物的爱恨情仇。小说在20世纪70年代结束时,叙述者回到他家扫墓,在田间他看到他家的红高粱已经被一个绿色的杂交版本所替代,不禁扼腕痛惜,那见证历史的红高粱终于是失去了。

本书的节选是小说开篇,故事是从“我”父亲童年的角度讲述的。余司令和他的军队正准备同日本人作战,但他们失败了,叙事者的记忆充满了童真和生动的意象。而另一条线,罗汉叔被日本人抓去做苦力,想要逃跑却被日本人抓住并活剥了皮,语言狂野血腥,让人身临其境感受到日军的残酷。

Ⅲ. 作品

1

THE NINTH DAY of the eighth lunar month, 1939. My father, a bandit's offspring who had passed his fifteenth birthday, was joining the forces of Commander Yu Zhan'ao, a man destined to become a legendary hero, to ambush a Japanese **convoy**① on the Jiao-Ping highway. Grandma, a padded jacket over her shoulders, saw them to the edge of the village. 'Stop here,' Commander Yu ordered her. She stopped.

'Douguan, mind your foster-dad,' she told my father. The sight of her large frame and the warm fragrance of her lined jacket chilled him. He shivered. His stomach **growled**②.

Commander Yu patted him on the head and said, 'Let's go, foster-son.'

Heaven and earth were in turmoil, the view was blurred. By then the soldiers' muffled footsteps had moved far down the road. Father could still hear them, but a curtain of

① 护卫队。
② 咆哮。

blue mist obscured the men themselves. Gripping tightly to Commander Yu's coat, he nearly flew down the path on **churning**① legs. Grandma receded like a distant shore as the approaching sea of mist grew more **tempestuous**②; holding on to Commander Yu was like clinging to the railing of a boat.

That was how Father rushed towards the uncarved granite marker that would rise above his grave in the bright-red sorghum fields of his hometown. A bare-assed little boy once led a white billy goat up to the weed-covered grave, and as it grazed in unhurried contentment, the boy pissed furiously on the grave and sang out: 'The sorghum is red—the Japanese are coming—**compatriots**③, get ready—fire your rifles and cannons—'

Someone said that the little goatherd was me, but I don't know. I had learned to love Northeast Gaomi Township with all my heart, and to hate it with **unbridled**④ fury. I didn't realise until I'd grown up that Northeast Gaomi Township is easily the most beautiful and most repulsive, most unusual and most common, most sacred and most corrupt, most heroic and most bastardly, hardest-drinking and hardest-loving place in the world. The people of my father's generation who lived there ate sorghum out of preference, planting as much of it as they could. In late autumn, during the eighth lunar month, vast stretches of red sorghum shimmered like a sea of blood. Tall and dense, it reeked of glory; cold and graceful, it promised enchantment; passionate and loving, it was **tumultuous**⑤.

The autumn winds are cold and bleak, the sun's rays intense. White clouds, full and round, float in the tile-blue sky, casting full round purple shadows onto the sorghum fields below. Over decades that seem but a moment in time, lines of scarlet figures shuttled among the sorghum stalks to weave a vast human tapestry. They killed, they looted, and they defended their country in a valiant, stirring ballet that makes us **unfilial**⑥ descendants who now occupy the land pale by comparison. Surrounded by progress, I feel a nagging sense of our species' regression.

After leaving the village, the troops marched down a narrow dirt path, the tramping of their feet merging with the rustling of weeds. The heavy mist was strangely animated, **ka-**

① 搅动。
② 暴乱的,剧烈的。
③ 同胞。
④ 无拘束的。
⑤ 吵闹的,喧嚣的。
⑥ 不孝的。

leidoscopic①. Tiny droplets of water pooled into large drops on Father's face, clumps of hair stuck to his forehead. He was used to the delicate peppermint aroma and the slightly sweet yet **pungent**②odour of ripe sorghum wafting over from the sides of the path-nothing new there. But as they marched through the heavy mist, his nose detected a new, sickly-sweet odour, neither yellow nor red, blending with the smells of peppermint and sorghum to call up memories hidden deep in his soul.

Six days later, the fifteenth day of the eighth month, the night of the Mid-Autumn Festival. A bright round moon climbed slowly in the sky above the solemn, silent sorghum fields, bathing the **tassels**③ in its light until they shimmered like mercury. Among the chiselled flecks of moonlight Father caught a whiff of the same sickly odour, far stronger than anything you might smell today. Commander Yu was leading him by the hand through the sorghum, where three hundred fellow villagers, heads pillowed on their arms, were **strewn**④ across the ground, their fresh blood turning the black earth into a sticky muck that made walking slow and difficult. The smell took their breath away. A pack of corpse-eating dogs sat in the field staring at Father and Commander Yu with glinting eyes. Commander Yu drew his pistol and fired—a pair of eyes was extinguished. Another shot, another pair of eyes gone. The howling dogs scattered, then sat on their haunches once they were out of range, setting up a deafening chorus of angry barks as they gazed greedily, longingly at the corpses. The odour grew stronger.

'Jap dogs!' Commander Yu screamed. 'Jap sons of bitches!' He emptied his pistol, scattering the dogs without a trace. 'Let's go, son,' he said. The two of them, one old and one young, **threaded**⑤ their way through the sorghum field, guided by the moon's rays. The odour saturating the field drenched Father's soul and would be his constant companion during the cruel months and years ahead.

Sorghum stems and leaves sizzled fiercely in the mist. The Black Water River, which flowed slowly through the swampy lowland, sang in the spreading mist, now loud, now soft, now far, now near. As they caught up with the troops, Father heard the tramping of feet and some coarse breathing fore and aft. The butt of a rifle noisily bumped someone else's. A

---

① 万花筒似的,千变万化的。
② 刺激性的。
③ 穗子。
④ Strew 过去分词,散落。
⑤ 穿过。

foot crushed what sounded like a human bone. The man in front of Father coughed loudly. It was a familiar cough, calling to mind large ears that turned red with excitement. Large transparent ears covered with tiny blood vessels were the trademark of Wang Wenyi, a small man whose enlarged head was tucked down between his shoulders.

Father strained and **squinted**① until his gaze bored through the mist: there was Wang Wenyi's head, jerking with each cough. Father thought back to when Wang was whipped on the parade ground, and how pitiful he had looked. He had just joined up with Commander Yu. Adjutant Ren ordered the recruits: Right face! Wang Wenyi **stomp**②ed down joyfully, but where he intended to 'face' was anyone's guess. Adjutant Ren smacked him across the backside with his whip, forcing a yelp from between his parted lips. Ouch, mother of my children! The expression on his face could have been a cry, or could have been a laugh. Some kids sprawled atop the wall **hoot**③ed gleefully.

Now Commander Yu kicked Wang Wenyi in the backside.

'Who said you could cough?'

'Commander Yu ...' Wang Wenyi stifled a cough. 'My throat itches ...'

'So what? If you give away our position, it's your head!'

'Yes, sir,' Wang replied, as another coughing spell erupted.

Father sensed Commander Yu **lurch**④ing forward to grab Wang Wenyi around the neck with both hands. Wang wheezed and gasped, but the coughing stopped.

Father also sensed Commander Yu's hands release Wang's neck; he even sensed the purple **welt**⑤s, like ripe grapes, left behind. Aggrieved gratitude filled Wang's deep-blue, frightened eyes.

The troops turned quickly into the sorghum, and Father knew instinctively that they were heading southeast. The dirt path was the only direct link between the Black Water River and the village. During the day it had a pale cast; the original black earth, the colour of **ebony**⑥, had been covered by the passage of countless animals: **cloven**⑦ hoofprints of oxen and goats, semicircular hoofprints of mules, horses, and donkeys; dried road apples

---

① 斜视。
② 跺脚。
③ 呼呼大笑。
④ 跨步。
⑤ 伤痕。
⑥ 乌木。
⑦ 劈开的。

left by horses, mules, and donkeys; wormy cow chips; and scattered goat pellets like little black beans. Father had taken this path so often that later on, as he suffered in the Japanese **cinder pit**①, its image often flashed before his eyes. He never knew how many sexual comedies my grandma had performed on this dirt path, but I knew. And he never knew that her naked body, pure as glossy white jade, had lain on the black soil beneath the shadows of sorghum stalks, but I knew.

The surrounding mist grew more **sluggish**② once they were in the sorghum field. The stalks screeched in secret resentment when the men and equipment bumped against them, sending large, mournful beads of water splashing to the ground. The water was ice-cold, clear and sparkling, and deliciously refreshing. Father looked up, and a large drop fell into his mouth. As the heavy curtain of mist parted gently, he watched the heads of sorghum stalks bend slowly down. The tough, **pliable**③ leaves, weighted down by the dew, **saw**④ed at his clothes and face. A breeze set the stalks above him rustling briefly; the **gurgl**⑤ing of the Black Water River grew louder.

Father had gone swimming so often in the Black Water River that he seemed born to it. Grandma said that the sight of the river excited him more than the sight of his own mother. At the age of five, he could dive like a duckling, his little pink asshole bobbing above the surface, his feet sticking straight up. He knew that the muddy riverbed was black and shiny, and as spongy as soft **tallow**⑥, and that the banks were covered with pale-green reeds and **plantain**⑦ the colour of goose-down; **coil**⑧ing vines and stiff bone grass hugged the muddy ground, which was **crisscross**⑨ed with the tracks of skittering crabs.

Autumn winds brought cool air, and wild geese flew through the sky heading south, their formation changing from a straight line one minute to a V the next. When the sorghum turned red, **horde**⑩s of crabs the size of horse hooves scrambled onto the bank at

---

① 炭窑。
② 停滞的。
③ 柔韧的。
④ 锯。
⑤ gurgle，汩汩地流。
⑥ 油脂。
⑦ 车前草。
⑧ 盘绕。
⑨ 交叉。
⑩ 群。

night to search for food—fresh cow dung and the rotting **carcass**①es of dead animals—among the clumps of river grass.

The sound of the river reminded Father of an autumn night during his childhood, when the foreman of our family business, **Arhat**② Liu, named after Buddhist saints, took him crabbing on the riverbank. On that grey-purple night a golden breeze followed the course of the river. The sapphire-blue sky was deep and boundless, green-tinted stars shone brightly in the sky: the ladle of **Ursa Major**③ (signifying death), the basket of **Sagittarius**④ (representing life); Octans, the glass well, missing one of its tiles; the anxious Herd Boy (Altair), about to hang himself; the mournful Weaving Girl (Vega), about to drown herself in the river. ... Uncle Arhat had been overseeing the work of the family distillery for decades, and Father scrambled to keep up with him as he would his own grandfather.

The weak light of the kerosene lamp bored a five-yard hole in the darkness. When water flowed into the halo of light, it was the **cordial**⑤ yellow of an overripe apricot. But cordial for only a fleeting moment, before it flowed on. In the surrounding darkness the water reflected a starry sky. Father and Uncle Arhat, rain capes over their shoulders, sat around the shaded lamp listening to the low gurgling of the river. Every so often they heard the excited screech of a fox calling to its mate in the sorghum fields beside the river. Father and Uncle Arhat sat quietly, listening with **rapt**⑥ respect to the whispered secrets of the land, as the smell of stinking river mud drifted over on the wind. Hordes of crabs attracted by the light **skitter**⑦ed towards the lamp, where they formed a shifting, restless **cloister**⑧. Father was so eager he nearly sprang to his feet, but Uncle Arhat held him by the shoulders.

'Take it easy! Greedy eaters never get the hot gruel.' Holding his excitement in check, Father sat still. The crabs stopped as soon as they entered the ring of lamplight, and lined up head to tail, **blot**⑨ting out the ground. A greenish glint issued from their shells, as

① 尸体。
② 罗汉。
③ 北斗七星。
④ 人马星座。
⑤ 亲切的。
⑥ 全神贯注的。
⑦ 掠过。
⑧ 回廊,圆圈。
⑨ 遮盖。

countless pairs of button eyes popped from deep **socket**[1]s on little stems. Mouths hidden beneath sloping faces released frothy strings of brazenly colourful bubbles. The long fibres on Father's straw rain cape stood up. 'Now!' Uncle Arhat shouted. Father sprang into action before the shout died out, **snatch**[2]ing two corners of the tightly woven net they'd spread on the ground beforehand; they raised it in the air, scooping up a layer of crabs and revealing a clear spot of riverbank beneath them. Quickly tying the ends together and tossing the net to one side, they rushed back and lifted up another piece of netting with the same speed and skill. The heavy bundles seemed to hold hundreds, even thousands of crabs.

As Father followed the troops into the sorghum field, he moved sideways, crablike, overshooting the spaces between the stalks and bumping them hard, which caused them to sway and bend violently. Still gripping tightly to Commander Yu's coat-tail, he was pulled along, his feet barely touching the ground. But he was getting sleepy. His neck felt stiff, his eyes were growing dull and listless, and his only thought was that as long as he could tag along behind Uncle Arhat to the Black Water River he'd never come back empty-handed.

Father ate crab until he was sick of it, and so did Grandma. But even though they lost their appetite for it, they couldn't bear to throw the uneaten ones away. So Uncle Arhat minced the leftovers and ground them under the bean-curd millstone, then salted the crab paste, which they ate daily, until it finally went bad and became mulch for the poppies.

Apparently Grandma was an opium smoker, but wasn't addicted, which was why she had the complexion of a peach, a sunny disposition, and a clear mind. The crab-nourished poppies grew huge and fleshy, a mixture of pinks, reds, and whites that assailed your nostrils with their fragrance. The black soil of my hometown, always fertile, was especially productive, and the people who tilled it were especially decent, strong-willed, and ambitious. The white eels of the Black Water River, like plump sausages with tapered ends, foolishly swallowed every hook in sight.

Uncle Arhat had died the year before on the Jiao-Ping highway. His corpse, after be-

---

① 孔。
② 抓。

ing **hack**[1]ed to pieces, had been scattered around the area. As the skin was being stripped from his body, his flesh jumped and quivered, as if he were a huge skinned frog. Images of that corpse sent shivers up Father's spine. Then he thought back to a night some seven or eight years earlier, when Grandma, drunk at the time, had stood in the distillery yard beside a pile of sorghum leaves, her arms around Uncle Arhat's shoulders. 'Uncle… don't leave,' she pleaded. 'If not for the sake of the monk, stay for the Buddha. If not for the sake of the fish, stay for the water. If not for my sake, stay for little Douguan. You can have me, if you want… You're like my own father…' Father watched him push her away and swagger into the shed to mix fodder for the two large black mules who, when we opened our distillery, made us the richest family in the village. Uncle Arhat didn't leave after all. Instead he became our foreman, right up to the day the Japanese confiscated our mules to work on the Jiao-Ping highway.

Now Father and the others could hear long-drawn-out brays from the mules they had left behind in the village. Wide-eyed with excitement, he could see nothing but the **congealed**[2] yet nearly transparent mist that surrounded him. Erect stalks of sorghum formed dense barriers behind a wall of vapour. Each barrier led to another, seemingly endless. He had no idea how long they'd been in the field, for his mind was focused on the fertile river roaring in the distance, and on his memories. He wondered why they were in such a hurry to squeeze through this packed, dreamy ocean of sorghum. Suddenly he lost his bearings. He listened carefully for a sign from the river, and quickly determined that they were heading east-southeast, towards the river. Once he had a fix on their direction, he understood that they would be setting an ambush for the Japanese, that they would be killing people, just as they had killed the dogs. By heading east-southeast, they would soon reach the Jiao-Ping highway, which cut through the swampy lowland from north to south and linked the two counties of Jiao and Pingdu. Japanese and their running dogs, Chinese collaborators, had built the highway with the forced labour of local conscripts.

The sorghum was set in motion by the exhausted troops, whose heads and necks were soaked by the settling dew. Wang Wenyi was still coughing, even though he'd been the target of Commander Yu's continuing angry outbursts. Father sensed that the highway was

① 劈，砍。

② 凝结的。

just up ahead, its pale-yellow outline swaying in front of him. Imperceptibly tiny openings began to appear in the thick curtain of mist, and one dew-soaked ear of sorghum after another stared sadly at Father, who returned their devout gaze. It dawned on him that they were living spirits: their roots buried in the dark earth, they soaked up the energy of the sun and the essence of the moon; moistened by the rain and dew, they understood the ways of the heavens and the logic of the earth. The colour of the sorghum suggested that the sun had already turned the obscured horizon a pathetic red.

Then something unexpected occurred. Father heard a shrill whistle, followed by a loud burst from up ahead.

'Who fired his weapon?' Commander Yu bellowed. 'Who's the prick who did it?'

Father heard the bullet pierce the thick mist and pass through sorghum leaves and stalks, lopping off one of the heads. Everyone held his breath as the bullet screamed through the air and thudded to the ground. The sweet smell of gunpowder dissipated in the mist. Wang Wenyi screamed pitifully, 'Commander—my head's gone—Commander—my head's gone—'

Commander Yu froze momentarily, then kicked Wang Wenyi. 'You dumb fuck!' he growled. 'How could you talk without a head?'

Commander Yu left my father standing there and went up to the head of the column. Wang Wenyi was still howling. Father pressed forward to catch a glimpse of the strange look on Wang's face. A dark-blue substance was flowing on his cheek. Father reached out to touch it; hot and sticky, it smelled a lot like the mud of the Black Water River, but fresher. It overwhelmed the smell of peppermint and the pungent sweetness of sorghum and awakened in Father's mind a memory that drew ever nearer: like beads, it strung together the mud of the Black Water River, the black earth beneath the sorghum, the eternally living past, and the unstoppable present. There are times when everything on earth spits out the stench of human blood.

'Uncle,' Father said, 'you're wounded.'

'Douguan, is that you? Tell your old uncle if his head's still on his neck.'

'It's there, Uncle, right where it's supposed to be. Except your ear's bleeding.'

Wang Wenyi reached up to touch his ear and pulled back a bloody hand, yelping in alarm. Then he froze as if paralysed. 'Commander, I'm wounded! I'm wounded!'

Commander Yu came back to Wang, knelt down, and put his hands around Wang's neck. 'Stop screaming or I'll throttle you!'

Wang Wenyi didn't dare make a sound.

'Where were you hit?' Commander Yu asked him.

'My ear . . .' Wang was weeping.

Commander Yu took a piece of white cloth from his waistband and tore it in two, then handed it to him. 'Hold this over it, and no more noise. Stay in rank. You can bandage it when we reach the highway.'

Commander Yu turned to Father. 'Douguan,' he barked. Father answered, and Commander Yu walked off holding him by the hand, followed by the **whimper**[①]ing Wang Wenyi.

The offending discharge had been the result of carelessness by the big fellow they called Mute, who was up front carrying a rake on his shoulder. The rifle slung over his back had gone off when he stumbled. Mute was one of Commander Yu's old bandit friends, a greenwood hero who had eaten fistcakes in the sorghum fields. One of his legs was shorter than the other—a prenatal injury—and he limped when he walked, but that didn't slow him down. Father was a little afraid of him.

At about dawn, the massive curtain of mist finally lifted, just as Commander Yu and his troops emerged onto the Jiao-Ping highway. In my hometown, August is the misty season, possibly because there's so much swampy lowland. Once he stepped onto the highway, Father felt suddenly light and **nimble**[②]; with extra spring in his step, he let go of Commander Yu's coat. Wang Wenyi, on the other hand, wore a crestfallen look as he held the cloth to his injured ear. Commander Yu crudely wrapped it for him, covering up half his head. Wang gnashed his teeth in pain.

'The heavens have smiled on you,' Commander Yu said.

'My blood's all gone,' Wang whimpered, 'I can't go on!'

'Bullshit!' Commander Yu exclaimed. 'It's no worse than a mosquito bite. You haven't forgotten your three sons, have you?'

Wang hung his head and mumbled, 'No, I haven't forgotten.'

The butt of the long-barrelled fowling piece over his shoulder was the colour of blood. A flat metal gunpowder pouch rested against his hip.

Remnants of the dissipating mist were scattered throughout the sorghum field. There were neither animal nor human footprints in the gravel, and the dense walls of sorghum on

---

① 抽泣。

② 敏捷的,灵活的。

the deserted highway made the men feel that something ominous was in the air. Father knew all along that Commander Yu's troops numbered no more than forty—deaf, mute, and crippled included. But when they were quartered in the village, they had stirred things up so much, with chickens squawking and dogs yelping, that you'd have thought it was a garrison command.

Out on the highway, the soldiers huddled so closely together they looked like an inert snake. Their motley assortment of weapons included shotguns, fowling pieces, ageing Hanyang rifles, plus a cannon that fired scale weights and was carried by two brothers, Fang Six and Fang Seven. Mute was toting a rake with twenty-six metal tines, as were three other soldiers. Father still didn't know what an ambush was, and even if he had, he wouldn't have known why anyone would take four rakes to the event.

2

I RETURNED TO Northeast Gaomi Township to compile a family chronicle, focusing on the famous battle of the banks of the Black Water River that involved my father and ended with the death of a Jap general. An old woman of ninety-two sang to me, to the accompaniment of bamboo clappers: 'Northeast Gaomi Township, so many men; at Black Water River the battle began; Commander Yu raised his hand, cannon fire to heaven; Jap souls scattered across the plain, ne'er to rise again; the beautiful champion of women, Dai Fenglian, ordered rakes for a barrier, the Jap attack broken...' The wizened old woman was as bald as a clay pot; the protruding tendons on her chapped hands were like strips of melon rind. She had survived the Mid-Autumn Festival massacre in '39 only because her **ulcerated**① legs had made walking impossible, and her husband had hidden her in a yam cellar. The heavens had smiled on her. The Dai Fenglian in her clapper-song was my grandma. I listened with barely concealed excitement, for her tale proved that the strategy of stopping the Jap convoy with rakes had sprung from the mind of my own kin, a member of the weaker sex. No wonder my grandma is **fêted**② as a **trailblazer**③ of the anti-Japanese resistance and a national hero.

At the mention of my grandma, the old woman grew expansive. Her narration was choppy and confused, like a shower of leaves at the mercy of the wind. She said that my

---

① 溃烂的。

② 招待。

③ 先驱。

grandma had the smallest feet of any woman in the village, and that no other distillery had the staying power of ours. The thread of her narrative evened out as she talked of the Jiao-Ping highway: 'When the highway was extended this far…sorghum only waist-high...Japs **conscript**[①]ed all able-bodied workers… Working for the Japs, slacked off, sabotage…took your family's two big black mules…built a stone bridge over the Black Water River… Arhat, your family's foreman…something fishy between him and your grandma, so everyone said…Aiyaya, when your grandma was young she sowed plenty of wild oats…Your dad was a capable boy, killed his first man at fifteen, eight or nine out of every ten bastard kids turn out bad…Arhat hamstrung the mule… Japs caught him and skinned him alive… Japs butchered people, shit in their pots, and pissed in their basins. I went for water once that year, guess what I found in my bucket, a human head with the pigtail still attached…'

Arhat Liu played a significant role in my family's history, but there is no hard evidence that he had an affair with my grandma, and, to tell the truth, I don't believe it. I understood the logic of what the old clay-pot was saying, but it still embarrassed me. Since Uncle Arhat treated my father like a grandson, that would make me sort of his great-grandson; and if my great-granddad had an affair with my grandma, that's **incest**[②], isn't it? But that's hogwash, since my grandma was Uncle Arhat's boss, not his daughter-in-law, and their relationship was sealed by wages, not by blood. He was a faithful old hand who embellished the history of our family and brought it greater glory than it would have had otherwise. Whether my grandma ever loved him or whether he ever lay down beside her on the kang has nothing to do with morality. What if she did love him? I believe she could have done anything she desired, for she was a hero of the resistance, a trailblazer for sexual liberation, a model of women's independence.

In country records I discovered that in 1938, the twenty-seventh year of the Republic, four hundred thousand mandays were spent by local workers from Gaomi, Pingdu, and Jiao counties in the service of the Japanese army to build the Jiao-Ping highway. The agricultural loss was incalculable, and the villages bordering the highway were stripped clean of draught animals. It was then that Arhat Liu, a conscript himself, took a hoe to the legs of our captured mule. He was caught, and the next day the Japanese soldiers tied him to a **tether**[③]ing post, skinned him alive, and mutilated him in front of his compatriots. There

---

① 征兵。

② 乱伦。

③ 拴马的绳。

was no fear in his eyes, and a stream of abuse poured from his mouth up until the moment he died.

3

SHE TOLD IT exactly like it was. When construction of the Jiao-Ping highway reached our place, the sorghum in the fields was only waist-high. Except for a handful of tiny villages, two crossing rivers, and a few dozen winding dirt paths, the marshy plain, which measured sixty by seventy-odd li—or about twenty by twenty-five miles—was covered with sorghum that waved like an ocean of green. From our village we had a clear view of White Horse Mountain, an enormous rock formation on the northern edge of the plain. Peasants tending the sorghum looked up to see White Horse and down to see black soil that soaked up their sweat and filled their hearts with contentment. When they heard that the Japanese were building a highway across the plain, they grew restive, awaiting the calamity they knew was coming.

The Japanese said they would come, and they were as good as their word.

My father was sleeping when the Japs and their puppet soldiers came to our village to conscript peasant labourers and confiscate their mules and horses. He was awakened by a disturbance near the distillery. Grandma dragged him over to the compound as fast as her bamboo-shoot feet would carry her. Back then there were a dozen or so huge vats in the compound, each brimming with top-quality white liquor, the aroma of which hung over the entire village. Two khaki-clad Japanese soldiers with fixed bayonets stood there as a couple of black-clad Chinese, rifles slung over their backs, untied our two big black mules from a catalpa tree. Uncle Arhat kept trying to get to the shorter puppet soldier, who was untying the tethers, but the taller comrade forced him back with the muzzle of his rifle. Since Uncle Arhat was wearing only a thin shirt in the early-summer heat, his exposed chest already showed a welter of circular bruises.

'Brothers,' he pleaded, 'we can talk this over, we can talk it over.'

'Get the hell out of here, you old bastard,' the taller soldier barked.

'Those animals belong to the owner,' Uncle Arhat said. 'You can't take them.'

The puppet soldier growled menacingly, 'If I hear another word out of you, I'll shoot your little prick off!'

The Japanese soldiers stood like clay statues, holding their rifles in front of them.

As Grandma and my father entered the compound, Uncle Arhat wailed, 'They're taking our mules!'

'Sir,' Grandma said, 'we're good people.'

The Japanese **squint**[1]ed and grinned at her.

The shorter puppet soldier freed the mules and tried to lead them away; but they raised their heads stubbornly and refused to budge. His buddy walked up and **prod**[2]ded one of them in the rump with his rifle; the angered animal pawed the ground with its rear hooves, its metal shoes glinting in the mud that sprayed the soldier in the face.

The tall soldier pointed his rifle at Uncle Arhat and bellowed, 'Come over here and take these mules to the construction site, you old bastard!'

Uncle Arhat squatted on the ground without making a sound, so one of the Japanese soldiers walked up and waved his rifle in front of Uncle Arhat's face. 'Minliwala, yala-limin!' he grunted. With the shiny **bayonet**[3] glinting in front of his eyes, Uncle Arhat sat down. The soldier thrust his bayonet forward, opening a tiny hole in Uncle Arhat's shiny scalp.

Beginning to tremble, Grandma blurted out, 'Do it, Uncle, take the mules for them.'

The other Jap soldier edged up close to Grandma, and Father noticed how young and handsome he was, and how his dark eyes sparkled. But when he smiled, his lip curled to reveal yellow buck teeth. Grandma staggered over to Uncle Arhat, whose wound was oozing blood that spread across his scalp and down his face. The grinning Japanese soldiers drew closer. Grandma laid her hands on Uncle Arhat's scalp, then rubbed them on her face. Pulling her hair, she leaped to her feet like a madwoman, her mouth agape. She looked three parts human and seven parts demon. The startled Japanese soldiers froze.

'Sir,' the tall puppet soldier said, 'that woman's crazy.'

One of the Jap soldiers mumbled something as he fired a shot over Grandma's head. She sat down hard and began to wail.

The tall puppet soldier used his rifle to prod Uncle Arhat, who got to his feet and took the tethers from the smaller soldier. The mules looked up; their legs trembled as they followed him out of the compound. The street was chaotic with mules, horses, oxen, and goats.

Grandma wasn't crazy. The minute the Japs and the puppet soldiers left, she removed the wooden lid from one of the wine vats and looked at her frightful, bloody reflection in the

---

① 斜视。

② 戳。

③ 刺刀。

mirrorlike surface. Father watched the tears on her cheeks turn red. She washed her face in the wine, turning it red.

Like the mules he was leading, Uncle Arhat was forced to work on the road that was taking shape in the sorghum field. The highway on the southern bank of the Black Water River was nearly completed, and cars and trucks were driving up on the newly laid roadway with loads of stone and yellow gravel, which they dumped on the riverbank. Since there was only a single wooden span across the river, the Japanese had decided to build a large stone bridge. Vast areas of sorghum on both sides of the highway had been levelled, until the ground seemed covered by an enormous green blanket. In the field north of the river, where black soil had been laid on either side of the road, dozens of horses and mules were pulling stone rollers to level two enormous squares in the sea of sorghum. Men led the animals back and forth through the field, trampling the tender stalks, which had been bent double by the shod hooves, then flattening them with stone rollers turned dark green by the plant juices. The **pungent**[①] aroma of green sorghum hung heavily over the construction site.

Uncle Arhat, who was sent to the southern bank of the river to haul rocks to the other side, reluctantly handed the mules over to an old geezer with festering eyes. The little wooden bridge swayed so violently it seemed about to topple as he crossed to the southern bank, where a Chinese overseer tapped him on the head with a purplish rattan whip and said, 'Start lugging rocks to the other side.' Uncle Arhat rubbed his eyes—the blood from his scalp wound had soaked his eyebrows. He picked up an average-sized rock and carried it to the other side, where the old geezer stood with the mules. 'Use them sparingly,' he said. 'They belong to the family I work for.' The old geezer lowered his head numbly, then turned and led the mules over to where teams of animals were working on the connecting road. The shiny rumps of the black mules reflected specks of sunlight. His head still bleeding, Uncle Arhat **hunker**[②]ed down, scooped up some black dirt, and rubbed it on the wound. A dull, heavy pain travelled all the way down to his toes.

Armed Jap and puppet soldiers stood on the fringes of the construction site; the overseer, whip in hand, roamed the site like a spectre. The eyes of the frightened labourers rolled as they watched Uncle Arhat, his head a mass of blood and mud, pick up a rock and take a couple of steps. Suddenly he heard a crack behind him, followed by a drawn-out,

① 刺鼻的。
② 盘坐。

stinging pain on his back. He dropped the rock and looked at the grinning overseer. 'Your honour, if you have something to say, say it. Why hit me?'

Without a word, the grinning overseer flicked his whip in the air and wrapped it around Uncle Arhat's waist, all but cutting him in half. Two streams of hot, stinging tears oozed out of the corners of Uncle Arhat's eyes, and blood rushed to his head, which began to **throb**① as though it might split open.

'Your honour!' Uncle Arhat protested.

His honour whipped him again.

'Your honour,' Uncle Arhat said, 'why are you hitting me?'

His honour flicked the whip and grinned until his eyes were mere slits: 'Just giving you a taste, you son of a bitch.'

Uncle Arhat choked off his sobs as his eyes pooled with tears. He bent over, picked up a large rock from the pile, and staggered with it towards the little bridge. The **jagged**② edges dug deeply into his gut and his rib cage, but he didn't feel the pain.

The overseer stood rooted to the spot, whip in hand, and Uncle Arhat trembled with fear as he lugged the rock past his gaze. With the whip cutting into his neck he fell forward, landed on his knees, and hugged the rock to his chest. It tore the skin on his hands and left a deep gash in his chin. Stunned, he began to blubber like a baby; a purple tongue of flame licked out in the emptiness inside his skull.

He strained to pull his hands out from under the rock, stood up, and arched his back like a threatened, skinny old tomcat. Just then a middle-aged man, grinning from ear to ear, walked up. He took a pack of cigarettes out of his pocket and held one up to the overseer, who parted his lips to accept the offering, then waited for the man to light it for him.

'Revered one,' the man said, 'that stinking blockhead isn't worth getting angry over.'

The overseer exhaled the smoke through his nose and said nothing. Uncle Arhat stared at the whip in his twitching yellowed fingers.

The middle-aged man stuffed the pack of cigarettes into the pocket of the overseer, who seemed not to notice; then, **snort**③ing lightly, he patted his pocket, turned, and walked away.

---

① 颤动。
② 参差不齐的。
③ 哼鼻子。

'Are you new here, elder brother?' the man asked.

Uncle Arhat said he was.

'You didn't give him anything to grease the **skid**[1]s?'

'Those mad dogs dragged me here against my will.'

'Give him a little money or a pack of cigarettes. He doesn't hit the hard workers, and he doesn't hit the **slacker**[2]s. The only ones he hits are those who have eyes but won't see.'

All that morning, Uncle Arhat desperately lugged rocks, like a man without a soul. The scab on his scalp, baked by the sun, caused terrible pain as it dried and cracked. His hands were raw and bloody, and the stiffened gash on his chin made him drool. The purplish flame kept licking at the inside of his skull -sometimes strong, sometimes weak, but never dying out completely.

At noon a brown truck drove up the barely negotiable road. Dimly Uncle Arhat heard a shrill whistle and watched the labourers stumble up to the truck. He sat mindlessly on the ground, showing no interest in the truck. The middle-aged man walked over and pulled him to his feet. 'Elder brother, come on, it's mealtime. Try some Japanese rice.'

Uncle Arhat stood up and followed him.

Large buckets of snowy white rice were handed down from the truck, along with a basket of white ceramic bowls with blue floral patterns. A fat Chinese stood next to the baskets, handing bowls to the men as they filed past. A skinny Chinese stood beside the buckets, ladling rice. The labourers stood around the truck, wolfing down their food, bare hands serving as chopsticks.

The overseer walked up, whip in hand, the enigmatic grin still on his face. The flame in Uncle Arhat's skull blazed, illuminating thoughts of the hard morning that he had tried to cast off. Armed Japanese and puppet **sentries**[3] walked up and stood around a galvanised-iron bucket to eat their lunch. A guard dog with a long snout and trimmed ears sat behind the bucket, its tongue lolling as it watched the labourers.

Uncle Arhat counted the dozen or so Japs and the dozen or so puppet soldiers standing around the bucket eating their lunch; the word 'escape' flashed into his mind. Escape! If he could make it to the sorghum field, these fuckers wouldn't be able to catch him. The

① 刹车器。

② 懒惰的人。

③ 哨兵。

soles of his feet were hot and sweaty; the moment the idea to flee entered his mind, he grew **fidgety**① and anxious. Something was hidden behind the calm, cold grin on the face of the overseer. Whatever it was, it made Uncle Arhat's thoughts grow muddled.

The fat Chinese took the bowls from the labourers before they were finished. They licked their lips and stared longingly at kernels of rice stuck to the sides of the buckets, but didn't dare move. A mule on the northern bank of the river brayed shrilly. Uncle Arhat recognised the familiar sound. Tethered to rolling stones beside the newly ploughed road-bed, the listless mules nibbled stalks and leaves of sorghum that had been trampled into the earth.

That afternoon a man in his twenties darted into the sorghum field when he thought the overseer wasn't looking. A bullet followed his path of retreat. He lay motionless on the fringe of the field.

The brown truck drove up again as the sun was sinking in the west. Uncle Arhat's digestive system, used to sorghum, was intent on ridding itself of this mildewy white rice, but he forced the food past the knots in his throat. The thought of escape was stronger than ever; he longed to see his own compound, where the pungent odour of wine pervaded the air, in that village a dozen or so li away. The distillery hands had all fled with the arrival of the Japanese, and the wine cooker now stood cold. Even more he longed to see my grandma and my father. He hadn't forgotten the warmth and contentment she had bestowed upon him alongside the pile of sorghum leaves.

After dinner the labourers were herded into an enclosure of fir stakes covered with **tarpaulins**②. Wires the thickness of mung beans had been strung between the stakes, and the gate was made of thick metal rods. The Jap and puppet soldiers were **billet**③ed in separate tents several yards away; the guard dog was tethered to the flap of the Jap tent. Two lanterns hung from a tall post at the entrance of the enclosure, around which soldiers took turns at sentry duty. Mules and horses were tethered to posts in a razed section of the sorghum field west of the enclosure.

The stench inside the enclosure was suffocating. Some of the men snored loudly; others got up to piss in a tin pail, raising a noisy liquid tattoo, like pearls falling onto a jade plate. The lanterns cast a pale light, under which the sentries' long shadows flickered.

---

① 坐立不安的。

② 雨衣,油布。

③ 分配住宿。

As the night stretched on, the cold became unbearable, and Uncle Arhat couldn't sleep. With his thoughts focused on escape, he lay there not daring to move; eventually he fell into a muddled sleep. In his dream his head felt as though it were being carved by a sharp knife, while his hand felt seared as if he clasped a branding iron. He awoke covered in sweat; his pants were soaked with piss. The shrill crow of a rooster floated over from the distant village. The mules and horses pawed the ground and snorted. Stars winked slyly through holes in the tattered tarpaulin above him.

The man who had come to his aid that day quietly sat up. Even in the relative darkness of the enclosure, Uncle Arhat could see his blazing eyes, and could tell that he was no ordinary man. He lay there, watching silently.

As the man knelt in the enclosure opening, he raised his arms slowly and deliberately. Uncle Arhat's eyes were riveted on his back and his head, around which hung an aura of mystery. The man took a deep breath, cocked his head, and thrust out his hands, like arrows from a bow, to grab two metal rods. A green glare shot from his eyes, and seemed to crackle when it struck an object. The metal rods silently parted, admitting more light into the enclosure from the lanterns and overhead stars, and revealing the shoe of a sentry. Uncle Arhat saw a dark shadow dart out of the enclosure. The Jap sentry grunted, then, in the man's **vicelike**① grip, crumpled to the ground. The man picked up the Jap's rifle and slipped silently into the darkness.

It took Uncle Arhat a moment to realise what had happened. The middle-aged man had shown him the way to escape! Cautiously, he crawled out through the opening. The dead Jap lay on the ground, face up, one leg still twitching.

After crawling into the sorghum field, Uncle Arhat straightened up and followed the **furrow**②s, taking care not to bump the stalks and get them rustling. He found his way to the bank of the Black Water River, where the three stars—Rigel, Betelgeuse, and Bellatrix—hung directly overhead. A heavy predawn darkness had fallen around him. Stars glistened in the water. As he stood briefly on the riverbank, he shivered from the cold, his teeth chattered, and the ache in his chin spread to his cheeks and ears, finally merging with the throbbing pain in his festering scalp. The crisp air of freedom, filtered through the juices of the sorghum plants, entered his nostrils, his lungs, and his intestines. The ghostly light of the two lanterns shone weakly through the mist; the dark outline of the fir-stake en-

① 紧紧的。
② 垄沟。

closure was like an immense graveyard. Astonished at having got away so easily, he strode onto the **rickety**① wooden bridge, above splashing fish and rippling water, as a shooting star split the heavens. It was as though nothing had happened. He was free to return to his village to let his wounds mend and to go on living. But as he was crossing the bridge, he heard the plaintive braying of a mule on the southern bank. He turned back for Grandma's mules. This decision would lead to a grand tragedy.

Horses and mules had been tied to a dozen or more tethering posts not far from the enclosure, in an area saturated with their foul-smelling urine. The horses were snorting and eating sorghum stalks; the mules were gnawing on the tethering posts and shitting loose stool. Uncle Arhat, stumbling three times for every step, stole in among them, where he smelled the welcome odour of our two big black mules and spotted their familiar shapes. Time to free his comrades in suffering. But the mules, strangers to the world of reason, greeted him with flying hooves.

'Black mules,' Uncle Arhat mumbled, 'black mules, we can run away together!' The irate mules pawed the earth to protect their territory from their master, who was unaware that the smell of his dried blood and new wounds had changed his identity to them. Confused and upset, he stepped forward, and was knocked down by a flying hoof. As he lay on the ground, his side started turning numb. The mule was still bucking and kicking, its steel-crescent shoes glinting like little moons. Uncle Arhat's hip swelled up painfully. He clambered to his feet, but fell back. As soon as he hit the ground, he struggled back up. A thin-voiced rooster in the village crowed once more, as the darkness began to give way to a glimmer of stars that illuminated the mules' rumps and eyeballs.

'Damned beasts!'

With anger rising in his heart, he stumbled around the area looking for a weapon. At the construction site of an irrigation ditch he found a sharp metal hoe. Now armed, he walked and cursed loudly, forgetting all about the men and their dog no more than a hundred paces distant. He felt free-fear is all that stands in the way of freedom.

A red solar halo crumbled as the sun rose in the east, and in the predawn light the sorghum was so still it seemed ready to burst. Uncle Arhat walked up to the mules, the rosy colour of dawn in his eyes and bitter loathing in his heart. The mules stood calmly, motionlessly. Uncle Arhat raised his hoe, took aim on the hind leg of one of them, and swung with

---

① 摇晃的。

all his might. A cold shadow fell on the leg. The mule swayed sideways a couple of times, then straightened up, as a brutish, violent, stupefying, wrathful **bray**① erupted from its head. The wounded animal then arched its rump, sending a shower of hot blood splashing down on Uncle Arhat's face. Seeing an opening, he swung at the other hind leg. A sigh escaped from the black mule as its rump settled earthwards and it sat down hard, propped up by its forlegs, its neck jerked taut by the tether; it bleated to the blue-grey heavens through its gaping mouth. The hoe, pinned beneath its rump, jerked Uncle Arhat into a squatting position. **Muster**②ing all his strength, he managed to pull it free.

The second mule stood stupidly, eyeing its fallen comrade and braying piteously, as though pleading for its life. When Uncle Arhat approached, dragging his hoe behind him, the mule backed up until the tether seemed about to part and the post began to make cracking sounds. Dark-blue rays of light flowed from its fist-sized eyeballs.

'Scared? You damned beast! Where's your arrogance now? You evil, ungrateful, parasitic bastard! You ass-kissing, treacherous son of a bitch!'

As he spat out wrathful obscenities, he raised his hoe and swung at the animal's long, rectangular face. It missed, striking the tethering post. By twisting the handle up and down, back and forth, he finally managed to free the head from the wood. The mule struggled so violently that its rear legs arched like bows, its **scrawny**③ tail was noisily sweeping the ground. Uncle Arhat took careful aim at the animal's face—crack—the hoe landed smack on its broad forehead, emitting a resounding clang as metal struck bone, the **reverberation**④ passing through the wooden handle and stinging Uncle Arhat's arms. Not a sound emerged from the black mule's closed mouth. Its legs and hooves jerked and twitched furiously before it crashed to the ground like a capsized wall, snapping the tether in two, with one end hanging limply from the post and the other coiled beside the dead animal's head. Uncle Arhat watched quietly, his arms at his sides. The shiny wooden handle buried in the mule's head pointed to heaven at a jaunty angle.

A barking dog, human shouts, dawn. The curved outline of a blood-red sun rose above the sorghum field to the east, its rays shining down on the black hole of Uncle Arhat's open mouth.

---

① 驴叫。

② 集结。

③ 骨瘦如柴的。

④ 回响。

Ⅳ. 思考题

1. What are the symbolic meanings of the red sorghum?
2. How do you appreciate Mo Yan's language? In what ways is his narrative vivid? Think about the ways in which linguistic apparatus functions in this novel.
3. What is Mo Yan's approach to construct history? How do we get to know the Sino-Japanese War? From whose narration do we get a complete picture?

Ⅴ. 文学批评

翻译的归化和异化

Culture-loaded words—also known as "lexical gap"—refers to that the information the words in the source language carried have no equivalents in the target language. And the characteristics of the culture-loaded words make it difficult to find the corresponding words and expressions in the target language in the process of their translation.

Meanwhile, while translating the culture-loaded words, there are commonly two strategies—"domestication" and "foreignization". With the continuous improvement of China's international status, the foreignization strategy, which renders Chinese culture as the end-result, will be more and more widely used in the translation of Chinese culture-loaded words.

This thesis respectively discusses the specific translation approaches under the guidance of "domestication" and "foreignization". Both "domestication" and "foreignization" are indispensable in transcultural translation; needless to say, naturalized translation has its significance of existence; however, with the advent of globalization, as foreignization of Chinese culture-loaded words can not only accurately convey the meaning of the words, but also facilitate the spread of oriental culture, thus to achieve the maximum transmission of Chinese culture and to promote the mutual understanding and exchange between the east and west; so as a result, foreignization would be more and more widely accepted by the world.

In practice, we usually have two main methods of domestication. One is "Free Translation", and the other is "Substitute method". From Chinese to English translation, for example,

"祖母在纳鞋底,她不说话。"

In this words, "纳" means "stitch, sew", and thus there is no equivalent word in English, so we, through applying the free translation method, translate the words into this:

"Remaining silent, grandmother was stitching a shoe sole."

As for substitute method, I hereby quote another example: "母老虎" (tigeress) in Chinese stands for courage, vitality and strength, and has the connotation of "shrew", however, in English, "tigeress" doesn't have such connotative meaning; this is called lexical gap or glossary vacancy, The phenomenon of lexical gap, a commonly encountered problem in cross-cultural communication, often causes trouble to translation in cross-cultural communication.

So in this case, we have "lioness" in English as a substitute for tigeress as it has the corresponding cultural connotation like "tigeress".

However, although domestication is quintessential in Chinese-English translation, yet with the fast development of China, foreignization will definitely play a more and more important role in the translation as it helps to spread the Chinese traditional culture to the world and promote the equality of cultures.

Foreignization has several concrete methods either:

1. Transliteration

We take this method as we cannot find equivalents in English for the Chinese words, for example, "国民党" - "Kuomintang", "麻辣烫" - "malatang", "花旦" - "huadan", "喇嘛" - "lama", etc.

2. Transliteration plus annotation

"抓周" translate into :"zhuazhou, a child told by his/her parents to choose one thing among many others to show his/her future".

3. Literal translation

Literal translation, as its name suggests, means to translate literally. For example:

"纸老虎": paper tiger

"鱼米之乡": a land of fish and rice

"三峡工程": the three gorges project

4. Literal translation plus annotation

This method can maintain the culture background. For example:

(1)三个代表:Three Represents(the Communist Party of China represents the trend of development of advanced production forces, the orientation of advanced culture, and the fundamental interests of the overwhelming majority of the people in China)。

(2)端铁饭碗: have an iron rice bowl (a stable, lifelong job regardless of one's performance).

To conclude, translation is not a bilingual communication, moreover, it's a cross-culture communication. In order to bridge the language barriers and realize the information exchange of cross-culture, we can adopt the strategy of "giving priority to domestication while using domestication strategy as a supplementary". And with the enhancing cultural development and assimilation, this strategy will become more and more feasible.

Ⅵ. 拓展阅读

Jonathan Stalling's "The Voice of the Translator: An Interview with Howard Goldblatt" (*Translation Review* 88.1 (2014): 1-12).

Ⅶ. 参考文献

Aliel. "*On the Translation of Chinese Culture-loaded Words from the Perspective of Domestication and Foreignization.*" Retrieved June 7th, 2020, https://www.ccjk.com/on-the-translation-of-chinese-culture-loaded-words-from-the-perspective-of-domestication-and-foreignization/.

Mo Yan. *Red Sorghum*. Trans. Howard Goldblatt. Random House, 2012.

Chapter 12 Alice Munro and "A Room of One's Own"

Ⅰ. 作者简介

艾丽丝·门罗(Alice Munro)(1931—)出生于加拿大安大略省温厄姆镇(Wingham)的一个以饲养狐狸和家禽为业的牧场主家庭。在一次访谈中,门罗称自己自幼喜爱随时编故事,写作的开端始于给童话《海的女儿》编造圆满结局。门罗十几岁时就开始写作,并于1950年在西安大略大学就读期间发表了第一篇作品《影子的维度》。1949年,门罗进入西安大略大学主修英语。1951年,她退学与詹姆斯·门罗结婚,移居温哥华。1963年,门罗夫妇移居维多利亚,在那里创办了门罗图书公司。1972年,门罗与丈夫离婚并回到安大略,成为西安大略大学的住校作家。1976年,门罗与第二任丈夫结婚,夫妇二人搬到安大略省克林顿镇外的一个农场,后来又从农场搬到克林顿镇,从此一直居住在那里。门罗于1968年出版了第一部短篇小说集《快乐阴影的舞蹈》(*Dance of the Happy Shades*),该作品获得了高度赞誉,一举赢得了当年加拿大的最高文学奖项——加拿大总督奖。在此之后她又出版了《女孩和女人的生活》(*Lives of Girls and Women*),书中讲述了一组相互关联的故事,合起来构成了一部长篇小说。1978 年,门罗的小说集《你认为你是谁?》(*Who Do You Think You Are?*)出版,这也是一组相互关联的故事,这本书为她赢得了第二次总督奖。1979 到 1982 年,门罗游历了澳大利亚、中国和斯堪的那维亚半岛。1980 年她同时担任不列颠哥伦比亚与昆士兰两所大学的住校作家。20 世纪 80 代和 90 年代这二十年里,门罗每隔四年就会出版一部短篇小说集,并给重要文学刊物如《纽约客》(*The New Yorker*)、《大西洋月刊》(*The Atlantic*)、《巴黎评论》(*Paris Review*)供稿。门罗共获过三次加拿大总督将,并于 2009 年凭借《逃离》(*Runaway*)获得当年的布克国际奖。

门罗的作品在题材上有两大鲜明的特点,一是作品中强烈的地方意识,二是其女性视角创作。门罗的作品充满浓厚的地域色彩,她的故事多以安大略省西南部的小镇为背景,门罗笔下的小镇生活虽表面平静,但在这之下却潜伏着阴森朦胧的悬念,人生各种料想不到而又在情理之中的转折都会出现:逃避、谎言、出轨、自私、出逃、死亡……因此,读门罗的小说会给人一种"于无声处听惊雷"的感觉。门罗的"小镇"叙事又常常与女性叙事纠缠在一起。门罗的女主人公通常是受过教育的知识女性,面对失败的爱、失败的生活,她们企图打破世俗的束缚和限制,却总在或堕落或澄明的关键点为自身矛盾的性格所困,最终陷入更深的绝望。

门罗坚持只创作短篇小说,作为一名现实主义者,门罗极其在意文学的"质地",在创作时坚持使用精确的措辞、适当的韵律,并始终不忘文学对人性的挖掘和探讨。阅读她的作品,读者能深切地感受其身处的文学经验和传统与人类共同命运的关系,促使读者重新思考日常生活中被忽视的细节和被贬低的人物。2013 年,门罗获得诺贝尔文学奖,颁奖词为"当代短篇小说大师"("master of the contemporary short story")。诺贝尔文学奖评审委员会将奖项颁给门罗无疑是对短篇小说这一文类的肯定,门罗的获奖或许会将短篇小说这个具有浓缩的感染力的艺术形式推向一个新高度。

Ⅱ. 内容提要

《办公室》的叙述者是一位生活条件优越的家庭主妇,因钟情于文学创作又不堪相夫教子的重负，决定去租一间办公室写作，一方面是为了实现自己的作家梦，另一方面也想逃离琐碎的家务。她在租借的办公室中写作，但在男房东持续不断的骚扰和干涉下，最终退掉了房间，放弃了写作梦，回归家庭生活。

英国现代主义作家、著名女性主义思想家弗吉尼亚·伍尔夫曾提出著名的论断："一个女人要写小说，她必须有钱，还要有一个她自己的房间。"门罗在故事中设想女性如果真的接受伍尔夫的这一建议并实际去做会遭遇什么。故事写于 20 世纪 60 年代平权运动兴起的时段，彼时写作并不是公认的适合女性从事的职业，门罗在这篇短篇小说中与女性主义先驱伍尔夫进行了隔空对话，表达了自己对女性职业发展、女权主义运动的思考。

Ⅲ. 作品

The solution to my life occurred to me one evening while I was **ning**① a shirt. It was simple but **audacious**②. I went into the living room where my husband was watching television and I said, "I think I ought to have an office."

It sounded fantastic, even to me. What do I want an office for? I have a house; it is pleasant and roomy and has a view of the sea; it provides appropriate places for eating and sleeping, and having baths and conversations with one's friends. Also I have a garden; there is no lack of space.

No. But here comes the **disclosure**③ which is not easy for me: I am a writer. That does not sound right. Too **presumptuous**④; **phony**⑤, or at least unconvincing. Try again. I write. Is that better? I try to write. That makes it worse. Hypocritical humility. Well then?

It doesn't matter. However I put it, the words create their space of silence, the delicate moment of exposure. But people are kind, the silence is quickly absorbed by the **solicitude**⑥ of friendly voices, crying variously, how wonderful, and good for you, and well, that

---

① 熨烫。
② 大胆的。
③ 揭露，披露。
④ 自以为是的。
⑤ 假的，虚伪的。
⑥ 渴望。

is intriguing. And what do you write, they inquire with spirit. Fiction, I reply, bearing my humiliation by this time with ease, even a suggestion of **flippancy**①, which was not always mine, and again, again, the perceptible circles of **dismay**② are smoothed out by such ready and tactful voices—which have however exhausted their stock of consolatory phrases, and can say only, "Ah!"

So this is what I want an office for (I said to my husband): to write in. I was at once aware that it sounded like a **finicky**③ requirement, a piece of rare **self-indulgence**④. To write, as everyone knows, you need a typewriter, or at least a pencil, some paper, a table and chair; I have all these things in a corner of my bedroom. But now I want an office as well.

And I was not even, sure that I was going to write in it, if we come down to that. Maybe I would sit and stare at the wall; even that prospect was not unpleasant to me. It was really the sound of the word "office" that I liked, its sound of dignity and peace. And purposefulness and importance. But I did not care to mention this to my husband, so I launched instead into a high-flown explanation which went, as I remember, like this:

A house is all right for a man to work in. He brings his work into the house, a place is cleared for it; the house re-arranges itself as best it can around him. Everybody recognizes that his work exists. He is not expected to answer the telephone, to find things that are lost, to see why the children are crying, or feed the cat. He can shut his door. Imagine (I said) a mother shutting her door, and the children knowing she is behind it; why, the very thought of it is **outrageous**⑤ to them. A woman who sits staring into space, into a country that is not her husband's or her children's is likewise known to be an offence against nature. So a house is not the same for a woman. She is not someone who walks into the house, to make use of it, and will walk out again. She is the house; there is no separation possible.

(And this is true, though as usual when arguing for something I am afraid I do not deserve, I put it in too emphatic and emotional terms. At certain times, perhaps on long spring evenings, still rainy and sad, with the cold bulbs in bloom and a light too mild for

---

① 轻蔑,玩世不恭。
② 惊愕。
③ 挑剔的。
④ 自我放任。
⑤ 无法容忍的,反常的。

promise drifting over the sea, I have opened the windows and felt the house shrink back into wood and plaster and those humble elements of which it is made, and the life in it subside, leaving me exposed, empty-handed, but feeling a fierce and lawless quiver of freedom, of loneliness too harsh and perfect for me now to bear. Then I know how the rest of the time I am sheltered and encumbered, how insistently I am warmed and bound.)

"Go ahead, if you can find one cheap enough," is all my husband had to say to this. He is not like me; he does not really want explanations. That the heart of another person is a closed book, is something you will hear him say frequently, and without regret.

Even then I did not think it was something that could be accomplished. Perhaps at bottom it seemed to me too improper a wish to be granted. I could almost more easily have wished for a **mink**① coat, for a diamond necklace; these are things women do obtain. The children, learning of my plans, greeted them with the most **dashing**② skepticism and unconcern. Nevertheless I went down to the shopping centre which is two blocks from where I live; there I had noticed for several months, and without thinking how they could **pertain**③ to me, a couple of "For Rent" signs in the upstairs windows of a building that housed a drugstore and a beauty parlour. As I went up the stairs I had a feeling of complete unreality; surely renting was a complicated business, in the case of offices; you did not simply knock on the door of the vacant premises and wait to be admitted; it would have to be done through channels. Also, they would want too much money.

As it turned out, I did not even have to knock. A woman came out of one of the empty offices, dragging a vacuum **cleaner**④, and pushing it with her foot, towards the open door across the hall, which evidently led to an apartment in the rear of the building. She and her husband lived in this apartment; their name was Malley; and it was indeed they who owned the building and rented out the offices. The rooms she had just been vacuuming were, she told me, fitted out for a dentist's office, and so would not interest me, but she would show me the other place. She invited me into her apartment while she put away the vacuum and got her key. Her husband, she said with a sigh I could not interpret, was not at home.

Mrs. Malley was a black-haired, delicate-looking woman, perhaps in her early forties,

---

① 貂皮。
② 劲头十足的,尖锐的。
③ 适合。
④ 吸尘器。

slatternly① but still faintly appealing, with such arbitrary touches of femininity as the thin line of bright lipstick, the pink feather slippers on obviously tender and swollen feel. She had the swaying passivity, the air of exhaustion and muted apprehension, that speaks of a life spent in close attention on a man who is by turns vigorous, **crotchety**② and dependent. How much of this I saw at first, how much decided on later is of course impossible to tell. But I did think that she would have no children, the stress of her life, whatever it was, did not allow it, and in this I was not mistaken.

The room where I waited was evidently a combination living room and office. The first things I noticed were models of ships—galleons, clippers, Queen Marys—sitting on the tables, the window sills, the television. Where there were no ships there were potted plants and a clutter of what are sometimes called "masculine" ornaments—china deer heads, bronze horses, huge ashtrays of heavy, veined, shiny material. On the walls were framed photographs and what might have been diplomas. One photo showed a poodle and a bulldog, dressed in masculine and feminine clothing, and assuming with dismal embarrassment a pose of affection. Written across it was "Old Friends." But the room was really dominated by a portrait, with its own light and a gilded frame; it was of a good-looking, fair-haired man in middle age, sitting behind a desk, wearing a business suit and looking preeminently prosperous, rosy and agreeable. Here again, it is probably **hindsight**③ on my part that points out that in the portrait there is evident also some uneasiness, some lack of faith the man has in this role, a tendency he has to spread himself too **bountifully**④ and insistently, which for all anyone knows may lead to disaster.

Never mind the Malleys. As soon as I saw that office, I wanted it. It was larger than I needed, being divided in such a way that it would be suitable for a doctor's office. (We had a **chiropractor**⑤ in here but he left, says Mrs. Malley in her regretful but uninformative way.) The walls were cold and bare, white with a little grey, to cut the glare for the eyes. Since there were no doctors in evidence, nor had been, as Mrs. Malley freely told me, for some time, I offered twenty-five dollars a month. She said she would have to speak to her husband.

---

① 不整洁的,邋遢的。
② 反复无常,爱发牢骚。
③ 事后的认识。
④ 丰裕的。
⑤ 脊椎按摩师。

The next time I came, my offer was agreed upon, and I met Mr. Malley in the flesh. I explained, as I had already done to his wife, that I did not want to make use of my office during regular business hours, but during the weekends and sometimes in the evening. He asked me what I would use it for, and I told him, not without wondering first whether I ought to say I did stenography①.

He absorbed the information with good humour. "Ah, you're a writer."

"Well yes. I write."

"Then we'll do our best to see you're comfortable here," he said expansively. "I'm a great man for hobbies myself. All these ship-models, I do them in my spare time, they're a blessing for the nerves. People need an occupation for their nerves. I dare say you're the same."

"Something the same," I said, resolutely agreeable, even relieved that he saw my behaviour in this hazy and tolerant light. At least he did not ask me, as I half-expected, who was looking after the children, and did my husband approve? Ten years, maybe fifteen, had greatly softened, spread and defeated the man in the picture. His hips and thighs had now a **startling**② accumulation of fat, causing him to move with a sigh, a **cushiony**③ settling of flesh, a ponderous matriarchal discomfort. His hair and eyes had faded, his features blurred, and the **affable**④, **predatory**⑤ expression had collapsed into one of troubling humility and chronic mistrust. I did not look at him. I had not planned, in taking an office, to take on the responsibility of knowing any more human beings.

On the weekend I moved in, without the help of my family, who would have been kind. I brought my typewriter and a card table and chair, also a little wooden table on which I set a hot plate, a kettle, a jar of instant coffee, a spoon and a yellow **mug**⑥. That was all. I **brooded**⑦ with satisfaction on the bareness of my walls, the cheap dignity of my essential furnishings, the remarkable lack of things to dust, wash or polish.

The sight was not so pleasing to Mr. Malley. He knocked on my door soon after I was settled and said that he wanted to explain a few things to me—about unscrewing the light

① 速记。
② 令人吃惊的。
③ 柔软的。
④ 和蔼的,友善的。
⑤ 掠夺性的,攻击性的。
⑥ 马克杯。
⑦ 沉思,孵蛋。

in the outer room, which I would not need, about the **radiator**① and how to work the **awning**② outside the window. He looked around at everything with gloom and mystification and said it was an awfully uncomfortable place for a lady.

"It's perfectly all right for me," I said, not as discouragingly as I would have liked to, because I always have a tendency to **placate**③ people whom I dislike for no good reason, or simply do not want to know. I make elaborate offerings of courtesy sometimes, in the foolish hope that they will go away and leave me alone.

"What you want is a nice easy chair to sit in, while you're waiting for inspiration to hit. I've got a chair down in the basement, all kinds of stuff down there since my mother passed on last year. There's a bit of carpet rolled up in a corner down there, it isn't doing anybody any good. We could get this place fixed up so it'd be a lot more homelike for you."

"But really," I said, "but really I like it as it is."

"If you wanted to run up some curtains, I'd pay you for the material. Place needs a touch of colour, I'm afraid you'll get **morbid**④ sitting in here."

"Oh, no," I said, and laughed, "I'm sure I won't."

"It'd be a different story if you was a man. A woman wants things a bit cosier."

So I got up and went to the window and looked down into the empty Sunday street through the slats of the Venetian blind, to avoid the accusing vulnerability of his fat face and I tried out a cold voice that is to be heard frequently in my thoughts but has great difficulty getting out of my cowardly mouth. "Mr. Malley, please don't bother me about this any more. I said it suits me. I have everything I want. Thanks for showing me about the light."

The effect was devastating enough to shame me. "I certainly wouldn't dream of bothering you," he said, with precision of speech and aloof sadness. "I merely made these suggestions for your comfort. Had I realized I was in your way, I would of left some time ago." When he had gone I felt better, even a little exhilarated at my victory though still ashamed of how easy it had been. I told myself that he would have had to be discouraged sooner or later, it was better to have it over with at the beginning.

---

① 电暖炉。

② 遮阳篷。

③ 安抚。

④ 病态的。

The following weekend he knocked on my door. His expression of humility was exaggerated, almost enough so to seem mocking, yet in another sense it was real and I felt unsure of myself.

"I won't take up a minute of your time," he said. "I never meant to be a nuisance. I just wanted to tell you I'm sorry I offended you last time and I apologize. Here's a little present if you will accept."

He was carrying a plant whose name I did not know; it had thick, **glossy** ①leaves and grew out of a pot wrapped **lavishly**② in pink and silver foil.

"There," he said, arranging this plant in a corner of my room. "I don't want any bad feelings with you and me. I'll take the blame. And I thought, maybe she won't accept furnishings, but what's the matter with a nice little plant, that'll brighten things up for you."

It was not possible for me, at this moment, to tell him that I did not want a plant. I hate house plants. He told me how to take care of it, how often to water it and so on; I thanked him. There was nothing else I could do, and I had the unpleasant feeling that beneath his offering of apologies and gifts he was well aware of this and in some way gratified by it. He kept on talking, using the words bad feelings, offended, apologize. I tried once to interrupt, with the idea of explaining that I had made provision for an area of my life where good feelings, or bad, did not enter in, that between him and me, in fact, it was not necessary that there be any feelings at all; but this struck me as a hopeless task. How could I confront, in the open, this craving for intimacy? Besides, the plant in its shiny paper had confused me.

"How's the writing progressing?" he said, with an air of putting all our unfortunate differences behind him.

"Oh, about as usual."

"Well if you ever run out of things to write about, I got a **barrelful**③." Pause. "But I guess I'm just eatin' into your time here," he said with a kind of painful **buoyancy**④. This was a test, and I did not pass it. I smiled, my eyes held by that magnificent plant: I

① 有光泽的。
② 华丽地。
③ 一桶之量。
④ 乐观,快乐。

said it was all right.

"I was just thinking about the fellow was in here before you. Chiropractor. You could of wrote a book about him."

I assumed a listening position, my hands no longer hovering over the keys. If cowardice and insincerity are big vices of mine, curiosity is certainly another.

"He had a good practice built up here. The only trouble was, he gave more adjustments than was listed in the book of chiropractory. Oh, he was adjusting right and left. I came in here after he moved out, and what do you think I found? Soundproofing! This whole room was **soundproofed**①, to enable him to make his adjustments without disturbing anybody. This very room you're sitting writing your stories in.

"First we knew of it was a lady knocked on my door one day, wanted me to provide her with a passkey to his office. He'd locked his door against her.

"I guess he just got tired of treating her particular case. I guess he figured he'd been knocking away at it long enough. Lady well on in years, you know, and him just a young man. He had a nice young wife too and a couple of the prettiest children you ever would want to see. **Filthy**② some of the things that go on in this world."

It took me some time to realize that he told this story not simply as a piece of gossip, but as something a writer would be particularly interested to hear. Writing and **lewdness**③ had a vague delicious connection in his mind. Even this notion, however, seemed so **wistful**④, so **infantile**⑤, that it struck me as a waste of energy to attack it. I knew now I must avoid hurting him for my own sake, not for his. It had been a great mistake to think that a little roughness would settle things.

The next present was a teapot. I insisted that I drank only coffee and told him to give it to his wife. He said that tea was better for the nerves and that he had known right away I was a nervous person, like himself. The teapot was covered with gilt and roses and I knew that it was not cheap, in spite of its extreme **hideousness**⑥. I kept it on my table. I also continued to care for the plant, which thrived **obscenely**⑦ in the corner of my room. I

---

① 隔音的。
② 肮脏下流的。
③ 色情,淫荡。
④ 渴求的,这里指一厢情愿。
⑤ 婴儿的,孩子气的,幼稚的。
⑥ 丑陋。
⑦ 令人发指地。

could not decide what else to do. He bought me a wastebasket, a fancy one with Chinese mandarins on all eight sides; he got a foam rubber cushion for my chair. I despised myself for submitting to this **blackmail**①. I did not even really pity him; it was just that I could not turn away, I could not turn away from that **obsequious**② hunger. And he knew himself my tolerance was bought; in a way he must have hated me for it.

When he lingered in my office now he told me stories of himself. It occurred to me that he was revealing his life to me in the hope that I would write it down. Of course he had probably revealed it to plenty of people for no particular reason, but in my case there seemed to be a special, even desperate necessity. His life was a series of **calamities**③, as people's lives often are; he had been let down by people he had trusted, refused help by those he had depended on, betrayed by the very friends to whom he had given kindness and material help. Other people, mere strangers and passersby, had taken time to torment him gratuitously, in novel and inventive ways. On occasion, his very life had been threatened. Moreover his wife was a difficulty, her health being poor and her temperament unstable; what was he to do? You see how it is, he said, lifting his hands, but I live. He looked to me to say yes.

I took to coming up the stairs on tiptoe, trying to turn my key without making a noise; this was foolish of course because I could not **muffle**④ my typewriter. I actually considered writing in **longhand**⑤, and wished repeatedly for the evil chiropractor's soundproofing. I told my husband my problem and he said it was not a problem at all. Tell him you're busy, he said. As a matter of fact I did tell him; every time he came to my door, always armed with a little gift or an errand, he asked me how I was and I said that today I was busy. Ah, then, he said, as he eased himself through the door, he would not keep me a minute. And all the time, as I have said, he knew what was going on in my mind, how I weakly longed to be rid of him. He knew but could not afford to care.

One evening after I had gone home I discovered that I had left at the office a letter I had intended to post, and so I went back to get it. I saw from the street that the light was on in the room where I worked. Then I saw him bending over the **card table**⑥. Of course,

---

① 胁迫。
② 谄媚的，卑躬屈膝的。
③ 不幸之事。
④ 消音。
⑤ 手写。
⑥ 折叠桌。

he came in at night and read what I had written! He heard me at the door, and when I came in he was picking up my wastebasket, saying he thought he would just tidy things up for me. He went out at once. I did not say anything, but found myself trembling with anger and gratification. To have found a just cause was a wonder, an unbearable relief.

Next time he came to my door I had locked it on the inside. I knew his step, his chummy **cajoling** ①knock. I continued typing loudly, but not uninterruptedly, so he would know I heard. He called my name, as if I was playing a trick; I bit my lips together not to answer. Unreasonably as ever, guilt **assailed**② me but I typed on. That day I saw the earth was dry around the roots of the plant; I let it alone.

I was not prepared for what happened next. I found a note taped to my door, which said that Mr. Malley would be obliged if I would step into his office. I went at once to get it over with. He sat at his desk surrounded by obscure evidences of his authority; he looked at me from a distance, as one who was now compelled to see me in a new and sadly unfavourable light; the embarrassment which he showed seemed not for himself, but me. He started off by saying, with a rather **stagey**③ reluctance, that he had known of course when he took me in that I was a writer.

"I didn't let that worry me, though I have heard things about writers and artists and that type of person that didn't strike me as very encouraging. You know the sort of thing I mean."

This was something new; I could not think what it might lead to.

"Now you came to me and said, Mr. Malley, I want a place to write in. I believed you. I gave it to you. I didn't ask any questions. That's the kind of person I am. But you know the more I think about it, well, the more I am inclined to wonder."

"Wonder what?" I said.

"And your own attitude, that hasn't helped to put my mind at ease. Locking yourself in and refusing to answer your door. That's not a normal way for a person to behave. Not if they got nothing to hide. No more than it's normal for a young woman, says she has a husband and kids, to spend her time rattling away on a typewriter."

"But I don't think that—"

---

① 哄骗的。
② 袭击。
③ 造作的。

He lifted his hand, a forgiving gesture. "Now all I ask is, that you be open and **aboveboard**① with me, I think I deserve that much, and if you are using that office for any other purpose, or at any other times than you let on, and having your friends or whoever they are up to see you—"

"I don't know what you mean."

"And another thing, you claim to be a writer. Well I read quite a bit of material, and I never have seen your name in print. Now maybe you write under some other name?"

"No," I said.

"Well I don't doubt there are writers whose names I haven't heard," he said genially. "We'll let that pass. Just you give me your word of honour there won't be any more deceptions, or any **carryings-on**②, et cetera, in that office you occupy—"

My anger was delayed somehow, blocked off by a stupid **incredulity**③. I only knew enough to get up and walk down the hall, his voice **trail**④ ing after me, and lock the door. I thought—I must go. But after I had sat down in my own room, my work in front of me, I thought again how much I liked this room, how well I worked in it, and I decided not to be forced out. After all, I felt, the struggle between us had reached a **dead-lock**⑤. I could refuse to open the door, refuse to look at his notes, refuse to speak to him when we met. My rent was paid in advance and if I left now it was unlikely that I would get any refund. I resolved not to care. I had been taking my manuscript home every night, to prevent his reading it, and now it seemed that even this precaution was beneath me. What did it matter if he read it, any more than if the mice scampered over it in the dark?

Several times after this I found notes on my door. I intended not to read them, but I always did. His accusations grew more specific. He had heard voices in my room. My behaviour was disturbing his wife when she tried to take her afternoon nap. (I never came in the afternoons, except on week-ends.) He had found a whiskey bottle in the garbage.

I wondered a good deal about that chiropractor. It was not comfortable to see how the legends of Mr. Malley's life were built up.

---

① 光明正大的。
② 丑闻。
③ 怀疑。
④ 跟踪。
⑤ 僵局,死胡同。

As the notes grew more **virulent**① our personal encounters ceased. Once or twice I saw his stooped, sweatered back disappearing as I came into the hall. Gradually our relationship, passed into something that was entirely fantasy. He accused me now, by note, of being intimate with people from Numero-Cinq. This was a coffee-house in the neighbourhood, which I imagine he invoked for symbolic purposes. I felt that nothing much more would happen now, the notes would go on, their contents becoming possibly more **grotesque**② and so less likely to affect me.

He knocked on my door on a Sunday morning, about eleven o'clock. I had just come in and taken my coat off and put my kettle on the hot plate.

This time it was another face, remote and transfigured, that shone with the cold light of intense joy at discovering the proofs of sin.

"I wonder," he said with emotion, "if you would mind following me down the hall?"

I followed him. The light was on in the washroom. This washroom was mine and no one else used it, but he had not given me a key for it and it was always open. He stopped in front of it, pushed back the door and stood with his eyes cast down, expelling his breath **discreetly**③.

"Now who done that?" he said, in a voice of pure sorrow.

The walls above the toilet and above the washbasin were covered with drawings and comments of the sort you see sometime in public washrooms on the beach, and in town hall lavatories in the little decaying towns where I grew up. They were done with a lipstick, as they usually are. Someone must have got up here the night before, I thought, possibly some of the gang who always **loafed**④ and cruised around the shopping centre on Saturday nights.

"It should have been locked," I said, coolly and firmly as if thus to remove myself from the scene. "It's quite a mess."

"It sure is. It's pretty filthy language, in my book. Maybe it's just a joke to your friends, but it isn't to me. Not to mention the art work. That's a nice thing to see when you open a door on your own premises in the morning."

I said, "I believe lipstick will wash off."

---

① 恶毒的。
② 荒诞不经的。
③ 小心谨慎地。
④ 游荡。

"I'm just glad I didn't have my wife see a thing like this. Upsets a woman that's had a nice bringing up. Now why don't you ask your friends up here to have a party with their pails and brushes? I'd like to have a look at the people with that kind of a sense of humour."

I turned to walk away and he turned heavily in front of me.

"I don't think there's any question how these decorations found their way onto my Walls."

"If you're trying to say I had anything to do with it," I said, quite flatly and wearily, "you must be crazy."

"How did they get there then? Whose lavatory is this? Eh, whose?"

"There isn't any key to it. Anybody can come up here and walk in. Maybe some kids off the street came up here and did it last night after I went home, how do I know?"

"It's a shame the way the kids gets blamed for everything, when it's the elders that corrupts them. That's a thing you might do some thinking about, you know. There's laws. **Obscenity**① laws. Applies to this sort of thing and literature too as I believe."

This is the first time I ever remember taking deep breaths, consciously, for purposes of self-control. I really wanted to murder him. I remember how soft and **loathsome**② his face looked, with the eyes almost closed, nostrils extended to the soothing **odour**③ of righteousness, the odour of triumph. If this stupid thing had not happened, he would never have won. But he had. Perhaps he saw something in my face that unnerved him, even in this victorious moment, for he drew back to the wall, and began to say that actually, as a matter of fact, he had not really felt it was the sort of thing I personally would do, more the sort of thing that perhaps certain friends of mine—I got into my own room, shut the door.

The kettle was making a fearsome noise, having almost boiled dry. I snatched it off the hot plate, pulled out the plug and stood for a moment choking on rage. This **spasm**④ passed and I did what I had to do. I put my typewriter and paper on the chair and folded the card table. I screwed the top tightly on the instant coffee and put it and the yellow mug and the teaspoon into the bag in which I had brought them; it was still lying folded on the shelf. I wished childishly to take some vengeance on the potted plant, which sat in the cor-

---

① 淫秽内容。

② 令人讨厌的。

③ 气味。

④ (能量、情绪的)突发。

ner with the flowery teapot, the wastebasket, the cushion, and—I forgot—a little plastic pencil sharpener behind it.

When I was taking things down to the car Mrs. Malley came. I had seen little of her since that first day. She did not seem upset, but practical and resigned.

"He is lying down," she said. "He is not himself."

She carried the bag with the coffee and the mug in it. She was so still I felt my anger leave me, to be replaced by an absorbing depression.

I have not yet found another office. I think that I will try again some day, but not yet. I have to wait at least until that picture fades that I see so clearly in my mind, though I never saw it in reality—Mr. Malley with his **rags**① and brushes and a pail of soapy water, **scrubbing**② in his **clumsy**③ way, his deliberately clumsy way, at the toilet walls, stooping with difficulty, breathing sorrowfully, arranging in his mind the bizarre but somehow never quite satisfactory narrative of yet another betrayal of trust. While I arrange words and think it is my right to be rid of himself.

Ⅳ. 思考题

1. What does the opening part of the story reveal in terms of the power relation between men and women?
2. "The Office" is an allusion to Virginia Woolf's famous feminist essay "A Room of One's Own" in which Woolf argues that "a woman must have money and a room of her own if she is to write fiction". However, in this story, the woman protagonist's practical attempt to follow Woolf's advice is failed at the end. Given this background knowledge, what do you make of Munro's intention of writing this story?

Ⅴ. 文学批评

女性主义文学批评

The historical implication of "**feminism**" usually means "movements for recognition

① 破布。

② 刷洗。

③ 笨拙的。

of the claims of women for rights (legal, political. familial, etc.) equal to those possessed by men." Women have never ceased to fight for their rights, though the feminist movement in the West did not take any visible shape till the nineteenth century in the name of women's liberation movement. This liberation movement began to subside in the twentieth century as women had gained most of these political and legal rights. The feminism starting in the 1960s has been concerned not so much with the traditional women's rights as with issues more deeply rooted than those for the previous liberation movement. The "feminism" in this unit refers chiefly to the theoretical speculations on women and women related subjects as the result of the contemporary women's movement, which is markedly different from the previous feminisms.

It is not easy to identify the origin of feminism. An "archaeology" would find women antagonists in the fifth century Greek literature, and similar images of women may have existed in the Chinese Tang poetry. In Europe the feminist tradition can be traced back at least to the fourteenth century, where French woman poet Christine de Pisan criticized the misogynist ideas in terms of court etiquette and the Christian tradition. The Dutch renaissance scholar E. Erasmus attacked the double standard in education and morality for women. The age of Enlightenment saw a hostile attitude toward women in France, but the *mujer esquiva* in the seventeenth century Spanish drama is a eulogy of woman identity.

Feminism is mostly found in the English speaking countries, thanks in part to *The Norton Anthology of Literature by Women*, one of the two most widely read feminist works in the West today (Leitch 1988: 307). The first conspicuous women writers appeared in the Eighteenth century England when industrial revolution increased the number of well-educated middle class women and greatly facilitated their publication. Writers for the first time shifted from the patronage of the court to the general reading public, and writing became largely a commercial activity. The nineteenth century brought about major changes to feminist movement. Inspired by the American and French Revolutions and the anti-slavery movement, women for the first time unmistakably claimed for the natural "Rights of Women" Darwinism shook the self-importance of man/male, Marxism further questioned the legitimacy of capitalist man, and Nietzsche denounced the validity of (the male) God. In this context women's liberation movement took a definite shape and made major progress in women's suffrage and property rights. Women became medical doctors, lawyers, or journalists, and women students went into Harvard, Oxford and Cambridge. This was also a golden age for literary women: Austin, Brontes, Eliot and Dickinson, to name only a few.

Women were still the subjects of unfair treatment, but there was an increasingly louder voice for social justice for women. The early twentieth century saw an unprecedented "anxiety" for man and, consequently, a further development of feminism. Einstein made relative the once unchangeable time and space, Freud suggested that man had an entirely different self within, anthropology and archaeology revealed that patriarchal society was not necessarily the only (not to say the best) form of social organization for humanity, Great Britain as a symbol of patriarchy was being challenged and inevitably declining, the two world wars deepened the suspicion of reason, science and technology. Meanwhile, women's contribution during the two world wars proved, better than anything else, that women were as capable as men, and the final approval of women's suffrage around 1920 in Great Britain and the US marked the climax of the women's liberation movement (Gilbert & Gubar 1985: 39-58, 162-83, 1215-38, 1654-76).

Compared with the long tradition of the feminist practice or women's lib, feminist theory started only in this century. The theoretical feminism is usually thought of in two parts, the Anglo-American and the French. The Anglo-American is believed to be more practically minded, and the French more theoretical, though this assumption tends to be over generalizing.

Virginia Woolf is the forerunner, indeed the "mother" of the contemporary Anglo-American feminism. This is so not only because she did more than what a woman was supposed to do: studied Greek, taught in a woman's college, argued for women's suffrage, explored lesbian experience, and wrote for the *Times Literary Supplement*. In her *A Room of One's Own*, perhaps the first important feminist document in the West, Judith the extraordinarily gifted sister of Shakespeare could only "have gone crazy, shot herself, or ended her days in some lonely cottage outside the village, half witch, half wizard, feared and mocked at." In a speech, Woolf calls on women to kill "the Angel in the House," the traditional image of women (charming, unselfish, pure, and above all mindless), even though this Angel "dies hard." But one should have to kill her, she asserts, before one could be a woman writer for women (Eagleton 1986: 48, 52).

The American feminism may be divided into three (though by no means necessarily chronological) phases: criticism oi male sexism in the "androtexts," discovery of the women writers in history or spade work for "gynotexts," and feminist discourse for female identity (Leitch 1988: 307). If Woolf's was still "bedroom farce," *Sexual Polities* (1970) is "raw guerrilla warfare" raged by Kate Millett, "the most famous mother of

American feminist criticism" (Todd 1988: 21). The book is a frontal attack on the sexual ideology in some classical male authors such as D. H. Lawrence, Henry Miller and Sigmund Freud, and reveals convincingly the inequality of power in the master narrative of the high modernism. The love between man and woman in Lawrence, for instance, is set against the distorted human relations under industrialization, but this love is based upon the male sexism (Millett 1977: 238-57). Though the book may be more emotional than academic, the call for an "unprecedented social revolution" has marked a climax of the first phase of feminist criticism.

The height of the spade work for "gynotexts" is *The Norton Anthology of Literature by Women, the Tradition in English* (1985). It is a collection of over 500 works by more than 170 women writers in the English speaking countries from the fourteenth century to the present, and many of these works and writers are discovered or rediscovered from a standard different from that of the male literary canons. Most importantly, Gilbert and Gubar delineate for the first time a systematic development of a feminist literary tradition, complimentary to the "lack" in the traditional literary history. A deficiency of the book is that while it is especially strong in the nineteenth century literature, the other parts of the book is comparatively weak, indicating that a feminist literary history is still largely dependent on the patriarchal literary canon.

If Millett conducts a "raw guerrilla warfare," Elaine Showalter helps to rage a more regular warfare. She proposes a set of strategies and principles, which contribute to the formation of the identity of an American feminist theory. The concept of "gynocriticism" for instance is introduced in "Towards a Feminist Poetics" (1979) for an appropriate form of feminist criticism, namely, to study women's writing in relation to female experience and develop out of it a theory appropriate to women. A similar appeal is made in "Feminist Criticism in the Wilderness" (1981) for a construction of feminist theory. What is typical of American feminism, however, is a combination of theoretical concern with textual analyses, and Showalter's discussion of how Ophelia is represented in Shakespeare's *Hamlet* is a clear indication of how the "responsibilities of feminist criticism" may be actualized. Similar analyses may be made of another Shakespeare's play, *Titus Atuironicus*, where the two women antagonists suffer a worse fate than Ophelia. Whether it is the "virtuous" Lavinia or the villainous Tamora. the bloody treatment awaits them for their submission or rebellion in a male dominated society.

In the words of Showalter, the French tradition differs from the Anglo-American in that

"French feminist criticism, essentially psychoanalytic, stresses repression; American feminist criticism, essentially textual, stresses expression." Take the concept of "woman" for instance. The woman in the Anglo-American tradition refers to the real woman and her lived experience, whereas in French feminism she tends to be a "writing effect." Heavily tinged by post-structural-ism, the French feminists are engaged in the subversion of the patriarchal ideology on the discursive level, while the Anglo-American feminists tend to keep some distance from "theory" as the latter is characterized by the phallocentric discourse.

Influenced by Derrida and Lacan, Lucy Irigaray tries to show how woman is being constructed by the Western metaphysical tradition. This master discourse both foregrounds the female difference as the negative of the male, and erases this difference so that man may speak for woman. In *This Sex Which Isn't One* (1977), she tries to define the female language (*parler-femme*) in terms of female biological difference. The metaphysical tradition valorizes identity and the same and diminishes the female presence for a "lack." The presence of female, she argues, has to be defined with a different discourse, a discourse of difference, since female is characterized by difference, diffusion, plurality, and multiplicity, logically and biologically (Gunew 1991: 204-11). The problem here is that this female identity is also based on the binary opposites, and the use of the Derridean discourse is another form of the female dependence.

Helene Cixous is another major French feminist theorist, known particularly for her idea of a feminist essentialism, or the peculiarly feminine characteristics that differentiate woman from man. Man expresses the female difference in Medusa, who in classical mythology is a woman known for her beauty and evil, in anthropology represents both fascination and abhorrence of man towards woman in the transition of the matriarchal society to the patriarchal, in Freudian psychoanalysis is the castration threat to the boy. All this explains the fact that woman is always negatively defined, who talks but never speaks. In "The Laugh of the Medusa" Cixous argues that woman should break loose from "the naivete," the "monster," the "self-disdain" imposed by the "parental-conjugal phallocentrism," and "speak out" her "strength" with her own "writing." Cixous' feminine essence (feminine as negative binary opposition and "dephallocentralize" the male power and knowledge (Adams& Scarle 1992: 309-20).

The American feminists are critical of their French counterparts for being too theoretically minded to be concerned with the real experience of the actual woman. Meanwhile, however, the French theory has become too important a part of feminism to be simply slighted. The feminist movement in the 1990s has made the feminists in both traditions realize that, in face of new challenges and backlashes, feminism has to be united for a common cause (Collier & Geyer-Ryan 1990: 199). Compared with the other critical theories, feminism has a greater impact on other intellectual movements and has brought about more substantial changes to society, but it has a tougher task lying ahead.

Ⅵ. 拓展阅读

Judith Butler's *Gender Trouble* (Routledge, 2006).
Virginia Woolf's *A Room of One's Own* (Penguin Classics, 2002).

Ⅶ. 参考文献

朱刚. 二十世纪西方文艺批评理论. 上海:上海外语教育出版社,2001.

Chapter 13 Svetlana Alexievich and the Literariness of Reportage

Ⅰ. 作者简介

斯维特拉娜·阿列克谢耶维奇(Svetlana Alexievich)(1948—)1948 年 5 月 31 日出生于乌克兰小镇伊凡诺弗兰克夫斯克。她的父亲是白俄罗斯人,母亲是乌克兰人,两人都在白俄罗斯当教师。阿列克谢耶维奇从明斯克大学新闻系毕业后,被派往布雷斯特地区的 Beresa 镇,在当地的报纸工作。几年后,她担任文学杂志《尼曼》的记者,很快就被提升为非小说类栏目的负责人。

阿列克谢耶维奇尝试用不同体裁创作,如短篇小说、散文和报告文学。她深受白俄罗斯著名作家阿达莫维奇的影响,后者定义了一种新型的文学体裁,他称之为"集体小说""小说证据""自叙"等(collective novel, novel- evidence, people talking about themselves)。

在对阿列克谢耶维奇的一次采访中,她说:"我一直在寻找一种文学方法,让它最接近现实生活。现实总是像磁铁一样吸引着我,它折磨和催眠着我,我想把它记录在纸上。因此,我立即采用了这类真实的录音、证据和文件。这就是我听到和看到世界的方式——作为个人声音的合唱和日常细节的拼贴。我的眼睛和耳朵就是这样运作的。这样,我所有的精神和情感潜能都得到了充分的发挥。这样我就能同时成为作家、记者、社会学家、心理学家和传教士。”

1983 年,她完成了《战争的非女性面孔》,但是没能出版,反而被抨击为诋毁英勇的苏联妇女。这部作品是由战争中的女性独白组成的,她们讲述了第二次世界大战中不为人知的一面。直到 1985 年,这部作品才得以出版,一同出版的还有她的第二部作品《最后一个证人》。这本书描述了通过妇女和儿童的眼睛看到的战争,开辟了一个全新的情感和思想领域。1989 年《锌皮娃娃兵》出版,这是一本关于苏联入侵阿富汗战争的书,这段历史被苏联隐瞒了十年。阿列克谢维奇在全国各地游历了四年,采访战争受害者的母亲和战争的退伍军人。这本书轰动一时,许多人无法原谅作者将这个被宣扬为正义神圣的战争拉下神坛。1997,她出版了《切尔诺贝利的悲鸣》。这本书与其说是关于切尔诺贝利核电站灾难,不如说是关于灾难之后的世界,即人们如何适应新的现实。

阿列克谢耶维奇于 2015 年获得诺贝尔文学奖,因为“她的复调书写是这个世界承受的灾难和人性勇气的丰碑”(“for her polyphonic writings, a monument to suffering and courage in our time”)。她认为她作品的主旨在于试图了解每个人身上包含着多少人性,以及如何保护一个人的人性。她创造了一个完全属于她自己的文学体裁。她认为自己写的是“声音小说”,基于数百千次的采访不断磨砺着她的纪实美学,她在这方面的技巧使她能够将民众的声音交织成一幅灵魂全景。阿列克谢耶维奇曾经写道:“我把世界看作是声音,是色彩。从一本书到另一本书,我变了,主题也变了,但叙述的主线不变。这是我认识的人的叙述线索……我可以用成千上万的声音创造——你很难称之为现实,因为现实仍然是难以理解的——我的时代、我的国家的形象……所有这些都形成了一种小百科全书,我这一代人的百科全书,我所遇到的人的百科全书。他们过得怎么样?他们相信什么?他们怎么死的,怎么杀人?他们是如何努力追求幸福,又是如何被现实打败的?”

Ⅱ. 作品简介

《切尔诺贝利的悲鸣》是一本关于切尔诺贝利灾难的书。灾难发生时,阿列克谢维奇住在明斯克,是一名记者。她花费超过 10 年,采访了超过 500 名目击者,包括消防员、清道夫、政治家、医生、物理学家和普通公民。这本书讲述了切尔诺贝利事故的心理和个人悲剧,探讨了个人的经历和灾难如何影响他们的生活。

这本书是一部典型的复调书写,这意味着在书中,有重叠的声音甚至是相反观点,但它也是由无数小片段拼凑成的一个新的整体。这本书有三个部分,部分主题重叠:“死亡之地”“活人的土地”和“出人意料的哀伤”。这三个部分都像一个“合唱团”,它允许个人的声音自由说话,有些甚至相互冲突。结尾处作者保留了自己的声音,但她没有做出判断,而是像其他见证者一样,讲述自己对切尔诺贝利的记忆。

这本书的开篇和结尾来自两位在灾难中丧失丈夫的女性:开篇是一个第一批到达灾难现场的普里皮亚特消防员的年轻妻子,结尾则是一个清道夫的妻子,清道夫的任务是负责掩盖表层土壤,射杀该地区的每一只动物。

本书节选的是文章的开篇,柳德米拉·伊格纳坚科的丈夫瓦西里是第一批应对切尔诺贝利的消防员之一。柳德米拉娓娓道来她记忆中的切尔诺贝利事件,她并没有像百科全书条目和报纸文章那样讲述这个故事的细节,而是从她失去的爱人这个角度切入,第一手的叙述给读者带来了巨大的震撼。柳德米拉的开场白是:“我不知道该说什么,关于死亡还是爱情?”在柳德米拉描述了她用绷带包扎自己的手,并在丈夫呕吐时从他嘴里取出部分内脏后,她说:“这事件不可能用言语表述,不可能用文字记录,甚至无法想象是怎么活过来的,但这一切都是我的,都是我爱的记忆。”

Ⅲ.作品

A SOLITARY HUMAN VOICE

We are air, we are not earth ... —Mesab Mamardashvili

I don't know what I should talk about—about death or about love? Or are they the same? Which one should I talk about?

We were **newlyweds**[①]. We still walked around holding hands, even if we were just

① 新婚夫妇。

going to the store. I would say to him, "I love you." But I didn't know then how much. I had no idea ... We lived in the dormitory of the fire house where he worked. On the second floor. There were three other young couples, we all shared a kitchen. On the first floor they kept the trucks. The red fire trucks. That was his job. So I always knew what was happening—where he was, how he was.

One night I heard a noise. I looked out the window. He saw me. "Close the window and go back to sleep. There's a fire at the **reactor**①. I'll be back soon."

I didn't see the explosion itself. Just the flames. Everything was radiant. The whole sky. A tall flame. And smoke. The heat was awful. And he's still not back.

The smoke was from the burning **bitumen**②, which had covered the roof. He said later it was like walking on tar. They tried to beat down the flames. They kicked at the burning **graphite**③ with their feet. . . . They weren't wearing their canvas gear. They went off just as they were, in their shirt sleeves. No one told them. They had been called for a fire, that was it.

Four o'clock. Five. Six. At six we were supposed to go to his parents' house. To plant potatoes. It's forty kilometers from Pripyat to Sperizhye, where his parents live. Sowing, plowing—he loved doing that. His mother always told me they didn't want him to move to the city, they'd even built a new house for him. He was **drafted**④ into the army. He served in the fire brigade in Moscow and when he came out, he wanted to be a fireman. And nothing else! [*Silence.*]

Sometimes it's as though I hear his voice. Alive. Even photographs don't have the same effect on me as that voice. But he never calls out to me ... not even in my dreams. I'm the one who calls to him.

Seven o'clock. At seven I was told he was in the hospital. I ran there, but the police had already **encircled**⑤ it, and they weren't letting anyone through. Only ambulances. The policemen shouted: the ambulances are **radioactive**⑥, stay away! I wasn't the only one there, all the wives whose husbands were at the reactor that night had come. I started looking for a friend, she was a doctor at that hospital. I grabbed her white coat when she

① 反应堆。
② 沥青。
③ 石墨。
④ 应征。
⑤ 包围。
⑥ 放射性的。

came out of an ambulance. "Get me inside!" "I can't. He's bad. They all are." I held on to her. "Just to see him!" "All right," she said. "Come with me. Just for fifteen or twenty minutes."

I saw him. He was all **swollen**① and puffed up. You could barely see his eyes.

"He needs milk, lots of milk," my friend said. "They should drink at least three liters each." "But he doesn't like milk." "He'll drink it now." Many of the doctors and nurses in that hospital, and especially the **orderlies**②, later got sick themselves and died. But we didn't know that then.

At ten in the morning, the cameraman Shishenok died. He was the first. On the first day. We learned that another one was left under the **debris**③—Valera Khodemchuk. They never did reach him. They buried him under the **concrete**④. And we didn't know then that they were just the first ones.

I said, "Vasya, what should I do?" "Get out of here! Go! You have our child." But how can I leave him? He's telling me: "Go! Leave! Save the baby." "First I need to bring you some milk, then we'll decide what to do." My friend Tanya Kibenok comes running in—her husband's in the same room. Her father's with her, he has a car. We get in and drive to the nearest village for some milk. It's about three kilometers from town. We buy a bunch of three-liter bottles, six, so it's enough for everyone. But they started throwing up from the milk. They kept passing out, they got put on IVs. The doctors kept telling them they'd been poisoned by gas. No one said anything about radiation. And the town was **inundated**⑤ right away with military vehicles, they closed off all the roads. The **trolleys**⑥ stopped running, and the trains. They were washing the streets with some white powder. I worried about getting to the village the next day to buy some more fresh milk. No one talked about the radiation. Only the military people wore surgical masks. The people in town were carrying bread from the stores, just open sacks with the loaves in them. People were eating cupcakes on plates.

I couldn't get into the hospital that evening. There was a sea of people. I stood under his window, he came over and yelled something to me. It was all so desperate! Some-

---

① 肿的。
② 卫生员。
③ 废墟。
④ 水泥。
⑤ 充满。
⑥ 电车。

one in the crowd heard him—they were being taken to Moscow that night. All the wives got together in one group. We decided we'd go with them. Let us go with our husbands! You have no right! We punched and clawed. The soldiers—there were already soldiers—pushed us back. Then the doctor came out and said, Yes, they were flying to Moscow, but we needed to bring them their clothes. The clothes they'd worn at the station had been burned. The buses had stopped running already and we ran across the city. We came running back with their bags, but the plane was already gone. They tricked us. So that we wouldn't be there yelling and crying.

It's night. On one side of the street there are buses, hundreds of buses, they're already preparing the town for **evacuation**①, and on the other side, hundreds of fire trucks. They came from all over. And the whole street is covered in white foam. We're walking on it, just cursing and crying. Over the radio they tell us they might evacuate the city for three to five days, take your warm clothes with you, you'll be living in the forest. In tents. People were even glad—a camping trip! We'll celebrate May Day like that, a break from routine. People got barbeques ready. They took their guitars with them, their radios. Only the women whose husbands had been at the reactor were crying.

I can't remember the trip out to my parents' village. It was like I woke up when I saw my mother. "Mama. Vasya's in Moscow. They flew him out on a special plane!" But we finished planting the garden. [*A week later the village was evacuated.*] Who knew? Who knew that then? Later in the day I started throwing up. I was six months pregnant. I felt awful. That night I dreamed he was calling out to me in his sleep: "Lyusya! Lyusenka!" But after he died, he didn't call out in my dreams anymore. Not once. [*She starts crying.*] I got up in the morning thinking I have to get to Moscow. By myself. My mother's crying: "Where are you going, the way you are?" So I took my father with me. He went to the bank and took out all the money they had.

I can't remember the trip. The trip just isn't in my memory.

In Moscow we asked the first police officer we saw, Where did they put the Chernobyl firemen, and he told us. We were surprised, too, everyone was scaring us that it was top secret. "Hospital number 6. At the Shchukinskaya stop."

It was a special hospital, for radiology, and you couldn't get in without a pass. I gave some money to the woman at the door, and she said, "Go ahead." Then I had to ask some-

① 撤离。

one else, beg. Finally I'm sitting in the office of the head radiologist, Angelina Vasilyevna Guskova. But I didn't know that yet, what her name was, I didn't remember anything. I just knew I had to see him. Right away she asked: "Do you have kids?"

What should I tell her? I can see already I need to hide that I'm pregnant. They won't let me see him! It's good I'm thin, you can't really tell.

"Yes," I say.

"How many?"

I'm thinking, "I need to tell her two. If it's just one, she won't let me in."

"A boy and a girl."

"So you don't need to have anymore. All right, listen: his central nervous system is completely **compromised**①, his skull is completely compromised."

Okay, I'm thinking, so he'll be a little **fidgety**②.

"And listen: if you start crying, I'll kick you out right away. No hugging or kissing. Don't even get near him. You have half an hour."

But I knew already that I wasn't leaving. If I leave, then it'll be with him, I swore to myself! I come in, they're sitting on the bed, playing cards and laughing.

"Vasya!" they call out.

He turns around:

"Oh, now it's over! Even here she found me!"

He looks so funny, he's got pajamas on for a size 48, and he's a size 52. The sleeves are too short, the pants are too short. But his face isn't swollen anymore. They were given some sort of fluid.

I say, "Where'd you run off to?"

He wants to hug me, the doctor won't let him. "Sit, sit," she says. "No hugging in here."

We turned it into a joke somehow. And then everyone comes over, from the other rooms too, everyone from Pripyat. There were twenty-eight of them on the plane. What's going on? How are things in town? I tell them they've begun evacuating everyone, the whole town is being cleared out for three or five days. None of the guys says anything, and then one of the women, there were two women, she was on duty at the factory the day of the accident, she starts crying.

---

① 损伤。
② 不安的。

"Oh God! My kids are there. What's happening with them?"

I wanted to be with him alone, if only for a minute. The guys felt it, and each of them thought of some excuse, and they all went out into the hall. Then I hugged and kissed him. He moved away.

"Don't sit near me. Get a chair."

"That's just silly," I said, waving it away. "Did you see the explosion? Did you see what happened? You were the first ones there."

"It was probably **sabotage**①. Someone set it up. All the guys think so."

That's what people were saying then. That's what they thought.

The next day, they were lying by themselves, each in his own room. They were banned from going in the hallway, from talking to each other. They knocked on the walls with their **knuckles**②. Dash-dot, dash-dot. The doctors explained that everyone's body reacts differently to radiation, one person can handle what another can't. They even measured the radiation of the walls where they had them. To the right, left, and the floor beneath. They moved out all the sick people from the floor below and the floor above. There was no one left in the place.

For three days I lived with my friends in Moscow. They kept saying: Take the pot, take the plate, take whatever you need. I made turkey soup for six. For six of our boys. Firemen. From the same **shift**③. They were all on duty that night: Bashuk, Kibenok, Titenok, Pravik, Tischura. I went to the store and bought them toothpaste and toothbrushes and soap. They didn't have any of that at the hospital. I bought them little towels. Looking back, I'm surprised by my friends: they were afraid, of course, how could they not be, there were rumors already, but still they kept saying: Take whatever you need, take it! How is he? How are they all? Will they live? Live. [*She is silent.*] I met a lot of good people then, I don't remember all of them. I remember an old woman janitor, who taught me: "There are sicknesses that can't be cured. You just have to sit and watch them."

Early in the morning I go to the market, then to my friends' place, where I make the soup. I have to grate everything and grind it. Someone said, "Bring me some apple juice." So I come with six half-liter cans, always for six! I race to the hospital, then I sit there until evening. In the evening, I go back across the city. How much longer could I

---

① 蓄意破坏。

② 关节。

③ 班次。

have kept that up? After three days they told me I could stay in the dorm for medical workers, it's on hospital grounds. God, how wonderful!

"But there's no kitchen. How am I going to cook?"

"You don't need to cook anymore. They can't digest the food."

He started to change—every day I met a brand-new person. The burns started to come to the surface. In his mouth, on his tongue, his cheeks—at first there were little **lesions**①, and then they grew. It came off in layers—as white film ... the color of his face ... his body ... blue ... red ... gray-brown. And it's all so very mine! It's impossible to describe! It's impossible to write down! And even to get over. The only thing that saved me was, it happened so fast; there wasn't any time to think, there wasn't any time to cry.

I loved him! I had no idea how much! We'd just gotten married. When we walked down the street—he'd grab my hands and whirl me around. And kiss me, kiss me. People are walking by and smiling.

It was a hospital for people with acute radiation poisoning. Fourteen days. In fourteen days a person dies.

On the very first day in the dormitory they measured me with a **dosimeter**②. My clothes, bag, purse, shoes—they were all "hot." And they took it all right away. Even my underthings. The only thing they left was my money. In exchange they gave me a hospital robe—a size 56—and some size 43 slippers. They said they'd return the clothes, maybe, or maybe they wouldn't, since they might not be possible to "launder" at this point. That is how I looked when I came to visit him. I frightened him. "Woman, what's wrong with you?" But I was still able to make him some soup. I boiled the water in a glass jar, and then I threw pieces of chicken in there—tiny, tiny pieces. Then someone gave me her pot, I think it was the cleaning woman or the guard. Someone else gave me a cutting board, for chopping my parsley. I couldn't go to the market in my hospital robe, people would bring me the vegetables. But it was all useless, he couldn't even drink anything. He couldn't even swallow a raw egg. But I wanted to get him something tasty! As if it mattered. I ran to the post office. "Girls," I told them, "I need to call my parents in Ivano-Frankovsk right away! My husband is dying." They understood right away where I was from and who my husband was, and they connected me. My father, sister, and brother flew out that very day to Moscow. They brought me my things. And money. It was the ninth of May. He al-

---

① 损伤。

② 放射测量仪。

ways used to say to me: "You have no idea how beautiful Moscow is! Especially on V-Day, when they set off the fireworks. I want you to see it."

I'm sitting with him in the room, he opens his eyes. "Is it day or night?"

"It's nine at night."

"Open the window! They're going to set off the fireworks!"

I opened the window. We're on the eighth floor, and the whole city's there before us! A bouquet of fire was exploding in the air.

"Look at that!" I said.

"I told you I'd show you Moscow. And I told you I'd always give you flowers on holidays ..."

I look over, and he's getting three carnations from under his pillow. He gave the nurse money, and she bought them.

I run over to him and I kiss him.

"My love! My one and only!"

He starts growling. "What did the doctors tell you? No hugging me. And no kissing!"

They wouldn't let me hug him. But I ... I lifted him and sat him up. I made his bed. I placed the thermometer. I picked up and brought back the sanitation dish. I stayed up with him all night.

It's a good thing that it was in the hallway, not the room, that my head started spinning, I grabbed onto the windowsill. A doctor was walking by, he took me by the arm. And then suddenly: "Are you pregnant?"

"No, no!" I was so scared someone would hear us.

"Don't lie," he sighed.

The next day I get called to the head doctor's office.

"Why did you lie to me?" she says.

"There was no other way. If I'd told you, you'd send me home. It was a sacred lie!"

"What have you done?"

"But I was with him . . ."

I'll be grateful to Angelina Vasilyevna Guskova my whole life. My whole life! Other wives also came, but they weren't allowed in. Their mothers were with me. Volodya Pravik's mother kept begging God: "Take me instead." An American professor, Dr. Gale—

he's the one who did the bone **marrow**① operation— tried to comfort me. There's a tiny ray of hope, he said, not much, but a little. Such a powerful organism, such a strong guy! They called for all his relatives. Two of his sisters came from Belarus, his brother from Leningrad, he was in the army there. The younger one, Natasha, she was fourteen, she was very scared and cried a lot. But her bone marrow was the best fit. [*Silent.*] Now I can talk about this. Before I couldn't. I didn't talk about it for ten years. [*Silent.*]

When he found out they'd be taking the bone marrow from his little sister, he flat-out refused. 'Td rather die. She's so small. Don't touch her." His older sister Lyuda was twenty-eight, she was a nurse herself, she knew what she was getting into. "As long as he lives," she said. I watched the operation. They were lying next to each other on the tables. There was a big window onto the operating room. It took two hours. When they were done, Lyuda was worse off than he was, she had eighteen **punctures**② in her chest, it was very difficult for her to come out from under the anesthesia. Now she's sick, she's an **invalid**③. She was a strong, pretty girl. She never got married. So then I was running from one room to the other, from his room to hers. He wasn't in an ordinary room anymore, he was in a special bio-chamber, behind a transparent curtain. No one was allowed inside.

They have instruments there, so that without going through the curtain they can give him shots, place the **catheter**④. The curtains are held together by Velcro, and I've learned to use them. I push them aside and go inside. There was a little chair next to his bed. He got so bad that I couldn't leave him now even for a second. He was calling out to me constantly: "Lyusya, where are you? Lyusya!" He called and called. The other bio-chambers, where our boys were, were tended to by soldiers, because the orderlies on staff refused, they demanded protective clothing. The soldiers carried the sanitary vessels. They wiped the floors down, changed the bedding. They did everything. Where did they get those soldiers? We didn't ask. But he—he—every day I would hear: Dead. Dead. Tischura is dead. Titenok is dead. Dead. It was like a **sledgehammer**⑤ to my brain.

He was producing stool 25 to 30 times a day. With blood and **mucous**⑥. His skin

---

① 骨髓。
② 穿刺。
③ 病人。
④ 导管。
⑤ 锤击。
⑥ 黏液。

started **cracking**[1] on his arms and legs. He became covered with **boils**[2]. When he turned his head, there'd be a clump of hair left on the pillow. I tried joking: "It's convenient, you don't need a comb." Soon they cut all their hair. I did it for him myself. I wanted to do everything for him myself. If it had been physically possible I would have stayed with him all twenty-four hours. I couldn't spare a minute. [*Long silence.*] My brother came and he got scared. "I won't let you in there!" But my father said to him: "You think you can stop her? She'll go through the window! She'll get up through the fire escape!"

I go back to the hospital and there's an orange on the bedside table. A big one, and pink. He's smiling: "I got a gift. Take it." Meanwhile the nurse is gesturing through the film that I can't eat it. It's been near him a while, so not only can you not eat it, you shouldn't even touch it. "Come on, eat it," he says. "You like oranges." I take the orange in my hand. Meanwhile he shuts his eyes and goes to sleep. They were always giving him shots to put him to sleep. The nurse is looking at me in horror. And me? I'm ready to do whatever it takes so that he doesn't think about death. And about the fact that his death is horrible, that I'm afraid of him. There's a fragment of some conversation, I'm remembering it. Someone is saying: "You have to understand: This is not your husband anymore, not a beloved person, but a radioactive object with a strong density of poisoning. You're not suicidal. Get ahold of yourself." And I'm like someone who's lost her mind: "But I love him! I love him!" He's sleeping, and I'm whispering: "I love you!" Walking in the hospital courtyard, "I love you." Carrying his sanitary tray, "I love you." I remembered how we used to live at home. He only fell asleep at night after he'd taken my hand. That was a habit of his—to hold my hand while he slept. All night. So in the hospital I take his hand and don't let go.

One night, everything's quiet. We're all alone. He looked at me very, very carefully and suddenly he said:

"I want to see our child so much. How is he?"

"What are we going to name him?"

"You'll decide that yourself."

"Why myself, when there's two of us?"

"In that case, if it's a boy, he should be Vasya, and if it's a girl, Natasha."

---

① 开裂。

② 疖子。

I had no idea then how much I loved him! Him ... just him. I was like a blind person! I couldn't feel the little pounding underneath my heart. Even though I was six months in. I thought that my little one was inside me, that he was protected.

None of the doctors knew I was staying with him at night in the bio-chamber. The nurses let me in. At first they **pleaded**[①] with me, too: "You're young. Why are you doing this? That's not a person anymore, that's a nuclear reactor. You'll just burn together." I was like a dog, running after them. I'd stand for hours at their doors, begging and pleading. And then they'd say: "All right! The hell with you! You're not normal!" In the mornings, just before eight, when the doctors started their rounds, they'd be there on the other side of the film: "Run!" So I'd go to the dorm for an hour. Then from 9 A. M. to 9 P. M. I have a pass to come in. My legs were blue below the knee, blue and swollen, that's how tired I was.

While I was there with him, they wouldn't, but when I left—they photographed him. Without any clothes. Naked. One thin little sheet on top of him. I changed that little sheet every day, and every day by evening it was covered in blood. I pick him up, and there are pieces of his skin on my hand, they stick to my hands. I ask him: "Love. Help me. Prop yourself up on your arm, your elbow, as much as you can, I'll smooth out your bedding, get the wrinkles and folds out." Any little wrinkle, that was already a wound on him. I clipped my nails down till they bled so I wouldn't accidentally cut him. None of the nurses could approach him; if they needed anything they'd call me.

And they photographed him. For science, they said. I'd have pushed them all out of there! I'd have yelled! And hit them! How dare they? It's all mine—it's my love—if only I'd been able to keep them out of there.

I'm walking out of the room into the hallway. And I'm walking toward the couch, because I don't see them. I tell the nurse on duty: "He's dying." And she says to me: "What did you expect? He got 1 600 **roentgen**[②]. Four hundred is a lethal dose. You're sitting next to a nuclear reactor." It's all mine ... it's my love. When they all died, they did a **remont**[③] at the hospital. They scraped down the walls and dug up the **parquet**[④].

And then—the last thing. I remember it in flashes, all broken up.

---

① 解释。
② 伦琴。
③ 装修。
④ 地板。

I'm sitting on my little chair next to him at night. At eight I say: "Vasenka, I'm going for a little walk." He opens his eyes and closes them, lets me go. I just walk to the dorm, go up to my room, lie down on the floor, I couldn't lie on the bed, everything hurt too much, when already the cleaning lady is knocking. "Go! Run to him! He's calling for you like mad!" That morning Tanya Kibenok pleaded with me: "Come to the cemetery, I can't go there alone." They were burying Vitya Kibenok and Volodya Pravik. They were friends of my Vasya. Our families were friends. There's a photo of us all in the building the day before the explosion. Our husbands are so handsome! And happy! It was the last day of that life. We were all so happy!

I came back from the cemetery and called the nurse's post right away. "How is he?" "He died fifteen minutes ago." What? I was there all night. I was gone for three hours! I came up to the window and started shouting: "Why? Why?" I looked up at the sky and yelled. The whole building could hear me. They were afraid to come up to me. Then I came to: I'll see him one more time! Once more! I run down the stairs. He was still in his bio-chamber, they hadn't taken him away yet. His last words were "Lyusya! Lyusenka!" "She's just stepped away for a bit, she'll be right back," the nurse told him. He sighed and went quiet. I didn't leave him anymore after that. I escorted him all the way to the grave site. Although the thing I remember isn't the grave, it's the plastic bag. That bag.

At the morgue they said, "Want to see what we'll dress him in?" I do! They dressed him up in formal wear, with his service cap. They couldn't get shoes on him because his feet had swelled up. They had to cut up the formal wear, too, because they couldn't get it on him, there wasn't a whole body to put it on. It was all—wounds. The last two days in the hospital—I'd lift his arm, and meanwhile the bone is shaking, just sort of dangling, the body has gone away from it. Pieces of his lungs, of his liver, were coming out of his mouth. He was choking on his internal organs. I'd wrap my hand in a bandage and put it in his mouth, take out all that stuff. It's impossible to talk about. It's impossible to write about. And even to live through. It was all mine. My love. They couldn't get a single pair of shoes to fit him. They buried him barefoot.

Right before my eyes—in his formal wear—they put him in that cellophane bag of theirs and tied it up. And then they put this bag in the wooden coffin. And they tied the coffin with another bag. The plastic is transparent, but thick, like a tablecloth. And then they put all that into a zinc coffin. They squeezed it in. Only the cap didn't fit.

Everyone came—his parents, my parents. They bought black handkerchiefs in Moscow. The Extraordinary Commission met with us. They told everyone the same thing: it's impossible for us to give you the bodies of your husbands, your sons, they are very radioactive and will be buried in a Moscow cemetery in a special way. In sealed zinc **caskets**①, under cement tiles. And you need to sign this document here.

If anyone got indignant and wanted to take the coffin back home, they were told that the dead were now heroes, you see, and that they no longer belonged to their families. They were heroes of the State. They belonged to the State.

We sat in the hearse. The relatives and some military people. A colonel and his regiment. They tell the regiment: "Await your orders!" We drive around Moscow for two or three hours, around the beltway. We're going back to Moscow again. They tell the regiment: "We're not allowing anyone into the cemetery. The cemetery's being attacked by foreign correspondents. Wait some more." The parents don't say anything. Mom has a black handkerchief. I sense I'm about to black out. "Why are they hiding my husband? He's—what? A murderer? A criminal? Who are we burying?" My mom: "Quiet. Quiet, daughter." She's petting me on the head. The colonel calls in: "Let's enter the cemetery. The wife is getting hysterical." At the cemetery we were surrounded by soldiers. We had a **convoy**②. And they were carrying the coffin. No one was allowed in. It was just us. They covered him with earth in a minute. "Faster! Faster!" the officer was yelling. They didn't even let me hug the coffin. And—onto the bus. Everything on the sly.

Right away they bought us plane tickets back home. For the next day. The whole time there was someone with us. He wouldn't even let us out of the dorm to buy some food for the trip. God forbid we might talk with someone—especially me. As if I could talk by then. I couldn't even cry. When we were leaving, the woman on duty counted all the towels and all the sheets. She folded them right away and placed them in a polyethylene bag. They probably burnt them. We paid for the dormitory ourselves. For fourteen nights. It was a hospital for radiation poisoning. Fourteen nights. That's how long it takes a person to die.

At home I fell asleep. I walked into the place and just fell onto the bed. I slept for three days. An ambulance came. "No," said the doctor, "she'll wake up. It's just a terrible sleep."

---

① 锌皮棺材。

② 护送队。

I was twenty-three.

I remember the dream I had. My dead grandmother comes to me in the clothes that we buried her in. She's dressing up the New Year's tree. "Grandma, why do we have a New Year's tree? It's summertime." "Because your Vasenka is going to join me soon." And he grew up in the forest. I remember the dream— Vasya comes in a white robe and calls for Natasha. That's our girl, who I haven't given birth to yet. She's already grown up. He throws her up to the ceiling, and they laugh. And I'm watching them and thinking that happiness—it's so simple. I'm sleeping. We're walking along the water. Walking and walking. He probably asked me not to cry. Gave me a sign. From up there.

[*She is silent for a long time.*]

Two months later I went to Moscow. From the train station straight to the cemetery. To him! And at the cemetery I start going into labor. Just as I started talking to him—they called the ambulance. It was at the same Angelina Vasilyevna Guskova's that I gave birth. She'd said to me back then: "You need to come here to give birth." It was two weeks before I was due.

They showed her to me—a girl. "Natashenka," I called out. "Your father named you Natashenka." She looked healthy. Arms, legs. But she had **cirrhosis**① of the liver. Her liver had twenty-eight roentgen. **Congenital**② heart disease. Four hours later they told me she was dead. And again: we won't give her to you. What do you mean you won't give her to me? It's me who won't give her to you! You want to take her for science. I hate your science! I hate it!

[*She is silent.*]

I keep saying the wrong thing to you. I'm not supposed to yell after my stroke. And I'm not supposed to cry. That's why the words are all wrong. But I'll say this. No one knows this. When they brought me the little wooden box and said, "She's in there," I looked. She'd been **cremated**③. She was ashes. And I started crying. "Put her at his feet," I requested.

There, at the cemetery, it doesn't say Natasha Ignatenko. There's only his name. She didn't have a name yet, she didn't have anything. Just a soul. That's what I buried there. I always go there with two bouquets: one for him, and the other I put in the corner

---

① 肝硬化。

② 天生的。

③ 火化。

for her. I crawl around the grave on my knees. Always on my knees. [*She becomes incomprehensible.*] I killed her. I. She. Saved. My little girl saved me, she took the whole radioactive shock into herself, she was like the lightning rod for it. She was so small. She was a little tiny thing. [She has trouble breathing.] She saved . . . But I loved them both. Because—because you can't kill something with love, right? With such love! Why are these things together—love and death. Together. Who's going to explain this to me? I crawl around the grave on my knees.

[*She is silent for a long time.*]

In Kiev they gave me an apartment. It was in a large building, where they put everyone from the atomic station. It's a big apartment, with two rooms, the kind Vasya and I had dreamed of. And I was going crazy in it!

I found a husband eventually. I told him everything—the whole truth—that I have one love, for my whole life. I told him everything. We'd meet, but I'd never invite him to my home, that's where Vasya was.

I worked in a candy shop. I'd be making cake, and tears would be rolling down my cheeks. I'm not crying, but there are tears rolling down.

I gave birth to a boy, Andrei. Andreika. My friends tried to stop me. "You can't have a baby." And the doctors tried to scare me: "Your body won't be able to handle it." Then, later—later they told me that he'd be missing an arm. His right arm. The instrument showed it. "Well, so what?" I thought. "I'll teach him to write with his left hand." But he came out fine. A beautiful boy. He's in school now, he gets good grades. Now I have someone—I can live and breathe him. He's the light in my life. He understands everything perfectly. "Mom, if I go visit grandma for two days, will you be able to breathe?" I won't! I fear the day I'll have to leave him. One day we're walking down the street. And I feel that I'm falling. That's when I had my first stroke. Right on the street. "Mom, do you need some water?" "No, just stand here next to me. Don't go anywhere." And I grabbed his arm. I don't remember what happened next. I came to in the hospital. But I grabbed him so hard that the doctors were barely able to **pry**① my fingers open. His arm was blue for a long time. Now we walk out of the house, he says, "Mommie, just don't grab my arm. I won't go anywhere." He's also sick: two weeks in school, two weeks at home with a doctor. That's how we live.

---

① 撬开。

[*She stands up, goes over to the window.*]

There are many of us here. A whole street. That's what it's called—Chernobylskaya. These people worked at the station their whole lives. A lot of them still go there to work on a provisional basis, that's how they work there now, no one lives there anymore. They have bad diseases, they're invalids, but they don't leave their jobs, they're scared to even think of the reactor closing down. Who needs them now anywhere else? Often they die. In an instant. They just drop—someone will be walking, he falls down, goes to sleep, never wakes up. He was carrying flowers for his nurse and his heart stopped. They die, but no one's really asked us. No one's asked what we've been through. What we saw. No one wants to hear about death. About what scares them.

But I was telling you about love. About my love ...

Lyudmilla Ignatenko, wife of deceased fireman Vasily Ignatenko

Ⅳ. 思考题

1. How is the author able to re-present the original story? What literary devices are adopted?
2. Under this seemingly objective narrative, is it possible to detect the author's stance?
3. In what ways do you think this excerpt is a literary piece?

Ⅴ. 文学批评

报告文学

The genre of literary reportage is situated between journalism and literature. It has in common with journalism its relation to actuality. Reportage refers to cultural and social reality, past developments, and current affairs.

Good journalism interprets events by contextualizing elements such as historical background and causality, presenting readers with material for a more enlightened interpretation of world affairs.

The imperatives of mass media, their standardized patterns, their competitiveness, their permanent quest for the latest sensation, and their view of information as a commodity, impose tight limitations on the journalist's radius of action. Journalism often has to isolate facts and events, sensationalizing and glamorizing them through personification. Likewise, much of today's journalism oversimplifies complex situations and their backgrounds, favoring a trivial and partial understanding. Furthermore, it is compelled to use a language appropriate for the busy and undiscerning reader. As a result, it can hardly avoid providing stereotyped interpretations of reality.

Literature, on the other hand, is born of imagination, invention, and fantasy. Literature need not be directly related to real life. Its protagonists exist in a fictional sphere. Literature embraces images, metaphors and allegories, and is nourished by the poetic impact of language. Literature uses rhythm. Literature can use cuts and montages like a film. Literature draws energy through condensation. Literature touches dimensions of actuality which journalism avoids—such as psychology, visions and introspection, emotion and imaginary reality—and is sensitive to the effects of geography on human modes, behaviors, and traditions.

In earlier times, newspaper journalism—the written report—was the medium for conveying the unknown, describing events which often happened far away. The reports had to communicate a high level of credibility. Attempting to transcend its own limitations, newspaper journalism was expected to deliver a depiction of events that the reader couldn't experience personally. The journalist was a substitute eye-witness. Consequently, his role was to stimulate the reader's imagination, evoking a complete, multifaceted, and lively image of the events reported.

Later, photography entered the realm of delivering representations of real life in accompanying written journalism. Subsequently, photography gained a journalistic value of its own, ranging from serious photo-reportage to sensationalist photo-journalism.

Meanwhile, we are witnessing a process of historical change in the field of journalism. The function of delivering representational images of distant situations has been widely passed on to television, whose influence is prevailing over written journalism.

Today, audiovisual media has become a powerful and dominant force, and images seem to have become synonymous with authentic reporting. In this context, language has deteriorated into a mere auxiliary element, accompanying the image content. In TV, it is the image flow which defines the length and speed of the text. Images may not last longer than a few seconds, and texts should not be long or complicated.

We are exposed to an overwhelming flood of images which trigger powerful sensations. We have to adapt ourselves to the speed of the image flow. Thus, TV diminishes the viewers' habit of, and capacity for concentration, manifesting itself in short attention spans.

However, life as a world citizen, on a planet with diverse interdependencies of increasing complexity, demands much more. This world requires many competencies of people: to integrate diversity, to comprehend heterogeneity, to reconcile different layers of information, to interpret context, and to appreciate historical background.

In terms of market and finance, technology and media, or mass culture and tourism, the process of globalization seems to be irreversible. This process creates a complex matrix of relations. Paradoxically, the ruling rhetoric of globalization is often characterized by a critical oversimplification of reality and claims that a homogeneous world will emerge following the imperatives of development. The power of simplified versions of events upon our thinking explains why we are frequently confronted with bolts from the blue.

Reportage writers, with their immersion in the subject, bring unknown, hidden or forgotten realities and intricacies to light. By witnessing with their own eyes and collecting and consolidating a mass of information, in forming a picture of the whole, the reportage writer can deliver a greater degree of accuracy than is generally possible with other media formats. This is what gives reportage writing its significance and authority.

Reportage writing, however, is not limited to merely documenting events. The combination of reportage with the techniques and subjects of literature allows for the creation of complexity, density, depth and multiple layers. In the field of reportage, creative nonfiction makes use of literary writing by taking advantage of its refinement of composition and its devices of introspection, interior monologue, dialogue, and polyphony. Literary reportage can draw on the visual arts, using changes of perspective, tempo and mood, cuts and montages, and it can make use of metaphors, parables, and allegories. Thus, reportage can be transformed into an art—the Art of Reportage.

Ⅵ. 拓展阅读

Anna Karpusheva's "Svetlana Aleksievich's Voices from Chernobyl: Between an Oral History and a Death Lament" (*Canadian Slavonic Papers* 59. 3/4 (Sep-Dec 2017): 259-280).

John C. Hartsock's "Literary Reportage: The 'Other' Literary Journalism" (*Genre* 42. (1-2) (2009): 113-134).

Ⅶ. 参考文献

Alexievich, Svetlana. *Chernobyl Prayer: A Chronicle of the Future*. Penguin UK, 2016.

"The Art of Reportage." Retrieved June 7th, 2020, https://www.lettre-ulysses-award.org/about/Art_of_Reportage.html.